SIELANKA,

AND OTHER STORIES

BARTEK, THE VICTOR.

Photogravured after a drawing by J. Rosen.

SIELANKA, *Frontispiece.*

SIELANKA:

A Forest Picture,

AND OTHER STORIES

BY

HENRYK SIENKIEWICZ,

AUTHOR OF "QUO VADIS," "WITH FIRE AND SWORD,"
"THE DELUGE," "PAN MICHAEL," ETC.

AUTHORIZED UNABRIDGED TRANSLATION
FROM THE POLISH

BY

JEREMIAH CURTIN.

Fredonia Books
Amsterdam, The Netherlands

Sielanka:
A Forest Picture, and Other Stories

by
Henryk Sienkiewicz

ISBN: 1-58963-590-6

Reprinted from the 1898 edition

Fredonia Books
Amsterdam, The Netherlands
http://www.fredoniabooks.com

CONTENTS.

INTRODUCTORY.

THE present volume and "Hania," which preceded it, contain all the stories in Sienkiewicz's collected works. Of seventeen titles in the contents of this volume, nine, beginning with "Yanko the Musician," and ending with "A Comedy of Errors," belong to stories which have appeared in the two small volumes, "Yanko the Musician" and "Lillian Morris."

It will not detract from the interest of that pathetic and beautiful story, "The Lighthouse Keeper of Aspinwall," to state that it is founded on fact.

The experiences of Bartek the Victor and the Tutor of Poznan touch German traits keenly. On a broader field, and in detail, German character will be exhibited in "The Knights of the Cross," a work of intense and deep interest which Sienkiewicz is writing at present. In this work the author shows us Poland just as she is emerging from desperate peril to become a strong Commonwealth; he shows us also the Knights of the Cross, the most effective German power of that period, a power which was striving to master all Eastern Europe and subject the Slav race wherever resident; finally he shows that same German power cast down by the Slavs at Tannenberg, cast down not to rise in its old form at any time.

JEREMIAH CURTIN.

BRISTOL. VERMONT. U. S. A.

SIELANKA.

A FOREST PICTURE

SIELANKA.

A FOREST PICTURE.

O
N a broad plain, in a deep forest, stood the cottage of the forester Stepan. The cottage was thatched with straw, and built of round logs, the spaces between which were stuffed with moss. At the side of the cottage were two outbuildings, in front of it a piece of inclosed field and a well with a sweep; the well, fallen in and sloping, held water covered with duck plant.

Before the windows grew sunflowers and wild hollyhocks, tall, slender, and covered with blossoms, as if with a swarm of butterflies; among the sunflowers peeped out the red heads of poppies; around the hollyhocks twined red and white sweet peas and morning-glories; close to the ground grew nasturtiums, yellow crocuses, marigolds, golden primroses, and asters, pale, because deadened and concealed from sunlight by the grayish leaves of the sunflowers, and by hollyhocks.

In the enclosure, on both sides of the path leading to the house, vegetables had been planted: carrots, beets, and cabbages; farther on, in separate fields, with every breath of wind moved waves of blue flax blossoms; farther was the dark green of potato leaves; and on the rest of the broad plain a fleece of grain changed now into a lighter, now into a darker color up to the edges of a lake which washed the plain on one side.

There were not many trees near the cottage, — a few cherry-trees with dark, glittering leaves, and one birch with long, slender branches, which stood so near the cottage that every breeze cast its green tress on the sunken moss-covered straw roof; a stronger wind bent the birch toward the wall, and when all the branches and all the waves of leaves touched the roof; one might think that the birch loved the cottage and was seizing it in its arms.

This birch was full of sparrows, and the sound of its branches was mingled with the twittering and noisy uproar of the birds. Doves busied themselves at the gable, and that place was full of their talk, their cooing and enticing, as it were with requests and questions, as happens usually among doves, a wonderfully noisy and talkative people.

At times some unknown alarm frightened them, then around the cottage rose the sound of wings; the air was filled with the whirl of flying, and with a multitude of white birds. We have heard the disturbance, the tumult, and the flapping of their strong tail-feathers. A whole flock has flown out on a sudden, and in rings and circles it wheels, draws near, flies off and separates in the blue; now it is glittering with white feathers under the sun; now it is hanging over the cottage, hesitating, fluttering in the air, and at last falls, like a cloud of snowflakes, on the gray straw roof of the cottage.

If this happened in the redness of the morning, or the evening, then in the gleams of the air those doves seemed not white, but rosy, and like little flames, or scattered rose leaves which were falling on the roof and the birch-tree.

In the evening when the sun had sunk behind the pine woods, the conversation at the gable, and twittering on the birch, grew quiet gradually. The sparrows and doves shook the dew from their wings, and prepared for rest; sometimes one of them cooed or twittered again;

but each time more rarely, more quietly, more drowsily, and at last was silent. Darkness fell from heaven to the earth; the cottage, the cherry-trees, and the birch grew dull in outline, mingled together, were concealed in and covered with mist, which rôse from the lake.

Around the plain, as far as the eye could see, extended a wall of dark pines and thicket. This wall was broken in one place, and, going to a distance in the form of a corridor, widened more and more. In the corridor and the widening the waves of the lake stammered, and washed the edge of the plain. The lake was long, for the other end of it was almost lost in the distance, and through a haze, as it were, one could see a red roof with a tower standing at the other side of a little church, and a dark strip of forest which shut out the horizon not far beyond the church.

The pine-trees looked down from the high, sandy shores of the lake as if into a mirror, and there seemed to be another forest in the water, and if the forest on land moved, that in the water moved also; when there was noise on land, there seemed to be noise in the water; when amid the silence of the air the forest stood motionless, on the smooth, unwrinkled water every needle of the pines was outlined distinctly, and the trees went straight down as rows of columns, going somewhere far, far into infinity.

In the centre of the lake the water reflected the sun in the daytime, in the morning and the evening a ruddy light, in the night the moon and stars; and it seemed as deep as the vault of heaven is high above us, high beyond the sun, the moon, and the stars.

In the cottage dwelt Stepan, the forester, and his daughter, sixteen years of age, Kasia by name. Kasia was in that cottage what the aurora is in the sky. She was reared in great innocence and fear of God. Her dead

uncle, who in his time had eaten bread from various ovens,
and in his old age was an organist in the neighboring
church, taught her to read pious books; and what her
uncle had not finished in his teaching, forest seclusion had
taught.   Hence the bees had taught her to labor; doves
to be pure; the gray sparrows to twitter joyously to her
old father; the still water of the lake, calmness; the
peace of the heavens, earthly peace; the early church
bell, piety; and the goodness of God, the goodness of
people.

Therefore Kasia and her father led a peaceful life, and
were as happy as in the calmness and seclusion of a
forest one may be happy in this world.

Once on the Saturday before Whitsuntide old Stepan
came home at noon.   He had gone around a piece of
forest, and was wearied, for he had returned from morasses
and swampy thickets.   Kasia put his dinner before him,
and after dinner, when she had fed the dog and washed
the plates and pots, she said, —

"Father?"

"What?"

"I will go to the forest."

"Go, go.   Let a wolf or some other vermin meet thee."

"I will go for plants.   To-morrow will be Whitsunday;
we must have plants for the church."

"Well, go."

Kasia put a yellow kerchief, with blue flowers worked
on it, over her head, and, looking for a basket to hold the
plants, began to sing, —

"Oi, the young falcon has come, the gray falcon has flown
     to us!"

The old man fell to scolding her good-naturedly.

"Hadst thou as much wish to work as to sing?" said he.

Kasia, who had risen on tip-toe to look on the shelf, turned her face toward her father, laughed joyously, and, showing her white teeth, sang on, as if teasing him:

"He shouts in the forest, he seeks his dear cuckoo, in the wood he seeks for her."

"Thou wouldst be glad also to coocoo a falcon to thyself," said the old man. "Perhaps a falcon from the tar pit? But that is folly. Thou wilt not earn a morsel of bread by thy singing."

To that Kasia answered, —

"'Oh, shout not young falcon, seek not, poor falcon!
Thy cuckoo is drowned in the lake, she is now at the bottom.'

"And let father keep the house, I will come back before evening and milk the cows. But some one must drive them from the oak grove." She found her basket, kissed her father's hand, and went out.

Stepan found his wicker net, which was already begun, went in front of the cottage and sat down. He took his cords and a needle, shut one eye and tried to thread the needle; he failed to the right, he failed to the left, he spat, at last he aimed well, struck, drew the cord through, and began to bind the net.

But from time to time he looked after Kasia. Kasia went along the left bank of the lake, and on the lofty edge of the bank she was as plainly seen as in a picture. Her white shirt, red petticoat, and yellow kerchief seemed many-colored from a distance, like a flower. Though spring, the heat was unendurable.

When she had gone about half a verst from the cottage, she turned to one side and entered the pine wood. The hour was after midday. It was hot in the world, but cool in the forest. Kasia went straight ahead all the time, suddenly she stopped, laughed, and blushed like a cherry.

Before her, on a path which vanished in the depth of the forest, stood a youth eighteen years of age perhaps.

This youth was the tar-boiler from the edge of the forest, who was going just then to Stepan's cottage.

" May He be praised !" said the tar-boiler.

" For the ages of ages !"

Kasia was silent, but she rubbed her eyes from bashfulness, and then, raising her apron, she covered her face with it, looking from under the edge of the apron with a smile into Yasio's face.

" Kasia ?"

" What, Yasio ?"

" But is thy father at home ?"

" He is."

The tar-boiler, poor fellow, did not want, perhaps, to inquire about the father; but somehow he was frightened and inquired in spite of himself. Then he was silent and waited. Would Kasia say something first ?

Kasia stood there doing nothing, but twisting the end of her apron, terribly bashful, till at last she said, —

" Yasio ?"

" What, Kasia ?"

" But is not the tar pit smoking to-day ?"

She too wanted to ask about something else.

" Why shouldn't it smoke? It never stops smoking. I left lame Franek there; but thou, Kasia, art twisting out somehow, like a fox, onto the tar pit."

" Ei ! because I am going for plants."

" I will go with thee, and when we come back, if thou refuse not, I will go to the cottage."

" I ought to refuse."

" If thou like me, refuse not : but if thou like me

not, then refuse. Say, Kasia, a little word. Dost like me?"

"Thou fate! Oh, my fate!" and Kasia covered her face with her hands. "What must I say? I like thee, Yasio, like thee, I like thee terribly," said she, in a low voice.

And then before the tar-boiler could give her an answer, she cried, uncovering her blushing face and eyes, —

"Let us go for the plants; let us go in a breath!"

They went then, the tar-boiler and Kasia. They were radiant with love; but these simple children did not dare yet to speak of it. They only felt it, they knew not themselves what they felt. But it troubled them in some way, and was sweet. And never had the forest above their heads sung to them so wonderfully with its sounds, never had the breath of the wind seemed so delicious, so fondling, never had the noise of the pine wood, the rustle of the breeze, the voices of birds, and that sound of the forest seemed such an angel's orchestra, sweet, though enormous, as just at that moment filled so with awkwardness and unconscious delight.

Oh, sacred power of love, what a good angel of light art thou, what a rosy dawn in darkness, what a rainbow on the weeping clouds of misfortune!

In the pine wood went a resonant echo from tree to tree; it repeated the barking of a dog, and soon Burek ran up; he had escaped from the cottage, had followed on Kasia's trail, had run up panting; with great delight he sprang onto Kasia with his big paws, and onto the tar-boiler, and then he looked at one and the other with his wise and mild eyes, as if wishing to say, —

"You are in love, I see! That is good!"

And he wagged his tail with delight; then he ran with a great rush, making larger and larger circles, till at last he stopped, barked once more joyfully, and dashed into the forest, looking around from time to time at the youth and the maiden.

Kasia put her hand to her forehead, and looking up through the leaves at the bright sun, exclaimed, —

"Oh, for God's sake! It is two hours after midday, and not a plant yet! Go thou, Yasio, to the left, I will go to the right, and collect. We must hurry, as God is dear to me!"

They separated and went into the forest, but they went forward not far from each other, and at the same pace, so that one never left the eyes of the other. In the ferns, as on a green wave, among the trees appeared the colored petticoat and the yellow kerchief of Kasia. The slender maiden appeared to sail on amid the berry-bushes, mosses, and ferns. One might have said that she was a rusalka, or a vila of the forest; every moment she bent down and stood erect again, and so on, and on; passing the pines, she vanished from the tar-boiler's eyes; then he stopped, put his hands to his mouth and called with a great voice, —

"Hoop, hooooop!"

Kasia, hearing this, stopped, with a smile, and pretending not to see, but to seek him, she answered, with a thin little voice, —

"Yasio!"

And the echo answered, —

"Yaa-a-sio!"

Meanwhile, Burek had sniffed a squirrel on a tree; so he stood at the foot of it, raised his eyes and jaws upward, and went to barking. The squirrel, sitting on the branch, covered itself roguishly with its tail, raised a paw to its snout, and rubbing its nose, seemed to play with fingers at Burek, and to ridicule his anger. Kasia, observing this, laughed with a silvery, resonant laugh; the tar-boiler followed her example, and the forest was filled with noise, and crying of people, and echoes, and laughter, and joyous happiness.

At times silence came down for some moments; nothing spoke but the sound of the forest. A slight breeze played in the leaves of the fern; the old pine-trees groaned once — and then all was stillness!

Next was heard distinctly the measured beating of a woodpecker. It seemed as if some one were knocking at some other one's door, and that after a while a mysterious forest voice asked, —

"Who is there?"

Then the wiewilga whistled with a sweet voice; the hoopoo raised the golden crown on his head, and opening his beak as long as a needle, cried, "Hu! hu! hu! hup! hup!" In the hazel thicket the linnets applauded; green titmice circled around among the leaves; from time to time on a pine-top some crow flapped his black wings, hiding in the forest from heat.

It was afternoon, the sky was very clear, not even a small cloud on it, and above the green dome of leaves extended the blue dome of heaven, immense, limitless, blue gray at the edges, deepest azure in the centre. In the sky was the great golden sun; space was filled with light; and the air was so clear and transparent that the most remote objects came out of the blue distance definite to the eye, clear in form, not hazy. From the height of heaven the kind Creator had taken in with His eye the whole region. In the field the grain with its golden wave bowed to Him; the heavy heads of wheat rustled; the thin heads of oats trembled like bells. In the air, filled with brightness of the sun and with azure, floated here and there a spring spider thread, blue from the azure, and golden from the sun, — a real thread from the distaff of the Mother of God.

In depressed valleys, between strips of wheat, the dark fleece of meadows looked green. Here and there, where a spring bubbled forth in the grass, the green was brighter, and that whole meadow spot was covered with yellow buttercups; the eye was struck by an excess of golden glitter. In wet places the alders looked dark; from these came a coolness and moisture.

But in the forest, among pines, it was sultry, and there was great silence. It seemed that a sort of drowsiness and faintness had embraced the whole region.

After a while the breeze stopped, and then the woods and wheat fields and grass remained motionless. The leaves hung on the trees as if cradled to sleep; the noise of birds had grown silent, — the moment of rest had arrived. But that seemed a rest from excess of sweetness, a drowsiness of nature. The great dome of heaven seemed to smile, and somewhere, high, high in the unattainable blue, the great God delighted Himself benevolently with the delight of the fields, the woods, the meadows, and waters.

Meanwhile the tar-boiler and Kasia wandered on in the forest, selecting plants, laughing or chatting joyously. A peasant, like a bird, sings when he can, for such is his nature. The tar-boiler sang a simple, but melancholy song. The last word of the song is drawn out according to its melody, prolonged, sad; and thus prolonged and sad did the tar-boiler and Kasia continue it, and the echo sang to them in accompaniment; in the dark depth of the forest, pine gave the echo to pine, and the song begun in words, ran through the row of pines in the forest distance with a sigh more and more indefinite, lighter, weaker, till it turned at last into silence.

Then Kasia sang a more gladsome song, beginning with the words, "I will become a gold ring!" This is a beautiful song. A young, wilful maiden contends with her lover and tells the methods by which she intends to escape.

But she has no weapons against him. When she declares that she will become a gold ring and roll along the gray highroad, he threatens to discover the ring with swift eyesight; when she wishes to become a golden fish in the river, he sings to her of a silken net; when a wild duck on the lake, he stands before her as a hunter. When at last the poor maiden sees that she cannot hide on earth from him, she sings, —

> "I will be a star in the sky,
> I will shine as men need me.
> I will not be thy love,
> I will not do thy will."

But the young man, disheartened by nothing, replies:

> "I will bow down in church nicely,
> I will pay for holy mass, and the star will fall.
> Thou must be my love,
> Thou must do my will."

The girl sees that there is no escape for her on earth, or in the sky, so she agrees with the will of Providence and sings, —

> "I see, God's judgment I see,
> Wherever I hide thou wilt find me.
> I must be thy love,
> I must do thy will."

"Seest thou, Kasia?" asked the tar-boiler.

"What, Yasio?"

And he sang, —

> "Thou must be my love,
> Thou must do my will."

Kasia was bashful again; but she laughed, and wishing to talk, said, —

"I have collected a lot of plants; I must put them in water, or they will wither in the heat before evening."

There was great heat indeed; the wind had ceased altogether. In the forest, even in the shade, the air was quivering with boiling heat, the pines gave out a strong, resinous odor. Kasia's delicate, golden-tinged face was moist, and her blue eyes looked wearied. She took the kerchief from her head and cooled herself; meanwhile the tar-boiler took the basket of plants from her hand, and said, —

"Hear me, Kasia. A quarter of a mile from here is a spring between the alders. Let us go and drink water."

Both went. In fact after a short time the forest earth yielded to the foot; among the trees, instead of bill-berries, ferns, and dry moss, appeared damp green turf, one alder appeared and another, after them whole rows. They entered a dark, damp grove where the sunlight, passing through leaves, took on their color and painted people's faces light green.

Yasio and Kasia went farther into shade and dampness. A pronounced coolness, pleasant after the heat of the forest, surrounded them, and soon among the rows of alders, they saw in the black, turfy ground a deep brook, overgrown here and there with sweet flag, reeds, or covered with great round leaves of the water-lily, which the peasants call "the white one."

It was a beautiful place, quiet, secluded, shady, even a little dark.

The clear brook wound among the trees. The lilies, rocked by the light movement of the water, swayed gently with their white flowers; bending toward one another, they seemed to kiss; above their broad leaves, which lay like shields on the surface of the water, dark sapphire-colored grasshoppers moved around in the air with broad and rustling wings, so delicate and slender that people call them "water maidens" justly; black butterflies, with white mourning borders, sat on the points of the flag. On the ruddy background of turf bloomed blue forget-me-nots. Here and there rustled a clump of slender reeds, on which the wind played its usual songs. On its banks grew gloomy thickets of the snowball, and under the thickets were heads of lilies of the valley and the water-bell, and the pimpernel hung its white head over the clear water; the silvery threads of larkspur, pulled out by the current, waved in long and thin tresses. As to the rest, solitude, that was it! wild seclusion, forgotten by people, peaceful, occupied only by the world of birds, flowers, and insects.

In such a silence nymphs and rusalkas dwell usually, as well as other good and bad forest divinities. So when Kasia, who went ahead, stopped first on the bank and looked at the water, in which her charming, slender form was reflected, she might have seemed indeed a beautiful apparition of the woodland, such as foresters meet in the woods sometimes, or as bargemen meet when floating down among trees with their flat-boats. She was without a kerchief on her head; the wind had blown her tresses apart somewhat, and stirred the hair on her forehead. She was bright-haired and sunburnt; she had eyes smiling, but blue as star-thistles, and lips also smiling. Besides, she was tall and slender, a perfect rusalka! Nobody would swear that, frightened by an eye, she would not spring into the water, or vanish in mist, in a rainbow, or in sunlight, that she would not change suddenly into a lily or a snowball, which, when thou shouldst wish to pluck it, would say in human speech, though in speech like the rustle of a tree,—

" Touch me not ! "

Kasia bent from the turf over the water till her tresses fell on her arms, then she turned to the tar-boiler, —

" But how shall we drink," asked she.

" As the birds drink," replied Yasio, and pointed at a number of wagtails, and to kingfishers, beautiful as a rainbow ; these were drinking at a distance, raising their bills toward the sky.

The tar-boiler knew how to help himself better than birds do, for he took an enormous leaf of water-lily, twisted it into a funnel, and, taking water, reached it to Kasia.

Kasia drank, and the tar-boiler drank. She plucked some forget-me-nots ; he took out his knife, cut a willow twig and made a whistle.

The whistle was finished soon. Yasio put it to his lips and played a simple song, like those which shepherds play in the evenings on a meadow. The pleasant sounds spread with inexpressible sweetness in that seclusion. After a time the tar-boiler took the whistle from his lips, and listened to catch, with his ear, the echoes playing in the alders ; and it seemed that together with them the clear brook heard that voice, and the dark alders, and the birds hidden in the reeds. Everything grew silent, but, after a while, as if in answer, as if in challenge, was heard a light whistle, after it a second and a third. It grew still more silent. That was the nightingale, the nightingale had challenged the whistle, and had begun to sing.

All listened to that singer of the Lord. The water-lilies raised their heads above the water ; the forget-me-nots nestled up to one another ; the reeds ceased to rustle ; no bird dared raise a voice : the unwise and ruffled cuckoo alone flew up over the water with quiet wing, sat on a knot, raised its head, opened its bill widely, and said inanely, " Ku-ku ! ku-ku ! "

But afterward it was evidently ashamed that it had acted so stupidly, for it was silent on a sudden.

In vain did Kasia, standing on the edge of the brook with forget-me-nots in her hand, turn to that side whence the voice of the cuckoo had come, and inquire :

"Cuckoo, oh, blue cuckoo, have I long to live ? "

The cuckoo said nothing in answer.

" Cuckoo, shall I be rich ? "

The cuckoo said nothing.

Then the tar-boiler said, —

" Cuckoo, gray cuckoo, will my wedding come soon ? "

The cuckoo said nothing.

"He will not answer," said Yasio. " Let us go back."

On returning they found the great stone near which they had left the basket and dry plants. Kasia sat on the grass under it and began to weave garlands. Yasio helped her. Burek planted himself before them, stretched forward his shaggy paws, dropped out his tongue, and began to pant from exertion, looking around carefully to discover some living creature at which to rush and make an uproar. But it was silent in the woods round about. The sun was inclining toward the west, and through the leaves and the needles of the pines its rays came in ever ruddier, covering the ground of the forest with great golden spots. The air was dry ; on the west the great golden light of evening was spreading like a sea of molten gold and amber. A calm, warm spring evening was burning in the sky. In the forest the labor of the day was ceasing gradually. The hammering of the woodpecker had grown still ; black and reddish ants were returning in rows to their ant-heaps, which were red from the evening light and the rays of the sun ; some of them were carrying pine-needles in their mouths, others, insects. Among the plants were whirling here and there small forest bees, buzzing gladly as usual : " Dana, oh, dana ! " completing the last load of honey dust. From cracks in the split bark of trees were emerging the gloomy, blind legions of the night : in the torrents of golden light moved swarms of moths, gnats scarcely visible to the eye ; mosquitoes began their sad songs. On the trees birds chose their places for sleep. At one moment a yellow-beaked blackbird or crow flapped its wings. After seizing a tree, the birds fought about the best branch. But those voices grew rarer and rarer and weaker. Gradually they ceased altogether, and silence was broken only by the rustle of the trees. The hazel bush raised its grayish leaves upward ; the royal oak muttered, or the birch moved its tresses. After that there was silence.

The evening grew still redder, and in the east the deep blue of heaven became darker ; now all the sounds of the forest were mingled in majestic and low, though immense, choruses, — that was the forest, which, before it goes to sleep, before night, prays and repeats its "Our Father :" the trees declare the praise of God to other trees, and thou mightst say that they were discoursing in human speech.

Ah ! only very innocent souls understand this mighty and blessed speech. Ah ! only very innocent hearts listen and understand when the first chorus of the fathers of oaks begins the converse, —

" Rejoice, sister pines, the Lord has given us a calm and warm day, and now a starry night is falling on the earth. The Great Lord, Mighty, mightier than we, but kind, hence praise be to Him on the heights, and on the waters, and on land, and in the air ! "

And the pines consider the words of the oak for a while, and then answer in a concordant chorus, —

"Ah, behold, O Lord, in Thy praise, as an offering of incense, we drop sweet balsam and a strong and mighty resinous odor. Our Father who art in heaven, hallowed be Thy name!"

And then the birches, —

"The twilight of evening is burning in the sky, O Lord, and in the gleams of it our leaves are golden and burning. Hence, with our golden leaves, we raise a hymn to Thee, O Lord, and our slender branches play like harps, O Thou, our good Father!"

And then the melancholy fir, —

"On our gloomy foreheads, tortured with heat, the evening dew is falling. Praise to the Lord! Brothers and sisters, rejoice, for the dew of the evening is falling!"

And amid these choruses the aspen alone trembles timidly, for the aspen gave wood for the cross to crucify our Redeemer, and at intervals only it groans in a low voice, "O Lord, have pity on me!"

And again, when the oaks and pines have grown silent for a space, from the foot of them rises a low, timid, small voice, as weak as the buzzing of a mosquito, as feeble as silence itself. That little voice sings, —

"I am a berry, O Lord! small and sheltered in the moss. But Thou wilt hear me, distinguish me, and love me; for though small, I am pious, and I sing to Thee to increase Thy glory!"

So prays the forest daily, and such a concert rises every evening to the heavens from the earth, and flies high, high, up, where there is no created thing, where there is nothing save the silver star dust and the Milky Way, and the stars — and above the stars — God!

At such a moment the sun sinks his radiant head in

the distant sea; the field-worker turns upward his plough-point and hastens to his cottage. The lowing cattle return from the field, sounding their wooden bells; the sheep raise clouds of golden dust. Then darkness falls. In the distant village the well-sweep squeaks, the windows gleam, and from afar, afar, comes the barking of dogs.

But when Kasia had sat down to weave garlands under the mossy stone, the sun had not sunk yet beyond the forest. On the contrary, its rays, broken by the shadows of limbs and leaves, threw light on her face. The work did not advance hurriedly, for Kasia was wearied by heat and running through the forest. Her sunburnt hands twisted the strands of the plants. The warm wind kissed her temples and face, and the sound of the trees lulled her to slumber. Her large sleepy eyes became gleaming; her lids began to close slowly; she rested her head on the stone; once more she opened her lids widely, like a child which looks on God's world with wonder, — then the sound of·trees, the rows of tree-trunks, the forest earth covered with pine-needles, and the heavens visible through the branches, grew indistinct before her, began to mingle, she smiled, and fell asleep.

Her head at that moment was in a mild shade, but the shirt over her bosom was covered with a light like that of morning, and it shone all rosy and purple. A slight breathing moved her bosom, and she was so wonderful in that sleep, and in those afternoon gleams, that Yasio looked on her as he would on an image in the church all glittering in gold, and like a many-colored rainbow.

Kasia's hands held a still unfinished green garland. She was sleeping evidently with a light and pleasant sleep, for she smiled in her sleep, like a child talking with angels. Perhaps too she was talking with angels, for she was as pure as a child, and she had served God all that day, weaving garlands for the church on the morrow.

Yasio sat near her, but he did not sleep. His simple breast was expanded by feeling; he felt as if his soul had gained wings, and was ready to fly into heavenly spaces. A hei! hei! he knew not himself what was happening within him, so he turned his eyes to the sky, and it might have been said that love had transfixed him.

And long yet slept Kasia, and long both sat thus.

Meanwhile the shade of evening came. The remnants of the purple light were struggling with shade. In the forest it had grown dark — silent. From the reeds of the lake, from the direction of the cottage and the plain, came the night calls of the bittern.

All at once, in the little church beyond the lake, the Angelus sounded. That sound flew over the peaceful lake, flew on the wings of the evening breeze, pure, resonant, and far reaching. This summoned the faithful to prayer, and at the same time announced rest, "Enough of toil and heat," said the bell; "fold yourselves to sleep under the wing of the Lord. Go, go, ye wearied, to God, in Him is rejoicing! Here is quiet, here is joy, here is sleep! here is sleep! here is sleep! here is sleep!"

The tar-boiler removed his cap at the sound of the bell. Kasia shook the sleep from her eyes, and asked,—

" Are they ringing ? "

" The Angelus."

Both knelt near the moss-covered stone, as near an altar. Kasia began to recite in a melancholy voice:

" The angel of the Lord declared unto Mary — "

" And She conceived of the Holy Ghost," answered Yasio.

" Behold the handmaid of the Lord — "

And thus kneeling, those simple children prayed. The

calm summer lightning flew from the east to the west, and in its light came down from heaven a crowd of winged angels, and hung over the heads of those two. And then they mingled with angels, and they were themselves almost angels, as it were, for there was nothing clearer, purer, and more innocent on earth than those two.

FOR BREAD

FOR BREAD.

I.

ON the broad waves of the ocean the German steamer
Blücher was rocking as it sailed to New York from
Hamburg.

That was its fourth day on the voyage; two days before
it had passed the green shores of Ireland, and had come
out on the open ocean. From the deck, as far as the eye
could see, nothing was visible save the green and gray
plain, ploughed into furrows and ridges, swaying heavily, in
places foaming, in the distance darker and darker and
blending with the horizon, which was covered with white
clouds.

The light of these clouds fell in places on the water
too, and on that pearly background the black body of the
vessel was outlined distinctly. The prow of that body
was turned to the west; now it rose on a wave with great
labor, now it plunged into the depth, as if drowning; at
moments it vanished from the eye; at moments, lifted on
the back of a billow, it rose so high that the bottom of it
was visible, but the steamer went forward. The sea
moved toward it, and it toward the sea, cleaving the
water with its breast. Behind it, like a giant serpent,
chased a white road of foaming water; sea-gulls flew after
the rudder, turning somersaults in the air and piping like
Polish lapwings.

The wind was favorable; the vessel was going with half steam, but all sails were raised on it. The weather grew better and better. In places among the rent clouds bits of blue sky could be seen changing their forms unceasingly. From the moment that the Blücher had left the port of Hamburg, the weather had been windy, but without storm; the wind blew toward the west, but at times it ceased; then the sails dropped with a flapping, to swell out again like the breast of a swan. The sailors, in close-fitting knit jackets, tightened the line in the lower yard of the mainsail, chanting a melancholy: "Ho — ho — o!" They bent and straightened themselves in time with the sound, and their voices were mingled with the midshipmen's whistles, and the feverish puffing of smoke-stacks which hurled out broken bundles or rings of black smoke.

The passengers had come out on deck numerously. In the stern of the steamer were those of the first-class, in black overcoats and caps; toward the prow had assembled the particolored multitude of emigrants who lived between decks. Some of these were sitting on benches, smoking short pipes; others, lying down; others, leaning against the bulwarks, were gazing into the water. There were women with children in their arms, and with tin cups fastened to their girdles; there were young people walking backward and forward from the prow to the bridge, preserving their balance with difficulty and staggering from moment to moment as they sang: "Wo ist das deutsche Vaterland!" and thinking, perhaps, that they would never again see that "Vaterland," still gladness did not leave their faces. Among the passengers were two, the saddest of all, and separated, as it were, from the others: an old man and a young girl. Neither understood German, and they were really alone and among strangers.   Who were they ? — each one of us [1] would have divined at the first glance that they were Polish peasants.

The man was called Vavron Toporek, and the girl was Marysia, his daughter. They were going to America, and had taken courage a moment before to come out on deck for the first time.   On their faces, thin from sickness, were depicted both fear and astonishment.   They looked with frightened eyes at their companions of the journey, at the sailors, at the steamer, at the smoke-stacks, belching forth mightily, at the terrible walls of water which hurled wreaths of foam to the deck of the steamer.   They said nothing to each other, for they dared not.   Vavron held the railing with one hand, and his four-cornered cap with the other, lest the wind might sweep it away from him ; Marysia held to her father, and when the ship inclined more steeply, she held to him more closely, and cried in a low voice from fear.   After a certain time the old man broke the silence, —

" Marysia ! "

" But what ? "

" Dost see ? "

" I see."

" And dost wonder ? "

" I wonder."

But she feared still more than she wondered ; it was the same with old Toporek.

Happily for them, the waves decreased ; the wind went down ; and the sun broke forth through the clouds. When they saw the " dear beloved sun," it became easier at their hearts ; for they thought to themselves that that sun was " just the very same as in Lipintse." Indeed everything was new and unknown to them ; that sun

---

[1] Poles, as the author is.

disk alone, gleaming and radiant, seemed as it were an old friend and guardian.

Meanwhile the sea became smoother and smoother; after a time the sails slackened; and from the lofty bridge was heard the whistle of the captain, and the sailors rushed to reef them. The sight of these sailors suspended, as if in the air above an abyss, filled Toporek and Marysia with wonder a second time.

"Our boys could not do that," said the old man.

"Wherever Germans go, Yasko can go," replied Marysia.

"Which Yasko? Is it Sobkov?"

"How Sobkov? I mean Smolak, the groom."

"He is a smart fellow, but drive him from thy head. Thou art not for him, nor he for thee. Thou art to be a lady; and he, as he is a groom, will remain a groom."

"But he has land too."

"He has, but it is in Lipintse."

Marysia said nothing; but she thought to herself that whatever was fated would not fail, and she sighed sadly. Meanwhile the sails were reefed; but the screw stirred the water so mightily that the whole steamer quivered from its movements. The rocking had stopped almost completely. In the distance the water seemed even now smooth and azure. From moment to moment new figures came up from below: laborers, German peasants, street idlers from various seaports, people going to America to seek fortune, not work; a throng took possession of the deck, so Vavron and Marysia, to crowd no one, sat on a coil of rope in the very point in the prow.

"Tatulo (papa), shall we go long through the water yet?" inquired Marysia.

"Do I know. Whomever thou may ask, no one will answer in Catholic fashion."

"But how shall we talk in America?"

"Have men not said that there is a cloud of our people there?"

"Tatulo?"

"What?"

"To wonder there is something to wonder at, still it was better in Lipintse."

"Better not blaspheme for nothing."

But after a while Vavron added, as if speaking to himself, —

"The will of God!"

The girl's eyes filled with tears; and both began to think of Lipintse.

Vavron Toporek considered why he was going to America, and how it had happened. How had it happened? Well, half a year before, in the summer, they had seized his cow in a clover field. The owner of the clover, who took her, wanted three rubles damages; Vavron would not give them. The man went to law. The case dragged on. The injured owner of the clover wanted now not only the damage for the clover, but the cost of keeping the cow, and the cost increased daily. Vavron refused it; since he was sorry for the money. He had spent no little for the suit itself; it dragged on, and dragged on. The cost increased all the time. Finally Vavron lost the case. Besides, for the cow he had incurred cost, God knows how much; as he had no money to pay, his horse was taken; and the court sentenced him to arrest for resistance. Toporek squirmed like a snake, for the harvest was just coming, so hands and energy were needed for work. He was late at bringing in his grain, then rain began to fall; the wheat grew in the bundles. Hence he thought that by the single damage to that clover all his little property would be wasted; that he had lost so much money, a part of his cattle, all his year's grain; and that before the new harvest either he and the girl would have to eat earth, or beg bread.

As the man had been well-to-do and successful before, so terrible despair seized him now, and he fell to drinking. In the public house he made the acquaintance of a German who was bargaining for flax, as he said, through the villages; but really he was luring people beyond the sea.

The German told Vavron miracles and wonders about America. He promised him more land for nothing than there was in all Lipintse, and with a forest, and with meadows; Vavron's eyes laughed. He believed and he did not believe; but the Jew dairy-man supported the German, and said that the Government there gave each man as much land "as he could use." The Jew had learned this from his nephew. On his part, the German showed an amount of money which not only a peasant's eyes, but even the eyes of an heir, had not seen in his lifetime. They tempted the man till they convinced him. Why should he stay at home? For one loss he had spent so much money that he might have kept a man for it. Was he to yield himself to ruin? Was he to take a staff in his hand and sing at the church: "Holy heavenly, angelic Lady?" "Nothing of that will come!" thought he. He struck hands with the German, sold out before Saint Michaels, took his daughter, and now he was sailing to America.

But the journey was not the success he had expected. In Hamburg people had dragged much money from him; on the steamer he and his daughter went between decks in the steerage. The rocking of the ship, and the endlessness of the ocean terrified them. No man could understand him, and he could understand no man. They were thrown around, each of them, like a thing, pushed aside like a stone on a highway; the Germans, their fellow-passengers, reviled him and Marysia. At dinner-time, when all crowded with their plates to the cook who distributed food, they were pushed away to the very last, so that more than once they had to suffer from hunger. On that ship it was strange and sad. Save the care of God, Vavron felt none other above him. He put on a bold face before the girl, raised his cap on the side of his head, told Marysia to admire things, admired everything himself, but trusted in nothing. At times he was seized by fear that perhaps those "pagans," as he called his fellow-passengers, would throw him and Marysia into the sea, perhaps they would force them to change their religion, or sign some paper, yes! even a "cyrograf."

The steamer itself, which went on day and night over the boundless ocean, shook and roared, raising water and foam, that steamer which puffed like a dragon, and drew after it at night a line of fiery sparks, seemed to him some kind of power which was suspicious and very uncanny. Childish fears, though he did not confess them, straitened his heart; for that Polish peasant, torn away from his native nest, was in truth a helpless child, and really at the mercy of God. Besides, he could understand nothing that he saw, nothing about him; so it is not a wonder that, when he was sitting on that coil of rope, his head bent under the weight of oppressive uncertainty and vexation, the breeze of the ocean sang in his ear and seemed to repeat the word: "Lipintse! Lipintse!" at times also it piped like the whistles of Lipintse; the sun said: "How art thou, Vavron? I have been in Lipintse." But the screw whirled the water with still mightier force, and the smoke-stack puffed more loudly, more quickly, — they were like two evil spirits drawing him farther and farther from Lipintse.

But other thoughts and memories were pursuing Marysia, like that foaming road, or the gulls which flew after the steamer. She remembered how one evening in the autumn, not long before their departure, she went to the well, which had a sweep above it, to draw water. The first stars were twinkling in the sky, and she was drawing the sweep, singing: "Yasio was watering the horses — Kasia had come to the well — ' and somehow she felt as sad as a swallow twittering before its departure. Then from the pine wood, from the dark one, the swamp gave forth a drawling sound; that was Yasko Smolak, the groom, letting her know that he saw the well-sweep inclining, and that he would come from the pasture immediately. Indeed there was trampling; he rode up; he sprang from his horse; he shook his yellow forelock; and she remembered what he said to her as if it had been music. She closed her eyes, and it seemed to her that Smolak was whispering again to her, in a quivering voice, —

"If thy father is stubborn, I will give up all in the mansion; I will sell my cottage, my village land, and go — My Marysia," said he, "wherever thou shalt be, I will fly through the air as a stork to thee, or swim as a duck through the water, or roll on the road as a gold ring, and find thee, thou, my only one! Have I fortune without thee? Whither thou turnest, I shall turn also. Whatever happens thee, will happen me also; one life and one death to us. And as I have promised here above the water of this well, so may God desert me as I desert thee, Marysia, my only one."

Remembering these words, Marysia saw the well and the great ruddy moon above the pine wood, and Yasko as if living. She found solace in that memory and great comfort. Yasko was resolute; hence she believed that he would do what he had promised. Then all she wished was that he might be there, and listen with her to the sounds of the ocean. In his company, all would be livelier and more cheerful, for he feared no man, and could help himself anywhere. What was he doing then in Lipintse? The first snows must have fallen. Had he gone with his axe to the forest, was he harnessing horses, had they sent him to some place from the mansion, with the sleigh? was he cutting openings in the ice of the pond? Where was he, dear fellow? Here Lipintse appeared to her just as it had been : snow squeaking on the road, the ruddy light of evening between dark, leafless tree branches, flocks of crows flying from the pine wood to the village with cawing, smoke rising skyward from the chimneys, the frozen sweep at the well, and in the distance pine woods ruddy in the light of evening, and snow-covered.

Ah, where is she now! Where has her father's will brought her! In the distance, as far as the eye can reach, nothing but water, green furrows, foaming ridges, and on those boundless fields of water that one ship, like a lost bird; heaven above them, a desert beneath, a mighty sound as it were the weeping of waves and the whistling of winds, and off there, before the beak of the vessel, the ninth land, or the end of the world.

Yasko, poor fellow, wilt thou meet her there? Wilt thou fly thither through the air in the form of a falcon? or wilt thou swim through the water disguised as a fish? or art thou thinking of her in Lipintse?

The sun inclined toward the west gradually, and was going down in the ocean. On the wrinkled billows the broad sunny pathway, stretched behind, shaped itself into golden scales, changed, glittered, shone, was consumed and perished somewhere in remoteness. The ship, sailing on

3

over that fiery ribbon, seemed to pursue the fleeing sun. The smoke, bursting from the smoke-stack, grew ruddy; the sails and damp ropes became rosy; the sailors fell now to singing; meanwhile the radiant circle increased and settled down lower toward the ocean. Soon only one half of the shield was seen above the water, then only rays, and after that the whole west was filled with one immense ruddiness, and it was unknown in those gleams where the brightness of the waves found its end, and the sky its beginning. The air and the water were penetrated in like manner with light, which quenched gradually; the ocean sounded with one great but mild voice, as if it were murmuring an evening prayer.

In such moments the soul in a man receives wings, and what he had to remember, he remembers; what he loved, he loves still more ardently; that after which he yearns, to that does he fly now.

Vavron and Marysia felt, both of them, that though the wind was bearing them like helpless leaves, the tree from which they were borne was not in the direction in which they were going, but that from which they were coming: the Polish land, that grain land, waving in one field, grown over with pine-trees, dotted with straw roofs, full of meadows, of golden buttercups, and gleaming water, full of storks and swallows, crosses by the road-side, white mansions among lindens; she, who with a pointed cap under her feet, with the word "Praised!" greets and answers "for the ages of ages," she the venerable, she the sweetest mother, so true, beloved above all others on the earth! Hence what their peasant hearts had not felt before, they felt then. Vavron removed his cap; the evening light fell on his hair, growing gray; his mind was laboring, for the poor man knew not how he was to tell Marysia what his belief was. At last he said: "Marysia, it seems to me as if something had remained there beyond the sea."

"Our fate has remained, and love has remained there," answered the girl, in a low voice, raising her eyes as if in prayer.

Meanwhile it had grown dark. The passengers had begun to leave the deck; on the ship, however, there was an unusual movement. The night is not always calm after a beautiful sunset, so the whistles of the officers were heard continually, and sailors were hauling ropes.

The last purple gleams were quenched on the sea, when a mist rose from the water; the stars twinkled in the sky, and then vanished. The mist thickened before the eye, hiding the heavens, the horizon, and even the vessel. Only the smoke-stack and the great central mast were now visible; the figures of the sailors seemed, from some distance, like shadows. An hour later, all was hidden in a whitish fog, even lanterns hanging on the mast-heads, even sparks flying out through the smoke-stack.

The vessel did not rock in the least; one might have said that the sea had grown feeble and had flattened out under the weight of the fog.

Night had come down, in fact, blind and silent. Suddenly, in the midst of the silence, and from the remotest rim of the horizon, were heard wonderful rustles, like the heavy breathing of some giant breast nearing the vessel. At times it seemed as if some one were calling in the darkness, then that a whole distant chorus of voices were answering with infinite sadness and complaining tearfully. Those calls were running from darkness and endlessness toward the steamer.

Sailors, when they hear these sounds, say that the tempest is calling winds out of hell.

In fact these calls grew more and more definite. The
captain, wearing a rubber coat with a hood, stood on
the highest bridge; an officer took his usual place before
a lighted compass. On the deck was no passenger now.
Vavron and Marysia had gone down to the common
cabin also. There was silence. The lamps, fastened in a
very low arch, shone with a gloomy light on the interior
and the crowds of emigrants sitting beside their bunks
near the walls. The cabin was large but gloomy, as
cabins in the fourth class are usually. Its ceiling and
walls were very nearly one, therefore those bunks at the
ends, divided by partitions, were more like dark dens than
beds, and the entire cabin produced the impression of one
immense cellar. The air in it was filled with the odor
of tarred canvas, ship cables, bilge water, and dampness.
Where could be found in it a comparison with the beautiful rooms of the first class ! A passage of even two weeks
in such cabins would poison lungs with bad air, bring
a sickly pallor to faces, and cause scurvy frequently.

Vavron and his daughter were out only four days;
still if one were to compare the former Marysia of
Lipintse, the healthy and blooming, with her of to-day,
made haggard by sickness, he would not have known
her. Old Vavron too had grown as yellow as wax, for
the first days neither of them had gone on deck. They
thought it forbidden. Or for that matter did they know
what was permitted and what was forbidden ? They
had hardly dared to move; moreover they feared to leave
their things. And now not only they, but all, were sitting
with their effects. The entire steerage was strewn with
bundles belonging to emigrants; this increased the disorder and gloomy appearance. Bedding, clothing, supplies of provisions, various utensils, and tin dishes, mixed
together, were thrown in smaller or larger heaps over the

whole floor. Upon them were sitting emigrants, nearly all Germans. Some were chewing tobacco, others smoking pipes; the rolls of smoke struck the low ceiling, and, forming a long streak, obscured lamp-light. A number of children were crying in the corners, but the usual noise had ceased, for the fog had penetrated all with a sort of fear, alarm, and gloom. The most experienced of the emigrants knew that it foreboded a storm. It was a secret at that time to no one, that danger was coming, and perhaps death was near. Vavron and Marysia could inform themselves in nothing, though when any one opened the hatchway for a moment those distant, ill-omened voices, coming up from infinity, were heard with distinctness.

Both were sitting in the depth of the room, in its narrowest portion, therefore not far from the prow of the steamer. The movement there was disagreeable; hence their fellow-passengers pushed them to that place. The old man strengthened himself with bread brought from Lipintse, and the girl, who disliked to do nothing, braided her hair for the night.

Gradually, however, the general silence, interrupted only by the crying of children, began to astonish the girl.

"Why do the Germans sit to-night so quietly?" inquired she.

"Do I know?" answered Vavron, as usual. "It must be that they have a holiday, or something."

All at once the ship trembled mightily, exactly as if it had shivered before something terrible. The tin dishes lying around rattled gloomily, the flame in the lamps danced and gleamed up, some frightened voices inquired:

"What is it? What is it?"

But there was no answer. A second shock, weightier

than the first, shook the steamer; the prow rose suddenly,
and went down with equal suddenness, and at the same
time a wave struck with dull force the round window
on one side.

"A storm is coming!" whispered Marysia in terror.

Meanwhile something howled around the steamer like
a pack of wolves, then it sounded like a pine wood when
a whirlwind is breaking it suddenly. The wind struck
once and a second time; it put the steamer on its
side, then turned it around, raised it aloft, and hurled
it into the depth. The rigging creaked, tin vessels,
bundles, bags, and utensils flew along the floor, hurled
from corner to corner. Some passengers fell flat; feathers
from pillows flew through the air, and the lamp chimneys
jingled mournfully.

All was noise and uproar: the plashing of water pour-
ing in on the deck, the struggling of the ship, the screaming of women, and the weeping of children, the chasing
for effects, and, in this disturbance and chaos, nothing
was heard but the shrill sound of whistles, and, from
moment to moment, the dull tramp of sailors hurrying
along on the upper deck.

"Virgin of Chenstohova!" whispered Marysia.

The prow of the ship, in which both were sitting, shot
into the air, and then went down as if frantic. Though
Vavron and Marysia held to the sides of their plank
berths, they were thrown so that at moments they struck
the ceiling. The roar of the billows increased; the groans
of the deck grew so piercing that it seemed as though beams
and planks would burst in with a crash any moment.

"Hold on, Marysia!" shouted Vavron, trying to out-
shout the roar of the tempest; but fear soon closed his
throat, and those of others. Children stopped crying;
women stopped screaming; all breasts breathed only

hurriedly, and hands held with effort to various fixed objects.

The rage of the tempest rose increasingly. The elements were unchained; the fog thickened with darkness, the clouds with water, the whirlwind with foam; billows struck the ship as if they had been sent from cannon, they hurled it to the right, to the left, and from the clouds to the bottom of the sea. At moments the foaming summits of waves passed over the whole length of the steamer; gigantic masses of water seethed in one awful disorder.

The oil lamps in the room began to quench. It became darker and darker; it seemed to Vavron and Marysia that the darkness of death was approaching.

"Marysia!" began the man, with a broken voice, for breath failed him. "Marysia, forgive me for delivering thee to death. Our last hour has come. We shall not look again on the world with our sinful eyes. We shall have no confession, no anointment; we are not to lie in the earth, but go from the water to the terrible judgment, poor girl!"

And while he was speaking thus, Marysia understood that there was no rescue. Various thoughts flew through her head, and something called in her soul, —

"Yasko, Yasko, my heart's love, dost thou hear me in Lipintse?"

Terrible sorrow pressed her heart, and she sobbed aloud. The sobbing filled the room where all were as silent as if at a funeral. One voice called out from a corner: "Still!" but stopped, as if frightened by its own sound. Then a lamp chimney fell to the floor, and the flame went out. It was still darker. The alarm of silence reigned everywhere, when Vavron's voice was heard suddenly in the silence, —

" Kyrie eleison ! "

" Chryste eleison," responded Marysia, sobbing.

" Christ listen to us ! "

" Father in heaven, God, have mercy on us ! " said the two, repeating the Litany.

In the dark room the voice of an old man, and responses, broken by sobbing, coming from a girl sounded with wonderful solemnity.   Some of the emigrants uncovered their heads.   Gradually the girl's weeping ceased, the voices grew calmer, clearer; outside the tempest howled a response to them.

All at once a scream was heard among those who were standing nearer the exit.   A wave had beaten the door in and rushed to the cabin; the water flowed to every corner with a plashing; women began to scream and save themselves on the bunks.   It seemed to all that the end had come.

After a while an officer on duty, all wet and red-faced, entered with a lantern in his hand.   He pacified the women with a few words, saying that the water had come only by accident; afterward he added, that as the vessel was on the open sea there was no great danger.   In fact an hour passed, two hours.   The tempest raged more and more madly.   The vessel groaned, went down prow foremost; the deck sank; it lay on one side, — but the vessel did not sink.   People were quieted a little; some went to sleep.   Again a number of hours passed; through the upper, grated window a gray light broke in.   Day came on the ocean, pale, as if frightened, gloomy, dark; but it brought a certain hope and solace.

When Vavron and Marysia had said all the prayers that they had in their memories, they climbed up to their plank beds and fell asleep, soundly.

They were roused only by the sound of the bell calling

to breakfast. But they could not eat. Their heads felt as heavy as if they had been leaden; the old man was worse still than the girl. In his benumbed brain nothing could fix itself. The German who persuaded him to go to America had told him, it is true, that he must cross water; but he had never supposed it such a great water that he would have to sail so many days and nights on it. He had thought that he would cross on a scow, as he had crossed water more than once in his lifetime. If he had known that the sea was so enormous, he would have remained in Lipintse. Besides, one other thought struggled in him unquietly: had he not given to damnation his own soul and the soul of his daughter? Was it not a sin for a Catholic from Lipintse to tempt the Lord God, and put himself into an abyss, over which he was sailing now the fifth day to another shore, if in general there was any shore on the other side? His doubts and fears had seven days more of increase to them.

The storm raged forty-eight hours longer, then it went down in some fashion. Vavron and Marysia made bold to go out on deck again; but when they saw rolls of water rocking yet, black, and, as it were, enraged, those mountains advancing against the ship, and those bottom-less, moving valleys, again they thought that only the hand of God, or some power not of man, could save them.

At last it became perfectly clear. But day followed day, and before the ship nothing was visible except always water and water without end, at one time green, at another blue, and mingling with the sky. On that sky passed at times, high up, small, bright clouds, which, growing red in the evening, laid themselves to sleep in the distant west. The ship pursued these clouds over the water. Vavron thought that perhaps in truth the sea did not end anywhere, but he took courage and resolved to ask.

Once he took off his cap and, bowing submissively to a passing sailor, inquired, —

"Great, mighty lord, shall we go quickly to the end of the voyage?"

Oh, wonder! the sailor did not snort with laughter, but stopped and listened. On his red face cut by the wind was to be recognized the working of memory, and of certain recollections which could not arrange themselves in conscious thought at first. After a while he asked, —

"*Was?*"

"Shall we come to land soon, great, mighty lord?"

"Two days, two days," repeated the sailor, with difficulty, holding up at the same time two fingers.

"I thank humbly."

"Whence are ye?"

"From Lipintse."

"What is that Lipintse?"

Marysia, who came up during the talk, blushed greatly, but raising her timid eyes on the sailor, she said, with that thin little voice with which village girls speak, —

"We are from Poznan."

The sailor looked thoughtfully at a bronze nail in the bulwark; then at the girl, at her hair, bright as flax, and something as it were emotion appeared on his weather-beaten face. After a while he said seriously:

"I have been in Dantzig — I understand Polish — I am a Kashub [1] — your brother; but that was long ago! Jetzt bin ich Deutsch."

When he had said this, he raised the end of the rope which he had held before in his hand, turned away, and calling out in sailor fashion: "Ho! ho! o!" he began to draw it.

[1] The Kashubs, a variety of the Poles, live southwest of Dantzig; they number between one and two hundred thousand; their language differs somewhat from the ordinary Polish.

From that time, whenever Vavron and Marysia were on deck, he smiled in a friendly manner at Marysia when he saw them. They were greatly delighted, for they had a living soul inclined to them on this German steamer. But the journey now was not to last long. The next morning, when they went out on deck, a wonderful sight struck their eyes. They saw something dancing on the sea, and when the ship approached that object, they saw that it was a great red cask moved gently by the waves; in the distance was a second like it, and a third, and a fourth. The air and the water were somewhat misty, but not greatly so, besides it was silvery and mild; the surface of the water was smooth, noiseless, and, as far as the eye reached, more and more casks were dancing on the water. Whole clouds of white birds with black wings were flying behind the ship, crying and whistling. On the deck there was an uncommon movement. The sailors had put on fresh clothing; some were washing the deck; others were cleaning the brass fastenings of the bulwarks and the windows; on the mast was hung out one flag, and at the stern of the steamer another, a larger one.

Animation and delight had seized all the passengers; everything living had run out on the deck: some brought up their bags and began to strap them.

Seeing all this, Marysia said, —

" Surely we are coming to land."

A more cheerful spirit entered her and Vavron. At last Sandy Hook showed itself on the west, and another island with a great edifice standing in the centre; in the distance was a condensed fog, as it were a cloud, as it were a collection of smoke, stretched in strips above the sea, indefinite, distant, dim, formless. At sight of this there was a great murmur; all pointed to it; the steamer, on its part, whistled shrilly, as if from delight.

"What is that?" inquired Vavron.

"New York," said the Kashub, who was standing at his side.

Now the columns of smoke seemed to separate, to be lost, and on the background on which they had been. in proportion as the steamer cleaved the silvery water, appeared the outlines of houses, roofs, chimneys; pointed spires were defined more clearly on the blue; with the spires were the tall chimneys of factories, over the chimneys columns of smoke spreading in soft, bushy forms above. Below, in front of the city, a forest of masts, and on the points of them thousands of flags which the breeze moved as if they were flowers on a meadow. The steamer drew nearer and nearer. The fair city rose as if from under the water. Great delight and astonishment seized Vavron; he removed his cap, opened his lips and gazed; he gazed, and then said to the girl,—

"Marysia!"

"O for God's sake!"

"Dost see?"

"I see!"

"Dost wonder?"

"I wonder."

But Vavron not only wondered, he desired. Seeing the green shores on both sides of the bay, and the dark lines of groves, he continued,—

"Well, praise be to God! If they would only give me land right away, here near the city, with that meadow, it would be close to the market. The fair would come: a man might drive a cow, drive a pig, and sell them. I see that people are here as numerous as poppy seeds. In Poland I was a peasant, but here I shall be a lord."

At that moment the splendid National Park deployed

before his eyes in all its length, and Vavron, when he saw those groups and clusters of trees, said again, —

"I will bow down low to the great, mighty commissioner of the Government, — I will talk to him cunningly to give me even sixty acres of this forest, and afterward an addition. If an inheritance, then an inheritance. I can send a man with wood in the morning to the city. Glory to the Highest! for I see that the German did not deceive me."

Lordship smiled somehow at Marysia also, and she knew not why that song came to her head which brides sang to bridegrooms at weddings in Lipintse, —

> "What sort of bridegroom art thou?
> Thy whole outfit is a cap and a coat."

Had she, perhaps, the design of singing something similar to poor Yasko, when he should come for her and she should be an heiress?

Now a little steamer from the quarantine flew toward the great one. Four or five men came on board. Conversation and outcries set in. Soon another steamer came up from the city itself, bringing agents of hotels and boarding-houses, guides, money-changers, railroad agents; all these shouted in heaven-piercing voices, crowding and circling around the whole deck. Vavron and Marysia had fallen, as it were, into a vortex, and could not tell what to do.

The Kashub advised the old man to change his money, and promised not to let people cheat him. Vavron followed his advice. He received forty-seven dollars in silver for what he had. Before all this was finished, the steamer had approached the city so nearly that not only the houses could be seen, but people on the streets. They passed every moment larger or smaller vessels; at last they reached the wharf and pushed into a narrow dock of the port.

The journey was ended.

People poured out from the steamer like bees from a hive. Along the narrow gangway, from the deck to the shore, flowed a many-colored throng; the first class, then the second, and at last the steerage passengers, bearing their effects.

When Vavron and Marysia, pushed by the throng, approached the gangway, they found the Kashub near them. He pressed Vavron's hand firmly, and said, —

"Bruder! I wish luck! and to thee, girl, God aid thee!"

"The Lord God repay!" answered both; but there was no time for further farewell. The crowd urged them along the gangway, and in a moment they found themselves in a broad custom-house building.

The custom-house officer, dressed in gray overcoat with a silver star, felt of their packages, then called, "All right!" and pointed to the exit. They went out, and found themselves on the street.

"Tatulo! but what shall we do?"

"We must wait. The German said that a commissioner would come from the Government and inquire for us."

They stood at a wall waiting for a commissioner; meanwhile the uproar of an unknown and immense city surrounded them. They had never seen anything like it. The streets were straight, broad, and on them were crowds of people, as in time of a fair; in the middle of the street were carriages, omnibuses, freight wagons. Round about sounded a strange, unknown tongue; the shouts of workmen and hucksters were heard. From moment to moment entirely black people pushed past; they had big woolly heads. At sight of these Vavron and Marysia made the sign of the cross on themselves, piously. Something marvellous to them was that city, so noisy, so full of voices, so full of whistling of locomotives, clatter of wagons, and shouting of men. All people there were running as quickly as if hunting down some one, or fleeing from some one, and besides what swarms of them! What strange faces; now black, now olive color, now reddish! Just where they were standing near the harbor the greatest activity reigned; from some steamers they were unloading bales; at other steamers they were putting them in. Wagons arrived every moment; trucks clattered on cross-walks; a hurly-burly and an uproar raged as in a sawmill.

In this way passed one hour and a second; they were standing at the wall waiting for the commissioner.

A strange sight on the American shore, in New York, was that Polish peasant, with long hair growing gray, in his square-topped cap, with lamb-skin body, that girl from Lipintse, in a dark-blue jacket, and with beads around her neck.

But strangers passed without even looking at them. In New York, people wonder at no face, at no dress.

Another hour passed; the sky became cloud-covered; rain fell, mixed with snow, a cold, damp wind came in from the sea.

They remained waiting for the commissioner.

The peasant nature was patient; but something in their souls began to grow heavy.

They had felt lonely on the steamer, amid strange people, and that desert of water had been terrible and evil. They had implored God to conduct them, like wandering children, over the abysses of the ocean. They had thought that if once they could put foot on land their misfortune would end. Now they had come; they

were in a great city; but in that city, in the uproar of
men, they felt all at once that it was lonelier still, and
more terrible than ever it had been on the steamer.

The commissioner was not coming. What would they
do if he should not come at all, if the German had
deceived them?

The poor peasant hearts quivered with dread at the
thought. What would they do? They would just
perish.

Meanwhile the wind passed through their clothing,
the rain wet them.

"Marysia, art thou not cold?" inquired Vavron.

"Cold, tatulo," answered the girl.

The city clock struck another hour; it was growing
dark in the world. The movement at the wharf ceased;
street lamps were lighted; one sea of gleaming lights
flashed through the city. Laborers from the wharf, singing with hoarse voices, strolled along in smaller or larger
groups into the city. Gradually the street was deserted
completely. The custom-house was closed.

They remained waiting for the commissioner.

At last night came, and it was quiet at the water, save
that, from time to time, the dark smoke-stacks of ferry-
boats belched out bundles of sparks with a hiss, which
died in the darkness, or a wave splashed, striking the
stone embankment. At times was heard the song of a
drunken sailor returning to his ship. The light of the
lamps became pale in the fog. They waited.

Even if they had had no wish to wait, where could
they go? What were they to do? Where were they to
turn? Where were they to lay their wearied heads?
The cold pierced them more sharply; hunger tortured
them. If they had even a roof above their heads, for
they were wet to the skin.

Ah! the commissioner had not come, and he would not come, for there was no such commissioner. The German was an agent of the transportation company; he took a percentage for each person, and cared for nothing more.

Vavron felt that the legs were tottering under him, that some gigantic weight was crushing him, that God's anger must be hanging over him.

He suffered and waited as only a peasant can. The voice of the girl, shivering from cold, roused him at last from his torpor.

" Tatulo."

" Be quiet. There is no mercy above us!"

" Let us go back to Lipintse."

" Go drown thyself —"

" O God, God!" whispered Marysia, quietly.

Grief seized Vavron.

" Oh, orphan, poor girl! May God take pity even on thee!"

But she heard him no longer. Leaning her head against the wall, she closed her eyes. Sleep came, broken, oppressive, feverish. And in a dream, as it were a picture in a frame, Lipintse, and as it were the song of Yasko, the groom, —

> " What bride art thou?
> Thy whole outfit
> Is a garland of rue."

The first rays of daylight in the port of New York fell on the water, the masts, and the custom-house building.

In that gray light one might have distinguished under a wall two sleeping figures with pallid, bluish faces; they were covered with snow, and were as still as if dead. But in the book of their misfortune only the first leaves had been turned. We will read the others later on.

II.

IN NEW YORK.

Passing in New York from wide Broadway toward the wharf, in the direction of Chatham Square, and crossing a number of adjacent streets, the traveller comes upon a part of the city which increases in poverty, squalor, and gloom. The narrow streets become ever narrower. The houses, built, it may be, even by the Dutch colonists, have cracked and bent over in course of time; the roofs on them have sagged, the plaster fallen in great part from the walls, and the walls themselves sunk into the earth, till the tops of the basement windows are barely above the street pavement. A marvellous crookedness is present there, instead of the favorite straight lines of America; roofs and walls, standing out of line, crowd together and rise, one above another, showing disordered aggregations of shaggy roofs.

Because of its position near the water, the puddles in the street-ruts in this part of the city hardly ever dry, and the small squares, securely closed, are like little ponds filled with thick, black, stagnant water. The windows of the tumble-down houses gaze gloomily into this water, the foul surface of which is varied with scraps of paper and pasteboard, bits of glass, wood, and pieces of tin from bales. With similar fragments, whole streets are covered, or rather the entire layer of mud which conceals them. Everywhere are visible human misery, dirt, and disorder.

In this division of the city are " boarding-houses," or inns, in which, for two dollars a week, it is possible to find lodging and entire maintenance; here also are drinking houses, or "bar rooms," in which whalers find every kind of rough men for their vessels; and secret agencies of Venezuela, Ecuador, and Brazil persuade people to tropical colonization, and obtain a respectable number of victims for the yellow fever; restaurants, feeding their guests with salt meat, rotten oysters, and fish, which surely the water itself brought to shore; secret places for dice playing; Chinese laundries; various refuges for sailors; finally dens of crime, hunger, misery, and tears.

Still that part of the city is active; for all the immigrants who cannot find even a temporary place in the barracks of Castle Garden, and who wish not, or are unable to go to the so-called "work houses," huddle together, live and die there. On the other hand, it may be said, that if immigrants are the scum of European society, the inhabitants of these retreats are the scum of immigration. The people here are idle, partly through want of work, and partly through desire.

Here in the night-time revolver shots are heard with sufficient frequency, shouts for help, hoarse screams of rage, drunken songs, or the howls of negroes butting their heads against one another. Every little while in the daytime whole crowds of loafers, in torn hats, and with pipes between their teeth, look on at fist battles, betting meanwhile from one to five cents on black eyes. White children and woolly headed little negroes, instead of passing their time at school, wander through the streets, playing with pieces of ox ribs, or looking in the mud for remnants of vegetables, bananas, or lemons; destitute women stretch their hands to a better dressed passer-by, in case he wanders in there.

In this human Gehenna we find our old acquaintances, Vavron Toporek and Marysia, his daughter. The "inheritance" which they had hoped for was a dream, and like a dream had it vanished; but reality presents itself to us now in the form of a little room sunk in the earth, having one window with broken panes. On the walls of the room is foul, black mould with streaks of dampness; at the wall stands a rusty little iron stove with holes in it, and a three-legged table; in one corner a small bundle of barley straw takes the place of a bed.

This is all. Old Vavron, kneeling before the stove, is searching in the cold ashes to find a potato somewhere, and to that search he returns now in vain — the second day; Marysia is sitting on the straw clasping her knees with her hands, and looking at the floor with fixed stare. The girl is ill and emaciated. She is the same Marysia, as it were: but her cheeks, once blooming, are deeply sunken; her complexion has grown pallid and sickly, her whole face as if smaller than before; her eyes are larger and staring. On her face the effects of foul air, gnawing grief and vile food are evident. They had lived on potatoes only; but for two days potatoes are lacking. Now they know not what to do or how to exist any longer. It is now the third month that they have lived on this street and inhabited this den; their money is gone. Old Vavron tried to find work; but no one understood even what he wanted; he went to the wharf to carry packages and load coal into ships; but he had no wheelbarrow, and, moreover, he got a black eye right away; he wanted to find work with an axe in building piers, men gave him a black eye the second time. Besides, what sort of a laborer is he who does not understand what people say to him? Wherever he thrust in his hand, to whatever he wished to betake himself, whithersoever he went, people laughed him out, threw him out, pushed him out, beat him; consequently he found nothing; he was neither able to earn money or beg it from any source. His hair whitened from gnawing grief; hope was exhausted, and hunger began.

In his own country, among his own people, were he to lose everything, were disease to harass him, were his children to drive him from his cottage, he would need simply to take a staff in his hand and stand under a cross at the roadside, or at the door of some church, and sing: "O God the merciful, hear Thou my cry!" A rich man, passing, would give him ten coppers; a lady would send from her carriage a little girl with money in her rosy hand, and with great eyes fixed on the grandfather (the beggar); a peasant would give a loaf of bread; a peasant woman, a bit of bacon, — and he might live, even as a bird which neither ploughs nor sows. Besides, whenever he stood at a cross, its arms would be over his head, above that the heavens, and round about fields. In that quiet of the country the Lord God would hear his complaint. There, in that city, something was roaring as terribly as in an enormous machine; each one, rushing straightforward, looked ahead so directly that no man saw another's misfortune. Dizziness seized the brain; a man's hands fell; his eyes could not take in all that thrust itself on them, nor could one thought catch another. All was so wonderful, foreign, repelling, and scattering that the man who could not turn in that whirl was shot out of the circle and broken, like an earthen pot.

"Ei! what a difference! There in quiet Lipintse, Vavron was a householder and a counsellor; he had land, the respect of people, a sure spoonful of daily food; on Sunday he went out before the altar with a candle; but here he was the last of all, he was like a dog which has wandered into a strange yard, timid, trembling, curled up, and famished.

In the early days of his misfortune memory said frequently, "It was better in Lipintse" His conscience cried to him, "Vavron, why hast thou deserted Lipintse?" Why? — because God had deserted him. The man would bear his cross, would suffer, if to that way of the cross there was an end in any place; but he knew well that every day would bring a still harder trial, and every morning the sun would shine upon still greater misery for him and Marysia. What then? Was he to twist a rope, say an Our Father, and hang himself? The man would not wink an eye in face of death; but what would happen to his daughter? When he thought of all this, he felt that not only had God deserted him, but that his mind was deserting him. There was no light in that darkness which he saw before him, and he could not even name the greatest pain that he felt.

The yearning for Lipintse was that greatest pain. It tortured him night and day, and tortured him the more terribly because he knew not what he needed, or whither the peasant soul in him was tearing, or why that soul was howling from torture; but he needed the pine wood, the fields, and the cottages thatched with straw, and lords and peasants, and priests, and all that over which a part of his native sky was hanging, and to which the heart becomes so attached that it cannot tear itself away, and if it is torn away it bleeds. The man felt that something was crushing him into the earth. At moments he would have been glad to seize his hair and smash his head against the wall, or throw himself on the ground, or howl like a dog on a chain, or call as if in frenzy — whom? — he knew not himself. Now he is just bending under this unknown burden, just falling, and here the strange city roars and roars. He groans and calls Jesus; but there is no crucifix there; no man answers; the city roars and roars; and on the straw sits his daughter with eyes staring at the floor, — famishing and suffering in silence. A wonderful thing! — he and the girl were always together, but often they did not speak one word to each other for days. They lived as if greatly offended. It was evil and oppressive for them to live in that way, but of what could they speak? It is better not to touch festering sores. What could they talk about except this, — that there was no money in the pocket, no potatoes in the stove, no counsel in the head.

Assistance they got from no one. Very many Poles inhabit New York, but none who are prosperous live near Chatham Square.

On the second week after the arrival they made the acquaintance, it is true, of two Polish families, — one from Silesia, the other from near Poznan itself; but those were dying of hunger a long time. The Silesians had lost two children already; the third child was sick, still for two weeks it slept under an arch of a bridge with its parents, and all lived only on what they found on the streets. Later they were taken to a hospital, and it was unknown what had happened them. Equal evil came to the second family, and even greater, for the father drank. Marysia saved the woman while she could; but now she herself needed rescue.

She and her father might have betaken themselves to the Polish church at Hoboken. The priest would at least have informed others concerning them; but did they know that there was any Polish church, or Polish priest; or could they speak with any one, or inquire of any one? So every cent expended was for them, as it were, a step toward the abyss of misery.

They were sitting at that moment, he at the little stove, she on the straw. One hour and a second hour passed.

In the room it had become darker and darker; for, though it was midday, mist had risen from the water, as is usual in spring-time, a dense, penetrating mist. Though it was warm out of doors, both were trembling from cold in that room; at last Vavron lost hope of finding anything in the ashes.

"Marysia," said he, "I cannot endure this any longer, and neither canst thou; I will go to the water to find driftwood; we will heat up the stove even, and I may find something to eat."

She made no answer, so he went. He had learned already to go to the river and fish out bits of boards from boxes and crates which the water brought to shore. So do all who have no means to buy coal. He was cuffed frequently while doing this, but frequently not; sometimes he happened to find a thing to eat,— certain remnants of spoiled vegetables thrown out of ships; and at that occupation, when he went about in the mist and sought what he had not lost, he forgot at moments his misfortune, and the grief which hunted him more than all.

He came at last to the water; and because it was "lunch" time there circled about the shore only a few little boys, who began, it is true, to cry at the man, throw black mud and mussels at him; but these did not hurt. Small boards enough were dancing on the water, one wave brought them in, another took them out to deep places. Soon he had captured enough of them.

Bunches of green stuff of some sort were floating on the water; perhaps there was something in these fit to eat; but, being light, they did not come to shore, hence he could not get them. The boys threw out lines and captured them in that way; he, having no line, merely looked on greedily and waited till the boys went away, then he searched the remnants and ate what seemed to

him fit to be eaten. He did not remember that Marysia
had eaten nothing.

But fate was to smile on him. On the way home he
met a large wagon with potatoes which had stuck fast in
a rut while going to the wharf. Vavron seized the
spokes straightway and pushed the wheel, together with
the teamster. The work was so hard that it made his
back ache; but at last the horses gave a sudden pull,
the wagon came out, and because it was loosely laden a
good number of potatoes fell to the mud from it. The
teamster did not even think of collecting them; he
thanked Vavron for his assistance, cried "Get up!" to
the horses, and drove on.

Vavron rushed immediately for the potatoes, gathered
them greedily with trembling hands, hid them in his
breast, and straightway a better feeling entered his
heart. In hunger a morsel of bread found seems a fortune discovered; hence the man, while returning home,
muttered, —

"Well, thanks be to God, the Highest, that He looked
down on our misfortune. There is wood, the girl will
make a fire; there are potatoes enough for two meals.
The Lord God is merciful! There will be more cheer in
the room right away. The girl has not eaten for a day
and a half; she will be delighted. The Lord God is
merciful!"

Thus talking to himself, he carried the wood in one
hand, with the other he felt every moment to be sure
that the potatoes were not falling from his bosom. He
bore a great treasure; hence he raised his eyes to heaven
and muttered, —

"I thought to myself: I will steal! and here, without
stealing, they fell from the wagon. We have not eaten,
but we shall eat. The Lord God is merciful! Marysia

will rise from the straw right away when she knows that
I have potatoes."

Meanwhile Marysia had not left the straw from the
time that her father had gone out. Formerly when
Vavron had brought wood in the morning, she would heat
the stove, bring water, eat what there was, and then gaze
for whole hours at the fire. She, too, had tried to find
work. They had even hired her in a boarding-house
to wash dishes and sweep; but since they could not
talk to her, and because she did her work badly, not
understanding her employers, they sent her away in two
days. After that she looked for nothing and found
nothing. She sat whole days in the house, afraid to go
out in the street, for drunken sailors would attack her
there. Through this idleness she was still more unhappy.
Homesickness devoured her as rust eats out iron. She
was even more unhappy than Vavron, for besides hunger,
and all those sufferings which she endured, besides the
conviction that there was no help, no salvation, no to-
morrow, to the terrible yearning for Lipintse was added
the thought of Yasko, the groom. He had promised her,
it is true, and said, " Whithersoever thou turnest, will I
turn;' but she went away to be an heiress and a lady,
and now how all had changed, —

He was a young man, working at a great house; he had
his inherited share in the village land: and she had
become as poor, and as hungry, as a mouse in the church
of Lipintse. Would he come, and even should he come,
would he take her to his bosom, would he say to her,
Poor girl, beloved of my heart! or would he say, Go off,
beggar's daughter? What is her dower now? — rags. The
dogs in Lipintse would bark at her; but still something
so draws her there that in truth the soul would be glad
to fly out of her and speed away as a swift swallow over

the water, and even to die, if only there. There he is, Yasko, mindful or not, but greatly beloved; only near him could she have peace, and joy, and gladness, of all people, only with him in the world.

When there was a fire in the stove, and hunger did not torment as to-day, the flames, hissing, shooting up sparks, jumping and glittering, spoke to her of Lipintse, and reminded her how she sat long ago with other girls spinning. Yasko, looking in from another room, cried, "Marysia, let us go to the priest, for thou art dear to me!" And she answered, "Be silent, you rogue!" And it was so pleasant for her, so joyous in her soul, as even at that time when he invited her from a corner to a dance in the middle of the room, he drew her by force, and she, covering her eyes with her arm, whispered, "But go away, I am ashamed!" When the flames reminded her of this, sometimes tears covered her face; but now, just as there was no fire in the stove, there were no tears in her eyes, for she had cried out all her tears. She felt great exhaustion and weariness; she lacked strength even to meditate; but still she endured patiently, merely looking forward with great eyes, like a bird which some one is torturing.

She was looking in that manner this time, also sitting on the straw. Meanwhile some one moved the door of the room. Marysia, with the thought that that was her father, did not move her head till the voice of a strange man called out to her, —

" Look here!"

This was the owner of the tumble-down house in which they were living, — an old mulatto, gloomy-faced, dirty, tattered, with cheeks puffed out with tobacco.

When she saw him, the girl was terribly frightened. They owed a dollar for the coming week, and had not

one cent. All that she might effect was through humility, so, approaching him, she took hold of his feet,
and kissed his hand.

"I came for the dollar," said he.

She understood the word dollar, and, shaking her
head, spoke in broken English, looked imploringly, and
tried to explain that they had spent everything, that
that was the second day since they had eaten, that
they were hungry, and that he ought to take pity on
them.

" God will repay thee, great, mighty lord," added she, in
Polish, not knowing what to say or what to do.

The great, mighty lord did not understand, it is true,
that he was great, mighty, but he divined that he would
not get the dollar. He divined so clearly indeed that,
seizing with one hand the bundles containing their effects,
he took the girl with the other by the arm, pushed her
lightly upstairs, conducted her to the street, and, throwing the things at her feet, opened the door of an adjacent
bar-room and called, —

"Hei! there is a room for you!"

"All right!" answered some voice from within. "I
will come in the evening."

The mulatto vanished then in the dark entrance, and
the girl remained alone on the sidewalk. She put her
bundles in a niche of the house, so that they might not
roll in the mud, and, standing near them, waited, humble
as ever, in silence.

The drunken men who passed by did not touch her
this time. It was dark in the room, but outside there
was much light, and in that light the girl's face seemed
as emaciated as after a great illness. Only her bright,
flaxen hair remained as before; her lips had grown blue;
her eyes were sunken and black underneath; the bones

stood forth in her cheeks. She was like a flower which is withering, or a girl who must die.

Passers-by looked at her with a certain consideration. An old negro woman asked her some question, but, receiving no answer, passed on offended.

Meanwhile Vavron hastened homeward with that pleasant feeling which in very poor people is roused by an evident proof of God's kindness. He had potatoes now; he was thinking how he and Marysia would eat them; how to-morrow again he would go around wagons; but of the day after to-morrow he was not thinking at that moment, for he was very hungry. When from a distance he saw the girl standing on the pavement in front of the house, he wondered greatly, and hastened still more.

" But why art thou standing here ? "

" The house-owner has driven us out, father."

" Has he driven us out ? "

The wood fell from Vavron's hand. That was too much indeed ! To drive them out at that moment when there was wood and potatoes ! What could they do now ; where could they cook the potatoes ; with what could they nourish themselves; whither could they go ? After the wood, Vavron hurled his cap into the mud. " O Jesus, O Jesus ! " he turned around; he opened his mouth; he looked wildly at the girl and repeated once more, —

" Did he drive us out ? "

Then he wished as it were to go somewhere, but turned at once, and his voice became deep, hoarse, and threatening, when he said again, —

" Why didst thou not beg him, thou blockhead ? "

She sighed.

" I begged him."

" Didst thou take him by the knees ? "

"I did."

Again Vavron turned on the spot, like a worm which some one has pierced. It became entirely dark in his eyes.

"Would to God thou wert dead!" cried he.

The girl looked at him with pain.

"Tatulo! how am I to blame?"

"Wait here, stir not. I will go and beg him to let us even cook the potatoes."

He went. After a while an uproar was heard in the entrance, a trampling of feet, loud voices, and then out flew Vavron to the street, pushed evidently by a strong hand.

He stood a moment, then said to the girl, mildly, —

"Come."

She bent down over the bundles to take them; they were very heavy for her exhausted strength; but he did not help her, as if he had forgotten, as if he did not see that the girl was barely able to carry them.

Two such wretched figures, the old man and the girl, would have attracted the attention of passers-by if those passers-by had been less accustomed to spectacles of misery. Whither could they go? Into what other darkness, into what other misfortune, into what other torture?

The girl's breath came with more and more difficulty; she tottered once, and a second time. At last she said, with entreaty in her voice, —

"Father, take the rags; I cannot carry them."

He was roused, as if from sleep, —

"Throw them away, then!"

'But they will be of use."

"They will not be of use."

Seeing all at once that the girl hesitated, he cried in a rage, —

"Throw them away, for I am going to kill thee!"

This time she obeyed in terror, and they went on. The man repeated a number of times yet, —

"If it is that way, then let it be that way!"

He was silent, but something uncanny was gazing out of his eyes. Through narrow streets, still muddier, they were approaching the remotest harbor. They went out onto a large pier resting on piles; they passed near a building with an inscription, "Sailors' Asylum," and went down close to the very water. Men were building a new dock in that place. The lofty timbers of a pile-driver rose high above the water, and among the plank and beams persons occupied with the work were circling about. Marysia, when she had come to a pile of timber, sat down on it, for she could not go farther. Vavron sat near her in silence.

It was four in the afternoon. The whole wharf was seething with life and movement. The mist had fallen away; the calm rays of the sun cast their light and gracious warmth on the two unfortunates. The breath of spring came to land, fresh, full of life, and joyous. Round about there was so much azure and light that the eyes blinked under the excess of them. The surface of the sea blended charmingly with the sky. In those blue expanses nearer the middle of the harbor were masts standing motionless, smoke-stacks, flags waving lightly in the breeze. On the horizon, vessels sailing into the harbor seemed to move upward, or to push themselves out of the water. The tightly raised and swollen sails, looking like clouds, all in sunlight shone with blinding whiteness on the azure of the sea. Some vessels going out to the ocean left a foaming trail behind them. They were going in the direction in which Lipintse lay, hence for them both toward the place of lost happiness, — that is, peace and a better lot. The girl thought how could they have sinned so greatly, what could they have done against the Lord God, that He, the merciful, had turned His face from them in the midst of strange people, and thrown them out on that distant shore? In His hand was the power to return them happiness; and how many ships were sailing away toward that land, and sailing away without taking them. She was wearied. Marysia's poor mind flew once more toward Lipintse and Yasko, the groom. Was he thinking of her? Did he remember her? She remembered him, for it is only in happiness that people forget; in misfortune, in loneliness, thought winds itself around the beloved one, as hops around a poplar tree. But he? Perhaps he has despised his former loving, and has sent matchmakers to another cottage. Besides, it would be even a shame for him to think of one so wretched, one who has nothing in this world but a garland of rue, and for whom, if any one is to send a matchmaker, it is death alone who will do so.

As she was sick, hunger did not torment her much, but sleep, which came of suffering and weakness, overcame her; the lids closed over her eyes, and her pallid face dropped toward her breast. At moments she woke and opened her eyes, then she closed them again. She dreamed that while walking along certain chasms and precipices she fell down like Kasia, in the peasant song: "Into the deep Dunayets," and immediately she heard distant singing clearly, —

> "Yasko on the high mountain saw that fall;
> He let himself down on a silken cord to Marysia;
> But the cord was too short, an ell was still wanting.
> Marysia, dear girl, give thy tress to me."

Here she woke suddenly, for it seemed to her that the tress was gone, and that she was falling into the abyss.

The dream vanished. Not Yasko was sitting near her, but Vavron; and not the "Dunayets" was visible, but the harbor of New York, currents, scaffoldings, masts, and smoke-stacks. Again certain vessels sail out into the open, and from them came the singing. A calm, warm, clear, spring evening was reddening the sky. The surface of the water became like a mirror; every vessel, every pile, was reflected as if another were beneath it, and all was beautiful round about. A certain happiness and great bliss were in the air; it seemed that the whole world was rejoicing. They two alone were unhappy and forgotten. The laborers began to return home; they alone had no home.

Hunger with iron hand was rending Vavron's entrails more and more. The man sat gloomy and cloudy; but something, which seemed a terrible determination, began to depict itself on his face. Whoso might look at him would be frightened, for that face had the expression of a beast and a bird, because of hunger; but, at the same time, it was as despairingly calm as the face of a dead man. For a whole hour he had not spoken one word to the girl; but when night had come, when the dock was deserted completely, he said, with a strange voice, —

"Let us go, Marysia."

"Where?" asked she, drowsily.

"To those platforms above the water. Let us lie down on the planks there, and sleep."

They went. In the utter darkness they had to creep along very carefully, so as not to fall into the water.

The American structure of beams and planks formed numerous windings, and as it were a wooden corridor, at the very end of which was a platform of plank, and beyond it a pile-driver. On this platform, covered with a roof to protect from rain, stood the men who drew the

ropes of the pile-driver; but now there was no one
there.

When they reached the very end, Vavron said, —

"Here we shall sleep."

Marysia fell rather than placed herself on the planks,
and, though a swarm of mosquitoes attacked them, she
fell asleep soundly.

Suddenly in the dark night Vavron's voice roused her:
"Marysia, rise up!"

There was something in that call of such nature that
she woke at once.

"What is it, tatulo?"

In the silence and darkness of night the voice of the
old peasant was deep and terrible, but calm, —

"Girl! Thou wilt famish no longer from hunger.
Thou wilt not go to strange thresholds for bread; thou
wilt not sleep out of doors. People have deserted thee.
God has deserted thee; thy fate is ended, — then let even
death show thee kindness. The water is deep; thou wilt
not suffer."

She could not see him in the darkness, though her eyes
were widely open from terror.

"I will drown thee, poor girl, I will drown myself,
too," continued he. "There is no salvation for us, no
mercy above us. To-morrow thou wilt have no wish to
eat; thou wilt be happier to-morrow than to-day."

But she had no wish to die. She was eighteen years of
age, and had that attachment to life, that fear of death,
which youth gives. The whole soul in her shuddered to
its depth at the thought that to-morrow she would be a
drowned corpse, that she would go into some darkness,
that she would be lying among fish and vile creatures
at the slimy bottom of the water. For nothing in the
world! Repugnance and terror indescribable seized her

at that moment, and her own father, speaking thus in the darkness, seemed to her some kind of evil spirit.

During this time his hands were resting on her emaciated shoulders, and the voice continued, with its terrible calmness, —

"If thou scream, no man will hear thee. I shall only push thee; the whole will not last two Our Fathers."

"I do not want to die, father. I do not!" cried Marysia. "Have you no fear of God? Oh, dear, golden father, take pity on me! What have I done to you? You know I have not complained of my fate; I have suffered hunger and cold with you — father!"

His breathing became quicker, his hands closed like vices; she begged more and more despairingly against death.

"Take pity on me! mercy! oh, mercy! but I am your child. I am poor; I am sick; I am not long for the world anyhow. Take pity on me! I am afraid."

Thus moaning, she clung to his coat, pressed her lips imploringly to those hands which were thrusting her into the abyss. But all this seemed merely to urge him on. His calmness passed into madness; he began to rattle in the throat, and snort. At moments there was silence between them, and if any man had been standing near he would have heard only the loud breathing and struggling, and the creaking of planks. The night was dark. It was late, and aid could come from no place, for that was the very end of the port, at which even in the daytime there were no people save laborers.

"Mercy! mercy!" cried Marysia, shrilly.

At that moment one hand drew her violently to the very edge of the scaffolding, a second began to beat her head to stifle her cries. But those cries roused no echo; some dog merely howled in the distance.

The girl felt that she was weakening. At last her feet were in emptiness; only her hands clung to her father, but her hands were weak. Her screams for rescue grew fainter and fainter; her hands at last tore off a piece of the coat, and Marysia felt that she was flying into the abyss.

She had indeed fallen from the platform, but on the way she grasped a brace and hung above the water.

The man bent over, and, dreadful to relate, fell to loosening her hands.

A crowd of thoughts, like a flock of frightened birds, fly through her brain in the form of images, and lightning flashes, — Lipintse, the well-sweep, the departure, the ship, the storm, the Litany, the misery of New York, finally that which is happening to her. Then she sees a ship, immense, with lofty prow, on it a throng of people, and out of that throng two hands are stretched toward her. As God lives! that is Yasko standing there; Yasko stretches his hand out, and, above the ship, and above Yasko, is the Mother of God smiling, surrounded with immense brightness. At sight of this she pushes apart the people on shore: "Most holy Virgin! Yasko! Yasko!" One moment more — once again she raises her eyes to her father: "Oh, father! the Mother of God is up there, the Mother of God is up there!"

The next moment those same hands which were pushing her into the water seize her weakening arms, and draw her up with a kind of preterhuman strength. Now she feels the plank of the structure under her feet; again an arm surrounds her, but the arm of a father, not an executioner, and her head falls on his breast.

When she recovered from her faint, she saw that she was lying quietly near her father; and, though it was dark, she saw him lying in the form of a cross, and saw that deep, penitent sobs were shaking him, and rending his breast.

"Marysia," said he, at length, in a voice broken with sobs, "forgive me, child."

The girl sought his hand in the darkness, and, putting it to her pale lips, whispered, —

"Father! may the Lord Jesus forgive you as I forgive."

Out of the pale clearness which for some time had been on the horizon came the moon at last, large, mild, full, and again something wonderful happened. Marysia saw whole swarms of little angels, like golden bees, and they floated to her on the moon-rays, buzzing with their little wings, circling, winding, and singing with childlike voices, —

"Maiden tormented, peace to thee! Poor little bird, peace to thee! Flower of the field, peace to thee! Patient and silent, peace to thee!"

Thus singing, they shook over her the cups of white lilies, and little silver bells which sounded, —

"Sleep to thee, maiden! sleep to thee! sleep! sleep! sleep!"

And it became so pleasant for her, so clear, so calm, that she fell asleep really.

The night passed, and began to grow pale. Dawn came. Light whitened the water. The masts and smoke-stacks came out of the darkness and drew nearer; Vavron was kneeling now, bent over Marysia.

He thought that she had died. Her slender form lay motionless; her eyes were closed her face, pale as linen, with a bluish tinge, calm and deathlike. In vain did the old man shake her arm, she quivered not, neither did she open her eyes. It seemed to Vavron that he too would die; but, putting his hand to her mouth, he felt that she was breathing. Her heart was beating, though faintly; he understood that she might die any moment. If a pleasant day rose from the mist of the morning, if the sun warmed her, she would waken, otherwise she would not.

The sea-gulls circled above her as if concerned for her safety; some of them sat on a neighboring pillar. The morning mist vanished slowly under the breath of wind from the west. It was a spring breeze, warm, full of sweetness.

Then the sun rose. Its rays fell first on the top of the pile-driver, then, descending lower and lower, cast their golden light on the deathlike face of Marysia. They seemed to kiss it, to fondle it, and as it were embrace it. In those rays, and in that garland of bright hair, dishevelled from the struggle of the night and from dampness, the face seemed simply angelic; but Marysia, too, was almost an angel through her suffering and misfortune.

A beautiful, rosy day came up from the water; the sun warmed with increasing strength; the wind blew with pity on the maiden; the sea-gulls, circling like a garland, cried, as if they wished to rouse her. Vavron, taking off his coat, covered her feet with it, and hope entered his heart.

Indeed the blueness left her face gradually; her cheeks gained a slight rose-color; she smiled once and a second time; and finally she opened her eyelids.

Then that old peasant knelt on the pier, raised his eyes heavenward, and tears flowed in two streams along his wrinkled face.

He felt once and forever that that child was now the sight of his eyes, the soul of his soul, and as it were a sacredness beloved above everything.

She not only woke, but she woke feeling better and

more lively than the day previous. The pure air of the harbor was more wholesome for her than the poison air of the room. She had returned to life indeed, for, sitting on the plank, she said immediately, —

"Father, I want very much to eat."

"Come, daughter, to the edge of the water, we may find something there," said he.

She rose without great effort and went. Evidently that day was to be somehow exceptional in the days of their misfortune, for barely had they gone a few steps when they saw there near them on the scaffolding a handkerchief thrust in between two beams, in it was cooked corn and salt meat. The simple explanation of this was that some laborer working at the wharf had put away yesterday a part of his food for to-day. Laborers there had that custom; but Vavron and Marysia interpreted it still more simply. Who put that food there? In their opinion He who thinks of every bird and flower, every grasshopper and ant.

God!

They repeated Our Father and ate, though there was not much there, and then went along the water to the main docks. New strength entered into them. Going to the custom-house, they turned up Water Street toward Broadway. With halts, this occupied two hours, for the road was a long one. At times they sat on boards or empty boxes. They went on, not knowing themselves why they went; but somehow it seemed to Marysia that they ought to go to the city. On the way they met a multitude of goods-wagons going to the wharf. On Water Street the movement was not slight. Doors opened and out came people who went hurriedly to their daily labor.

In one of these doorways appeared a tall, gray-mustached gentleman with a young boy. When he came out, he looked at Vavron and Marysia, at their dress; his mustache quivered, astonishment appeared on his face, then he looked more quickly, and smiled.

A human face smiling at them in a friendly manner in New York was a wonder, a witchery, at sight of which both were astounded.

The gray-haired man approached them, and asked, in the purest Polish, —

"And you people, whence come you?"

A thunderbolt as it were had struck them. Vavron, instead of answering, became as pale as a wall and tottered, believing neither his ears nor his eyes. Marysia, recovering first, fell at once to the feet of the old gentleman, embraced them, and said, —

"From Poznan, serene heir, from Poznan."

"What are ye doing here?"

"We are in need, in hunger, in terrible misfortune, dear master."

Here her voice failed. Vavron cast himself flat at the feet of the old gentleman, kissed the hem of his overcoat, and, holding to it, thought that he had caught a piece of heaven.

"This is a lord for thee, and he is our lord. He will not let a man die; he will save, he will not let us perish."

The young lad who was with the gray-haired gentleman stared; people gathered around, gaped, and looked wonderingly at one man kneeling before another and kissing his feet. In America this is unheard of. The old gentleman grew angry at the gapers.

"This is no 'business' of yours," said he to them in English; "go about your own business!" Then he turned to Vavron and Marysia, —

"We will not stand on the street; come with me."

He conducted them to the nearest restaurant, where they entered a room apart, and he shut himself in with them and the boy. Again they fell at his feet, which he forbade, and scolded them angrily, —

"An end to this! We are from the same country, children of one mother."

Here, evidently, smoke from a cigar which he had in his mouth began to affect his eyes, for he wiped them with his hand, and asked, —

"Are you hungry?"

"For two days we have eaten nothing; but to-day we found a little near the water."

"William!" said he to the lad, "order them something to eat." Then he continued, —

"Where do you live?"

"Nowhere, serene lord, nowhere."

"Where have you slept?"

"Above the water."

"You were driven from your lodgings?"

"Driven."

"You have no things except those on your bodies?"

"We have not."

"You have no money?"

"We have not."

"What will you do?"

"We know not."

The old gentleman, inquiring quickly, and as it were angrily, turned all at once to Marysia, —

"How old are you, girl?"

"I shall finish the eighteenth year Assumption day."

"You have suffered much?"

She made no answer, but bowed to his feet with humility.

The smoke began evidently to bite the old gentleman's eyes again.

At that same moment beer and hot meat were brought in. The old gentleman commanded them to begin eating at once, and they answered that they dared not do that in his presence; he told them that they were fools. But, in spite of his temper, he seemed an angel from heaven to them.

When they had eaten, clearly that delighted him much; he asked them to tell how they had come to America, and through what they had passed. So Vavron told him all, withheld nothing, just as he would confess to a priest. The old gentleman was angry, he scolded; and when it came to telling how Vavron wanted to drown his own daughter, he cried, —

"I would have flayed thee!"

Then he said to Marysia, —

"Come here, girl!"

When she went up to him, he took her head between his hands and kissed her on the forehead; then he thought a while, and said, —

"You have passed through misery. But this is a good country; only a man must know how to manage."

Vavron stared at him: this worthy wise gentleman called America a good country!

"It is true, stupid fellow," said he, observing Vavron s astonishment, "a good country! When I came here, I had nothing; now I have a morsel of bread. For you peasants, though, land-tilling is the work, not wandering about the world. When you go away from home, who will remain over there? You are of no use in this country; but to come here is easy, to go back is difficult."

He was silent a time, then added, as if to himself, —

"I am here forty and some years, and I have forgotten

the country over there. But at times homesickness seizes me. William must go there; let him see how his fathers lived. This is my son," said he, pointing to the boy. "William, thou wilt bring me a handful of earth from home to put under my head in the coffin."

" Yes, father," answered the boy, in English.

" And for my breast, William, and for my breast ! "

" Yes, father."

The smoke now affected the old gentleman's eyes so terribly that his eyeballs were as if covered with glass. Then he was angry and, pointing to the boy, said, —

" This fellow understands Polish, but he likes English better. It has to be so here. What falls here is lost for the old thresholds. Go, William, tell thy sister that we shall have guests for dinner and for the night."

The boy rushed away quickly. The old gentleman fell to thinking, and was silent a long time; then he said, as if to himself, —

"Even send them home, the cost would be great, and, besides, what would they return to? They have sold what they had; they would go to begging. In service God knows what would happen to the girl. Since they are here, they must try to find work. Send them to some colony; the girl will marry after a while. She and her husband will save something; if they want to go home, they will take the old man. Hast heard of our colonies in this country ? " said he then to Vavron.

" I have not heard, great, mighty lord."

" Oh, people ! how they start here ! By the dear God ! You will not be lost. In Chicago there are twenty thousand like thee, in Milwaukee as many, in Detroit a good number, in Buffalo many. They work in factories; but for a peasant, farming is better. We might send thee to Radomia, to Illinois, — hm ! land is dear there. They are founding a new Poznan on the prairies of Nebraska; but that is far away. The railroad fare is costly. There is the Panna Maria (Virgin Mary) colony in Texas; that is far away also. Best of all is to go to Borovina, especially since I can get free tickets, and what I give thee in hand save for housekeeping."

He thought a while still more deeply.

"Listen, old man," said he on a sudden. "They are founding a new colony in Borovina in Arkansas. That is a nice country and warm, and the land is almost vacant. There thou wilt get a hundred and sixty acres from the Government for nothing, and from the railroad for a small price — dost understand? To begin housekeeping, I will give money, and I will give thee tickets, for I can do so. Ye will go to Little Rock; from that place thou must go in a wagon. Thou wilt find others there who will go with thee. Besides, I will give thee letters. I wish to help thee, for I am thy brother; but I care more a hundred times for thy daughter than for thee. Dost understand? Thank God who sent you both to me!"

Here his voice became perfectly mild.

"Listen, child," said he to Marysia, "here is my card; keep it sacredly. Whenever trouble presses thee, shouldst thou be alone in the world and without assistance, find me. Thou art a poor child and good. If I die, William will care for thee. Do not lose the card. Come with me now."

On the road he bought linen for them and clothing; then he took them to his house and entertained them. That was a house filled with kind people, for William and Jennie occupied themselves with both as if they had been relatives. William treated Marysia as if she had been some "lady;" this embarrassed her terribly. In the evening a number of young girls, nicely dressed

and kind, with bangs on their foreheads, visited Panna
Jennie. These took Marysia among them, wondered that
she was so pale, and so pretty, that she had such bright
hair, that she bent to their feet and kissed their hands,
— at this they laughed greatly.

The old gentleman went among the young people,
shook his white head, muttered, was angry at times,
spoke now in English, now in Polish, spoke with Marysia
and Vavron of his and their distant native places, recalled, forgot, and from time to time the smoke of the
cigar affected his eyes evidently, for he rubbed them
often in secret.

When all separated to sleep, Marysia could not restrain
her tears, seeing that Panna Jennie prepared the bed for
her with her own hands. Oh, how kind these people
were! But what wonder, — the old gentleman was also
from Poznan!

On the third day Vavron and Marysia were on the
way to Little Rock. The old man had a hundred dollars
in his pocket, and had forgotten his misery altogether.
Marysia felt above her the visible hand of God, and believed that that hand would not let her perish; that as it
had brought her out of misfortune, it would bring Yasko
also to America, and watch over both, and would let
them even return to Lipintse.

Meanwhile cities and farms shot past the car-windows.
That was different entirely from New York. There were
fields and pine woods in the distance, and cottages and
trees growing around them; a fleece of every kind of grain
was green in great streaks on the earth, exactly as in
Poland. At sight of this Vavron's breast swelled so that
he had the wish to shout, " Hei, ye pine woods, ye green
fields!" Herds of cows and flocks of sheep were pasturing on meadows; on the edges of forests men with

axes were visible. The train flew farther and farther. Gradually the country became less populated. The farms vanished, and the country opened out into a wide and unoccupied prairie. The wind bent waves of grass on it, and it glittered with flowers. In places there wound, in the form of a golden ribbon, roads covered with yellow blossoms, upon which no wagon had ever passed. Lofty grass plots, mulleins, and thistles nodded their heads as if greeting the traveller. Eagles floated on broad wings over the prairie and surveyed the grass carefully. The train tore on, as if wishing to fly to that place where those prairie expanses are lost to the vision and blend with the sky. From the car-window were seen whole flocks of rabbits and prairie dogs. At times the horned head of a deer appeared above the grass. Nowhere were church spires, or towns, or villages, or a house, — nothing save stations, and between stations and behind them no living soul.

Vavron looked at all this, tortured his brain, but could not understand how so much "goodness," as he called land, should lie idle.

Day and night passed. One morning they entered forests in which the trees were entwined with plants as thick as the arm of a man, which made the forest so dense that one would have to cut with an axe through it, as through a wall. Unknown birds were singing in these green densities. Once it seemed to Vavron and Marysia that amid these labyrinths they saw certain horsemen with feathers on their heads, and faces as red as polished brass. Seeing those forests, and unoccupied prairies, and empty pine woods, all these unknown wonders and strange people, the old man could not restrain himself at last, and said, —

"Marysia?"

"What, father?"

"Dost see?"

"I see."

"And dost wonder?"

"I wonder."

They passed a river now three times wider than the Varta, and late that night they arrived at Little Rock.

From there they had to inquire for the road to Borovina. We will leave them here for the moment. The second division of their wandering for bread is finished. The third was to be worked out in the woods, amid the sound of axes, and in the oppressive heat of life in a colony. Whether there were fewer tears in it, less suffering and misfortune, we shall know before long.

III.

LIFE IN THE COLONY.

WHAT was Borovina? A colony to be founded. But evidently the name was thought out in advance, starting from the principle that where there is a name there must be a thing. Preliminarily Polish, and even American, papers, published in New York, Chicago, Buffalo, Detroit, Milwaukee, Manitowoc, Denver, Calumet, in a word, in all places where it was possible to hear Polish speech, announced, *urbi et orbi* (to the city and the world) in general, and to Polish colonists in particular, that whoever of them wished to be healthy, rich, happy, eat fatly, live long, and after death receive salvation surely, should inscribe himself for a share in an earthly paradise, or in Borovina.

The advertisements declared that Arkansas, in which Borovina was to rise, was a country still unoccupied, but

the wholesomest on earth. It is true that the town of
Memphis, lying at the very border on the other bank of
the Mississippi, was a hotbed of yellow fever; but, according to the advertisements, neither yellow, nor any other
fever could cross such a river as the Mississippi. On
the higher bank of the Arkansas River it did not exist,
because the neighboring Indians, the Choctaws, would
scalp it without mercy. Fever trembles at sight of a
redskin. Because of this combination of circumstances,
colonists of Borovina would dwell in a perfectly neutral
zone between fever on the east and Indians on the west.
Having before it, moreover, such a future, Borovina would,
in a thousand years, contain, beyond doubt, two million
inhabitants; and land, for which to-day one dollar and
fifty cents an acre was paid, would be sold at auction for
no less than a thousand dollars a square yard.

It was difficult to resist such promises and prospects.
Those to whom the neighborhood of the Choctaws was
less pleasing, were assured by advertisements that this
valiant tribe was animated by a most particular sympathy for Poles, that therefore it was proper to look forward to most agreeable relations. Moreover, it was
known that when the railroad passed through the prairies,
and there would be telegraph poles in the form of crosses,
those crosses would soon serve as monuments above the
graves of Indians; and since the land of Borovina was
obtained from the railroad, the disappearance of the
Indians was a question of time, nothing more.

The land had been acquired, indeed, from the railroad;
this assured the colony connection with the world, an out-
let for products, and future development. The advertisements had forgotten to add, it is true, that this railroad
was only projected, and that the sale of sections of
land, granted roads by the Government in uninhabited

places, was to guarantee, or rather to complete, the capital needful to build. This omission was, however, pardonable in business so complicated. Moreover, it involved this difference for Borovina, that the colony, instead of being on the line of the road, was in a deep wilderness to which one had to go amid immense difficulties, with wagons.

From these omissions, various disputes might rise, which were only temporary, however, and would cease at once with the building of the road. Besides, it is known that advertisements in America are not to be taken literally, for as plants transferred to American soil flourish surely, but at the cost of their fruit, in like manner advertisements in American papers increase so in every direction that at times it is difficult to separate the one grain of truth from rhetorical chaff.

But putting aside everything which in the advertisements touching Borovina should be considered as *humbug*, so called, it might still be supposed that that colony would not be worse than a thousand others, the rise of which was announced with no less exaggeration.

The conditions appeared in many respects favorable, hence a multitude of persons, and even of Polish families, scattered throughout the Union, from the Great Lakes to the palm forests of Florida, from the Atlantic to the coast of California, inscribed themselves as settlers in the colony about to be founded. Mazovians from Prussia, Silesians, people of Poznan, Galicia, Lithuanians from Augustov, and Mazovians from near Warsaw, who worked in factories in Chicago and Milwaukee, and who for a long time had been sighing for a life which a peasant should lead, seized the first opportunity to escape from stifling cities, blackened with smoke and soot, and betake themselves to the plough and axe in the broad

6

fields, forests, and prairies of Arkansas. Those for whom it was too hot at Panna Maria in Texas, or too cold in Minnesota, or too damp in Detroit, or too hungry in Radomia in Illinois, joined with the first, and a number of hundreds of people, mostly men, but still a good many women and children, moved to Arkansas. The name "Bloody Arkansas" did not overmuch terrify the colonists. Though, to tell the truth, this section abounds yet in thieving Indians, and so-called outlaws or robbers, fleeing from justice, and wild squatters who cut timber on Red River in defiance of Government, and various other adventurers or scoundrels avoiding the gallows; though hitherto the western part of the State was famous for savage struggles between Indians and the white buffalo-hunters, and for the terrible "lynch" law, — still it was possible to help one's self in all this. The Mazovian who feels a knotty club in his fist, and especially when he has a Mazovian at each side of him and a Mazovian behind, will not yield much to any one, and to the man who crawls into his path he is ready to shout, "Do not move, do not push in here, or we will pound you till you are lame!" It is also known that Mazovians like to keep together and settle so that Matsek may hurry at any moment to help another Matsek with a club.

The rallying point for the majority was Little Rock; but from Little Rock to Clarksville, the settlement nearest Borovina was a little farther than from Warsaw to Cracow, and, what was worse, colonists had to pass through an uninhabited country, and make their way through forests and deep water. In fact a number of people, unwilling to wait for the whole company, started on alone, and perished without tidings; but the main camp arrived successfully, and fixed itself in the midst of the forest.

When the colonists reached the place, they were in truth greatly disenchanted. They had hoped to find in the colony lands, forests, and fields; they found only forests, which had to be felled. Black oak, redwood, cottonwood, the light-colored sycamore, and the dark hickory stood side by side in one mass.

That wilderness was no joke, lined with chaparral below, entangled with hanging plants above, which went from tree to tree like cables and ropes, forming, as it were hanging bridges, curtains, as it were, festoons covered with flowers, and so dense, so packed and entangled, that the eye could not see in the distance as in our forests; and whoso went into them more deeply could not see the sky above his head, but had to wander in darkness, and might go astray and be lost forever. One and another Mazovian looked at his fist, at his axe, then at those oaks, a number of yards in circumference, and more than one man grew sad. It is well to have timber for a cottage and for fuel; but for one colonist to cut down a forest of a hundred and sixty acres, pull the stumps out of the ground, level the land, and then plough it, is the work of years.

But there was nothing else to be done, hence the day after the arrival of the company each man made the sign of the cross on himself, spat on his hands, caught up his axe, grunted, whirled the axe, struck; and from that time forth the noise of axes was heard in that Arkansas forest, and at times too songs attended with echoes, —

> "Kasenko came. He came from the mansion,
> Dear, darling Kasenko.
> Come to the pinewood,
> Come to the pinewood, come to the dark one."

The camp stood at the bank of a river, or rather on a broad plain at the edge of which were to stand in a quad-

rangle the cottages; in the middle, with time, was to be
a church and a school. But that was far ahead; meanwhile the wagons in which the colonists' families had arrived were put in line. Those wagons were arranged in
a triangle so that in case of attack people might defend
themselves behind them as in a fortress. Beyond the
wagons, on the rest of the plain, were the mules, horses,
oxen, cows, and sheep, watched by a guard composed of
armed young men. The people slept in the wagons, or
inside the triangle at fires.

In the daytime women and children remained in the
camp; the presence of men was known only by the
sound of axes, which filled the whole forest. At night
wild beasts howled in the thickets, jaguars, Arkansas wolves, and coyotes. Terrible gray bears, which fear
the glare of fire less than other beasts, approached rather
near the wagons at times; wherefore gunshots were heard
frequently in the darkness, and shouts of "Hurry to kill
the beast!" Men who had come from the wild regions
of Texas were trained hunters, for the greater part, and
those obtained with ease, for themselves and their families, the flesh of wild beasts; namely, antelopes, deer, and
buffaloes, for that was the time of spring migration when
those animals went northward. The rest of the colonists
nourished themselves with supplies bought in Clarksville
or Little Rock, and composed of Indian corn and salt
pork. Besides, they killed sheep, a certain number of
which had been brought by each family.

In the evening, when a large fire was made near the
wagons, the young people danced, after supper, instead
of going to sleep. A certain man who could play had
brought with him a violin; on this he played the Obertas
by ear, and when the sound of the violin was lost
amid the noise of the forest and under the open sky,

others helped the player in American fashion with tin plates.

Life passed noisily in hard work, and moreover without order. The first thing was to build cottages; in fact, on the green plain there soon appeared the bodies of a number of them, and all the surface of the place was covered with shavings, pieces of bark, and similar leavings of wood. Redwood was easily worked; but often they had to go far to find it. Some put up temporary tents of canvas taken from the wagons. Others, especially the unmarried, who were less careful of having a roof above their heads, and were more averse to pulling stumps, began to plough in places where the forest had no undergrowth, and where oak and hickory were rarer. Then was heard for the first time since that Arkansas forest was a forest, "Hets, kso, bys!" [1]

But in general such a weight of work fell on the colonists that they knew not where to put their hands first, whether to build houses, or clear the land, or hunt.

At the very beginning it came out that the agent of the colony had bought the land from the railroad on hearsay, and had never been there, otherwise he would not have taken a dense forest, since it was equally easy to buy pieces of prairie partly covered with timber. He and the agent of the railroad came, it is true, to the place to survey the sections, and show each man his own; but when they saw how matters stood really, they delayed a couple of days, then quarrelled, went away as if for surveying tools to Clarksville, and showed themselves never again in the colony.

Soon it appeared that some colonists had paid more than others; and, what was worse, no man knew where his section lay, or how to survey that which fell to him.

[1] Polish exclamations used in driving oxen.

The colonists remained without leadership, without any
authority which might bring their affairs into order and
settle disputes. They did not know well how to work.

Germans would have begun surely to cut down the
timber in company, and, after they had cleared a certain
space, put up the houses with combined labor; then they
would have measured out the land at each house. But
every Mazovian wanted to occupy his own ground immediately, put up his own house, and cut the forest on his
own section. Besides, each man wanted to take his place
in the middle of the plain where trees were fewest, and
water nearest. From this rose disputes, which increased
quickly, when the wagon of a certain Grünmanski appeared as if it had fallen from the sky. This Pan Grünmanski, in Cincinnati where Germans live, called himself,
simply Grünman; but in Borovina he added " ski," so
that his business might go on better. His wagon had a
lofty canvas top, on both sides of which was a black
inscription in great letters, " Saloon," and underneath, in
smaller letters, " Brandy, whiskey, gin."

How that wagon had passed the dangerous wilderness
between Clarksville and Borovina, how prairie adventurers had not broken it, why Indians, who were maraud-
ing in small bands, frequently very near Clarksville, had
not taken the scalp from Pan Grünmanski's head is his
secret; it is enough that he arrived and began a perfect business that very day. But that same day also the
colonists began to quarrel. To the thousand disputes
about sections, tools, sheep, and places at the fire, were
added very foolish things; for instance, among the colonists a certain provincial American patriotism was roused.
Those who had come from Northern States began to
praise their former homes at the expense of the colony
and of colonists from Southern States. and *vice versa*.

Where separation from the mother country and life among strangers had eaten through the native character, one might have heard frequently this North American Polonism, colored by the slang, "I don't care a d——!"

"But why praise your Southern country?" asked a young fellow from Chicago. "With us in Illinois, wherever you look is a railroad, and wherever you are in a car a short mile brings you to a city. You want to farm, you want to build a house, you don't need to gnaw timber; you buy lumber and that is the end of it."

"With us one cañon is worth whole blocks in your place."

"And you, God d——! What do you touch me for? I was there, sir, and I am here, sir, and what sort of a fellow are you?"

"Quiet, or I will take a shingle, or I will wet your head in the creek, if you get mad. What do you want of me?"

. . . .

In the colony evil was done directly; that society brought to mind a drove of sheep without a shepherd. Quarrels about land grew more violent. It came to fights in which comrades of certain towns or settlements joined against those who came from others. The more experienced, the elder or wiser secured, it is true, respect and importance gradually; but they were not always able to keep them. Only in moments of danger did the common instinct of defence command those colonists to forget their quarrels. Once on an evening when a company of renegade Indians stole sheep, the men rushed together in pursuit, without a moment's hesitation. The sheep were recovered; one of the Indians was so beaten that he died soon after; the most perfect harmony reigned that day, but the next morning there was quarrelling again at the forest. Concord returned when, in the evening, the fiddler played, not a dance, but various songs, which each man had heard long before under thatched roofs, then conversation stopped. All surrounded the musician in a great circle; the sound of the forest accompanied him; the blazing fires hissed and shot up sparks; some dropped their heads gloomily as they stood there, the souls flew out of them and went beyond the sea. More than once the moon rose high above the forest, and still they were listening. But except these short intervals, everything became more and more unhinged in the colony. Disorder increased, hatred burrowed into them. That little society, cast away among those forests, almost separated from the rest of humanity, deserted by its leaders, had neither the power nor the knowledge to help itself.

Among the colonists we find two figures known to us: the old man, Vavron Toporek, and his daughter, Marysia. Arriving in Arkansas, they had to share the common lot in Borovina. Indeed, at first they were in a better condition than others. Whatever a forest may be, it is not the pavement of New York; moreover, in New York they had nothing; here, they had a wagon, some live-stock bought cheaply in Clarksville, and a few tools for fieldwork. There, a terrible yearning was gnawing them; here, hard work did not let the mind wander from the present.

The old man felled trees from morning till evening; he hewed off chips and prepared logs for the cottage. The girl washed clothes in the river, made a fire, cooked; but, in spite of heat, exercise and the air of the forest obliterated gradually the traces of her sickness which she had incurred through want in New York. The burning breeze from Texas tanned her pale face and covered it with a slightly golden hue. Young men from San Antonio, and from the Great Lakes, who jumped at each other with fists on any pretext, were agreed only in this, that Marysia's eyes looked from under her bright hair as star-thistles in wheat, and that she was the prettiest girl that human eye had ever seen.

The beauty of Marysia was useful to Vavron. He picked out for himself a strip of the nicest forest, and no one opposed him, for all the young men were on his side. More than one helped him in the felling of trees, the hewing of beams, or in putting them in place for hewing; but the old man, since he was shrewd, knew their reasons, and said from time to time, —

"My daughter walks the plain like a lily, like a lady, like a queen. To whom I wish, to him I will give her; but I shall not give her to this man or that, for she is a landowner's daughter. Whoso will bow lower and please better, to him I will give her, not to a straggler."

So whoever helped Vavron thought that he was helping himself.

Vavron was better off even than others; and in general he would have been quite well to do if the colony had had any future before it. But things grew worse daily. One week passed and another. Round about the plain they cut trees; the ground was covered with chips; here and there rose the yellow walls of houses; but what was done was a trifle in comparison with what those men should have done. The green wall of the forest yielded only slowly before the axes. Those who went into the forest more deeply brought back strange tidings: that that forest had no end whatever; that farther on there were terrible swamps and bayous in it, morasses, and some kind of sleeping water under the trees; that wonderful creatures of some sort were dwelling there; that certain steaming things, like spirits, pushed along through the thickets, serpents of some kind hissed there; that voices cried, "Do not come!" Certain imps seized men by the clothing and would not let them go. A young man from Chicago declared that he had seen the very devil in person, that Satan raised his terrible shaggy head from the mud and snorted at him so that he was barely able to run home.

A colonist from Texas explained to the man from Chicago that he must have seen a buffalo; but he would not believe this. So the superstition of fear added to the terrible position. A few days after seeing the devil, it happened that two smart young men went into the forest and were seen no more. Some people fell ill with pain in the back from overwork, and then fever attacked them. Quarrels about division of land increased to the degree that it came to wounds, blood, and battles. If any man failed to brand his cattle, others denied his ownership. The camp lost cohesion; wagons were removed to all corners of the plain, so as to be as far from one another as possible. They could not agree as to who should go out to guard the cattle; sheep began to die.

Meanwhile one thing became more and more evident: before the grain sown on the edge of the forest would be green, and the increase of cattle come, the supply of provisions would fail, and hunger appear. Despair seized people. The sound of axes in the forest decreased, for patience and courage had begun to fail. Every man would have continued his work if some one could have said to him, "Here, this is thine forever." But no one knew what was his, and what was not his. The just complaints against leaders increased. People said that they had been led into the wilderness to die for nothing.

Whoever had some money yet sat in his wagon and drove away to Clarksville. But there were more who, having put their last copper into the colony, had nothing with which to return to their former homes. These wrung their hands, seeing certain ruin.

At last the axes stopped cutting; but the forest sounded as if jeering at men's helplessness. "Cut for two years, and then die of hunger," said man to man. But the forest sounded as if it were jeering. A certain evening Vavron came to Marysia and said, —

"I see that everything is going to ruin, and we also are going to ruin."

"The will of God," answered the girl. "He has been merciful and will not desert us now."

Thus speaking, she raised her blue eyes to the stars, and in the gleams of the fire she looked like a church image. And the young men from Chicago, and the hunters from Texas, looking at her, said, —

"And we will not desert thee, Marysia, thou morning dawn."

She thought to herself that there was only one with whom she would go to the end of the earth, — one, Yasko in Lipintse. But he, though he had promised to swim through the sea after her, to fly as a bird after her, roll as a ring after her on the highway, had not swum, had not flown, he alone had deserted her, hapless girl.

Marysia could not but know that evil was going on in the colony, but she had been in such distress, God had freed her from such abysses; her soul had become so serene in misfortune that nothing could deprive her of faith in Heaven's aid.

Besides she remembered that the old gentleman in New York, who had helped them to rise out of misery and reach that place, had given her his card, saying, that should misfortune oppress her to call to him, he would save her always.

Every day brought new peril for the colony. People flew from it by night, and what happened to them it is difficult to tell. Round about the forest sounded and mocked.

At last old Vavron fell ill from exertion. Pain began to pass through his spine. For two days he paid no attention to it, but on the third he could not rise. The girl went to the forest, collected moss and covered with it the wall of the house, which was ready and lying on the grass; she placed her father on the moss and prepared for him mèdicine with whiskey.

"Marysia," muttered the old man, "death is coming to me now through the forest; thou wilt remain alone in the world, poor orphan. God is punishing me for my grievous sins; I took thee beyond the sea, and ruined thee. Painful will my end be."

"Father," answered the girl, "God would have punished me if I had not come with you."

"If thou wert not alone when I leave thee, if I might bless thee for marriage, I should die more easily. Marysia, take Black Orlik as husband; he is good, he will not desert thee."

Black Orlik, an unerring hunter, from Texas, who heard this, threw himself on his knees at once.

"O father! bless us!" said he, "I love this maiden as my own life. I know the forest, and I will not let her die."

Saying this he looked with his falcon eyes on Marysia as on a rainbow; but she, bending down to the feet of her father, said, —

"Do not force me, father, I shall be his whom I promised. or no man's."

"Thou wilt not be his whom thou hast promised, for I will kill him. Thou must be mine, or else no man's," answered Orlik. "All will perish here; thou wilt perish with them unless I rescue thee."

Orlik was not mistaken. The colony was going to nothing; again a week passed and a second week. Supplies were near the end. They had begun to kill working cattle. The fever seized new victims day by day; people began now to curse, now to cry in loud voices to Heaven for deliverance.

One Sunday, the old men, boys, women, and children, all knelt on the ground and sang a supplication. A hundred voices repeated, "Holy God, Holy Mighty, Holy and Invincible, have mercy on us!" The forest ceased to move, ceased to sound, and listened. Only when the hymn was ended did the forest sound again, as if speaking terribly. "Here I am king; here I am lord; here I am the mightiest."

But Orlik, who knew the forest, fastened his black eyes on it, looked at it somehow strangely, and then said aloud, —

"Well, let us grapple."

The people looked in turn at Orlik, and a certain consolation entered their hearts. Those who knew him when in Texas had great trust in the man, for he was famed even in Texas. He had really grown wild in the prairies, and was as strong as an oak-tree. He used to go alone against a bear. In San Antonio, where he had lived before, they knew well that sometimes, when he took a gun and went to the desert, he was absent for two months, and always returned in health, sound. They nicknamed him "Black," because he was burned from the sun. They said even that on the Mexican boundary he had been a bandit, but that was untrue.

He brought back only skins; he brought Indian scalps sometimes till the local priest threatened to curse him. Now in Borovina he was the only man who cared for nothing and was concerned about nothing. The forest gave him food and drink; the forest clothed him. So when people began to flee and lose their heads, he took everything in hand, and managed like a gray goose in the sky, having behind him all who were from Texas. When, after the prayer, he challenged the forest, people thought to themselves: "He will invent something."

Meanwhile the sun went down. High among the black branches of the hickories the brightness of gold shone for a while yet, then reddened, and was quenched. The wind shifted to the south at nightfall. Orlik took his gun and went to the forest.

Night had begun when, in the dark distance, people saw as it were a great golden star, as it were a coming dawn, or a sun which rose with tremendous swiftness, spreading red and bloody light.

"The forest is burning! The forest is burning!" shouted people in the camp.

Clouds of birds rose with a clatter from every side of the forest, screaming, croaking, twittering. Cattle in the camp began to bellow pitifully; dogs howled; people ran about in terror, not knowing but the fire might come on them, though the strong south wind could only drive the flames away from the plain. Meanwhile in the distance rose a second red star, then a third. Both of these were merged quickly in the first, and the conflagration roared on over increasing expanses. The flames spread like water; they ran along dry, interlaced lianas and wild grape-vines; the forest trembled. The wind tore burning leaves away and bore them, like fiery birds, farther and farther.

Hickories burst in the fire with a report like the sound of cannon. Red serpents of fire wound themselves over the resinous bark of the wilderness. Hissing, roaring, the breaking of limbs, the deep howl of flames, mingled with the uproar of birds, and the bellowing of beasts filled the air. Heaven-touching trees tottered like flaming pillars and columns. Climbing plants, burned at the windings, broke away from the trees and, swinging terribly, like satanic arms, passed forward sparks and fire from tree to tree.

The sky grew red as if another conflagration were there. It was as clear as daylight. Then all the flames blended into one sea of fire, and went through the forest like the breathing of death, or the anger of God.

Smoke, heat, and the odor of burning filled the air. People in the camp, though no danger threatened them, shouted and cried to one another; when all at once, from the direction of the burning, came Orlik in the sparks, in the glare. His face was darkened with smoke, and terrible. When all stood around him in a circle, he leaned on his musket, and said, —

"You will not cut timber; I have burned the forest. To-morrow you will have on that side fields, as many as each man may wish for." Then, approaching Marysia, he said, —

"You must be mine; it was I who burnt the forest. Who here is stronger than I?"

The girl shivered through her whole frame, for the conflagration shone in the eyes of Orlik, and he seemed to her terrible. For the first time since their coming, she thanked God that Yasko was far away in Lipintse.

Meanwhile the roaring conflagration receded farther and farther. The dawn was cloudy, and threatened rain.

At daybreak, some people went to look at the burned

region; but they could not go near, because of heat. The second day, smoke like a fog filled the air, so that one man could not see another twenty steps distant. That night rain began, which soon passed into a frightful downpour. Perhaps the fire, by disturbing the air, had caused the settling of clouds; but, besides, it was the spring season, during which on the lower Mississippi, at the meeting of the Arkansas and Red River, enormous rains fall. Another cause of these rains is the evaporation of water, which, in Arkansas, covers the whole country in the form of swamps, small lakes, and streams, which are increased in spring by the melting of snow on the distant mountains.

The whole plain grew soft, and turned gradually into a great pond. People who had been wet for whole days now fell ill. Some left the colony for Clarksville; but they returned quickly, with news that the river had risen, that the ford was impassable.

The condition of affairs had grown terrible; a month had passed since the coming of the colonists; supplies might give out, and it was impossible to replenish them from Clarksville. But hunger threatened Vavron and Marysia less than others, for the strong hand of Orlik was over them. Every morning he brought to the wall of the house on which Vavron was lying game, either shot or trapped by him. Orlik put up his own tent to protect the old man and Marysia from rain. They had to accept the assistance which he almost imposed, and be bound by gratitude; he would not take pay, he wanted nothing but Marysia.

"Am I the only one on earth?" pleaded the girl. "Go seek some one else, since I love another."

"Though I should walk the world through," said Orlik. "I should not find another like thee. For me thou art the only one, and must be mine. What wilt thou do when thy father dies? Thou wilt come to me thyself, and I will take thee, as a wolf takes a lamb; I will bear thee to the forest, but I will not eat thee. Thou art mine, thou alone! Who will forbid me to take thee? Whom do I fear in this place? Let thy Yasko come, I want him."

As to Vavron, Orlik seemed to be right. The old man grew worse and worse; at times he was raving, and spoke of his sins, of Lipintse, and said that God would not let him see it again. Marysia shed tears for him, and for herself. Orlik's promise that if she would marry him, he would go with her, even to Lipintse, was bitterness, not consolation. To return to Lipintse where Yasko was, and return there another's, not for anything!—better die under the first tree she came to. She thought that it would end thus.

A new trial fell on the colony.

Rain poured down more and more. One dark night, when Orlik had gone to the forest as usual, a shrill, despairing cry was heard in the camp, "Water! water!" When the people rubbed their sleepy eyes, they saw in the darkness, as far as vision extended, one white plain, plashing under the downpour, and moved by the wind. The broken and dimmed light of night showed a steel-like reflection on the wrinkles and ripples of the water. On the side of the forest, where stumps were sticking up, and where, from the burnt forest, was heard the plashing and sound of new waves flowing, as it seemed, with great impetus. A cry rose in the whole camp. Women and children took refuge in the wagons; men ran with all their might to the western side of the plain, where the trees were not cut. The water hardly reached to their knees, but was rising rapidly. The sound from

the side of the forest increased, and was blended with
shouts of alarm, with the calling of names, and with
prayers for rescue. Soon larger animals began to retreat
from place to place before the weight of the water. It
was evident that the force of the current was increasing.
Sheep swam along, and, with plaintive bleating, called
for assistance, till they vanished, carried off toward the
trees. Rain poured as if from a bucket, and became
every moment more terrible. The distant sound changed
into one immense thunder and roar of mad waves; wagons
trembled under the pressure of them. It was evident
that this was no common rainfall, but that the Arkansas
River, and all streams running into it, had overflown.
That was a deluge, a tearing out of trees by the roots, a
rending of forests, a terror, an unchaining of elements,
darkness, death.

One wagon, standing near the burnt forest, turned over.
In answer to the piercing screams for help from the
women enclosed in it, a few dark figures rushed out of
the forest; but the water swept these men away, whirled
them around, and bore them toward the trees, to destruction. On other wagons other men climbed to the canvas
coverings. The rain roared more and more; greater and
greater darkness fell on that gloomy plain. At moments
some beam with a human figure clinging to it shot past,
hurled up and down; at moments the dark figure of a
beast, or a man, emerged; sometimes an arm was thrust
up from the deluge and then fell back forever.

The water roared with increasing rage, and drowned
everything, — drowned the bellows of perishing beasts,
and the cries "Jesus! Jesus! Mary!" On the plain were
formed eddies and whirlpools; the wagons vanished.

And Vavron and Marysia? That house wall on which
the old man lay, under Orlik's tent, saved them, for it

floated on like a raft. The water carried it around the whole field, and bore it toward the forest, there knocked it against one tree and another, and, pushing it finally into the current of the river, bore it farther in the darkness.

The girl, kneeling near her old father, raised her hands to Heaven, calling for salvation; but only blows of waves driven by the wind gave her answer. The tent was torn away, and the raft itself might be broken any moment, since before and behind were floating uprooted trees, which might crush or upset it.

At last it stuck in the branches of some tree, only the top of which was visible above water; out of that top at that moment came the voice of a man, —

"Take my gun and·stand on the other side, so the raft will not tip when I jump on it."

She and Vavron had barely done what was commanded, when some figure sprang from a limb to the raft.

It was Orlik.

"Marysia," said he, "as I have said, I will not leave thee. God aid me! I will bring thee out of this deep water also."

With the hatchet which he had he cut a straight limb from the tree, trimmed it in a twinkle, pushed the raft away, and paddled.

When he had worked into the regular current, they went on with lightning speed. Whither? — they knew not, but on they went.

Orlik from time to time pushed away trees, branches, or he turned the raft to avoid a standing tree. His gigantic strength seemed to increase. His eyes, in spite of the darkness, descried every danger. Hour succeeded hour. Every other would have fallen from weariness, but in him toil left no trace. Toward morning they came out of the forest, for no tree-tops were visible. But the whole circle of the world seemed one sea. Immense whirls of yellow, foaming water went around with a roar on that empty flatness.

Daylight grew clearer. Orlik, seeing no tree in the neighborhood, ceased paddling for a moment and turned to Marysia, —

"Marysia, thou art mine now, for I snatched thee from death."

His head was uncovered, and his face, wet and flushed from heat, warmed by the battle with the flood, it had such an expression of strength that Marysia for the first time dared not answer that she had promised another.

"Marysia," said he, softly, "Marysia of my heart!"

"Where are we floating to?" asked she, wishing to change the conversation.

"What care I, if with thee, my beloved."

"Paddle on, while death is before us."

Orlik paddled again.

Vavron felt worse and worse. At times he had a fever, at times it left him; but he weakened. The suffering was too great for his worn-out, old body. He was approaching the end, eternal relief, and great peace. At midday he woke, and said, —

"Marysia, I shall not wait till to-morrow. Oi, my daughter, would to the Lord that I had not left Lipintse, and had not brought thee here! But God is merciful! I have suffered not a little; He will forgive me my sins. Bury me, if thou shalt be able, and let Orlik take thee to the old gentleman in New York. He is a good man; he will pity thee and give thee means for the road, and thou wilt return to Lipintse. I shall never return. God, Thou the merciful, let my soul fly there as a bird and even look at the place!"

Here delirium seized him again, and he began to speak,

"To Thy protection I flee, Holy Mother of God!" cried he, on a sudden. "Do not throw me into the water, for I am not a dog!" and then, evidently, it occurred to him that he had wished to drown Marysia because of their misery, for again he cried, "My child, forgive! forgive!"

She, poor thing, was lying near his head, sobbing; Orlik was paddling, and tears were stopping his throat.

In the evening it became clear. The sun, at the moment of setting, appeared over the flooded country, and was reflected in the water with a long, golden streak. The old man was dying. But God took pity on him, and gave him a peaceful death. At first he said, in a sad voice:

"I went away from Poland, from that land over there," but afterward, in the wandering of his fever, it seemed to him that he was returning to it. He thought that the old gentleman in New York had given him money for the road, and to buy land, so he and Marysia were going back. They are on the ocean; the steamer is sailing night and day; the sailors are singing. Then he sees the port in Hamburg from which they had sailed; various places appear before his eyes. German speech is heard around him; but the train is flying onward, so Vavron feels that he is nearer and nearer home; a sure joy swells his breast; another atmosphere, beloved, greets him from his native place. What is that? — the boundary! The poor peasant heart is beating like a hammer. He is going on! O God! O God! and here are the fields of the Matseks, and their pear-trees; here are gray cottages and the church. There a villager follows the plough in his sheepskin cap. He stretches his hands to him from the train. O man! O man! — I cannot speak. They go farther. But what is that? That is Pryremble, and beyond Pryremble is Lipintse. He and Marysia are moving along the road, and weeping from joy. It is spring. The wheat is in blossom; the beetles are droning in the air; in Pryremble they are ringing the Angelus. O Jesus! Jesus! why is there so much happiness for him, sinful man? Over that hill, and there a cross and guide-post, and the boundary of Lipintse. They are not walking now, but flying as if on wings; now they are on the hill, at the cross, at the guide-post. The man throws himself on the ground; he bellows from happiness; he kisses the ground, and crawling up to the cross embraces it, — he is in Lipintse. Yes. He is now in Lipintse, for only his dead body is resting on that stray raft on the flood of water; his soul has flown to the place of its rest and its happiness.

In vain did the girl work over him. "Father, father!" Poor Marysia, he will not return to thee. He is too happy in Lipintse.

Night came. The stick was dropping out of Orlik's hand from fatigue; hunger tormented him. Marysia, kneeling over her father's body, was repeating with broken voice an "Our Father;" all round, to the remotest verges of the horizon, there was nothing but water.

They had come out above the bed of some large river, for the current was bearing them away again quickly. It was impossible to steer the raft. Perhaps that was merely a current circling about a hollow in the prairie, for frequently it carried them in a circle. Orlik felt that his strength was deserting him. On a sudden he sprang to his feet, and cried, —

"By the wounds of Christ, there is a light!"

Marysia looked in the direction in which he had stretched his arm. In fact some light gleamed in the distance; from it a line was reflected on the water.

"That is a boat from Clarksville!" cried Orlik, "sent out to save people. If only it would not miss us; Marysia, I will save thee. Hoop! hoop!"

At the same time he paddled with all his might. Indeed the flame increased, and in the red light from it something which looked like a large boat was outlined. It was very far away yet, but they were approaching each other. After a time, however, Orlik saw that the boat was not pushing forward; the raft had floated into a great and broad current, going in a direction opposite to that of the boat.

All at once the pole broke in Orlik's hand from pressure. They were without an oar. The current carried them farther and farther; the light decreased.

Happily a quarter of an hour later the raft struck a lone tree in the prairie, and it stuck in the branches. Both cried for help, but the noise of the current extinguished their voices.

"I will shoot," said Orlik; "they will see the light, they will hear the report."

He had barely thought of it when he raised the barrel of his musket, but instead of a report came the dull click of the hammer. The powder was wet.

Orlik threw himself at full length on the raft. There was nothing to be done. He lay as if dead for a while, then he rose, and said, —

"Marysia, I would have taken another girl long ago, in spite of her, and carried her to the forest. I thought to do so with thee; but I dared not, I loved thee. I went alone about the world like a wolf, and the common herd feared me, but I feared thee. Marysia! Thou must have given me some philter? But thou wilt not marry me : death is better! I will save thee, or perish; but if I perish, do thou of my heart take pity and say an 'Our Father' for Orlik. In what have I offended thee? I have done thee no wrong. Ei! Marysia, Marysia, farewell, thou my love and my sun! — "

And before she had noted what he wished to do, he threw himself into the water and began to swim. For a while she saw his head in the darkness, and his arms breaking the water against the current, for he was a strong swimmer. But soon he disappeared from her eyes He was swimming to the boat to find rescue for her. The swift current hampered his movements, as if some one were dragging him from behind; he pulled himself out, pushed forward. If he could avoid that current, if he could strike another, a favoring one, he would swim to the boat, he would do so most certainly. Meanwhile, in spite of superhuman efforts, he could move only slowly. Thick, yellowish water, often threw foam in his eyes; then he raised his head, took breath, and strained his eyes in the darkness to see where the boat with the light was. Sometimes a stronger wave pushed him back, sometimes it hurled him upward; he breathed with increasing difficulty; he felt that his knees were stiffening. He thought, "I shall not swim there;" then something whispered in his ear, as if it were the beloved voice of Marysia, "Save me!" and again he cut the water with his hands desperately. His cheeks swelled; his mouth threw out water; his eyes were protruding from his head. If he should turn, he could swim back to the raft with the current; but he did not even think of doing so, for the light of the boat was nearer and nearer. In fact the boat was coming toward him, borne by the same current with which he was struggling. All at once he felt that his knees and his legs were stiff altogether. A few more desperate efforts, the boat ever nearer, "Help! Rescue!"

The last word was drowned by the water which filled his throat. He sank, a wave passed over his head; but he swam out again. The boat was right there, right there. He hears the plash and the noise of the oars in the rowlocks; for the last time he strains his voice and cries for help.

They hear him, for the plash becomes quicker.

But Orlik went down again; an immense eddy bore him away. For a moment yet he was black on the wave, then one hand rose above the water, after that the other, and then he vanished.

Meanwhile Marysia, alone on the raft with the corpse of her father, was looking at the distant light like a person demented.

But the current bore it toward her. She saw the boat with a number of oars, which in the light moved like the red legs of a giant worm. Marysia began to call desperately.

"Eh, Smith," said some voice in English. "Hang me, if I don't hear cries for help, and if I don't hear them a second time."

After a while strong arms bore Marysia to the boat; but Orlik was not there.

Two months later Marysia came out of the hospital in Little Rock, and, with money collected by kind people, she went to New York.

But this money was not enough. She had to make a part of the road on foot; but, speaking a little English now, she was able to beg of conductors to take her free. Many people had pity on the poor, sick, pallid girl, with the great blue eyes, more like a shadow than a person, and begging alms with tears. It was not people who were tormenting her, but life and its conditions. What had that field flower of Lipintse to do in the whirl of America, in that gigantic " business " ? How was she to help herself? The car there had to pass over her and crush her frail body, as every car passes over a flower which has fallen in front of it.

A hand, emaciated, trembling from weakness, pulled a bell on Water Street. That was Marysia, who had come to seek aid of the old gentleman from Poznan.

Some stranger opened the door to her, an unknown person.

"Is Pan Zlotopolski at home?"

"Who is he?"

"An old gentleman." Here she showed his card.

"He is dead."

"He is dead? And his son? — Pan William?"

"He has gone away."

"And Panna Jennie?"

"She has gone away."

The door was closed before her. She sat on the doorstep and rubbed her face. She was in New York again, alone, without assistance, without protection, without money, dependent on the will of God.

Will she stay there? Never! She will go now to the wharf, to the German docks, to seize the captain's feet, and beg him to take her; and if they will have kindness, she will go through Germany on begged bread, and return to Lipintse. Her Yasko is there. Besides him she has no one in the broad world now. If he will not take her in, if he has forgotten her, if he will reject her, she can even die near him.

She went to the wharf and crawled at the feet of the German captains. They would have taken her; for were she to freshen up a little she would be a nice girl. They would be glad but then the rules did not permit — besides, it is a vexation. So let them alone.

The girl went to sleep on that same place where she had slept once with her father on that night when he wanted to drown her. She nourished herself with what the water threw up, as she had in New York with her father. Happily, the summer was warm.

Every day, just after dawn, she was at the German docks begging a favor, and every day vainly. She had peasant endurance, but strength was deserting her. She felt that if she could not go back quickly she would die soon, as all had died with whom fate had connected her.

A certain morning she dragged herself to the German docks with effort, and thinking that that was the last time, for to-morrow her strength would not be sufficient. She resolved not to beg, but to walk onto the first steamer sailing for Europe and hide somewhere quietly; when they sailed out and found her, they would not throw her into the water; if they should, well, let them do so. It is all the same to her how she dies, if die she must. But at the gangway leading to the steamer persons going on board are watched carefully, and the guard pushed her away at the first trial.

She sat on a post near the water, and thought to herself that fever might seize her. She began to laugh, and muttered, —

"I am an heiress, Yasko, but I kept faith with thee. Dost thou not know me?"

The hapless girl caught no fever, but insanity seized her. Thenceforward she went every day to the wharf to look for Yasko. People grew accustomed to her and gave her alms sometimes. She thanked them with humility, and laughed like a child. This lasted two months perhaps. One time, however, she did not go to the wharf, and was seen there no more. But the "Police Gazette" announced on the following morning that at the very end of the pier had been found the body of a dead girl, of unknown name and origin.

ORSO

ORSO.

THE last days of autumn are for Anaheim, a small town in Southern California, days of amusement and celebration. The grape-gathering is finished then altogether, so the town swarms with laboring people. Nothing is more picturesque than the view presented by that population, formed, in its minority, of Mexicans, but mainly of Cahuilla Indians, who come for work from the wild mountains of San Bernardino, which lie in the depth of the country. Both Indians and Mexicans dispose themselves on the streets and market squares, or so-called "lolas," where they sleep under tents, or simply under the naked sky, always serene at that season.

The pretty town, surrounded by groups of eucalyptus, castor, and pepper trees, is seething as though with a bustling and noisy fair, and forms an astonishing contrast to the deep and dignified silence of the cactus-covered desert, which begins immediately beyond the vineyards. In the evening, when the sun hides its shining circle in the depth of the ocean, and when, on the ruddy sky, are seen also the rosy bright lines of wild geese, ducks, pelicans, mews, and cranes, stretching in thousands from the mountains toward the ocean, fires are kindled in Anaheim and amusement begins. Negro minstrels shake their tambourines, and at every fire are to be heard the sound of drums and the plaintive tones of the banjo. The Mexicans dance on spread-out ponchos their favorite bolero; the Indians accompany them, holding in their teeth long white reeds of kiotte, or giving out shouts of " E viva !" The fire, nourished with redwood, crackles and shoots sparks, and in its bloody gleams are seen leaping figures, while round about are local settlers, with their handsome wives and daughters on their arms, witnessing the amusement.

The day, however, on which the last cluster of grapes is trodden out by Indian feet, is the greatest holiday ; for then comes from Los Angeles the travelling circus of Herr Hirsch, a German, and also the owner of a menagerie, composed of monkeys, cougars, African lions, one elephant, and a number of parrots, grown foolish from age, — this is "the greatest attraction of the world !"

The Cahuillas, indeed, give the last " pesos," which they have not been able to drink away, only to see, not so much wild beasts, for of those in San Bernadino there is no lack, but circus women, athletes, clowns, and all the wonders of the circus, which to them, at least, seem "great medicine," that is, magic, possible of accomplishment only through supernatural powers.

The man who should think, however, that the circus was an attraction merely for Indians, negroes, and Chinamen, would draw upon himself the just and, God knows, the dangerous wrath of Herr Hirsch. The arrival of the circus brings after it a gathering not only of the surrounding settlers, but even of inhabitants of the neighboring smaller towns, Westminster, Orange, and Los Nietos. Orange Street is so packed with wagons and buggies, of forms the most varied, that it is impossible to push through ; all the great world of settlerdom has risen as one man. Young, smart, little misses, with bright bangs over their eyes, sitting in the front seats, drive over people charmingly along the streets, twittering and showing their teeth as they do so ; Spanish señoritas

from Los Nietos, cast long shaded glances from under
their tulle veils; married dames, from the neighborhood,
dressed in the latest fashion, lean with pride on the arms
of sunburnt farmers, for whom a torn hat, jeans pantaloons, and a flannel shirt, which, for want of a cravat, is
fastened with hooks and eyes, serve as an entire costume.

All that world exchanges greetings, calls, looks with
careful eye at dresses to see how far they are " very fashionable," and gossips a little.

Among American buggies covered with flowers and
looking like great bouquets young men ride on mustangs
and bend forward on their high Mexican saddles, as they
glance stealthily under the hats of young maidens. The
half-wild horses; frightened by the uproar and noise, roll
their bloody eyes, rear, and neigh; but the daring riders
do not even seem to take note of their movements.

All speak of " the greatest attraction," or the details
of the evening representation, which is to surpass in
splendor everything seen hitherto.

Indeed, the gigantic show-bills announce real wonders.
The director himself, Herr Hirsch, " an artist at the whip,"
is to give a concert with the wildest known African lion.
The lion is to hurl himself, according to programme, on the
director, whose only defence is the whip. But that ordinary weapon becomes, in his wonder-working hands (always according to programme), a fiery sword and a shield.
The end of that whip is to bite like a rattlesnake, flash like
lightning, hit like a thunderbolt, and keep continually at a
distance the monster, which struggles in vain and tries to
rush on the artist. But that is not the end yet. The
sixteen-year-old Orso, the "Hercules of America," born
of a white father and an Indian mother, is to carry six
men, three on each shoulder; besides this, the director
offers a hundred dollars to any man, " without regard to

8

color of skin," who can throw the young athlete in
wrestling. An indefinite report is circling through Anaheim, that Grizzly-killer has come purposely from the
San Bernardino mountains for a trial with Orso. He is
a trapper, celebrated for courage and strength, who, since
California became California, is the first man who dared
to attack a grizzly bear with an axe and a knife.

The probable victory of the "bear-killer" over the sixteen-year-old athlete of the circus rouses all the male
population of Anaheim to the utmost; for, if Orso, who
hitherto had thrown the strongest "Yankees" between
the Atlantic and the Pacific, comes off victorious, immortal glory will settle on all California.

The minds of the women are not less roused by the
following item of the programme, which states that the
same powerful Orso will carry on a thirty-foot pole little
Jennie, "the wonder of the world," of whom the hand-
bill announces that she is the most beautiful maiden that
has lived on earth "during the Christian era."

Though Jennie is only thirteen, the director offers one
hundred dollars to any girl, "without reference to the
color of her skin," who will compete in beauty with
"the angel of the air." The misses, the little misses,
and the smallest misses from Anaheim and the environs
turn up their noses in contempt, when they read this
part of the programme, and declare that it would not
be "ladylike" to undertake such competition. Still, each
of them would rather give up her rocking-chair than not
be present at the evening exhibition, and not see that
childlike rival, in whose beauty, however, in comparison, for instance, with the sisters Bimpa, no one believes.

The two sisters Bimpa, the elder, Refugio, and the
younger, Mercedes, are sitting carelessly in a beautiful
"buggy," just reading the bill. On their wonderful faces

not the least emotion is noticeable, though they feel that
the eyes of Anaheim are turned to them at that moment,
as if imploring them to save the honor of the whole
county, and turned also with patriotic pride, founded on
the conviction that more beautiful than those two flowers of California, there are not in all the mountains and
cañons of this world. Oh! but they are beautiful, those
sisters Refugio and Mercedes! It is not for nothing that
pure Castilian blood is flowing in their veins; to this blood
their mother refers continually, expressing at the same
time her lofty contempt for all kinds of colored people, as
well as for persons with light hair, — that is, " Yankees."

The forms of the two sisters are slender, lithe; in their
movements are certain mysteries, languid, and so luxurious that when any young man approaches them the heart
struggles in his breast from unconfessed and unknown
desire. A charm breathes from Refugio and Mercedes, as
odor from magnolias. Their faces are delicate, their complexions transparent, though blushing with a slight rosi-
ness, like the gleam of dawn ; their eyes are dreamy and
black, sweet, and in expression innocent and sensitive.
Wrapped in the folds of their muslin rebozos, in a buggy
filled with flowers, they are sitting there so pure, calm,
and beautiful that they seem even not to know their
own beauty. Anaheim looks at them, devours them with
its eyes, is proud of them, is in love with them. What
must that Jennie be if she is to bear away the victory
from them? "The Saturday Weekly Review" wrote, it
is true, that when little Jennie climbs to the end of the
pole, resting on the powerful shoulder of Orso, when she
is on the point of that pole, hanging over the earth, exposed to death, and begins to spread out her arms and
flutter like a butterfly, it grows silent in the circus, and
not only eyes, but hearts follow, with trembling, every

movement of the wonderful child. "Whoever has seen her once on the pole, or on horseback," concludes the "Saturday Review," "will never forget it, for the greatest artist on earth, even Mr. Harvey of San Francisco, who painted the Palace Hotel, would not have been able to paint anything like her."

The youth of Anaheim, sceptical and enamoured of the sisters Bimpa, assert that there is "humbug" in that; still, it will be decided finally only in the evening.

Meanwhile the movement around the circus increases with every moment. From the midst of the long wooden sheds surrounding the canvas circus proper, comes the roaring of lions and of the elephant; parrots, attached to rings hung at the sheds, make an uproar with heaven-piercing voices; the monkeys hang by their own tails, or are teased by the public, held at a distance by ropes stretched around the buildings.

Finally, a procession emerges from the chief building, the object of which is to excite curiosity to the degree of amazement. The head of the procession is formed by an enormous chariot drawn by six horses with plumes on their heads. Grooms, in the French costume of postilions, drive from their saddles. On wagons are cages with lions, in each cage sits a lady with an olive branch. After the wagons marches an elephant covered with a carpet, a tower is fixed on his back, and bowmen are sitting in the tower.

Trumpets sound, drums are beaten, lions roar, whips are cracked; in a word, the whole caravan moves forward like a brawl, with outcry and uproar; that is not enough, behind the elephant rolls a machine with a boiler as in a locomotive, an organ on which steam plays, or rather bellows and whistles out in the most infernal manner, the national "Yankee Doodle." At times the steam is stopped in the pipes, and then comes out the ordinary whistle from the pipe, which does not decrease, however, the enthusiasm of the crowd, who cannot contain themselves from delight, when they hear that roaring music by steam. The Americans cry, "Hurrah!" the Germans, "Hoch!" the Mexicans, "E viva!" the Cahuillas howl like wild beasts, with ecstasy.

Crowds follow the procession; places around the circus are deserted; the parrots cease their uproar; the monkeys cease to jump. "The greatest attraction" does not take part, however, in the procession. In the chariots are neither the director, "incomparable at the whip," nor the "invincible Orso," nor "Jennie, the angel of the air." All that is reserved till evening, to produce then the greatest impression.

The director is sitting somewhere in the shed, or peeping in at his cash office, where his negroes show their white teeth to the public; he looks in and is angry in every case. Orso and Jennie have their own exercise in the circus. Under the canvas reign silence and gloom.

The background, where seats rise higher and higher, is almost completely dark; the greatest amount of light falls through the canvas roof on the arena, which is sprinkled with sawdust and sand. By those gray rays of light, which pass through the canvas, is seen a horse, standing at the barrier. There is no one near him; the large, broad beast is wearied evidently; he drives away flies with his tail, and nods as much as he can with his head, which is tied with white reins, and bent toward his breast. By degrees the eye discovers other objects too, such as a pole lying on the sand, the pole on which Orso carries Jennie usually, and a number of hoops with blotting paper pasted across them, through which Jennie has to spring; but all these are lying cast about carelessly. The whole half-lighted arena, and the circus, altogether gloomy, makes the impression of an empty house, with windows broken long before. The seats, rising in tiers, shone on only in some places, look like a ruin; the horse, with drooping head, does not enliven the picture.

Where are Orso and Jennie? One of the rays of light stealing in through the openings, in which the dust turns and dances, falls like a spot of gold on the seats of the farther benches. That spot advances according to the movement of the sun, and at last illuminates the group composed of Orso and Jennie.

Orso is sitting on a bench, near him, Jennie; her pretty, childish, little face is nestled up to the shoulder of the athlete, her arm is around his neck, and holds by the other shoulder. The eyes of the little girl are lifted, as if listening attentively to the words of her comrade, who, bent above her, moves his head sometimes, as if explaining and interpreting something. Thus nestled up to each other, they might be taken for two lovers, were it not that the legs of Jennie, clothed in pale rose-colored tights, without reaching the ground, were swinging back and forth with a movement perfectly childlike, which is called also making pots, her raised eyes express listening, and a powerful exertion of thought, rather than any romantic feeling. Also her form is only taking on the first outlines of a woman.

In general, Jennie is still a child, but such a charming one that, without offence to Mr. Harvey of San Francisco, who painted the Palace Hotel, it would be difficult for him to imagine anything similar. Her little face is simply angelic; her great, pensive blue eyes, of a deep, sweet, confiding expression, her dark brows are outlined with incomparable purity, on a forehead, white, and as it were sunk in thought, on which a yellow, silky, and a

trifle disordered forelock casts its shadow, which not
only Mr. Harvey, but a certain other painter named
Rembrandt, would not have been ashamed of. The little
maid reminds one of both Cinderella and Gretchen;
and the nestling posture, which she has taken, betrays a
timid disposition, requiring protection.

By this posture, in the manner of Greuze, is set off
wonderfully the circus costume formed of a short gauze
skirt embroidered with silver tinsel, so short that it does
not cover her knees, and rose-colored tights.

Sitting in the beam of golden light, on a deep and dark
background, she looks like some sunny, transparent vision,
and her slender figure presents a direct contrast to the
angular form of the young athlete.

Orso, dressed in flesh-colored tights, seems naked at a
distance; and that same beam illuminates his overgrown,
unsymmetrical limbs, his too prominent breast, his lank
stomach, and his legs too short in proportion to his body.
His powerful form seems to be merely struck out
roughly with an axe. He has all the traits of a circus
athlete, but carried to such a degree that they are
almost a caricature. Besides he is ugly. At times, when
he raises his head, his face is visible; the features are
regular, perhaps, even very regular, but somehow stiff,
and, as it were, hewn out. His low forehead, and black
hair, falling down to his nose, like the forelock of a horse,
inherited undoubtedly from his Indian mother, give his
face a threatening and gloomy appearance. He is at
once like a bull and a bear, and in general he has tremendous, but vicious power. In fact, he is not at all
kindly.

When Jennie passes near the stalls of the horses,
those honest creatures turn their heads, look at her with
their wise eyes, and neigh quietly as if they wished to

say, " How do you do, darling ? " but at sight of Orso,
they crouch from fear. He is a self-concentrated fellow,
gloomy and muttering. Herr Hirsch's negroes, who perform the duties of jockeys, clowns, minstrels, and rope-
walkers, cannot endure him, and annoy him as much
as they can; because he is a half-breed, they make
nothing of him, and express aloud their contempt. The
director, who, to tell the truth, does not risk much in
setting up a hundred dollars against every one who
may wish to try him, hates the youth, and also fears
him, but in the same way in which a trainer of wild
beasts fears, for example, a lion, that is, he flogs him for
any reason.

It is done also for this cause, that Herr Hirsch considers that if he should not beat the youth, he would
himself be beaten by him; but in general he holds the
principle of that Creole woman who looked on beating as
a punishment, and not beating as a reward.

Such is Orso. For some time, however, he has become
better, for he began to love little Jennie greatly. It
happened a year before that when Orso, who looked after
animals, was cleaning the cage of a cougar, the beast
thrust out his paw between the bars, and wounded him
in the head rather severely. The athlete went into the
cage then, and, after a terrible struggle between him
and the beast, he was the only survivor. He was so
severely wounded, however, that he fainted, and was sick
after that for a long time, especially since the director
flogged him for breaking the spine of the cougar.

In the time of his illness, little Jennie showed him
much sympathy, dressed his wounds in the absence of any
one else, and, in unoccupied hours, she sat near him, and
read to him the Bible, that is, " the good Book," which
mentions loving one another, and forgiveness, and

charity, — in one word, things concerning which mention was never made in Herr Hirsch's circus.

Orso, hearing that Book, labored a long time with his Indian head, and at last came to the conclusion that, if life in the circus were as in that Book, he would not be so cross-grained. He thought, too, that he would not be beaten, and, perhaps, he would even find some one to love him. But who? Not the negroes, and not Herr Hirsch, perhaps little Jennie, whose voice sounded as sweetly in his ears as the voice of a maukawis bird.

Because of this thought, he wept much on a certain evening; he began to kiss Jennie's little hands, and from that time he loved her greatly. Thenceforth, when during the evening exhibition the little girl rode on horseback, he was always in the arena, and followed her with careful eye. Holding before her hoops with blotting paper pasted across, he smiled at her, and when to the accompaniment of the music, "Ah, death is near!" he carried her on the point of the pole, to the great terror of the spectators, he was alarmed himself. He knew well at that time, that if she fell, there would be no one in the circus with the "good Book;" he did not let her out of his sight therefore, and that carefulness of his, and that alarm, as it were, in his movements added to the terror of the spectacle. When, called out by a storm of applause, they ran together into the arena, he pushed her ahead always, so that most of the applause should fall to her, and he muttered with delight. That surly fellow could talk with her only, and he opened his mind only before her. He hated the circus, and Herr Hirsch, who was quite different from the people of the "good Book."

Something always drew him to the edge of the horizon, to woods and to prairies. When the travelling company in its journeys happened to be near uninhabited regions, such instincts rose in him as rise in a tame wolf, on seeing a forest for the first time. That inclination, perhaps, he inherited not from his mother only, for his father was certainly some trapper, wandering over the plains. He confided these desires to little Jennie, and related to her also how people live in the wilderness. For the greater part he divined that, but he knew a little of it from the hunters of the plains, who came to the circus occasionally, sometimes to bring game to Herr Hirsch, sometimes to try for the hundred dollars which the director appointed for overcoming Orso.

Little Jennie listened generally to these conversations and Indian visions, opening her blue eyes widely, or thinking. Orso himself never went into the desert. She was always with him, and it was so pleasant for them, that it was just wonderful. Every day they saw something new; they had their own housekeeping; they had, therefore, to take everything into consideration.

They were sitting then in the streak of light and talking, instead of trying new jumps. The horse was standing in the arena, annoyed. Little Jennie, leaning up to Orso's shoulder, had her thoughtful eyes fixed in space, and was swaying her legs persistently and weighing in her little head how it would be in the wilderness; and at times she threw out a question so as to know better how it would be.

"And where is one to live?" asked she, raising her eyes to her comrade.

"It is full of oak-trees there. A man takes an axe and builds a house."

"Well," said Jennie, "but till the house is built?"

"It is always warm there. Grizzly Killer said that it was very warm."

Jennie began to swing her legs still more energetically, in sign that if it was warm she did not care for anything else; but after a while she stopped again. She has in the circus a dog which she calls Mr. Dog, and a cat called Mr. Cat; she wanted therefore to decide something touching them.

"But will Mr. Dog and Mr. Cat go with us?"

"They will," answered Orso, and he muttered with delight.

"Shall we take the 'good Book' with us too?"

"Yes!" said Orso, and he muttered still more loudly.

"Well," twittered the little maiden, "Mr. Cat will catch birds for us, and Mr. Dog will bark if anything ugly wants to come to us; and you will be husband, and I shall be wife, and they will be our children."

Orso was made so happy that he could not even mutter, so Jennie continued, —

"And there will be no Herr Hirsch, and there will be no circus, and we will never do any work! And only — but no," added she, after a while, "the good Book says that we must labor, so sometimes I will jump through a hoop, or two hoops, or three hoops, or four hoops!"

Evidently Jennie could not imagine to herself labor in another form than jumping through hoops. After a while she asks again, —

"Orso, and shall I really be with you all the time?"

"Yes, Jee, I love you very much."

His face lighted up when he said that, and he became almost good-looking. Still he did not know how he loved that little bright-haired head. He loved her as a mastiff his mistress. But for the rest in his whole life only her. He looked like a dragon near her; but how does that hurt him? In no way.

"Jee, listen to what I say."

Jennie, who a moment before had stood up, wishing to look at the horse, now, so as not to lose any of Orso's words, rested her elbows on his knee, and putting her chin on both palms, began to listen with upraised head.

At this moment, however, to the misfortune of the children, the artist of the whip came into the circus, and came in the very worst humor, for the trial with the lion had failed utterly. The beast had lost his hair from age, and would have been glad had they given him holy peace even once. He would not rush at the artist for anything, under blows of the club he only hid in the interior of the cage. The director thought, in despair, that if that loyal disposition did not leave the lion before evening, the concert on the whip would fail, for to beat a lion which slinks away is no greater trick than to eat a lobster tail first.

The humor of the director was still worse when the negro who was selling tickets for the standing-room reported that apparently the Cahuillas had drunk away all the money received from grape-gathering; they had come, it is true, in large numbers to the office, but instead of money for tickets, they offered blankets, marked U. S., or their wives, especially the old ones.

A failure of money with the Cahuillas was no small loss to the artist, for he had counted on a " crowded house," and there could be no " crowded house " unless the standing-room were occupied; therefore the director wished at that moment that all the Indians had only one back, and that he could give a concert on that back in presence of all Anaheim. He entered the circus building in this state of mind, and seeing, at the barrier, the horse standing idle, with a wearied look, he wanted to turn a handspring from anger. Where could Orso and Jennie be? Shading his eyes with his hand, so that the light coming through the canvas might not dazzle him, the director looked into the interior and saw Orso, and Jennie kneeling before him with her elbows on his knees. At this sight, he dropped the end of the whip to the ground.

"Orso!"

A thunderbolt striking the group of two children could not have produced in them greater astonishment. Orso sprang to his feet and went by the passage between the benches, with that hurried movement of a beast going to the voice of his master; after him followed little Jennie, with eyes widely opened from astonishment, catching the benches along the way.

Orso, when he had·come down to the arena, stopped at the parapet, gloomy and silent. The gray light falling from above illuminated sharply his Herculean body on short legs.

"Nearer!" cried the director, with hoarse voice.

Meanwhile the end of his whip was moving along the sand with the ominous movement of the tail of a tiger while waiting in ambush.

Orso advanced a few steps, and for some time both looked into each other's eyes.

On the whole, the director had the face of a tamer who has entered a cage to flog a dangerous beast, but at the same time observes him.

Rage gained the upper hand of wariness. His thin legs, in elkskin breeches and high-top boots, were dancing under him from anger. Maybe, too, it was not the idleness of the children alone which roused that anger.

Above between the benches Jennie was looking on both, as a doe might look on two bucks.

"Hoodlum! dog-catcher, low cur!" hissed the director.

The whip described a circle with the swiftness of light-

ning; it whistled, hissed, and struck. Orso whined with
a low sound, and threw himself forward a step; but
another blow stopped him at once, then a third, a fourth,
a tenth. The concert had begun, though there were no
spectators yet. The raised arm of the great artist
scarcely moved; his hand merely turned, as if it had been
a part of some machine fixed on a pivot, and every turn
was answered with a blow on the flesh of Orso. It
seemed that the whip, or rather the poisonous end of it,
filled all the space between the athlete and the director,
who, exciting himself gradually, fell into genuine artistic
ecstasy. The master was simply improvising. The lash,
gleaming in the air, had twice described on the neck of
the athlete bloody traces, which powder was to cover in
the evening.

Orso was silent in the dance; but after every blow he
moved a step forward, the director a step backward.
In this way they went around the whole arena; and then
the director pushed out of the arena, precisely as a beast-
tamer out of a cage, and finally vanished at the entrance
to the stables, exactly like a tamer.

But, in passing out, his glance fell upon Jennie.

"To horse!" cried he. "Reckoning with you will
come later!"

His voice had not ceased sounding when the white
skirt gleamed in the air, and Jennie sprang in a twinkle
to the horse's back, like a monkey.

The director vanished behind the curtain; the horse
began to gallop around, striking the barrier sometimes
with his hoofs.

"Hep! hep!" cried Jennie, in a thin voice. "Hep!
hep!" but that "hep! hep!" was at the same time a sob.
The horse, running faster and faster, struck with his
hoofs, bending away from the barrier more vigorously.

The little maiden, standing on the saddle, with her feet pressed one to the other, seemed hardly to touch it with the tips of her toes; her bare, rosy arms kept her balance with quick movements; her tresses and the gauze circus skirt, borne back by the current of air, flew after her slight form, which was like a bird circling in the air.

"Hep! hep!" cried she again. Meanwhile tears filled her eyes, so that she had to raise her head to see anything; the running of the horse made her dizzy; the rising tiers of benches, the walls, and the arena began to whirl around her. She staggered once, a second time, and at last fell into Orso's arms.

"Oh, Orso! poor Orso!" said the child, sobbing.

"What is the matter, Jee?" whispered the youth. "Why are you crying? Don't cry, Jee! It does n't pain me much, not much at all."

Jennie threw both of her arms around his neck, and began to kiss his cheeks. Her whole body trembled from excitement, and her weeping passed almost into spasms.

"Orso! Oh, Orso!" repeated she, unable to speak further, and her arms pressed violently around his neck. If she had been flogged herself, she could not have cried more; at last he fell to soothing in turn and pacifying her. Forgetting his pain, he took her in his arms, pressed her to his heart; and his nerves, roused by the flogging, caused him to feel for the first time that he loved her not merely as a mastiff loves his mistress. He breathed quickly, and his lips began to whisper, with interrupted breath, —

"Nothing pains me any more; when you are near me, I am very happy — Jennie, Jennie!"

Meanwhile the director was striding through the stables and foaming from rage. Jealousy was diving

into his heart. He had seen the little maiden on her
knees before Orso, and for a certain time the wonderful
child had begun to rouse in him as it were the dawn of
low feelings, not sufficiently developed yet. But he suspected her and Orso of a romance, hence he desired vengeance. He would find a wild delight in beating her, —
in beating her very soundly ; and he could not resist this
desire. After a while he called her.

She tore away from the arms of the athlete, and in a
twinkle disappeared in the dark entrance to the stables.
Orso was as if dazed, for, instead of following her, he
went with tottering step to a bench, and, sitting down,
began to pant violently.

The girl, when she had run into the stable, saw no·one
at first, for it was darker there than in the arena. But,
fearing that she might be censured for not obeying the
command at once, she called, in a low and alarmed
voice, —

"I am here, sir, I am here!"

At that moment the hand of the director seized her
little hand, and a hoarse voice said, —

"Come ! "

If he had been angry at her, or had shouted, it would
have frightened her less than that silence in which he led
her toward the dressing-room of the circus. She held
back, and, resisting with all her strength, repeated as
quickly as she could, —

"Dear, kind Herr Hirsch ! I will never — "

But he took her by force to the long, closed chamber
in which was the store of costumes, and locked the door.

Jennie threw herself on her knees, and, with upraised
eyes and crossed hands, trembling like a leaf, covered with
tears, she tried to bend him by entreaty ; but he, taking
a whip from the wall, said, in answer, —

"Lie down!"

Then she seized his feet in despair, for she was almost dying of terror. Every nerve in her was quivering like a distended chord in a musical instrument. But in vain did she press her pale lips imploringly to his polished boot-legs. On the contrary, her terror and prayers seemed to excite him still more. Grasping her by the girdle of her skirt, he placed her on a pile of robes lying on the table; then, for a while yet, he stopped the violent movement of her feet, and at last struck.

"Orso! Orso!" screamed the girl.

At that same moment the door shook on its hinges, cracked from top to bottom, and the whole half of it, broken out by gigantic strength, fell with a crash to the ground.

In the opening stood Orso.

The whip fell from the director's hand, and his face was covered with the pallor of a corpse, for Orso had a terrible look indeed. Instead of eyes only the whites of them were visible. His large mouth was covered with foam; his head was bent forward like the head of a bull, and his whole body was collected, as if for a plunge.

"Out of here!" shouted the director, striving to cover his fear with a shout.

But the bond was broken; Orso, usually as obedient as a dog to every motion, simply bent his head lower and moved on ominously toward the artist of the whip, stretching as if by superior force his iron muscles.

"Help! Help!" shouted the artist.

They heard him.

Four immense negroes ran in with all speed from the stables through the broken door and rushed at Orso. A terrible conflict began at which the director gazed with chattering teeth. For a long time only a group of inter-

9

woven dark bodies were to be seen struggling in convulsive whirls, moving, winding round each other, storming; in the silence which surrounded them was heard at one time a groan, at another, a snorting or the wheezing of nostrils. But after a while one of the negroes, hurled out as if by superhuman force from that formless mass, balanced in the air and fell at the side of the director, striking his head with a dull thump on the floor; soon a second man flew out; and finally above the crowd of strugglers rose only Orso, more terrible than ever, bloodstained, his hair standing on his head. His knees were still pressing down two negroes in a swoon. He sprang up and rushed at the director.

The artist closed his eyes.

In that same second he felt that his feet were no longer touching the earth, he felt that he was flying through the air; after that he felt nothing, for striking the remaining half of the door with his whole body, he fell on the ground without consciousness.

Orso wiped his face, and approached Jennie.

"Come!" said he, mildly.

He took her by the hand, and they walked out. The whole town was just running after the procession of wagons, and the machine playing "Yankee Doodle," therefore it was perfectly empty around the circus. Only the parrots, swinging in their hoops, were filling the air with their cries.

The children went hand in hand, straight ahead toward the place where at the end of the street an immense field of cactuses was visible. In silence they passed houses covered by the shade of eucalyptus, then they passed the slaughter-house, around which were circling thousands of black starlings with red wings. They sprang across the great irrigation ditch, entered a forest of orange-trees, and coming out of that found themselves among cactuses.

They were now in the desert.

As far as the eye could reach the thorny plants rose higher and higher; the intricate leaves growing from other leaves stopped the road, catching Jennie's dress with their thorns. Sometimes the cactuses rose so high that the children were as if in some forest, but neither in that forest could any one find them. They went on, turning now to the right, now to the left, only to be farther. In places where the pyramids of cactuses were fewer, they could see on the very edge of the horizon the blue mountains of Santa Ana. They went toward the mountains. Ash-colored locusts were singing in clumps of cactuses; sun rays came down in floods to the earth; the dried soil was varied with a network of cracks; the stiff cactus leaves seemed to grow soft from the heat; flowers were drooping and half withered.

The children went on, silent and thoughtful. But everything about them was so new that soon they both yielded to their impressions completely and forgot even suffering. Jennie's eyes ran from one clump to another; now she dropped her inquisitive glance into the middle of the cactuses, asking from time to time, in a low voice, —

"Is this the desert, Orso?"

But the desert did not seem empty. From the farther clumps came the calling of cock partridges, and round about were heard various wonderful clapping, clicking, mutterings, in a word, the most varied voices of small creatures living among cactuses. Now a whole flock of partridges rose on the wing, now crested runners fled on long legs, black squirrels sprang into the ground at the approach of the children; on all sides hares and rabbits were running; susliks, sitting on their hind legs before their holes, were like fat German farmers standing in the doors of their houses.

After a short time the children went on. Soon Jennie was thirsty. Orso, in whom Indian inventiveness had been roused, evidently, helped her by plucking prickly pears. There was a multitude of them growing on the same leaves with blossoms. It is true that in gathering them both pricked their hands with the thorns which were as delicate as hair, but to them the fruit tasted excellently; being both sweetish and sourish, it destroyed thirst and hunger. The desert fed the children, like a mother. When strengthened, they were able to go farther. The cactuses towered higher and higher; it might be said that one plant was growing on the head of another.

The ground on which they travelled rose gradually, but continually. Looking around once more from the foothills, they saw Anaheim, half lost in the distance, like a great group of trees growing on a low plain. There was no longer a trace of the circus. For whole hours they went on very enduringly toward the mountains, which were outlined more and more clearly. The region about began to take on another aspect. Among the cactuses appeared various bushes, and even trees. The woody part of the foothills of Santa Ana began. Orso broke one of the smaller trees and, trimming off the branches, made a club, which in his hand might be a terrible weapon. The instinct of the Indian whispered to him that in the mountains it was better to have even a stick than empty hands, especially since the sun had begun to sink toward the west, gradually. Its great fiery shield had passed far beyond Anaheim, and was dropping toward the ocean. After a while, it disappeared, but in the west red, golden, and orange lights of evening were stretched over the whole sky, like long belts and stripes. The mountains bristled up in those gleams; the cactuses took on various fantastic forms, like men and animals. Jennie felt wearied and sleepy; but both hastened with all their strength to the mountains, though they did not themselves know why. In fact they soon saw cliffs, and, coming to them, discovered a stream; after they had drunk water, they went farther along its course. Meanwhile the cliffs, at first scattered and broken, were changed into solid walls, then into walls still higher, and soon they entered a cañon or ravine.

The evening lights were quenched; darkness, ever increasing, embraced the earth. In places where the lianas threw themselves from one side of the cañon to the other, making, as it were, a vault over the stream, it was perfectly dark and quite terrible. Above was to be heard the noise of trees, which could not be seen from below. Orso divined that this was the wilderness, and that surely it was full of wild beasts. From time to time there came from it various suspicious voices; and when night fell they heard distinctly the hoarse bellowing of bucks, the roar of cougars, and the mournful voices of coyotes.

"Are you afraid, Jee?" inquired Orso.

"No!" answered the little maiden.

But she was very tired, and could not walk farther. Orso took her in his arms and carried her. He advanced continually with the hope of coming upon some squatter, or upon Mexican tents. Once or twice it seemed to him that he saw in the distance the gleaming eyes of a wild beast. He pressed to his bosom, with one arm, Jennie, who was sleeping, and with the other held his club firmly. He was greatly wearied him-

self. In spite of his gigantic strength, Jennie began to
weigh him down, all the more since he carried her with
his left arm; the right he wished to have free for defence. At times he stopped to draw breath; then he
went farther. He halted on a sudden and listened carefully. It seemed to him that from a distance came the
sound of bells such as the squatters hang on cows and
goats for the night. Going forward hurriedly he soon
came to a turn in the stream. The sound of the bells
became more distinct, and finally the barking of dogs
was added to it. Orso was certain now that he was approaching some dwelling. It was high time for him; he
had exhausted himself during the day, and strength began to fail him. He passed another turn and saw a light;
as he went forward his quick eyes discerned a fire. A
dog, evidently tied to a tree, was pulling and barking. At
last he saw a man sitting near the fire.

"God grant," thought he, "that this is a man from the
good ' Book.' "

Then he decided to rouse Jennie.

"Jee!" cried he, "wake up; we shall eat!"

"What is it?" asked the maiden. "Where are we?"

"In the wilderness."

She woke up.

"But what light is that?"

"Some man lives there. We shall eat."

Poor Orso was very hungry.

By this time they were near the fire. The dog barked
more violently, and the old man sitting by the fire
shaded his eyes and looked into the darkness. After a
while he asked, —

"Who is there?"

"It is we," answered Jennie, with her thin little voice;
" and we want very much to eat."

"Come near!" said the old man.

Coming from behind a great rock which had concealed them, they stood before the fire, holding each other by the hand. The old man looked at them with astonishment, and out of his mouth came the involuntary cry:

"What is this?"

For he beheld a spectacle which, in the uninhabited mountains of Santa Ana, might astonish any man. Orso and Jennie were wearing their circus costumes. The comely little maiden, dressed in rose-colored tights and a short skirt, appearing suddenly, looked, in the gleam of the fire, like some fantastic sylph. Behind her stood the uncommonly sturdy youth, dressed in flesh-colored tights, through which his muscles were visible like knots on an oak.

The old squatter looked on them with staring eyes.

"What kind of people are you?" asked he.

The little woman, counting evidently more on her own eloquence than on that of her comrade, began to twitter:

"We are from the circus, dear sir. Herr Hirsch beat Orso terribly, and then he wanted to flog me; but Orso would not let him flog me, and he beat Herr Hirsch and four negroes; and then we ran away into the wilderness; and we walked a long time through the cactuses, and Orso carried me; then we came here, and we want very much to eat."

The old hermit's face brightened slowly, and his eyes rested with a kind, fatherly expression on the charming child who hurried in talking, as if she wanted to tell everything in a breath.

"What is your name, little one?" asked he.

"Jennie."

"Well, then, welcome, Jennie, and you, Orso! I see people seldom. Come to me, Jennie."

The little maiden, without hesitation, threw her bare arms around the old man's neck, and kissed him heartily. He seemed to her to be out of the "good Book."

"But will Herr Hirsch find us here?" asked she, removing her rosy lips from the withered face of the settler.

"He will find a bullet!" replied the old man. And after a while he added, "Do you say that you want to eat?"

"Oh, very much!"

The squatter raked in the ashes and took out a splendid hind leg of a deer, the odor of which spread all around. Then they sat down to eat.

The night was magnificent; in the sky high above the cañon rolled the moon; in the thicket the mauhawis began to sing sweetly, the fire crackled joyfully, and Orso muttered from delight. He and the little girl ate as if paid for it; but the old hermit could not eat, and it is unknown why. In looking at little Jennie, he had tears in his eyes. Maybe he had been a father long ago, and maybe in the mountains he saw people rarely.

From that time on those three persons passed their lives together.

WHOSE FAULT?

A DRAMATIC PICTURE IN ONE ACT

WHOSE FAULT?

A DRAMATIC PICTURE IN ONE ACT.

CHARACTERS:

YADVIGA KARLOVETSKI.
LEO, *A Painter*.
A SERVANT.

In the dwelling of YADVIGA KARLOVETSKI.

SCENE I.

SERVANT (*conducts* LEO *in*). The lady will come immediately.

LEO (*alone*). I cannot repress my emotion, or the throbbing of my heart. Three times did I grasp the bell, and three times I wished to withdraw. Alarm seizes my whole being. Why did she summon me? (*Takes out a letter*.) " Would you have the kindness to come to me on an affair which will not suffer delay. Notwithstanding all that has passed and perished, I trust that you will not refuse a woman's prayer. Yadviga Karlovetski." Perhaps I should have acted far more wisely, safely, and honestly, had I left this letter unanswered; but I tempted myself, I persuaded myself that nothing could happen, that it would be simply brutal not to come. The soul, poor moth, flies to the light which may burn it, but can neither warm nor enlighten it. What drew me hither? Was it love? Or can I myself tell whether I love yet this woman, so unlike my former white maiden, — this half

lioness whose reputation is rent by people's tongues?
No! It was rather a kind of painful curiosity which
attracted me; that immense sorrow which two years
could not assuage; that thirst for every explanation of
"Why?" repeated amid sleepless nights. Well, let her
see this emaciated face, let her look from near by at a
broken life. I could not resist: such revenge belongs to
me. But I shall preserve dignity, set my teeth and not
groan. What has happened cannot be undone, and I
swear to myself, that is the word (*clenching his fists*), that
it shall never be undone.

Scene II.

YADVIGA (*entering*). I beg pardon for letting you
wait so long.

LEO. It is my fault, of course. I came too early,
though I tried to come at the appointed hour.

YADVIGA. No. I must be frank and say how it was.
Formerly we were so well acquainted — but we have not
seen each other for two years. I invited you, but I was
not sure that you would come; so, when the door-bell
rang — after two years (*with a smile*) — I needed a little
time to control my emotion. I thought that time was
needed somewhat by both of us.

LEO. I am calm, madam, and listen to you.

YADVIGA. I wished too that we should greet each
other as people who have forgotten the past, who know
that it will not return, and are immediately as good
friends — I dare not say as brother and sister; so, here
is my hand, and now pray be seated, and say if you accept
the agreement.

LEO. I accommodate myself to your wishes.

YADVIGA. In that case I will say further, that such
an agreement, resting on mutual good-will, excludes ex-

cessive coldness. We must be natural, sincere, and outspoken.

LEO. All that will be a little difficult indeed, but —

YADVIGA. It would be difficult, were it not for the first condition: not a word touching the past! If we hold to this point, both of us, good-will may appear of itself, and we may become friends in time. What have you been doing these two years?

LEO. Pushing the wheelbarrow of life, like all mortals. Every Monday I thought to myself that in a week there would be another Monday. There is a certain amusement in this, I assure you, to see how such days unwind like thread from a ball, and how everything which has happened goes off and vanishes gradually from the eye, like a bird which flies away.

YADVIGA. That amusement is pleasant for those to whom a new bird will fly from the future with a new song. But in the opposite case —

LEO. In the opposite case we may imagine greater amusement, — this, that when everything is unwound from the ball nothing will remain. Memories are very painful on occasions. It is lucky that time dulls them, otherwise they would prick like a thorn.

YADVIGA. Or burn like fire.

LEO. Wise Nature has invented a cure for that. Fire without fuel must die, and dead coals do not burn.

YADVIGA. We both chase, in spite of us, the bird that has flown. But no matter. Have you painted much recently?

LEO. I never do anything else: I think, and I paint. True, I have not invented much thus far, and I have not finished much painting. That is not my fault, however. But tell me plainly, why have you summoned me?

YADVIGA. That will reveal itself. First, even my

curiosity to see a great man should be an explanation. You have painted so much that your name is known in all Europe to-day.

LEO. You may suspect me of conceit, but I think really that I have not been a chance pawn on the society chessboard, and this is the reason perhaps, that for two years I have been thinking, but could not understand why I was killed and thrown aside, like a common pawn.

YADVIGA. But our agreement ?

LEO. That is a story told circumstantially, as it were, by a third person. Satisfying another condition of our agreement, sincerity, I add that I have grown accustomed to my wheelbarrow.

YADVIGA. Let us not mention it.

LEO. I forewarn you that that will be difficult.

YADVIGA. It should be easier for you. You are the chosen one of art, the glory of a whole people, and at the same time a spoiled child. You have something to live for, something to draw from. From the flowers cast at his feet, a man may always select the most beautiful, or not select, and walk ever on flowers and flowers.

LEO. Till he drops.

YADVIGA. No ! passes on to immortality.

LEO. Yearning for death on the road.

YADVIGA. That is too pessimistic ; it is like the man who says that he is accustomed to his wheelbarrow.

LEO. I wished merely to paint the reverse of the medal. Besides pessimism is very fashionable to-day. I beg you not to take my words literally. In a drawing-room expressions are shifted on the thread of conversation like beads in a rosary. That is simply an amusement.

YADVIGA. Let us amuse ourselves then — (*After a while.*) But how many changes ! I cannot take them in. If any one had told me two years ago that we should be sitting here to-day so distant, conversing as we are, and looking at each other with such watchful curiosity, like two utter strangers, I should not have believed it. Oh, this is very entertaining indeed !

LEO. It does not become me to recall our agreement.

YADVIGA. And still you recall it — I thank you ! This melancholy turn is the fault of my nerves. But I feel that it does not become me. Even though vanity were my only restraint, I shall not enter that thorny path again, be assured. I too amuse myself as I can, and return to former memories only because I am bored. For some days past I have suffered atrociously.

LEO. And therefore commanded me to come. I fear that my person will not be a very rich source of amusement. I am a man with a poor disposition for joyousness; as a subject of diversion, I have too much value, I am too proud and too honest. Permit me to take leave.

YADVIGA. I beg you to pardon me. I had no wish to offend you. Without returning to former memories, I can say, that pride is your greatest defect; had it not been for pride, many very sad things would not have happened.

LEO. Without returning to former memories, I answer you that that is the only sail which has remained on my bark. The wind of life has torn all the others. Had it not been for this last one, I should have gone, I think, to the bottom long ago.

YADVIGA. On the contrary, I judge that to be a rock on which has been shattered not only your ship — But no more of this ! So much the worse for those who had faith in good weather and a smooth sea. Let us not permit even this time the current to bear us to places where we do not wish to sail.

LEO. And where beyond doubt there are shallows —

YADVIGA.   Ei! we are carrying on a strange conversation.   It seems to me that this is a net in which truth at the bottom of the soul is struggling in vain, without power to break the meshes.   But, perhaps, it is better so.

LEO.   It is far better.   You wrote to me that you summoned me on an affair which does not suffer delay — I am listening to you.

YADVIGA.   Yes! (*With a smile.*)   A society lady is free to have fancies and whims, at times inexplicable fancies, which however gentlemen are not free to refuse.   Now I wish to have my portrait painted by the hand of the master Leo.   Are you willing to paint it ?

LEO.   Madam —

YADVIGA.   Ah! the forehead of the lion is wrinkled precisely as if by this wish I had desired to inflict some insult on him.

LEO.   I think only that society ladies have fancies at times very hard to explain, and quite unlike pleasantries.

YADVIGA.   This question has two sides.   The first, the formal one, appears in this form : Pani Yadviga Karlovetski begs most politely the renowned master, Leo, to paint her portrait.   That is all !   The master, who, as is known, paints many portraits, has no reason to refuse.   An artist cannot refuse a portrait any more than a doctor advice.   Only another side remains — the past.   But we have agreed not to mention it.

LEO.   Permit me, madam —

YADVIGA (*interrupting*).   Ah ! my woman's diplomacy knows how to tie the knot and hide the ends in water.   How I am amused by your vexation !   But there is something else in this.   Admit that I am an empty creature, full of female vanity, petty envy, and jealousy.   Now you have painted the portraits of Pani Zofia and Pani Helena, I wish to have mine also.   This is a thing not refused women. Your fame reaches me from all sides; round about I hear the words, "Our great master!" Society is tearing you to pieces. God knows how many bosoms are heaving for you with a sigh. All can have your works; all may approach you, see you, boast of your acquaintance; I alone, the comrade of your childhood's years, your old acquaintance, I alone am banned.

LEO. Pani Yadviga!

YADVIGA. Ah, you have called me by name! I thank you, and beg pardon earnestly for what I hàve said. It was woman's vanity that spoke, nothing more; I beg you not to be frightened at my nerves. You see how dangerous it is to excite me. At times I am very lonely, afterward I am unendurable. But now I am calm. For that matter, I give you three days for reflection. If you will not come, I beg you to write me (*smiling sadly*). Only I warn you, that if you neither write nor come, I shall tell on all sides that you are afraid of me, and thus I shall pacify my vanity. Meanwhile, out of regard for my nerves, not another word about refusal, not a word. I am a trifle ill, and therefore capricious.

LEO. In three days I will write (*rising to go*); and now I beg leave —

YADVIGA. Oh! ho! Not so easily! I think seriously that you are afraid of me. I know indeed that I have the reputation of a flirt and of being fickle; I know that people even speak ill of me; but really I am not so black as I seem. Besides we are such good acquaintances, who once — who have not seen each other for two years. So let us talk a little. I beg you to give me your hat. That is right! Now let us talk. Indeed, we can be friends yet. I at least — What have you in view for the future, besides painting my portrait?

LEO. We should exhaust a conversation about me **very**

10

quickly. Let us choose another subject, more interesting.
Speak of yourself, of your life, your family.

YADVIGA. My husband, as usual, is in Chantilly.
Mamma is dead! Poor mamma, she was very friendly
to you; she loved you much — (*After a while.*) I, as you
see, have grown old; I have changed beyond recognition.

LEO. At your age the words, " I have grown old," are
simply a bold challenge thrown out by a woman who is
not afraid that people will believe her.

YADVIGA. I am twenty-three years of age, hence I am
not speaking of years; but one may grow old morally.
I feel to-day that I resemble in no way that Yadvinia of
Kalinovitse whom you knew so well. My God! when
I remember that trust, that faith in life, those illusions
of a maiden desiring to be happiness to herself and some
one else, that enthusiasm for everything good and noble!
— whither has all that vanished, whither has it gone?
And to think that I was really that honest field-flower,
and to-day —

LEO. To-day — a grand lady —

YADVIGA. To-day, when I see such a sceptical smile
as I saw on your face a moment ago, it seems to me that
sometimes I am ridiculous, — that I am so even often; as
often as I sit down to an ideal embroidery-frame, and on
the canvas of the forgotten, vanished, and despised past
embroider faded flowers. That is an old fashion of the
time when faithfulness was taken seriously, and people
sang songs about Philo.

LEO. At this moment you are dropping into a strain
of the newest fashion.

YADVIGA. Am I to weep, or can I take up a broken
thread? Difficult! Times change. Be assured that I
have my better moments, in which I laugh heartily at
everything (*giving him a cigarette*). Do you smoke!

LEO. No, madam.

YADVIGA. I do. This is also a diversion. Sometimes I hunt *par force* with my husband; I read Zola's novels; I make visits; I receive; and every morning I think how to kill time. One day I succeed — another I fail. *Apropos,* you know my husband, of course ?

LEO. I knew him long ago.

YADVIGA. He is very fond of hunting, but only *par force.* We never hunt otherwise.

LEO. Let us be sincere. Cast aside this false note.

YADVIGA. On the contrary. In these times we need impressions which rouse the nerves. The latest thing in music, as well as in life, is composed of dissonances. I do not wish to say by this that I am unhappy with my husband. It is true that he lives always in Chantilly, so I see him only once in three months; but this shows confidence on his part. Does it not ?

LEO. I know not, and have no wish to decide, and above all I ought not to know of it.

YADVIGA. It has seemed to me that you ought to know of it. I beg you to be assured that with no other person should I be so outspoken; but we are such old acquaintances. I do not complain. I surround myself with young people who feign to be in love with me. There is not substance to the value of a copper in what they say; they lie till one's ears wither; but the form is very beautiful, for they are all well-bred. Count Skorzevski visits me also, you must have heard of him. I recommend him to you as a model for Adonis. Ha! ha! you could not recognize the "field-flower [1] from Kalinovitse."

LEO. True, I could not recognize it.

---

[1] Yadviga, or Yadvinia, as she calls herself on page 146, par. 3, is from Kalinovitse, hence she calls herself here the "field-flower of Kalinovitse."

YADVIGA. Ha! but life rolls on.

LEO. In jests —

YADVIGA. At which one does not wish always to laugh. If this were not such a sceptical age, I should pretend to be a wild, romantic nature striving to deaden some despair. But romantic times have passed, hence I wish really to fill up a great void. I too unwind my ball, though not always with pleasure. At times I seem to myself so mean, vain, and miserable that I run to that praying-stool there, which I inherited from my mother; I cry out my fill over it, and I pray — and then again I laugh at the weeping and the praying. So it goes round and round! Do you know that people weave scandal about me?

LEO. I do not listen to them.

YADVIGA. How kind of you! So I will tell you why they weave these scandals. A certain missionary asked a negro what his idea of evil was. The negro thought a while, and answered, "Evil is when somebody steals my wife." "And good, what is that?" asked the missionary. "Good," answered the negro, "is when I steal some other man's wife." My husband's friends agree with that negro. Each one of them would be glad to do such a good deed, and steal another man's wife.

LEO. That depends on the wife.

YADVIGA. True! but every word and look is the bait. When the fish avoids the hook, the fisherman's vanity is indignant. That is why they invent lies about me. (*After a while.*) You great people are full of simplicity. Hence you assert that this depends on the wife.

LEO. True, it does.

YADVIGA. *Morbleu!* as my husband says, and if the wife is bored?

LEO. I take farewell of you.

YADVIGA. Why? Does what I say offend you?

LEO. More than offends — it pains. Perhaps this may seem ridiculous to you to-day, but here in my bosom 1 bear flowers, withered, it is true, long since dead; but, for me, they are precious, and you are trampling them at this moment.

YADVIGA (*with an outburst*). Oh, if those flowers had not died! —

LEO. They are lying in my heart — and that is a grave. Let us leave the past in peace.

YADVIGA. True, you are right, let us leave it in peace. What is dead will not rise again. I wish to speak calmly. Look at my position: What defends me, what arm sustains me, what shields me? I am young, and not ugly perhaps; so no one approaches me with a simple, honest heart, but always with a snare in his eyes and on his lips. What have I to raise against that — weariness, regret, emptiness? In life, even a man must hold to something; but I, a weak woman, am like a boat without a rudder, without an oar, without a light to which I might steer. Still my heart is tearing forth to happiness. Will you understand that a woman must be loved, and must love somebody in the world, otherwise, through lack of genuine feeling, she will grasp after the first semblance of it, the first shadow —

LEO (*feverishly*). Poor —

YADVIGA. Do not laugh sneeringly. Be kinder, be less harsh to me. I have not even any one before whom I could complain, and for that reason I do not dismiss Count Skorzevski. I am disgusted with his beauty; I despise his perverse mind; but I do not dismiss him, for he plays like a trained actor, and when I look at his play the echoes of ancient memories are roused in me — (*After a while.*) With what shall I fill life?

Science? art? — even if I loved them they will not love me, for they are not living beings. No! — in truth they are not! No duties are pointed out to me, no objects, no basis. Everything with which other women live, which forms their world, their happiness, their heartfelt consolation, their strength, their tears and smiles, are closed to me. Morally, I am like a beggar; I have nothing to live on. Like an orphan, I have no one to live for. I am not even free to yearn for an honest life and a quiet one; I may only nourish myself with regret, and defend myself with the fragments of faded flowers, and remembrances of the past, pure, honest, and beloved Yadvinia. Ah! again I am breaking the agreement — I beg your pardon!

LEO. Pani Yadviga! — life has become a tangle for both of us. If I were very unhappy, if everything abandoned me, the love of an idea, love of country would remain.

YADVIGA (*thoughtfully*). The love of an idea — of country. In this there is something very great. You bring glory to the country by every picture you paint, you glorify its name; but what can I do?

LEO. Whoever lives simply, suffers, fulfils obligations in silence, serves it.

YADVIGA. What obligations? Let me have them. One great ideal love does not suffice me for daily life. I am a woman; I must cling to something, wind around something, like an ivy; otherwise I shall fall to the ground indeed, and people will walk on me. (*With an outburst.*) If I could even respect that —

LEO. Pani Yadviga! Stop before you come to him whom you have in mind. I have not even the right to know of your family relations.

YADVIGA. True! not only not the right, but not the

duty, or the wish. Friendly hearts alone know how to give solace; only suffering ones know how to give sympathy. You are lost gazing at the stars; the wheel of human misfortune passes by, and you do not turn your head, though that misfortune should shout at you: this is your fault.

LEO. My fault?

YADVIGA. Oh, do not wrinkle your brow and press your lips (*folding her arms*). I wish to make no reproach — I have forgiven long ago, and now I, the giddy woman, whom people see joyous and smiling, am so poor that I should not have strength even for hatred.

LEO. Enough — I have heard your history; do not bring me to tell you mine. Should you hear it, a still greater burden would fall on your shoulders.

YADVIGA. No! no! We might have been happy, and — we are not. This is the fault of both. What despair to think that we parted for a mere nothing, for one inconsiderate expression, and parted forever (*she covers her face with her hands*) — without hope, without salvation!

LEO. That expression was for you, madam, a nothing; but I remember it to this moment with my heart and brain. I was not then what I am to-day. I was poor, unknown, and you were all my future, my object in life, my wealth.

LADVIGA. Oh, Leo! Leo! what a golden dream that was —

LEO. But I was proud, for I felt that there was a spark of divinity in me. I loved you beyond everything, and nothing darkened the sky above me, till one evening Pan Karlovetski appeared, and the very next evening you told me that you were giving more than you received —

YADVIGA. Leo!

LEO. What inclined you to give that slap on the face
to my proud wretchedness, I do not know to this moment. You could not have loved that man then, but
barely had he shown himself, when you humiliated me.
There are wrongs which a man who feels his dignity cannot endure, hence those were the last words which I
heard from you.

YADVIGA. In truth, when I hear what you say, I need
to keep myself in check. Hardly had that man shown
himself, when you burst out in jealousy. I said that I
gave more than I received. You thought, did you, that I
was speaking of money, not of feeling? And suspected
that I wished to throw my wealth in your eyes. You
considered me capable of that? Was that why you did
not pardon? Was that why you went away? Was that
why you broke your life and mine?

LEO. It is too late to speak of this! Too late! You
knew then, and you know to-day, that I could not understand your words otherwise. In him you felt a man of
your society of which you were so fond that more than
once it seemed to me that this society was dearer to you
than even our love. In these doubts of suffering you did
not set me at rest. You were amused by the idea of
extending a hand to me first. I, in a moment when
the measure was passed, in a moment of humiliation,
rejected that hand. You knew this then, you know it
to-day.

YADVIGA. I know it to-day, but I did not know it then.
I swear to you by the memory of my mother! But even
had it been so, why did you not forgive? O God! in
truth one might lose one's senses. And there was
neither time nor means to explain anything. You went
away and showed yourself no more. What could I do?

When you became angry, when you so confined yourself within your own person, sorrow pressed my heart — and I am ashamed even to-day to tell it; but I looked into your eyes like a lap-dog which wishes to dissipate anger with submission. What could I do! I thought to my-self: At parting, I will press his hand so honestly and so cordially that he will understand and forgive. At parting, my hand dropped, for you bowed from a distance. I swallowed my tears and humiliation, and thought: He will return to-morrow. A day passed, two, then a week, a month —

LEO. Then you married.

YADVIGA (*with an outburst*). Yes! useless tears and time taught me that that parting was forever; hence anger rose in my heart, the wish for revenge on you and myself. I wanted to be lost, for I said to myself: That man does not love me and never has loved me. I married then as if I were to spring from a window — through despair, for I believed yet that you did not love me.

LEO. Madam, do not blaspheme! Do not bring me to an outburst — I not love you? Look at the pit which you opened under my feet. Count the sleepless nights in which I tore my breast from pain; count the days in which I called to you, as if from a cross; look at this thin face, at these trembling hands, and say again that I did not love you! What has happened to me? What has my life been without you? To-day this head is in laurels; but here in my breast it is dumb, empty; inex-haustible sorrow is here, with unwept tears; but in my eyes are eternal darkness. Oh, by the living God! I loved you with every drop of my blood, with every thought; and I could not have loved otherwise. Losing you, I lost everything: my star, my strength, my faith, my hope, my wish for life, and not only happiness, but the power of happiness. Woman, do you understand the meaning of this expression: I lost the power of happiness? Did I not love you? Oh, despair, God alone knows how many nights I called to Him: O Lord! take my talent, take my fame, take my life, and return for one moment to me my Yadviga, as she once was —

YADVIGA. Enough. O God! what is happening to me! Leo! I love thee.

LEO. My Yadviga! (*Presses her to his bosom. A moment of silence.*)

YADVIGA. I have found thee again. I loved thee always. Ah! how wretched I was in the world without thee. I have defended that love thus far from every one. Thou knowest not of this, but I used to see thee! That caused me delight and pain. I could not live longer, so I summoned thee. I did that purposely. If thou hadst not come, something terrible would have happened. Now we shall not separate; we shall never be angry with each other, — shall we? (*A moment of silence.*)

LEO (*wakening as if from sleep*). Madam, forgive me. The present moment thrust itself in instead of the past, so I let myself be borne away by an illusion. Pardon me!

YADVIGA. What sayest thou, Leo?

LEO (*severely*). I forgot for a moment, madam, that you are the wife of another.

YADVIGA. Oh, thou art ever just and honorable. No, we shall not carry on a guilty romance. I know thee, my great, noble Leo! The hand which is extended to thee is pure, I swear it. Pardon me also a moment of forgetfulness. I stand here now, and I say that I will not be thine till I am free. But I know that my husband will consent to a divorce. I will leave him all my property, and, since I wounded at one time your pride, for the fault was mine; yes! only mine!—you will take me poor, in this one dress—will you not? It will be well so? Then I shall be your lawful wife. O my God! and I shall be honest, and loving, and loved. I yearned for it so much with all my soul. Of our future I cannot think without tears. God is so good! When thou shalt return from thy studio in the evening, thou wilt not return to empty walls, or to regrets, but I shall wait for thee, I will share every delight with thee, every sorrow. I will share them with thee as a crust of bread. In truth, I cannot keep from tears. See, I am not so wicked, so malicious; I was only poor. I loved thee always! Oh! thou art not kind; had it not been for thy pride this would have happened long ago. Tell me once more that thou lovest me, that thou wilt consent to take me when I am free,— wilt thou not, Leo?

LEO. No, madam —

YADVIGA. Leo, my beloved! Perhaps I have not heard clearly, for it cannot find place in my head that when I am hanging over an abyss of despair and am grasping the brink with my hands, thou, thou, instead of giving me a hand, art treading on my fingers with a foot! No, that cannot be! Thou art too good to do that. Do not reject me! Life now would rend me still worse. I have no one in the world but thee, and thou seest that with thee I lose at once, not only happiness, but all that is best in me yet, which calls for life, quiet, and sacredness. But now it would be finished forever. Thou knowest not how happy thou wouldst be thyself, if thou wouldst forgive and save me. But thou dost love me. Thou hast said so; I have heard it! Now I, as if drowning, stretch my hands to thee, Leo,—save me?

LEO. It is time to finish this mutual torture. Madam,

I am a weak man! I should give way if — I should wish to spare you were it not that my suffering and dead heart can give nothing now except tears and compassion.

YADVIGA. Dost thou not love me?

LEO. I have no strength for happiness. I loved you. My heart quivered for a moment at the memory of it, as for the memory of a dead woman; but that woman is dead. In pain and torture I tell you that I do not love you.

YADVIGA. Leo!

LEO. Have pity on me, and forgive me.

YADVIGA. Dost thou not love me?

LEO. What is dead will not rise again. I take farewell of you.

YADVIGA (*after a while*). If you think that you have humiliated me sufficiently, that you have trampled me enough, that you have taken vengeance enough, then go. (*He wishes to go.*) No! no! remain — take pity on me —

LEO. Let God take pity on you — and on me, Yadviga. God! (*He goes out.*)

YADVIGA. It is over!

THE SERVANT (*enters*). Count Skorzevski!

YADVIGA. Ah! Beg him to enter! Beg him to enter! Ha! ha! ha! (*laughs spasmodically*).

THE DECISION OF ZEUS

THE DECISION OF ZEUS.

ONE evening Apollo and Hermes met on the Pnyx, and, standing on the edge of the rock, looked at Athens.

The evening was wonderful; the sun had advanced from the Archipelago to the Ionian Sea, and was bringing his radiant head slowly into the smooth turquoise-colored liquid plain. But the summits of Hymettus and Pentelicus were gleaming yet, as if covered with molten gold. The brightness of evening was in the sky; and the whole Archipelago was sunk in the gleams of it. The white marbles of the Propyleus, the Parthenon, and the Erechtheum seemed rosy, and as light as if the stone had lost all weight, or as if those buildings were a dream-vision. The point of the gigantic spear of Athene Promachus blazed in the gleam like a torch lighted above Attica.

In the sky floated, with outspread wings, a few falcons moving toward their night repose, to nests concealed in mountain cliffs.

People were returning in crowds from field labor to the city. Along the road from the Piræus passed mules and asses carrying panniers at their sides, full of olives or golden grapes; behind them, in ruddy clouds of dust, came flocks of crooked-horned goats, in front of each flock a white bearded he-goat, at the sides watchful dogs, behind herdsmen playing on bagpipes or slender whistles of thin oat-straw.

Among the flocks wagons bearing the divine barley moved slowly on drawn by sluggish oxen; here and there passed divisions of hoplites arrayed in brass armor, hastening to their night watch at the Piræus or in Athens.

Lower Athens was still seething with life. At the great fountain near the Poikile, young girls in white garments were drawing water, laughing loudly, or defending themselves against boys, who were throwing ivy or grapevine fetters over them. Others, who had taken water already, had amphoras on their shoulders, and, with arms raised upward, were moving toward their homes, graceful and charming, like immortal nymphs.

A mild breeze, blowing from the plain of Attica, brought to the ears of the two divinities sounds of laughter, singing, and kisses.

The Far-shooting Apollo, for whose eyes nothing under heaven was more precious than a woman, turned to the Slayer of Argus, and said, —

"O son of Maia, how beautiful are the women of Athens!"

"And virtuous, my Radiant One," answered Hermes; "for they are under the tutelage of Pallas Athene."

The god of the Silver-bow was silent, and looked, and continued to listen. Meanwhile the red of evening quenched slowly; movement stopped by degrees. Scythian slaves closed the gates, and finally all things were silent. Immortal night cast a dark curtain, dotted with stars, over the Acropolis, the city, and the region about.

But darkness did not last long. Soon pale Selene rose from the Archipelago, and sailed like a silver boat through the expanse of the sky. Again the marbles of the Acropolis shone, but this time with a light which was bright green, and they resembled still more a dream-vision.

"It must be confessed," said the Far-shooter, "that Athene has chosen a marvellous abode."

"Ha, she is wise! Who could choose better than she?" answered Hermes. "Besides, Zeus has a wonderful weakness for her. If she just begs him for something, strokes his beard; straightway he calls her his Tritogeneia, beloved daughter, promises and permits everything with a nod of his head."

"Tritogeneia annoys me at times," muttered the son of Latona.

"I, too, have noticed that she becomes annoying," answered Hermes.

"As an old peripatetic, and besides she is disgustingly virtuous, just like Artêmis, my sister."

"Or like her own wards, the women of Athens."

The Radiant Apollo turned to the Slayer of Argus:

"Thou speakest a second time, as if purposely, of the virtue of Athenian women. Are they in truth so unbending?"

"Fabulously so, O son of Latona!"

"Is it possible!" said Apollo. "But thinkest thou that there is even one in this city who could resist me?"

"I think there is."

"Resist me, Apollo?"

"Thee, O Radiant Divinity."

"Me, the god who subdues by poetry, who charms by music and song?"

"Thee, O Radiant One!"

"If thou wert an honest god, I should be willing to wager with thee. But, Slayer of Argus, if thou lose, thou wilt fly off at once with thy sandals and staff, and that is the last that I shall see of thee!"

"No. I will put one hand on the earth, the other on the sea, and swear by Hades. This oath is re-

spected not only by me but even by the magistrates of
Athens."

"Well, thou art exaggerating again! But I agree! If
thou lose, thou must bring to me, in Thrinacia, a herd of
long-horned oxen, which thou wilt steal from whomever
thou wishest, as thou didst steal, in thy time, when a boy,
my herds in Pieria."

"Agreed. But what shall I get if I win?"

"Make thy own choice."

"Listen to me, Far-shooter, I will be outspoken, which,
as thou knowest, does not happen with me often.
Once sent by Zeus, I do not remember on what errand,
I was flying over thy Thrinacia, and I saw Lampetia
with Phæthusa, who was guarding thy cattle there. From
that moment I have had no peace. Lampetia does not
leave my eyes, does not leave my memory; I love her, and
sigh night and day to her. If I win, if in Athens there
be found a woman so virtuous as to resist thee, thou shalt
give me Lampetia. I ask nothing more."

He of the Silver-bow nodded.

"Very gladly, since love can fix itself even in the
heart of the patron of merchants. I will give thee
Lampetia, the more readily since now she cannot agree
with Phæthusa; I may say, in parenthesis, that both are
in love with me, and, therefore, are quarrelling."

Great joy shot from the eyes of the Slayer of Argus.

"The wager is made, then," said he. "But one thing, —
I will select for thee the woman on whom thou art to try
thy divine power."

"If she is beautiful."

"She will be worthy of thee."

"Confess that thou hast already selected one."

"I confess."

"A maiden. a wife. or a widow?"

"Of course a wife. Thou mightst influence a maiden or a widow by a promise of marriage."

"What is her name?"

"Eriphyle, she is the wife of a baker."

"Of a baker?" asked the bright god, with a wry face; "that pleases me less."

"What dost thou wish? I move most frequently in those circles. Eriphyle's husband is not at home now; he has gone to Megera. The woman is the most beautiful person that has ever walked mother earth."

"I am curious."

"One condition more, my Silver-bowed. Promise me that thou wilt use only means worthy of thee, and that thou wilt not act, for instance, like that boor, Ares, or even, speaking among ourselves, like our common father, the Cloud-compeller."

"For whom dost thou take me?" asked Apollo.

"Then all the conditions are accepted, and I can show thee Eriphyle."

The air bore away immediately both gods from the Pnyx, and soon they were hanging over a house at some distance from the Stoa. The Slayer of Argus raised the whole top of the house with his powerful hand, as easily as a female, cooking food, might raise a pot-lid; and, pointing out a woman sitting in a shop, closed from the street by a copper grating and a woollen curtain, he said, —

"Look!"

Apollo looked, and was petrified.

Never had Attica, never had the Grecian land, given forth a more beautiful flower than that woman. She was sitting at the light of a triple lamp, bent over a table, and was writing something diligently on marble tablets. Her long, drooping lashes cast a shadow on her cheeks; at times she raised her head and eyes as if pondering and calling to mind what she had to write yet; and then her marvellous eyes could be seen, — so blue, that, compared with them, the turquoise surface of the Archipelago would have seemed pale and faded. It was simply the face of Kypris, — white as sea-foam, rosy as the morning dawn, with lips of the color of Syrian purple, and golden waves of hair, — beautiful, the most beautiful on earth, beautiful as a flower, as light as a song.

When she dropped her eyes, she seemed calm and sweet; when she raised them in thought, inspired. The divine legs began to tremble under the Radiant Apollo; all at once he rested his head on the shoulder of Hermes, and whispered, —

"Hermes, I love her! This one, or none!"

Hermes smiled shrewdly, and would have rubbed his palms under the folds of his robe, had he not held his staff in the right hand

Meanwhile the golden-haired woman took a new tablet, and began to write on it. She opened her divine lips, and her voice whispered, like the sound of a lyre, —

"Melanocles, a member of the Areopagus, for bread during two months, forty-five drachmæ and four oboli; for the sake of round numbers let us write forty-six drachmæ. By Athene! let us write fifty; my husband will be satisfied. Ah, Melanocles, if thou wert not able to fasten onto us for false weights, I would not give thee credit. But one must be on good terms with that locust."

Apollo did not hear the words; he only intoxicated himself with the sound of her voice, the charm of her figure, and whispered, —

"That one, or none!"

The golden-haired woman wrote on, —

"Alcibiades, for unleavened cake on honey from Hymettus, for the hetæra Chrysalis, three minæ. He never verifies accounts, besides, he slapped me on the shoulder once in the Stoa; we will write down, then, four minæ. If he is a fool, let him pay. And this Chrysalis, too! She feeds, I suppose, her carp in the pond with cakes, or, maybe, Alcibiades is fattening her purposely to sell her afterward to Phœnician merchants for ivory rings to put on his harness."

Apollo did not hear the words; he was intoxicated with the voice, and whispered to Hermes, —

"That one, or none!"

But Maia's son covered the house on a sudden, and the wonderful vision disappeared. To the Radiant god, it seemed that the stars were vanishing, the moon blackening, and the whole world hiding under the darkness of Cimmerian regions.

"When is the wager to be decided?" inquired Hermes.

"To-day, immediately!"

"During her husband's absence, she sleeps in the shop. Thou mayst stand on the street before the grating. If she pushes the curtain aside, and opens the grating, I have lost my wager."

"Thou hast lost!" cried the Far-shooting Apollo.

And not so swiftly does summer lightning pass at night from the east to the west, as he shot over the salt waves of the Archipelago. There, when he had begged Amphitrite for an empty turtle-shell, he fastened on it sun rays, and returned to Athens with a finished lyre.

In the city all was perfectly silent; the lights were extinguished; only houses and temples stood white in the gleam of the moon, which was sailing high in the heavens.

The shop was situated in a gap of the wall; and in it,

behind the grating and a curtain, slept the most beautiful
Eriphyle. The Radiant Apollo, halting on the street, began to touch the strings of his lyre. Wishing to rouse
his beloved gently, he played at first as low as the song
of mosquitoes in a spring evening above the Ilissus. But
the song rose gradually, like a mountain stream when
divine rain is falling, and more and more powerful,
sweeter, more entrancing; it filled the whole air, which
now quivered voluptuously. Athene's mysterious bird
flew in silent flight from the direction of the Acropolis,
and sat motionless on a column near by.

Then a bare arm worthy of Phidias or Praxiteles, whiter
than the marble of Pentelicus, pushed the curtain aside.
The heart in the Radiant god quivered from emotion.

But the voice of Eriphyle was heard, —

"What wretched fellow is that, dragging about in the
night and thrumming. It is not enough that one works
to weariness in the day; they won't let us sleep at night!"

"Eriphyle! Eriphyle!" cried the Bearer of the Silver-
bow. And he sang, —

> "From Parnassus of lofty peaks,
>   Where, in light, amid azure,
>   Inspired muses circle
> And sing inspired songs to me,
> I, divine, adored light,
> Have descended. Open thy arms,
> A moment on thy bosom, Eriphyle,
> Will to me be eternity."

"By the sacred, sacrificial flour!" called the baker's
wife, "that scapegrace is singing to me, and wants to turn
my head. But wilt thou not go home, thou torment!"

Apollo, wishing to convince her that he was no common mortal, shone all at once so that from the light of

him the earth and the air became radiant; but Eriphyle seeing that, exclaimed, —

"The good-for-nothing has hidden a lantern under his skirt, and gives himself out as some god! O daughter of mighty Zeus! they know how to torment us with taxes, but keep not even a Scythian guard in the city to take giddy heads like this one to prison."[1]

Apollo did not own himself beaten yet, and sang on, —

> "Ah, open thy white arms!
> I will give endless glory,
> Thy name shall be heard through the world,
> Above every goddess of the sky.
> Thou shalt have immortality;
> I will adorn thee, O beautiful,
> Through the power of a divine word,
> So that no Grecian queen
> Will have the like homage.
>
> "Ah, open, open thy arms!
>
> . . . .
>
> I will rob the sea of its azure,
> The dawn of its purple and gold,
> The stars of their sparks, the dew of its flowers,
> And of this brilliant web
> I will make for my only one
> The rainbow robes worn by Kypris."

The voice of the god of poetry sounded so marvellously that it called forth a miracle. There, in the immortal night, the golden spear quivered in the hands of Athene as she stood on the Acropolis, and the marble head of the gigantic statue turned somewhat toward the lower city, to hear the words of the song more distinctly. Heaven and earth listened; the sea ceased to roar, and lay in silence at its shores; even pale Selene (the moon)

[1] Scythian slaves were used in Athens to watch over the order and safety of the city.

stopped her night journey through the sky, and halted over Athens, immovable.

When Apollo ceased, a light breeze rose and bore the song through all Greece, and wherever a child in the cradle heard even one note of it, that child became a poet.

But before Latona's son had finished, the angry Eriphyle screamed loudly, —

"What a fool! He wishes to traffic here in stars and dew. Because my husband is not at home, thou thinkest that everything is permitted. Ei! a scandal that my servants are not here, I would teach thee sense! But I will break thee, O soap, of straggling in the night with thy music!"

Then, she seized a kneading-bowl with acid for making yeast, and throwing the liquid through the grating, she covered the bright face of Apollo, his radiant shoulders, his radiant robe and lyre with it.

Apollo groaned, and, covering his inspired head with the skirt of his wet robe walked away abashed and angry.

Hermes, who was waiting on the Pnyx, seized his sides from laughter, stood on his head, and brandished his staff with delight. But when the suffering son of Latona approached him, the cunning guardian of merchants feigned sympathy, and said, —

"I grieve that thou has lost, O Far-shooter."

"Be off, thou rascal!" answered Apollo, in anger.

"I will go only when thou givest Lampetia."

"May Cerberus rend thy calves! I will not give Lampetia; and I say, be off, or I will break thy staff on thy own head!"

The Slayer of Argus knew that when Apollo was angry, there were no jokes with him, so he pushed aside, with forethought, and said, —

" If thou wish to deceive me, be Hermes in future, and I will become Apollo. I know that thou art more powerful than I, and canst do me wrong; but happily there is one above thee, and he will judge us. I summon thee, Apollo, to the court of the son of Chronos! Come with me ! "

Apollo was frightened at mention of the son of Chronos (Zeus); he dared not refuse, and they went.

Meanwhile, it had begun to dawn. Attica was emerging from the shade. Rosy-fingered Aurora had appeared in the sky in the direction of the Archipelago.

Zeus had passed the night on the summit of Ida; but whether he had slept, or had not slept, or what he was doing there, no one knew, for the Mist-gatherer had sheltered himself with a cloud so dense that Hera herself could not see him.

Hermes trembled a little as he drew near the father of gods and men.

"Justice is on my side," thought he; "but suppose Zeus wakes up angry, suppose before hearing the case that he takes each of us by a leg, whirls us above his head, and hurls us about three hundred Athenian stadia. He has some regard for Apollo; but with me he will make no ceremony, though I am his offspring."

But the fears of Maia's son were vain. Zeus was sitting on the ground, gladsome, since for him the night had passed pleasantly; and in cheerful glory he was enjoying the circle of the earth with gleaming eyes. The earth, delighted under the father of gods and men, produced beneath him the bright grass of May, and young hyacinths. He leaned on his arms, passed his fingers over the curling flowers, and rejoiced in his lofty heart.

When he saw this, the son of Maia recovered, and.

giving obeisance to his parent, began boldly to inculpate Apollo; and flakes of snow fall not so thickly in a storm as fell the eloquent words of Hermes.

When he had finished, Zeus was silent for a while, and then spoke to Apollo.

"Is all this true, Radiant One?"

"True, father," answered Apollo, "but if thou command me to pay the wager, after the shame which has met me, I will go to Hades, and give light to the shades there."

Zeus reflected and considered.

"Then this woman," asked he, at last, "remained deaf to thy music, to thy song, and rejected thee with contempt?"

"She poured a pot of yeast on my head, O Wielder of Thunderbolts!"

Zeus frowned, and from that frown Ida trembled immediately. Fragments of cliffs rolled to the sea with tremendous report, and forests fell like stalks of grain broken by wind.

Both gods were frightened, and waited with throbbing hearts for the sentence.

"Hermes," said Zeus, "cheat men as much as may please thee, for men like to be cheated. But let the gods alone, for if I should flash up in anger and hurl thee into the ether, thou wouldst fall and sink in the ocean so deeply that even my brother, Poseidon, could not dig thee out with his trident."

Divine terror seized Hermes by the smooth knees; but Zeus spoke on, with an ever-increasing voice, —

"A virtuous woman, especially if she loves another, is able to resist Apollo. But certainly and always a stupid woman will resist him. Eriphyle is stupid, not virtuous; and that is why she resisted him. In this thou hast cheated the Radiant — and thou wilt not get Lampetia. Now, go in peace !"

. . . .

The gods departed.

Zeus sat alone in joyful glory for a while. He looked in silence after the departing Apollo, and muttered, —

"Oh, it is true, a stupid woman can resist him !" And immediately after, since he had not rested much, he beckoned to Sleep, who, sitting on a neighboring tree in the form of a sparrow-hawk, was awaiting orders from the father of gods and men.

ON A SINGLE CARD

PERSONAGES.

ON A SINGLE CARD.

PERSONAGES.

PRINCE STAROGRODSKI.
STELLA, *his daughter*.
YERZY PRETVITS, STELLA'S *betrothed*.
KAROL, COUNT DRAGOMIR, *a friend of* PRETVITS.
COUNTESS MILISHEVSKI.
YAN, COUNT MILISHEVSKI.
ANTONI JUK, *Secretary of the District Council*.
DOCTOR YOZVOVICH.
PANI GHESKI.
PODCHASKI.
SERVANT.

ACT I.

The stage represents a drawing-room with the main door opening on a garden. In the side walls are doors to adjoining chambers.

SCENE I.

PRINCESS STELLA, PANI CHESKI.

PANI CHESKI. Why tell me the news only now? Indeed, my dear Stella, I am inclined to be angry at thee. How is this? I live one verst away; I taught thee before thou wert given into the hands of French and English governesses; I see thee almost daily; I love thee, little girl, with my whole soul; and for weeks thou hast not brought thyself to say: I am betrothed. Do not torment me longer, at least now, and say who he is.

STELLA.   Guess, mother.

PANI CHESKI.   Since thou sayest mother, do not ask me to guess.

STELLA.   But I wish thee to guess, to say: "Naturally it is he and no other." Thou wilt not believe how that will flatter me, how it will please me.

PANI CHESKI.   Ah, then it is Count Dragomir.

STELLA.   Ah!

PANI CHESKI.   Dost thou blush? True, he has not been long here; but how pleasant, how sympathetic, how gladsome he is! Oh, my old eyes see clearly, and when I looked at you together, I thought right away: A beautiful couple! perhaps something will come of that.

STELLA.   Nothing will come of it, mother. Count Dragomir is very sympathetic indeed, but my betrothed is Pan Yerzy.

PANI CHESKI.   Pan Yerzy Pretvits?

STELLA.   Yes. Does this astonish thee?

PANI CHESKI.   No, my dear child. May God bless thee; why should I be astonished? Only I like Count Dragomir so much that I thought him the man — Pan Yerzy Pretvits! Oh, not in the least! I do not wonder at all that he fell in love with thee. But that too was rather sudden. How long hast thou known him? In my Bervinko I hear nothing of what happens in the neighborhood.

STELLA.   Three months. My betrothed inherited an estate here from the Yazlovetskis, and came, as thou knowest, from a great distance. He was a near relative of the Yazlovetskis, and is descended himself from a great family. Thou, beloved lady, hast heard of the Pretvitses?

PANI CHESKI.   Nothing and nothing. What do I care for heraldry!

STELLA.   On a time, but whole ages ago, the Pretvitses

were related to us. That family is very famous. Oh,
otherwise papa would not have consented. Well, Pan
Pretvits came here, received the estate left him by the
Yazlovetskis, became acquainted with us and —

PANI CHESKI. And fell in love with thee. In his
place I should have done the very same. That raises him
in my eyes.

STELLA. But did he need it?

PANI CHESKI. No, dear kitten — be at rest. People
laugh at me, I assure thee, because always I see in persons everything that is best. Of a nice family, young,
rich, genteel, well-bred, but —

STELLA. But what?

PANI CHESKI. Some birds have sung to me, for even I
do not remember who told me, that he is somewhat like
a storm.

STELLA. His life was like a storm, but that high-
hearted man was not broken in it.

PANI CHESKI. All the better. Listen, my child, such
men are the best, the truest. The more I think over the
matter, the more sincerely do I congratulate thee.

STELLA. Thanks, and I am glad that I have been outspoken with thee. I am indeed very lonely here. Papa
is always ailing; our doctor has not been in the house for
three months.

PANI CHESKI. But do not annoy us with that doctor.

STELLA. Thou hast never liked him.

PANI CHESKI. Thou knowest that I am not prepos-
sessed against people; but I cannot like him.

STELLA. Dost thou know that they have offered him
a chair in the University, and that he is striving for
election to the diet? Mother, thou art unjust indeed, for
he simply sacrifices himself for us. Such a famous man,
and well-to-do, and learned, still he stays with us, though

12

the whole world is open to him. I should certainly have asked his advice.

PANI CHESKI. Love, my dear Stella, is not a disease — never mind the doctor, let God help him. Tell me better, kitten, but sincerely, dost thou love much ?

STELLA. Seest thou, all passed suddenly. True, Countess Milishevski came also with her son. I saw that I was in question; and I was afraid, though needlessly, that papa might be on their side.

PANI CHESKI. Thou dost not answer my question —

STELLA. How speak definitely. Yerzy's life, mother, is a series of heroic deeds, sacrifices, and dangers. Once he was near death, and would not be living to-day had it not not been that Count Dragomir saved him. How he loves the Count for that act ! Distant deserts, loneliness, continuous suffering are evident on my betrothed. But when his life is unfolded before me, it seems, indeed, that I love that iron man greatly. If thou knew how timidly, and still how lovingly he declared what he feels for me, and added afterward that he knew that his hands were too rough —

PANI CHESKI. Not too rough, because honest. After what thou hast said, I give all my soul to him.

STELLA. But still, mother, in spite of all this, I feel at times very unhappy.

PANI CHESKI. And how is that, Stella ? Why ?

STELLA. Because at times we are unable to understand each other. Feelings, mother, are of two classes: one as firm and immovable as cliffs, the other like streams which are transparent. Now when I examine Yerzy's feelings, I see their greatness and unshaken character; but my soul is not reflected in them as a face in a clear river. I love him, that is true; but at moments it seems to me that I could love him more, that I do not put all the strength of my heart into this attachment, and then I feel unhappy.

PANI CHESKI. I can hardly understand thy words, I take life simply: İ love, or not. Ei! Stella dear, the world is so wisely arranged, and God is so good, that nothing is simpler than happiness. But one must not confuse God's affairs. Be calm, child! Thou art in love terribly. What is the use in talking!

STELLA. Oh, I need just thy confidence in the future, thy optimism. I knew that thou, dear sincerity, would frown, and say, "What is the use in talking." Right away I am brighter and more joyous. Only I am a little afraid of our doctor. But what is this? (*Looking through the window.*) Our gentlemen: Pan Yerzy and Count Dragomir.

PANI CHESKI (*looking through the window*). Thy betrothed looks nicely; but so does Count Dragomir. Has he been visiting Yerzy long?

STELLA (*looking through the window*). Two weeks. Pan Yerzy invited him purposely. They are coming now.

PANI CHESKI. And the little heart is going, puk! puk!

STELLA. Oh, be not my enemy, evil woman!

SCENE II.

PANI CHESKI, STELLA, YERZY, COUNT DRAGOMIR. DRAG-
OMIR *has his left arm in a sling.*

SERVANT (*opening the door*). The Princess is in the drawing-room.

STELLA (*greeting*). Are you not somewhat late to-day, Pan Yerzy.

YERZY. Yes, the sun is just setting. But we could

not come earlier. Do you know that there was a fire in the neighboring village ? We went to it.

PANI CHESKI. We have heard of it. I suppose a number of houses were burned.

YERZY. The fire broke out in the morning, and has been quenched just now. About twenty families are without a roof and without bread. We are late also, because the Count had an accident.

STELLA (*with animation*). True ! His arm is in a sling.

DRAGOMIR. Nothing serious. If there were no worse wounds in the world, courage would be sold on all market squares. A slight scratch —

STELLA. How did he get it, Pan Yerzy ?

YERZY. I was at the other end of the street at the time, and I could see nothing through the smoke. They told me simply that Karol had rushed into a burning house —

STELLA. O my God !

DRAGOMIR (*laughing*). I think that my deed gains by distance.

PANI CHESKI. Well, let the gentleman tell it himself.

DRAGOMIR. People shouted before me that in a house, the roof of which had just begun to burn, was a woman. Then, judging that that female salamander, fearless of fire, was some enchanted beauty, perhaps, I went in through pure curiosity. It was a little dark there from smoke. I looked, and convinced myself firmly that I have no luck in anything; for my salamander was only an old Jewess who was packing broken feathers into a bag. Amid flakes of goose-down she looked like whatever may please you; but not like an enchantress. I screamed that the house was burning ; she, in the darkness, took me evidently for a thief, and screamed also, or — we both screamed. At last, seeing that there was no help, I seized the salamander in my arms, and bore her out, fainting from fear, not by the window even, but by the door.

YERZY. But thou hast not added that the roof fell in and a rafter struck thy arm.

DRAGOMIR. If that is the way, I will break the bonds of modesty and add, that the mayor made a speech to me. He said something, I think, about a monument which they are to raise in the square to me. But, believe me, Yerzy and his men put the fire out. •I think that the village ought to raise two monuments.

PANI CHESKI. I know that one of you is worthy of the other.

STELLA. God be praised that nothing worse has met you, Count.

DRAGOMIR. Something very good has met me, your sympathy.

PANI CHESKI. And you have mine too; as to Pan Yerzy, I have a question with him.

YERZY. Touching what, dear lady?

PANI CHESKI. Ei, Pan Yerzy, Pan Yerzy! (*To Stella and* DRAGOMIR.) Go you to the Prince, and we will have a little talk here.

STELLA. Ah, mother, thou, I see, hast the wish to turn Pan Yerzy's head.

PANI CHESKI. Quiet, thou rogue! I am just the one to vie with thee. But know, my dear, that every autumn had its spring. Well, go!

STELLA (*to* DRAGOMIR). Let us go. Papa is in the garden, and I fear that he is worse again. A pity that the doctor is not here.

Scene III.

PANI CHESKI, YERZY, *and, later*, STELLA.

PANI CHESKI. I ought to scold you, Pan Yerzy, as I scolded my young lady, for secrecy. But Stella has told me everything, so I only say : God bless you both !

YERZY (*kissing her hand*). Thank you.

PANI CHESKI. I reared that child from being the smallest little mite; I was ten years with her, so I know what a treasure you are getting. You told her that your hands were too rough. I answered her at once: "Not too rough, because they are honest." But Stella is a very delicate flower; there is need to love her much, and to guard her. You will be able to do that, — will you not ?

YERZY. What shall I say to you ? As far as it is in human power to give happiness to that being who for me is sacred, I wish to give it.

PANI CHESKI. With all my soul I say : God bless you !

YERZY. The Princess looks on you as a mother, hence I will talk as frankly as with a mother. My life has been very difficult. At one moment it hung on a thread. I was saved then by Count Dragomir, whom I love and esteem as a brother; but later on—

PANI CHESKI. Stella told me. You were living far away—

YERZY. I was among empty steppes, half wild, among strangers, so very lonely and yearning for my country, and the last member of a noble family. Besides a proud soul, though struck by misfortune, as by a hammer, is ashamed to groan, and shuts pain within itself, and great torture comes through this. Indeed, at times, there was not a living being near me.

PANI CHESKI. God was above the stars, Pan Yerzy.

YERZY. Oh! that is another thing. But the heart cast on earth must love some one on earth and have some person near it. So with all that need of loving, I prayed God to let me love some person. He heard me and gave her. Do you understand now?

PANI CHESKI. Oh, I understand!

YERZY. How soon all changed after that! I inherited an estate here, and returned; then I became acquainted with the Princess, and now I love her as the accomplishment of my prayer, as the reward for my suffering, as my heartfelt *everything* on earth. Oh, be at rest, Pani!

PANI CHESKI. Indeed I will. My honest Pan Yerzy, be of good cheer, you are worthy of Stella, and with you she will be happy. My golden, my beloved Stella!

STELLA (*appearing in the garden door, and clapping her hands*). Perfect news! Perfect news! The doctor will come in a moment; he is in the village. Papa is already calmer and in better humor.

PANI CHESKI. But do not flutter about, do not run too fast, and grow red from over-exertion. Where is the Prince?

STELLA. In the garden, he is drinking coffee. He invites you to come.

YERZY. We will go.

STELLA (*goes in advance, and then halts*). But, I beg you not to tell the doctor what has happened between us —I wish to tell him first. I have begged papa already to keep the secret.   [*They go out.*

SCENE IV.

DOCTOR YOZVOVICH *enters through the principal door.*

DOCTOR (*to* SERVANT). Yan! take my things upstairs, the package which I left at the entrance send by a messenger to Pan Antoni, the secretary of the district council.

SERVANT (*bowing*). I obey, Pan Doctor!   [*Goes out.*

DOCTOR (*coming to the front of the stage*). At last! after three months of absence. How quiet and calm everything is here! After a while I will greet them as the future member. I have thrown six years into this abyss between us, — iron labor, sleepless nights, science, reputation, and now — let us see! (*He approaches the door to the garden.*) Here they are; she has not changed any.

SCENE V.

Through the garden door enters STELLA, PANI CHESKI, *at their side* YERZY, *behind*, DRAGOMIR, *on the arm of* PRINCE STAROGRODSKI.

STELLA. Oh, our doctor! our beloved doctor! How are you, Pan Stanislav? We had grown weary waiting for you.

PANI CHESKI (*inclining coldly*). Especially the Prince.

DOCTOR (*kissing* STELLA'S *hand*). Good-evening, Princess! And I was in a hurry to return. I have come for a longer time to rest a little. And the Prince, how is he, in health?

PRINCE (*embracing him*). Dear boy! Weak, weak! Thou hast acted perfectly in coming. Thou wilt see at once how I am.

DOCTOR. Now, Prince, perhaps you will have the kindness to present me to the rest of the society.

PRINCE. Ah, of course? Doctor Yozvovich, my minister of the interior — I said well, did I not? for thou art occupied with my health, Count Karol Dragomir.

DRAGOMIR. Your name is at present strange to no one, hence, properly, I should be presented.

PRINCE (*presenting*). Pan Yerzy Pretvits, our neighbor,

and — (STELLA *makes a sign to her father*) and this — I wish to say, and this —

YERZY. I, if I mistake not, am a comrade of your school days.

DOCTOR. I did not wish to mention it first.

YERZY. I greet a former comrade heartily. The time is long passed, but we lived intimately. Indeed I am delighted, sincerely, especially after what I have heard of you.

DRAGOMIR. As of the good spirit of this house.

STELLA. Oh, that is true!

PRINCE. Wait, let me tell what I have to say of him.

YERZY. How many times did the first scholar, Yozvovski, solve problems for Pretvits.

DOCTOR. You have a rare memory.

YERZY. Yes, comrade, for I remember also that in those days we did not say "Pan" to each other. So now again I greet thee heartily, Stanislav.

DOCTOR. The heartiness is mutual.

YERZY. But I remember that after finishing the course, thou didst study law.

DOCTOR. Later, I became a doctor of medicine.

PRINCE. Well, sit down. Or will you stand? Yan, here! a light!

STELLA. How pleasant it is that you gentlemen are acquainted!

DOCTOR. The school bench, like misery, unites people. But afterward society divides them. Yerzy had a brilliant position secured; I had to find mine.

PRINCE. He found his, but in blows.

DRAGOMIR. In two parts of the world.

PANI CHESKI. That was really manful.

DOCTOR. Ha, he followed his instinct! While in school he rode, shot, wielded the sword.

YERZY. Better than he learned?

DOCTOR (*laughing*). Yes! We called him the hetman, for he led us in our student wars.

DRAGOMIR. Yerzy, I recognize thee.

PANI CHESKI. But now I think that he will stop warring.

STELLA. Who knows?

YERZY. Beyond doubt he will.

DOCTOR. As for me, I was the worst among those in the ranks; I never had a taste for such amusements.

PRINCE. For those are the amusements of nobles, not of doctors.

DOCTOR (*laughing*). We are beginning to quarrel already! Prince, you are proud that your forefathers, who were knights, killed crowds of people. If you will learn how many I have killed with my medicines, I will guarantee that no ancestor of your princely race can boast of such numbers.

DRAGOMIR. Bravo, that is perfect!

PRINCE. What does this worthless man say? And he is my doctor!

STELLA. Papa, the doctor is joking.

PRINCE. I thank him for such jokes. But the world is going topsy-turvy, that is undoubted.

DOCTOR. And, Prince, we shall live a hundred years yet. (*To* YERZY.) Come, tell me thy adventures. Those present know thy life; but for me it is new. (*They go toward the window*)

PRINCE. You cannot believe how unhappy I am not to be rid of this worthless fellow. He is the son of a blacksmith from Stanislavov. I sent him to school, for I wished to employ him, and then he went himself to the University.

DRAGOMIR. And is a doctor of law and of medicine. A clever man, that is evident.

STELLA. Oh, such a clever one !

PANI CHESKI. So wise that I am afraid of him.

DRAGOMIR. But the Prince must be glad?

PRINCE. Glad, glad ! People have turned his head; they have made of him some kind of democrat or *sans culotte*. But he is a good doctor, and I am weak. I lack juices in the stomach. (*To* DRAGOMIR.) Do you know this?

DRAGOMIR. Your complaint is an old one —

PANI CHESKI. Twenty years.

PRINCE. My Cheski! Sorrow and public service have taken my health away.

PANI CHESKI. Pshaw ! the Prince is well.

PRINCE (*angrily*). I say that I am ill. Stella, dear, I am ill, am I not?

STELLA. Now, papa, you will be better right away.

PRINCE. He alone keeps me on my feet. Stella also would die of heart affection were it not for him.

DRAGOMIR. If that be true, he is a man beyond price.

STELLA. Oh, we owe him eternal gratitude.

PRINCE (*looking at* YERZY) Pretvits will need him. What thinkest thou, Stella, will he need him?

STELLA (*laughing*). How am I to know, papa?

DRAGOMIR. Indeed, more than once I envy those iron men who take the world by storm. In this battle they develop strength in themselves; our strength fades and vanishes, for nothing ever rouses it. We may be of sufficiently noble metal, but rust weakens us; they strengthen themselves in life. That is a sad necessity.

PANI CHESKI. But, Pan Yerzy?

DRAGOMIR. Yerzy, also, has passed through much. But there is a difference between them, which is felt, though to define it is difficult. Look, gentlemen, at those two men. When the storm blows, Yerzy resists like a tree of a hundred years' growth; but a man like the doctor controls the wind and commands it to push on his boat. There is in him a certain greater capacity for life. Hence the result is easily foreseen. The older the tree, though strong, the more it is pulled by storms, the earlier must it wither.

PRINCE. More than once I have said that we are withering like old trees. Some other kind of brush is growing; it is nothing but a thicket though. I have dried up and withered already three fingers' length at least.

STELLA. Whoever is good has a right to life, therefore we should not doubt ourselves.

DRAGOMIR Hence I do not doubt, even because of what the poet says: "He is a saint on earth who has been able to gain the friendship of saints." (*Bowing to* STELLA.)

STELLA (*threatening*). If he has not gained this friendship through flattery.

DRAGOMIR. Only let me not envy the doctor.

STELLA. Friendship is not exclusive, even if I look on the doctor as a brother

PRINCE. What art thou chattering, Stella ? He is as much a brother of thine as I am a radical. I cannot endure the man, though I cannot dispense with him.

PANI CHESKI. How, Prince, whom can you not endure ?

DRAGOMIR (*laughing*). And why ?

PRINCE. Why ? Have I not told you ? He does what he likes with us, disposes of the whole house as he wishes. Believes in nothing, except in some, there — what is it, Stella — what ? And besides, he is as ambitious as Satan. He is a professor of the Academy already, like some spiritual person, and, moreover, is trying to be elected to the diet. Have you heard ? He will be a deputy, then serene, great, mighty! But I should not be Starogrodski, if I permitted that. (*Aloud.*) Yozvovich!

DOCTOR (*under the window*). What do you command, Prince?

PRINCE. Is it true that thou art canvassing for election?

DOCTOR. At your service, Prince.

PRINCE. Pani Cheski, have you heard? Is not the world topsy-turvy? Yozvovich!

DOCTOR. What, Prince?

PRINCE. And perhaps thou wilt become a minister?

DOCTOR. Perhaps.

PRINCE. You have heard? And perhaps thou thinkest that I shall say of thee His Excellency?

DOCTOR. It would fall out so; every station has its honor

PRINCE. I take the company to witness. Yozvovich, dost wish that my bile should overflow?

DOCTOR. Let the Prince be at rest. My Excellency will always look after his Serene bile.

PRINCE. True. Irritation injures me Does it not, Yozvovich, injure me?

DOCTOR. Injures as to bile, but gives appetite. (*He and* YERZY *approach the speakers.*)

STELLA. Of what were you talking, gentlemen?

DOCTOR. I was listening to Yerzy's narratives. Wonderful, terrible things! Yerzy made a mistake; he should have come to the world two hundred years earlier. It is bad for Bayards at present.

PANI CHESKI. Providence is above all men.

DRAGOMIR. I believe in that also.

DOCTOR. If I were a mathematician, without contradicting you, I should simply say that since in many cases the value of X is unknown, it is necessary to help one's self.

PRINCE.   What is he saying ?

STELLA.   Oh, dear doctor, I beg you not to talk so sceptically, for you will have war, not with papa, but with me.

DOCTOR.   My scepticism ends where your words begin — so I yield unconditionally.

STELLA.   What a polite deputy !

SCENE VI.

The above and a servant.

SERVANT.   Tea is on the table !

YERZY.   I must take leave of you, Prince, and, you Princess.

STELLA.   How is this ? So far we have always had to be the first to say : "It is late," but now you leave us so early.

DOCTOR (*aside*).   My old comrade is on an intimate footing here.

YERZY.   Pardon me.   It is pleasanter here than ever ; but to-day I must be at home without fail.   Besides I leave Dragomir to take my place.

STELLA.   To grow angry would be to fix conceit in you ; still I beg an explanation.

YERZY.   The people who were burnt out are at my house.   I must arrange to give them food and a sleeping place.

PANI CHESKI (*aside*).   He knows how to renounce pleasure for duty.   (*Aloud.*) Stella !

STELLA.   I listen, mother.

PANI CHESKI.   To-morrow we will occupy ourselves with a collection and take them some clothing.

DOCTOR.   And I will go with you.   This will be the

first case when not misery seeks the doctor, but the doctor misery.

PANI CHESKI. Perfect!

PRINCE (*striking with his cane*). Pretvits!

YERZY. What do you command, Prince?

PRINCE. You say that those poor people are in terrible need?

YERZY. Very terrible need.

PRINCE. Do you say that they will die of hunger?

YERZY. Almost, Prince.

PRINCE. Justice to them. God is punishing them for choosing such deputies as this. (*Pointing to the* DOCTOR.)

DOCTOR (*with a bow.*) They have not chosen me yet.

STELLA. Papa!

PRINCE. Stella, what did I want to say? Aha! Pretvits!

YERZY. I hear, Prince.

PRINCE. Didst thou say that they would die of hunger?

YERZY. I said, almost.

PRINCE. Well! Go to the cashier Florkevich; tell him to give a thousand florins for those needy people (*strikes with his cane*). Let them know that I will not allow any man to die of hunger where I am.

STELLA. Dear, beloved father!

DRAGOMIR. I knew that it would end that way.

DOCTOR. This is in true princely fashion.

PRINCE. And so, Pan Yozvovich, *Noblesse oblige.* Does His Excellency understand, Pan Yozvovich?

DOCTOR. I understand, Serene Prince.

PRINCE (*giving his arm to* PANI CHESKI). And now let us go to tea.   [YERZY *takes farewell, and departs.*

DOCTOR. I must take leave too. I am tired, and besides I must write letters.

PRINCE. As God lives, one might think that he was a minister already. But come later to see me, for without thee I shall not go to sleep.

DOCTOR. I shall come, Prince.

PRINCE (*muttering*). A man is immediately healthier and gladder the moment that Robespierre comes.

STELLA. Pan Stanislav, wait a moment. I do not drink tea, so I will only seat papa, and return at once, I have something to say to you.

DOCTOR. At your service, Princess.

SCENE VII.

DOCTOR, *alone, then*, STELLA.

DOCTOR. What are those men doing here, and what does she want to tell me? Can it be? But no! That is impossible. I am somehow disquieted, but still all will be explained soon. Oh, what a fool I am! She wishes simply to tell me what she knows of the Prince's health. This moonlight evening so acts on me that I would just take a guitar in my hand.

STELLA (*entering*). Pan Stanislav.

DOCTOR. I am here, Princess.

STELLA. I tried not to keep you waiting long. I will sit here near you, and we will talk, as we talked long ago, when I was small and weak, and you cured me. I remember that more than once I fell asleep, and you carried me, sleeping, in your arms.

DOCTOR. The pet of the whole house was very weak in those days.

STELLA. If I am healthy at present, it is owing only to you; I am a plant reared by your hand.

DOCTOR. And therefore my merit and greatest

praise. In the life which I have passed there were few calm, warm moments, and I found peace only in this house.

STELLA. You were always uniformly kind, and I consider you an elder brother. You are not angry over this?

DOCTOR. Such words of yours are the only smile of my life. Not merely do I honor you, but I love you very deeply — as a sister, as my own child.

STELLA. I thank you. In no one's reason and justice have I so much confidence as in yours, therefore I have wished to speak of important things. I hope even that what I say will give you pleasure, as it does me, because you rise more and more above common people. Is it certain that you are to be a deputy?

DOCTOR (*unquietly*). That is only probable. But speak of that which relates to yourself.

STELLA. O my God! But you will not leave papa, will you?

DOCTOR (*with a deep breath of relief*). You wish to speak of the Prince's health.

STELLA. I know that papa is better now. Indeed, I did not think that this was so difficult. I am a little afraid of your harsh judgments on people.

DOCTOR (*with forced calmness*). But do not torture my curiosity.

STELLA. Then I will close my eyes and tell, though this is not easy for any young lady. Have you known Pan Yerzy a long time?

DOCTOR (*still more uneasily*). I know him, Princess.

STELLA. How does he please you?

DOCTOR. Of what use is my opinion to you?

STELLA. He — he is my betrothed.

DOCTOR (*rising*). Betrothed!

13

STELLA. My God! Then my choice does not please you? (*A moment of silence.*) Pan Stanislav —

DOCTOR. A moment only — a moment. Your choice, if it came from the heart and will, must be good. But for me this news was unexpected, so I received it with too much interest perhaps. But I could not take it indifferently, through good-will for your house. For that matter, my opinion here means nothing. I wish you happiness, and desire your happiness, Princess. I wish your happiness with all my heart.

STELLA. I shall be calmer now. Thank you.

DOCTOR. Return to your father. The happiness which has fallen on your house has taken me a little off my feet, for it fell unexpectedly. I need to recover. I need to accustom myself to the thought. In every case I congratulate you on the choice. Return to your father.

STELLA. Good-night! (*She halts in the door a moment, looks at the* DOCTOR *and goes out.*)

SCENE VIII.

DOCTOR YOZVOVICH, *alone.*

DOCTOR. Too late, too late!

(*The curtain falls.*)

END OF FIRST ACT.

ACT II.

The same drawing-room.

SCENE I.

DOCTOR YOZVOVICH *and* ANTONI JUK.

DOCTOR. Antoni, come this way! Here we can talk freely. They are renovating my rooms. What do you bring from the city?

ANTONI. Good news. In an hour a deputation of electors will come. You must say something to them — you understand? — Something about enlightenment, roads, bridges, unjust taxes on salt and grinding. But for that matter, you know this better than I do.

DOCTOR. I know, I know; and how is my programme?

ANTONI. An immense impression. The thing was written with coolness, dignity, and scientific accuracy. Though the figures strike the eye, they are unanswerable. The conservative journals are in a rage, all the more that nothing is left them to do but spit.

DOCTOR. That is well. What further?

ANTONI. Three days ago you were tottering in the suburbs; but I discovered this, assembled the electors, and fired off a little speech. 'Citizens,' said I, in conclusion, 'for all your troubles and those of society, I know only one cure: It is called Yozvovich! Long life to progress!' I lashed the conservatives also a little, but moderately. I called them belly-feeders.

DOCTOR. It is impossible to say how moderate that was on thy part. Thou art a practical man, Antoni. There is hope then of victory?

ANTONI. Almost a certainty of it. But whether we win now or not, the future is before us. And do you know why? Because avoiding all election outbursts, we, meeting here two of us, and speaking of our affairs, need not break into laughter before each other, like Roman augurs. Progress and truth are on our side, and every day makes new breaches in that rotten wall which we are undermining. We are merely assisting the ages, hence we must conquer. I speak with coolness. This people of ours, those electors, are sheep yet; but we wish to make men of them, and in this is our strength. The opposite camp will howl, will be enraged, will hurl mud at us, will undermine us, will blacken us; but we have sharp teeth. On our side is justice, intelligence, science; on theirs, escutcheons which the mice are gnawing. As to me, did I not feel that justice and progress were in my principles, I should be the first to spit on all this and go to a monastery.

DOCTOR. Still it would be fatal if we were not to win this time.

ANTONI. I am certain that we shall win. Among them there is a panic as after a defeat. For them, you are a terrible candidate. There is only one dangerous opponent, — Husarski, a rich noble; he is popular. The other, Milishevski, is an advantage to you. By his candidacy they merely divide themselves. I pushed him forward a little myself.

DOCTOR. Once in the diet, I shall work for influence.

ANTONI. And you will get it. I believe this and therefore spare no labor. Ha, ha! "They have taken everything from us," said Count Hornitski, in the club, yesterday, " significance, money, even good manners." Well, I, at least, have not borrowed their good manners. Devil take them!

DOCTOR. True, thou hast not taken good manners from them.

ANTONI. But people say in the city that thy Prince has given a thousand florins to the people who were burned out. This may make a bad impression for us. Thou, too, shouldst do something.

DOCTOR. I have done what was proper.

ANTONI. And now, I will tell thee something more — Well then, yesterday — But what the deuce is the matter? I am speaking, and thou art thinking of something else.

DOCTOR. Pardon. A great personal misfortune has struck me. I cannot think so freely as usual.

ANTONI. What is there new?

DOCTOR. Thou couldst not understand, Antoni.

ANTONI. On the contrary I could. I am the driver of the carriage in which thou art travelling. I should know of everything.

DOCTOR. No. This in no way concerns thee.

ANTONI. But it concerns thy energy, which, as it seems, thou art losing. We need no Hamlets.

DOCTOR (gloomily). Thou art mistaken, Antoni. I have not yielded the victory.

ANTONI. I see. In speaking of this thy teeth are gritting somehow; besides, hang me, if it lies in thy character to yield the victory.

DOCTOR. Perhaps not. Work to make me deputy. I shall lose two games, if thou losest.

ANTONI. They must have burnt thee devilishly, for thy hissing is terrible.

DOCTOR. An old story. A peasant slept not for six years; he ate not; he made his hands bloody; he bent his back and carried planks to build his cottage; after six years the lord came, kicked the cottage, and said, "Here must my castle stand." We are sceptical enough to laugh at this.

ANTONI. He was a genuine lord.

DOCTOR. A lord descended from lords, with a head so lofty that he paid no attention to what was cracking under his feet.

ANTONI. That history is to my taste. And what did the peasant do ?

DOCTOR. Agreeable to old peasant tradition, he is thinking of punk and steel [1]

ANTONI. A splendid thought! In truth, we despise tradition too much. There are very wholesome things in it.

DOCTOR. Enough. Let us speak of something else.

ANTONI (*looking around*). An old house, and imposing. What a cottage it would be !

DOCTOR. Of what art thou speaking ?

ANTONI. Nothing. Yozvovich, has the old Prince a daughter ?

DOCTOR. Yes. What of it ?

ANTONI (*laughing*). Ha, ha ! As God lives, ladies' perfumes have come to me. From thy misfortune and thy history, I catch the odor of some princess's petticoat. Behind the deputy is Yozvovich, as behind a dresscoat is the dressing-gown. Be greeted in the dressing-gown, beloved deputy ! Oh, what an odor of perfumes here !

DOCTOR. Sell thy subtleties at another market. This is a personal question.

ANTONI. By no means, for it signifies that thou art putting only half thy soul in affairs of the public. This is giving them to the deuce. Look at me : they hunt me like a dog in the daily papers ; they ridicule me in comedies ; but I care not, I will say more, I feel that I shall remain always below, though I lack neither power nor intelligence. I might strive for the first place in the

[1] For setting fire.

camp, for leadership; but still I do not do so. Why? Because I know myself thoroughly. I know that I have neither firmness, dignity, nor tact. I have been, and I am, an impulsive fellow, a tool which those like thee make use of, and which may be kicked out to-morrow, when it ceases to be useful. But vanity does not blind me; I care not myself; I work for my convictions, that is the end. They may eject me from my office any day; in my house want appears frequently, and though I love my wife and my little boys — Let us leave all this. When the play is on, let it continue; and when it is a question of convictions, I will live, agitate, and storm for it. I have put my whole soul into this. But in thy case a princess's petticoat stands in the way! I did not expect this of thee, Yozvovich. Tfu! spit on everything, and come with us!

DOCTOR. Thou art mistaken, Brutus. I wish not martyrdom, but victory; and the more personal ties there are which bind me to the cause, the more zealously shall I serve it with mind, heart, and action, — with everything that makes a man — dost understand?

ANTONI. Amen! His eyes are glittering like those of a wolf. I know thee.

DOCTOR. What more dost thou wish?

ANTONI. Ei! nothing now. I will say only that our programme is: Strike opposing principles, not people.

DOCTOR. Let thy maiden virtue be at rest; I shall poison no man.

ANTONI. I believe. Still I should say something more. I know thee well, I value thy energy, thy science, thy sound sense, but I should not like to stand in thy path.

DOCTOR. All the better for me.

ANTONI. For that matter, if it is a question of the

nobility; then, in spite of our programme, I give them to thee. But thou art not to take their heads off.

DOCTOR. Of course. Now go back and work for me, or rather for us.

ANTONI. For us, Yozvovich. Do not forget that.

DOCTOR. Without an oath, I shall not forget it.

ANTONI. But how manage that young noble?

DOCTOR. Dost wish to extort assurances?

ANTONI. To begin with, I do not need them, since in our camp there is shrewdness enough. The question is simply of the Prince's daughter. My thought comes always to this, that thou mayst sacrifice the cause for her. Working for thee, I answer for thee; so let us be outspoken.

DOCTOR. Let us be outspoken.

ANTONI. Then thou hast said to thyself: I will unhorse that young noble; well, unhorse him. That is thy affair, but I ask again: Dost thou wish to be a deputy for us, or for the Princess? This again is my affair.

DOCTOR. I place my cards on the table before thee. I, thou, and all of us new men have this in us, — that we are not dolls cut out of paper, and painted in one color. There is in us room for convictions, love, hatred, in a word, as I have said already, for everything of which a complete man is made. Nature gave me a heart, and the right to life, so I desire happiness. It gave me a mind, so I serve a chosen idea. What harm does one do the other? Why oppose the Princess to the cause? Art thou a reasonable and sober-minded man? Why dost thou wish to put a phrase in place of reality? I have a right to happiness, and I shall win it, and I shall be able to reconcile life with an idea, like a sail with a boat. I shall advance all the more securely. Understand me. In this is our strength, that we are able to reconcile; and in this is our superiority over them, for they simply do not know how to live. What my value will be without that woman — I know not. Thou hast called me Hamlet. I might become one; but the people need no Hamlets.

ANTONI. Thou art whirling my head around as in a mill, and it seems to me again that thou art right. Still, thou wilt fight two battles instead of one, and thou wilt divide the forces.

DOCTOR. I have forces enough!

ANTONI. Tell me briefly, is she betrothed?

DOCTOR. She is.

ANTONI. And she loves her betrothed?

DOCTOR. Or deceives herself.

ANTONI. In every case, she does not love thee.

DOCTOR. Him, first of all, must I set aside. Meanwhile do thou fly away and work.

ANTONI (*looking at his watch*). In a moment the deputation to thee will be here.

DOCTOR. That is well. The Prince is coming with Countess Milishevski, and her son is my opponent. Let us go.

SCENE II.

PRINCE, STELLA, PANI CHESKI, COUNTESS MILISHEVSKI, YAN MILISHEVSKI, PODCHASKI.

COUNTESS. So I say, Prince, that one cannot understand such a thing. At present the world is growing utterly wild, it seems.

PRINCE. I say the same, Countess. Stella, do I not?

STELLA. Oh, very often.

COUNTESS (*in a whisper to her son*). Sit near the Princess, and entertain her, Jean, do thy best.

YAN. Yes, mamma!

COUNTESS. But this insolence has passed the measure. I sent Pan Podchaski to the electors, and they answered, "We want no deputies without heads." I am only astonished that the Prince is not indignant. To what has it come, and to what will it come? I fly about here; I run, I circle around like a fly; I move heaven with my prayers, and they dare oppose to my son one Yozvovich.

PRINCE. Gracious lady, what can I do to remedy the position?

COUNTESS. But who is this Pan Yozvovich? A doctor! What is a doctor? Jean has influence, significance, connections, relatives, but who is Yozvovich? Whence did he bring himself to this place? Who has ever heard of him? In truth, I cannot speak calmly, and think that the end of the world must be coming. Is that not the case, Pan Podchaski?

PODCHASKI (*with a bow*). True, Countess, my benefactress! The anger of God! — never has it thundered so often —

PRINCE. Thundered? Pani Cheski, has it thundered?

PANI CHESKI. It is usual at the end of spring. No significance.

COUNTESS (*whispers*). Jean, do thy best.

YAN. I am doing so, mamma.

COUNTESS. Prince, you will see that they will not elect Yan deputy purely through hatred of us, through spite against us. Would he not be a successful deputy? Has he not finished a scientific course in Metz? They say that he is ignorant of the country, has no knowledge of its needs. But first of all we should not permit Yozvovich to mean anything in the country. Should we, Prince?

PRINCE. Not permit him, Countess, when he permits himself!

COUNTESS. This is precisely the end of the world, that men like him can permit themselves what they like. They have the insolence to say that my son cannot be a good deputy, but Pan Yozvovich can. Jean always excelled in science at Metz. Jean, didst thou not always excel in science and talent?

YAN. I excelled, mamma.

PODCHASKI. The end of the world! Your words, Countess, are sacred.

STELLA. What did you devote yourself to, specially?

YAN. I, Princess, studied the history of heresies.

PRINCE. What did he study, Pani Cheski?

COUNTESS. They have always reproached us with this, that so far we have not had talents among us, and still, for diplomacy, no small talent is needed.

PODCHASKI. The Count has the mien of a diplomat, indeed.

PRINCE. No, as God lives — not greatly!

PANI CHESKI. The Count is reticent and dignified.

YAN. On the contrary, madam, I speak enough sometimes.

COUNTESS. As to me, I declare in advance, that if Jean is not elected, it will be the Prince's fault.

PRINCE. My fault?

COUNTESS. How can you, Prince, permit such a person as Yozvovich to oppose people of society? How can you retain him?

PRINCE. To tell the truth, it is not I who retain him, but he me, for had it not been for him — (*He makes a sign with his hand.*)

COUNTESS. All the greater reason to restrain him. He is needed in your house, and when he is at the diet, who will look after you?

PRINCE. That is true. Stella, is it not true?

COUNTESS. You must forbid him, Prince. I will not go till you promise to forbid him. This is an unheard-of thing! You have the right; besides he is with you; you have reared him, and you have power over him.

STELLA. Dear lady, the doctor is papa's friend. Papa can only pray him, and I know not whether his prayer would be effectual.

COUNTESS (*with anger*). Has it come to this, then? So the Prince will support him, and become a tool in his hands, and through him serve the democracy?

PRINCE. What? I serve the democracy? Stella, dost thou hear? I serve the democracy? (*He strikes with his cane.*)

COUNTESS. All men will say so. Pan Yozvovich is the candidate of the democracy.

PRINCE. But I am not, and if it comes to this, I will not permit him to be its candidate. We have had enough of this, let it end once for all. Those democracies of Pan Yozvovich have become fish-bones. They must not say that I am a tool of the democracy! (*He rings, the* SERVANT *enters*) Beg the doctor to come this minute.

COUNTESS. This time he is a genuine prince.

PRINCE. I serve the democracy!

STELLA. Papa! papa!

COUNTESS. Meanwhile we will take leave of the Prince. Jean, make ready. Adieu, dear Stella, adieu, my child. (*To her son.*) Kiss the Princess's hand.

SCENE III.
The above, DOCTOR YOZVOVICH.

DOCTOR. I beg your pardon, Prince, if I am late, but a deputation waited on me. I had to finish with it.

COUNTESS. What? — is there a deputation here? Jean, do your best!

DOCTOR (*with a bow*). Hurry, Count, for they are going.

PODCHASKI. Serene Prince, I fall at your feet.

> [*The* COUNTESS, YAN, *and* PODCHASKI *go out;*
> *after them,* STELLA *and* PANI CHESKI.

SCENE IV.

DOCTOR YOZVOVICH *and the* PRINCE. *A moment of silence.*

PRINCE (*striking the floor with his cane*). I give notice, Pan Yozvovich, that I forbid you to stand for election.

DOCTOR. But if I do not obey?

PRINCE. You will enrage me.

DOCTOR. Prince, you close my future.

PRINCE (*in a passion*). I reared you from early boyhood.

DOCTOR. I preserve your life.

PRINCE. I have been a father to you.

DOCTOR. Let us speak more calmly, Prince. If you have been a father to me, I have shown the attachment of a son. But a father should not close the road to a public career against his son.

PRINCE. A public career is not for such persons as you.

DOCTOR (*smiling*). A moment ago, Prince, you called me a son.

PRINCE. What son? What kind of a son?

DOCTOR. As the sonship, so the obedience.

PRINCE. Ah, he wriggles out, he wriggles out! Stella! But she is gone!

DOCTOR. Prince, were I really your son, I should have a title, property, — in a word, all that you have; but as a poor man, I must open the road to myself, and no one has the right to close it against me, especially when it is straightforward and honorable (*laughing*); unless, Prince, you wish to adopt me, so that the family might not die out.

PRINCE.   What are you saying, Yozvovich?

DOCTOR.   I was only jesting.   No, dear Prince, let us not irritate each other, for that is harmful.

PRINCE.   True, irritation harms me.   Why the devil will you not give up that election, my boy?

DOCTOR.   You should put yourself in my position. That is my future.

PRINCE.   Meanwhile, people attack me here, irritate me, and bring me to my bed.   When young, I was in many a battle and feared nothing; I can show my decorations.   I had no fear of death in battle; but these Latin diseases of the doctors —   Why look at me so?

DOCTOR.   I look as usual.   But as to disease, I will tell you, Prince, it is more in your imagination than in reality.   Your organism is strong, and, with my aid, you will live to the years of Methuselah.

PRINCE.   Are you certain of that?

DOCTOR.   Most certain.

PRINCE.   Honest lad, and you will not leave me?

DOCTOR   You may be sure that I shall not.

PRINCE.   Then become a deputy or a devil, if you like!   Stella!   But she is not here!   As God lives, that Milishevski, have you noticed him, is a fool, is he not?

DOCTOR.   I cannot contradict.

SCENE V.

The same, STELLA, PANI CHESKI.

STELLA.   I came in because I was afraid that you gentlemen might contradict each other too much.   How has it ended?

PRINCE.   How?   That worthless man does what he

wishes. It lacked little of his commanding me to beg him to accept the nomination.

DOCTOR. Indeed, the Prince has been pleased to agree to my plans, and permits me to try for election.

PRINCE. Yes, I have permitted.

STELLA (*threateningly*). Ah, dear doctor!

PANI CHESKI. So many endeavors and disputes! Would it not be better for one to yield to the other? For that matter, the proverb says: "The wise yield to the foolish."

DOCTOR. We hold to this principle so far in all questions.

STELLA. Papa, come now to the garden. Pan Yerzy and Count Dragomir have come. They are waiting at the boats, for we are to sail over the lake. The Count is to come here for me, when all is ready.

PRINCE. Pani Cheski, let us go, then. (*They go.*) Have you noticed that Milishevski?

SCENE VI.

DOCTOR YOZVOVICH, STELLA; *later*, COUNT DRAGOMIR.

STELLA. How is father's health, dear doctor?

DOCTOR. The very best. But you are really pale.

STELLA. Oh, I am well.

DOCTOR. Then a little pensive it must be.

STELLA. Not even that. Perhaps more serious than formerly.

DOCTOR. As usual with a betrothed.

STELLA. Yes.

DOCTOR. Still you should be amused and diverted, for health's sake.

STELLA. Really, I have no wish for amusement.

DOCTOR. If not amusement, at least gladsomeness —

We are all of us here too serious for you; often, perhaps, we cannot understand you.

STELLA.   You are all even too kind, doctor.

DOCTOR.   At least anxious.   If you have a moment of time, Princess, let us sit down and talk.   Let my anxiety explain this boldness.   With the dignity of a betrothed is joined usually serenity and happiness.   Whoso gives away a heart without regret cannot be sad at anything, and looks serenely toward the future.

STELLA.   In every future there is something which at moments may fill the most daring soul with disquiet.

DOCTOR.   What is that, Princess ?

STELLA.   Even this, that that future is coming for the first time.

DOCTOR.   More than once you have called me a sceptic, and still I say, Whoso loves believes.

STELLA.   What is to be inferred from that, doctor ?

DOCTOR.   That whoso doubts —

STELLA.   Pan Stanislav !

DOCTOR.   I make no inquiry, Princess.   At moments I see that serenity vanishes from your face ; therefore I ask as a doctor, as a friend.   Set me at rest, Princess.   I pray you remember that this question is put by a man whom you have called a brother, and who alone knows how dear to him is the happiness of such a sister.   I have no one in the world ; all my family feelings are bound up with this house.   I have a heart which is solicitous.   Quiet my alarms, that is all I ask of you ?

STELLA.   What alarms ?   I cannot tell —

DOCTOR.   Alarms which I hardly dare to confess. Since I have come, my eyes have not left you ; and the more I see, the more I fear.   You dread the future ; you do not look at it with trust and hope —

STELLA.   Permit me to go —

DOCTOR. No, Princess, I have the right to ask ; and if you dare not look into the depth of your own heart, I have the right to say even, that this is weakness, and a lack of courage, and later such culpable weakness is punished by loss of one's own happiness and that of others. I, too, suffer while asking you ; but there is need to ask, there is need. Listen to me, Princess. In whomever there is even a shadow of doubt, that person is mistaken as to the nature of his or her feelings.

STELLA. Doctor ! Is it possible to mistake so ?

DOCTOR. It is possible. Sometimes it is possible to mistake sympathy for compassion, and pity for love.

STELLA. What a ghastly mistake !

DOCTOR. Which one recognizes when the heart rushes in another direction. Then the seriousness of a betrothed becomes a secret pain. If I mistake, pardon me.

STELLA. Pan Stanislav, I do not wish to think of such things.

DOCTOR. Then I am not mistaken. Do not look at me with fear ; I wish to save you, dear child. Where is your heart ? If you recognize at this moment that you do not love Yerzy, this very moment will inform you whom you do love. No, I will not withdraw the question ! Where is your heart ? As God lives, if you love some one not your equal, he will raise himself to you. But no ! I am going mad !

STELLA. I wish to withdraw, and I must.

DOCTOR (*stopping her*). No ! you will not go till you answer — whom do you love ?

STELLA. Spare me, doctor, or I shall doubt everything ! Take pity on me !

DOCTOR (*violently*). Whom do you love ?

14

SCENE VII.

The same and COUNT DRAGOMIR.

DRAGOMIR. Princess !

STELLA. Ah !

DRAGOMIR. What is this ? Have I frightened you ?
I have come only to say that we are waiting at the boats.
What is the matter ?

STELLA. Nothing. Let us go.

[DRAGOMIR *gives her his arm ; they go out.*

SCENE VIII.

DOCTOR YOZVOVICH, *alone.*

DOCTOR (*looking after them*). Ah, I un-der-stand.

(*Curtain falls.*)

END OF SECOND ACT.

ACT III.

The same drawing-room.

SCENE I.

PODCHASKI *enters first, after him, the* SERVANT.

PODCHASKI. Tell the doctor that Pan Podchaski salutes
him, and is waiting for him, on urgent business.

SERVANT. The doctor is very busy, for the Princess is
ill ; but I will tell him.   [*Goes out.*

PODCHASKI (*alone*). Fiu! Fiu! The Countess sends me
to the suburbs. "Podchaski fly! Podchaski agitate!
Podchaski persuade !" But money she gives not. I fly ;
I bow down; I persuade ; I press the hands of vulgar
people till their eyes start ; but when I ask her to lend
me a hundred florins, she says, "We shall see after

election!" Is that the case? Well indeed! So I have
to lend to the woman and not she to me? Must I drink
with shopkeepers at my own expense? I would rather
drink alone! To the deuce with such a service! I fall
at the feet of the Countess, my benefactress. I kiss her
feet. If that's to be the way, I shall succeed somewhere
else. This is a fool's service! I would rather go over to
the doctor. Persons like him pay, for they are clever.
And since he will take the whole party, one would rise
in significance. She is an aristocrat, but refuses to lend
a noble a hundred florins.

Scene II.
PODCHASKI, DOCTOR YOZVOVICH.

PODCHASKI. I salute you, Pan Doctor, I extend myself
at the feet of the doctor, my benefactor.

DOCTOR. With what can I serve you, Pan Podchaski?

PODCHASKI. My benefactor, I come directly without
delay to my business. It is known to you, my benefactor,
that I have given my services to Countess Milishevski.

DOCTOR. Somewhat.

PODCHASKI. As a former country resident, for I had
land here —

DOCTOR. After losing the land, you live in Lychakov;
and you are agitating for young Count Milishevski against
me.

PODCHASKI. God forbid — That is, I did; but I opened
my eyes in season. What was possible happened. The
Milishevskis have certain relations among shopkeepers —
among citizens who respect descent. But be confident,
my benefactor.

DOCTOR. In brief, what do you want?

PODCHASKI. God knows, my benefactor, I served the
Countess faithfully, and spent no little money; but when

I consulted my conscience, I could not go against such a wise man as you, unless to the harm of the country, and that I do not wish.

DOCTOR. I recognize your feelings of a citizen. You do not wish to go against me?

PODCHASKI. No, my benefactor, I do not.

DOCTOR. You are right. So you are with me?

PODCHASKI. If I may be bold to offer my services.

DOCTOR. I accept.

PODCHASKI (*aside*). I understand such a man — a hundred florins are the same as in my pocket. (*Aloud.*) My gratitude —

DOCTOR (*interrupting*). My gratitude will appear after election.

PODCHASKI. After e-lec-tion!

SCENE III.

The above, YAN MILISHEVSKI, *later*, ANTONI.

YAN. Good-day, doctor! Is mamma not here?

DOCTOR. No, Count, she is not.

YAN. We came here together, but mamma went straight to the Prince's apartments; I stopped behind a little, and now I cannot find the Prince's apartments. (*Seeing* PODCHASKI, *who bows to him.*) Ah! Podchaski, what are you doing here?

PODCHASKI. I fall at the feet of the Count. Oh, I came for advice. I have rheumatism in my feet, rheumatism in my head —

YAN. Will you have the kindness, doctor, to show me where the Prince's chambers are?

DOCTOR. On the left, in the amphitheatre.

YAN. Thanks. But later I should like to see you.

DOCTOR. At your service. (YAN *goes to the door, where he stumbles against* ANTONI.)

ANTONI. I beg your pardon!

YAN. Pardon! (*He puts up his eye-glasses, looks at him with curiosity, then goes out.*)

ANTONI (*to the* DOCTOR). I looked for thee in thy rooms, and did not find thee, so I hurried here, for they told me that thou wert here. Listen to me. Immensely important things. (*Sees* PODCHASKI.) How is this? You, our opponent, here?

PODCHASKI. No longer an opponent, my benefactor.

ANTONI (*looking at him a moment*). All the better. But leave us alone now.

PODCHASKI (*aside*). Oh, that is bad! (*Aloud.*) I commend myself to the memory of my benefactors. (*Aside.*) The devils have taken the hundred florins. [*Goes out.*

ANTONI. What did he want here?

DOCTOR. Money.

ANTONI. But he offered votes — I thought so. Didst give him anything?

DOCTOR. No.

ANTONI. That is well. We shall not bribe. Agitation is another thing. But never mind. Dost know? It was lucky that they put up Milishevski, otherwise you would have lost, for Husarski would have had a majority. As it is even, he is terrible; he has a majority in some districts.

DOCTOR. Will they beat us, Antoni?

ANTONI. No! I shall prevent that. Uf, how tired I am! I will rest even for five minutes. (*Sits down.*) Oh, as I love God, what soft sofas there are here. In Husarski's districts we need to give money for some public purposes. Hast thou money?

DOCTOR. A little.

ANTONI. Some beginning — afterward thou wilt have support from the diet. We will found some small school. Uf, how tired I am!

DOCTOR.   Well, here is the key to the bureau; there is a little ready money there and a bank check.

ANTONI.   Very well, but I must rest. Meanwhile, what news have we here? Thou hast grown thin; thy eyes are sunken. Thou must be in grief. As God lives, I did not love my wife in that way. Speak, while I rest, but speak sincerely.

DOCTOR.   Have no fear, I shall be frank with thee.

ANTONI.   What more?

DOCTOR.   That marriage will not take place.

ANTONI.   Why?

DOCTOR.   A time has come when these people succeed in nothing.

ANTONI.   To the garret with thy peacocks! What is that man-eater, Pretvits, doing?

DOCTOR.   It would take long to tell. The Princess has mistaken her pity and sympathy for something deeper. To-day she knows that she does not love him.

ANTONI.   Thou art kind. In truth, one might say that some fatality pursues these people. It is the lot of races who have outlived themselves.

DOCTOR.   The relentless logic of things.

ANTONI.   So she will not marry Pretvits? Really, I am sorry for them. But deuce take them!

DOCTOR.   She would marry him, even if she had to keep her word at the price of her life. But some third man is mixed up in the business — Count Dragomir.

ANTONI.   Wherever one moves there is a count! So he is betraying Yerzy?

DOCTOR   Let the man who taught thee to judge people return thy money.

ANTONI.   To tell the truth, I would not give five coppers for all your drawing-room great questions.

DOCTOR.   She and Dragomir do not understand that

they are in love. But some irresistible force attracts them to each other; what it is they do not inquire. They are innocent children.

ANTONI. Therefore, I ask, what benefit will come to thee of this?

DOCTOR. Listen, O democrat! When two knights are in love with one castellan's daughter, the love usually has a dramatic ending, and the castellan's daughter falls to some third man.

ANTONI. But the knights?

DOCTOR. The least thought for them; let them perish!

ANTONI (declaiming).

"On his grave moss is growing.
Ah! but the cockerel is dead!"

What will happen, thinkest thou?

DOCTOR. I know not. Pretvits is a violent man. I prophesy nothing; I see only the logic of things, which favors me, and I shall not be such a fool as to oppose my own fortune.

ANTONI. Oh, I am certain that if the need come thou wilt even help it!

DOCTOR. Ha! I am a doctor. My duty is to help nature.

ANTONI. Here is the programme ready! I know thee! But one thought occurs to me: How dost thou know that it is as thou sayest? Perhaps all this is random talk.

DOCTOR. I can get most perfect information through the former governess of the Princess, Pani Cheski.

ANTONI. Learn at the earliest.

DOCTOR. Pani Cheski will come here soon; I asked her purposely.

ANTONI. Then I shall be off. One thing more: Do not help nature too much, for that would be —

Scene IV.

The same, Pani Cheski.

Pani Cheski (*entering*). Did you wish to speak with me?

Doctor. I did.

Antoni (*bows to* Pani Cheski, *then to the* Doctor). I am going for the money and will return soon with the receipts.

Doctor. Very well.   [Antonio *goes out.*

Pani Cheski. Who is that gentleman?

Doctor. A steersman.

Pani Cheski. How is that?

Doctor. He is steering the ship on which I sail; for the rest he is a wonderfully honest man.

Pani Cheski. I do not understand well. Of what did you wish to speak with me?

Doctor. Of the Princess. You and she are like mother and daughter, so you must know everything. What is the matter with her? She is hiding some disappointment. As a doctor, I ought to know everything; for to cure physical illness one should often know moral causes. (*Aside.*) Spirit of Esculapius, forgive me this phrase!

Pani Cheski. My good Pan Yozvovich, of what are you asking?

Doctor. I told you that the Princess is concealing some disappointment.

Pani Cheski. I know not.

Doctor. You and I love her equally, hence let us be outspoken.

Pani Cheski. I am ready.

Doctor. Well, does she love her betrothed?

Pani Cheski. What do you ask, doctor? If she did

not, would she be his betrothed? In truth, you so like to reason about everything that sometimes you interfere more than is needful. Whom should she love? Naturally, since she is his betrothed, she loves him. I consider this so simple that I do not even talk any more with Stella about it.

DOCTOR. You say, madam, that you do not talk any more; therefore you have talked before?

PANI CHESKI. True. She told me that she knew not whether she loved him enough. But every pure soul fears that it may not do its duty. What could come to your mind?

DOCTOR. I only wished to know. (*Aside.*) A waste of time here!

SCENE V.

The same, YAN MILISHEVSKI.

YAN. So far I have not been able to find mamma. Good-day, Pani. Perhaps I interrupt?

PANI CHESKI. No, we have finished. She will do her duty, be quiet on that point.

DOCTOR. Thank you.   [PANI CHESKI *goes out.*

YAN. Doctor?

DOCTOR. I hear.

YAN. I must talk of things that are very delicate.

DOCTOR. I beg you to be outspoken.

YAN. Let us make an agreement like good people. Mamma wishes me to become a deputy, but I have no wish that way.

DOCTOR. Excess of modesty.

YAN. You are not sincere, and I know not how to defend myself. I should not be a candidate at all were it not for mamma. You see the affair is in this way: when

mamma wants anything, it must come. All the Srokos-
hynskis are of that kind; mamma is a Srokoshynski.

DOCTOR. But you have your own will.

YAN. In this lies the misery, that things have so
shaped themselves that the Milishevskis alway obey
women. We are distinguished for that.

DOCTOR. A knightly characteristic. But how can I
serve you?

YAN. I shall not hinder you as a candidate.

DOCTOR. Sincerity for sincerity. Thus far instead
of hindering, you have helped me.

YAN. I know not how, but if that be true, then help
me in turn.

DOCTOR. How?

YAN. This matter is especially delicate. But a secret
from mamma.

DOCTOR. Naturally.

YAN. Mamma wishes me to marry the Princess; but
I do not wish to marry her.

DOCTOR. You do not wish?

YAN. You are astonished?

DOCTOR. I confess —

YAN. I do not wish to marry her, because I do not
wish. When a man has no desire to marry, well, he has
no desire. Imagine that I love another. Perhaps I do.
It is enough that she is not the Princess. Naturally,
when mamma says, "Jean, do your best!" I go on, for
what am I to do? The Milishevskis know how to
manage men, but as for women, oh, ho!

DOCTOR. But I cannot understand how I may be
useful.

YAN. Doctor, you know that you can do anything in
this house, so bring it about in secret from my mother,
that I should be refused.

DOCTOR.   Count, for you I shall do what is humanly possible.

YAN.   I thank you.

DOCTOR.   And I will undertake this the more gladly since the Princess is betrothed.

YAN.   But I did not know that any one was climbing into my way here.

DOCTOR (*aside*).   A good idea! (*Aloud.*) Pan Yerzy Pretvits.

YAN.   Then they wished to make a fool of me!

DOCTOR.   Pan Pretvits is an insolent man.   I even confess to you that you were right when you called this a delicate affair.   Pan Pretvits is feared; so if you yield people may think —

YAN.   They may think that I am afraid? Well, I will not give way.   Oh, my dear sir, I see that you do not know the Milishevskis at all.   It is only women that we are not able to manage; but no Milishevski was ever a coward.   I know that people laugh at me; but if any one calls me a coward, I will teach him not to laugh.   I will show quickly whether I am a coward. What about Pan Pretvits?   Where is he now?

DOCTOR.   At this moment in the garden. (*Pointing through the window.*)   You see him there by the lake.

YAN.   Till we see each other!

SCENE VI.

DOCTOR, *alone, later*, ANTONI.

DOCTOR.   Many fathers are childless! Ha! ha!

ANTONI (*running in*).   Art thou at home? Here are the receipts.   Why art thou laughing?

DOCTOR.   Milishevski has rushed off to challenge Pretvits to a duel.

ANTONI. What? Are they mad?

DOCTOR. Pretvits will stand before her in a pretty light, this knight without reproach, if he has an encounter with such a fool. In a pretty light!

ANTONI. But hast thou wound it up so?

DOCTOR. As I told thee, I will help nature.

ANTONI. Assist for thyself, but I am off.

DOCTOR. Farewell! But no, I will go with thee; I cannot permit that the adventure go too far.

ANTONI. I wanted to tell thee, besides, that with thy money I bought food for my little boys. I will return it later. Do you permit?

DOCTOR. How canst thou ask, Antoni? [*He goes out.*

SCENE VII.

STELLA, *with a hat in her hand*, COUNT DRAGOMIR.
They enter the door from the garden.

STELLA. The walk has tired me a little. You see, Pan Karol, how feeble I am. (*Sits down.*) Where is Pan Yerzy?

DRAGOMIR. With young Milishevski, who asked for a talk with him. The Countess is discussing with the Prince. It seems to me that there is a little scene there. The Countess did not know that you were betrothed, and likely she had her plans. But, pardon me, Princess, I laugh, and that causes you suffering.

STELLA. I should wish to laugh, did I not know that this caused papa trouble. Also, I am sorry for Count Milishevski.

DRAGOMIR. I understand what in his position a truly loving heart may feel; as to Yan, I am at rest. He will console himself, if his mother commands him.

STELLA. At times it is possible to mistake people greatly.

DRAGOMIR. Are you talking of me, or Milishevski?

STELLA. Let it be of you. Before we met, people mentioned you to me as a collection of all the perfections.

DRAGOMIR. And you have found me a collection of all the faults.

STELLA. I have not said that.

DRAGOMIR. But you think it, I believe. As to me, I am not mistaken, the portrait of you painted by Yerzy and the doctor agrees with reality.

STELLA. How was it painted?

DRAGOMIR. With wings at the shoulders.

STELLA. That means that I have as much dignity as a butterfly?

DRAGOMIR. The wings of angels are consonant with dignity.

STELLA. Real friendship should tell the truth. I pray for some bitter truth.

DRAGOMIR. Shall it be very bitter?

STELLA. As wormwood, or as life is at times.

DRAGOMIR. You are not kind toward me.

STELLA. For what sin must I do penance?

DRAGOMIR. For lack of friendship toward me.

STELLA. I am the first to appeal to friendship; but in what condition of it do I fail?

DRAGOMIR. You share with me joyousness, amusement, laughter; but when a moment of sadness or bitterness comes, you keep the bitter flowers and the thorns for yourself. Share such moments too, I beg earnestly.

STELLA. I have never wished to disturb your joyousness; it was not egotism on my part.

DRAGOMIR. Neither is my joyousness egotistic. Yerzy told me of you when I came here; he said, "I can only gaze at her, and pray to her; thou art younger, more gladsome, try to amuse and divert her." So I brought all my joyousness here, as wares on my shoulders, and laid them at your feet. But for some time I have seen that I only torture you. I see a cloud on your face; I suspect some secret sorrow and, as a real friend, I would give my life to dispel it.

STELLA (*in a low voice*). Count.

DRAGOMIR (*clasping his hands*). Permit me to speak. In life I have been a thoughtless fellow; but I followed the voice of my heart, and with my heart I divined your sadness. From that moment a shadow fell on my joyousness; but I conquered it. Tears once shed never return; but a friendly hand may arrest a tear on the way to the eye. I overcame myself, so as not to let tears go to your eyes. If I have erred, if I have chosen the wrong road, I beg forgiveness. Your life will be arranged like a bouquet of flowers, so be joyous, be gladsome.

STELLA (*gives him her hand, with emotion*). I shall be in your company. I am a capricious girl, petted, and a little ill. Often I do not know myself what the trouble is. I am happy, really happy. Those are passing moments; I promise amendment. We shall spend more than one moment joyously yet.

DRAGOMIR. In that case what do we care, as Pani Chęski says. Let us try to overcome ourselves; we will laugh, run in the garden, play tricks on Mamma Milishevski and her son.

STELLA. I divine the secret of your gladsomeness and happiness, — it is honesty of heart and kindness.

DRAGOMIR. No, I am very heedless. But so far I have lived peacefully enough; real happiness, however, does not lie in peace.

STELLA. Sometimes I think that it does not exist in the world at all.

DRAGOMIR. Reason cannot seize it, and cannot fly after that winged vision. Sometimes, perhaps, it flits past near us; but before a man looks around, before he stretches out a hand, he is too late.

STELLA. What torturing words, — too late.

SCENE VIII.

The same, DOCTOR YOZVOVICH.

DOCTOR (*comes in laughing*). Ha! ha! do you know what has happened?

STELLA. Is it something amusing, doctor?

DOCTOR. Something awful, tragic, terrible, but above all ridiculous! Milishevski wanted to challenge Yerzy.

STELLA. My God!

DOCTOR. Laugh with me, Princess. If this were something dangerous, I should not have frightened you.

DRAGOMIR. How did it end?

DOCTOR. Do you know that I went so far as to be angry with Yerzy. Imagine that he took the matter seriously.

DRAGOMIR. But I pray you, what had he to do?

DOCTOR. But for a man like Yerzy, it would be a shame to have a pistol duel with such a pitiful person!

STELLA. The doctor is right. I cannot understand Pan Yerzy.

DOCTOR. Let not our Princess be angry, I reconciled them. But Yerzy did not penetrate the heart of the question; his native impulsiveness carried him away. Now, however, he has halted, and when I explained the whole affair to him, he agreed that it would have been at least ridiculous. He has much judgment.

DRAGOMIR.   What did Milishevski do?

DOCTOR.   I sent him to his mamma. He is a good fellow also.

STELLA.   But I shall open a storm on Pan Yerzy.

DRAGOMIR.   Only be not too severe.

STELLA.   You are laughing, gentlemen; but to me it is painful that there was need to explain this to Pan Yerzy. In truth he shall have a storm right away.   [*Goes out.*

SCENE IX.

DRAGOMIR, DOCTOR YOZVOVICH.

DRAGOMIR.   What an angel that Princess is!

DOCTOR.   True, there is not one taint in her crystalline nature.

DRAGOMIR.   It must be so, since even you, doctor, a sceptic, speak of her with such warmth.

DOCTOR.   Six years have passed since I came here. When I arrived the first time, she ran out to me in a short dress, and with her hair in papers, — such a little thing. Since then she has grown up before me. Six years have their rights; it would have been difficult not to grow attached to her.

DRAGOMIR.   I believe that. (*After a moment of thought.*) You people of work have wonderful hearts though.

DOCTOR.   Why?

DRAGOMIR.   I know what you might say of her social position; but that has no meaning, hearts are equal, hence how has it happened that, being so near the Princess, you have been able to master yourself and not — and not —

DOCTOR (*interrupting him*).   What is that?

DRAGOMIR.   It is difficult for me to find the expression.

DOCTOR. I have found it. You ask me why I have not fallen in love with her?

DRAGOMIR. I hesitated before the over-bold question.

DOCTOR. In truth, if you are lacking in decision, I will help you out and inquire: But you?

DRAGOMIR. Doctor!

DOCTOR. What lyric chord has groaned?

DRAGOMIR. Let us finish this conversation.

DOCTOR. As may please you, though I can talk calmly yet, and so to change the conversation I would ask you, Will she be happy with Yerzy?

DRAGOMIR. What a question! Yerzy loves her beyond everything.

DOCTOR. No doubt, but their natures are not in accord. Her thoughts and feelings are as subtle as spiderwebs, and Yerzy? Have you seen how it pricked her, that he accepted the challenge?

DRAGOMIR. Why did you mention the affair to her?

DOCTOR. I did wrong. But Yerzy —

DRAGOMIR. How happy he will be with her!

DOCTOR. Any man would be happy with her, and to every man one might give the advice, find one like her. Yes, Count, find one like her. [*He goes out.*

SCENE X.

COUNT DRAGOMIR, *alone.*

DRAGOMIR (*to himself*). Find one like her. But if she is found — too late. (*He sits with his face covered with his hand.*)

SCENE XI.

STELLA, DRAGOMIR.

STELLA (*seeing* DRAGOMIR, *looks at him in silence for a while*). What is the matter, Count?

15

DRAGOMIR. Are you here? (*A moment of silence.*)

STELLA (*confused*). I am looking for papa — I beg your pardon, I must go.

DRAGOMIR. Go, Princess.

[STELLA *goes, stops on the threshold for a moment, and vanishes.*

DRAGOMIR. I must leave here as soon as possible!

SCENE XII.

DRAGOMIR, PRINCE, *at the end, the* DOCTOR.

PRINCE (*rushing in panting*). Till this moment she has tormented me. O Jesus, Mary! And is that thou, Dragomir?

DRAGOMIR. I, Prince.

PRINCE. She tormented the life out of me!

DRAGOMIR. Who?

PRINCE. Countess Milishevski. My dear man, how is he to be a deputy when he is a fool?

DRAGOMIR. True, Prince.

PRINCE. And, seest thou! after that, when the mother made a proposal to me for Stella, I was just terrified Besides, she is betrothed, but they did not know it. O Jesus!

DRAGOMIR. How did you get off?

PRINCE. The doctor got me off. When he is absent the Countess does not leave a dry thread on him; but when he is here, she is like a mouse in a corner. That's a head, that Yozvovich! He has more sense than all of us.

DRAGOMIR. That is certain.

PRINCE. But thou hast sense also, Dragomir, hast thou not?

DRAGOMIR. How contradict or agree in this case? The doctor has another kind of mind. Prince.

PRINCE. But that is it! — another kind. I cannot endure him, I fear him, and I like him; but I say to thee that I could not live without him. Dost hear?

DRAGOMIR. He is a shrewd and honest man.

PRINCE. Honest? That is well; but thou art better, for thou art not a democrat. I love thee, Dragomir! Stella, I love him. But she is not here.

DRAGOMIR (*kissing him on the shoulder*). Thank you, Prince.

PRINCE. As God lives, if I had another daughter, I would give her to thee.

DRAGOMIR. Oh, do not say that, Prince. (*Aside.*) I must be off!

PRINCE. Come for a cigar. We will call those people and talk a little. Hei, Yozvovich! Pretvits!

DOCTOR (*entering*). What do you command, Prince?

PRINCE. Come for a cigar, Robespierre! I thank thee, my boy, for having freed me from that Countess.

DOCTOR. Go on, gentlemen, I will send for Pretvits, and we will come right away. (*He rings, a* SERVANT *appears; the* PRINCE *and* DRAGOMIR *go out.*) Ask Pan Pretvits to come! (*The* SERVANT *goes.*) (*Alone.*) Antoni was right! I am helping the logic. But it is disagreeable for me to undermine, I am accustomed to smash.

SCENE XIII.
YERZY, YOZVOVICH.

YERZY. I was looking for you.

DOCTOR. The Prince asks us to a cigar.

YERZY. Wait a little. In the name of God, tell me what all this means? Stella changes before one's eyes; there is something oppressive in the air. What does it mean?

DOCTOR.   Melancholy.   Melancholy is in fashion.

YERZY.   Thou art jesting with me ?

DOCTOR.   I know nothing.

YERZY.   Pardon me. Somehow the blood is rushing to my head in a wonderful way; some storm is above me. I thought that thou wouldst find a calming word for me ; I thought thee friendly to me.

DOCTOR.   Dost doubt it ?

YERZY.   Give me thy hand, and then some word of explanation or advice.

DOCTOR.   Advice ?   Art thou ill, then ?

YERZY (*with an effort*).   Indeed, thou art playing with me, as a cat with a mouse.

DOCTOR.   I know nothing of forebodings.

YERZY.   Didst thou tell me that she was not ill ?

DOCTOR.   She is bored.

YERZY.   Thou sayest that strangely, as though not knowing what pain that word causes me.

DOCTOR.   Distract her.[1]

YERZY.   How ? How ?

DOCTOR.   Not as a wolf a lamb, but, for example, as Count Dragomir does.

YERZY.   Does she like his society ?

DOCTOR.   And he hers. Such poetic souls come to each other mutually.

YERZY.   What dost thou mean by that ?

DOCTOR (*sharply*).   And how dost thou take my words ?

YERZY (*rising*).   Not another syllable, dost understand me, I am not always able to forgive !

DOCTOR (*rises too, approaches* YERZY, *and looks him in the eyes*).   I judge that it is thy wish to frighten me ? Besides this, what dost thou wish ?

---

[1] The Polish word means also to tear apart; hence, the different use of it by the doctor in the second line following.

YERZY (*after a moment of struggle with himself*). Ask what I have wished, for now I wish nothing. Thou knowest her longer than I; so I came to thee as to her friend and mine. Thou hast answered with jests. In thy eyes glitters hatred for me, though I have done thee no harm, and I was the first man to greet thee as a former comrade. Judge thyself! I should have more right to ask what thou wishest of me were it not for this (*with pride*), that all is one to me.   [*Goes out.*

DOCTOR. We shall see.

SCENE XIV.

DOCTOR YOZVOVICH, *the* SERVANT.

SERVANT. A special messenger from Pan Antoni has brought a letter.

DOCTOR. Give it. (*The* SERVANT *goes out. The* DOCTOR, *looking at the door through which* YERZY *went out.*) Oh! neither can I master my hatred any longer. I will crush thee in the dust; now I will hesitate before nothing. (*Breaks the seal hastily.*) A curse! I must go there to-day!

SCENE XV.

DOCTOR YOZVOVICH, PANI CHESKI.

PANI CHESKI (*coming in quickly*). Doctor, I am looking for you through the whole house.

DOCTOR. What has happened?

PANI CHESKI. Stella is ill. I found her in her chamber in tears.

DOCTOR (*aside*). Poor girl! (*Aloud.*) I hasten this minute.   [*They go.*

END OF THIRD ACT.

ACT IV.

The same drawing-room.

SCENE I.

YOZVOVICH, DRAGOMIR. *The* DOCTOR, *sitting at a small table, is noting in a catalogue ;* DRAGOMIR *enters.*

DRAGOMIR.   I come to take farewell, doctor.

DOCTOR (*rises suddenly*).   Ah! are you going away?

DRAGOMIR.   I am.

DOCTOR.   A sudden decision.   And for a long time?

DRAGOMIR.   I start this evening for Svetlenitse, to see Yerzy, to-morrow I go abroad.

DOCTOR.   One word more.   Have you told any one of this plan?

DRAGOMIR.   So far no one knows of it.   My intention became a decision only a couple of hours ago.

DOCTOR.   Is it irrevocable?

DRAGOMIR.   Irrevocable.

DOCTOR.   Then not even Yerzy knows of it yet?

DRAGOMIR.   Not even Yerzy.   Why do you ask?

DOCTOR (*aside*).   It has come.   There is need to act quickly, else all will be lost.   (*Aloud.*)   Count, I cannot speak in this moment at length with you, for Antoni is coming with an affair on which my whole future depends. But hear me, I implore you in the name of the peace and health of the Princess not to mention to any one that you are going away, neither to her, nor to Yerzy, nor to the Prince.

DRAGOMIR.   I do not understand you.

DOCTOR.   You will understand me.   At this moment I cannot say more.   I beg for a little time.   Half an hour hence, give me a moment's conversation, I pray.   You will

understand me, I assure you.   But here is Antoni.   You
see, Count, that at present I cannot —

DRAGOMIR.   Then till we meet again.

SCENE II.

ANTONI, DOCTOR YOZVOVICH.

ANTONI.   To-morrow the result will be known.   It is
a hot affair.   Is the address ready ?

DOCTOR.   Here it is.   And how are things going ?

ANTONI.   So far, everything goes well ; but I tell thee
that it is a hot affair.   If thou hadst not come the last
time, thou wouldst have been lost ; for Milishevski has
withdrawn, and now his partisans are on Husarski's
side.   Thy speech in the city hall was brilliant.   May a
thunderbolt split thee !   To-day we will give thee an ova-
tion.   Even thy enemies do justice to thy programme.
Oh, at last we shall come to have a voice !   These three
days I sleep not, neither do I eat, I only work, and I
have time, for they have dismissed me from office.

DOCTOR.   Have they driven thee out of office ?

ANTONI.   For agitation, and for the affair with
Husarski.

DOCTOR.   Hast found means against him ?

ANTONI.   I have scratched off a little article.   I will
give it to thee — here it is.   He has brought a suit
against me, and will win.   They will put me in prison ;
but the action will end only after election, while the
article will hurt him before election.

DOCTOR.   Well !

ANTONI.   But when I shall be sitting in prison, think
of my wife and children.   I love my little boys immensely.   I have a few too many of them ; but nature is
a hard law.

DOCTOR.   Be at rest.

ANTONI.   Thou wouldst not believe, but I am almost happy.   At times it seems to me that our province is a cabin with foul air, and that I open the window and let in a fresh breeze.   We will work, even if we have to wear off our arms to the elbows.   I believe in thee, for thou art a monster made of iron.   As God is true, thou hadst taken possession of us before we saw it.

DOCTOR.   I shall die, or gain two victories.

ANTONI.   Two?

DOCTOR.   Yes, and the other even here to-day. Events have anticipated me in some measure.   Facts turned against me.   I had to frame my plan of action quickly, a moment ago.

ANTONI.   Ei! if we can only win there.   Knowest thou, lord leader of our party, I would rather thou threw the other victory to the deuce.

DOCTOR.   In this thou art mistaken, Antoni.

ANTONI.   Thou grievest; thou sufferest; thou hast grown thin.   Look in the mirror!   What a face!

DOCTOR.   That is no harm; when I spring the mine here I shall be calmer, and the mine is now ready.

ANTONI.   But it will cost thee something.

DOCTOR.   Still I shall not go back.

ANTONI.   Deuce take it!   But do not blacken thy hands too much with the powder.

Scene III.

The same, STELLA.

STELLA (*entering, sees* ANTONI).   Ah, I beg pardon!

DOCTOR.   Pan Antoni Juk, my friend.   (ANTONI *bows*.) What do you command, Princess?

STELLA.   You prescribed the bed; but it is so hard to

lie down. Pani Cheski went to the chapel, so I fled. Do you permit?

DOCTOR. What am I to do, Princess, though I might have the wish to scold a disobedient child. Not long since some one else interceded for you.

STELLA. Who was that?

DOCTOR. Count Dragomir; and he begged so that I promised to let you rise in an hour. He wishes to talk with you to-day, I believe, even later, as he cannot —

STELLA (*aside*). What does this mean?

DOCTOR. About five, that is an hour from now, he will be here.

STELLA. Very well.

DOCTOR. Now I beg that you will return to your own room, for you are lightly dressed. [*She goes out.*

SCENE IV.

DOCTOR YOZVOVICH, ANTONI.

ANTONI. Ah, that is the Princess then. I saw her for the first time.

DOCTOR. Yes, that is she.

ANTONI. Very shapely. But somehow as if made of mist. I prefer women like my wife. From the Princess thou wilt not get sturdy democrats.

DOCTOR. Enough of this.

ANTONI. So I weigh anchor and sail. I will scatter thy address to-day, and at the same time another stiff article on Husarski. If they are to put me in prison, let people know why. Be well!

DOCTOR. And when thou shalt meet the servant, tell him that I am waiting for Count Dragomir.

SCENE V.

DOCTOR YOZVOVICH, *later*, DRAGOMIR.

DOCTOR. Then let this golden-haired page go away, but let him take farewell of her. That farewell will be a red rag for the bull. (DRAGOMIR *enters.*) I am waiting for you. Is Pretvits here?

DRAGOMIR. He is with the Prince.

DOCTOR. Sit down, Count; let us talk.

DRAGOMIR (*unquietly*). I listen.

DOCTOR. Do you love the Princess?

DRAGOMIR. Pan Yozvovich!

DOCTOR. On your honor, — yes or no.

DRAGOMIR. God might have the right to ask me a question which I dare not ask myself.

DOCTOR. And your conscience.

DRAGOMIR. And no one else.

DOCTOR. Then in another way! And she loves you.

DRAGOMIR. Be silent! O great God!

DOCTOR. Pride is broken! You knew of this?

DRAGOMIR. No, I did not wish to know.

DOCTOR. You know now.

DRAGOMIR. I am going away forever.

DOCTOR. Too late, Count! You have involved her life, and now you are leaving her.

DRAGOMIR. But what am I to do? In God's name!

DOCTOR. Go away, but not for good, and not without taking leave.

DRAGOMIR. Why add another drop to the overflowing cup?

DOCTOR. A pretty phrase! Do you not understand what people will think of her here, if you go away suddenly, without farewell, without return. Besides, she is ill, and may not survive your departure.

DRAGOMIR. I see no escape.

DOCTOR. There is only one. Find an occasion; take farewell of her calmly, and say that you will return. Otherwise the blow may exceed her strength. You must leave her hope. She ought not to suspect anything. Afterward she may grow used to your absence, then forget it.

DRAGOMIR. Better let her forget it.

DOCTOR. I shall use all my efforts to bring that about. I shall be the first one to throw a handful of dust on your memory.

DRAGOMIR. What am I to do, then?

DOCTOR. Find a cause for taking farewell, mention your return to all, and go away. Yerzy also is not to know of anything.

DRAGOMIR. When am I to take farewell of her?

DOCTOR. In a little while. I have forewarned her. I shall occupy Pretvits while you are with her. He will come here soon.

DRAGOMIR. All is so arranging itself that I would rather have a ball in my heart.

DOCTOR. No one is sure of his to-morrow. Go now

[DRAGOMIR goes out.

SCENE VI.

DOCTOR YOZVOVICH, later, the SERVANT.

DOCTOR. How hot it is here, my head is splitting! (Rings, SERVANT enters.) Ask Pan Pretvits here immediately. (SERVANT goes out.) My head is splitting, but afterward there will be a long rest.

Scene VII.

Doctor Yozvovich, Yerzy.

Yerzy (*entering*). What didst thou wish of me?

Doctor. I wish to give thee some advice touching the Princess's health.

Yerzy. How is she now?

Doctor. Better. I have permitted her to rise now, for she and Dragomir begged me to do so.

Yerzy. And Dragomir?

Doctor. Yes. He wishes to talk with her. They are to come in here a quarter of an hour from now.

Yerzy. Doctor, rage and pain are suffocating me. Dragomir avoids me.

Doctor. But still thou dost not suspect him.

Yerzy. I swear that I have warded off suspicions as a dying man keeps off crows; that I have gnawed my hands from pain and despair. I ward them off yet; but I cannot do so longer. I cannot. Reality strikes me on the head with the back of a hatchet. He avoids me, he — By the mercy of God! tell me that I am fool, that I have lost my senses, for everything is breaking in me.

Doctor. Restrain thyself. Even if he has loved the Princess, no man controls his own heart.

Yerzy. Enough, enough! Thou wert right in joining his name the first time with hers. I rejected the thought then, but it has lived here! (*Striking his breast.*) The grain is ripe now. Oh, what a terrible and ridiculous rôle I have played, till reality convinced me—

Doctor. But he saved thy life.

Yerzy. To take it when it began to have value. It is paid for already, paid for with torment, murdered happiness, broken hope, faith in him destroyed, in myself, in her. And knowest thou how many days and nights have passed; how I repress in myself the shriek of pure despair.

DOCTOR. Calm thyself.

YERZY. I loved that man. Tell me am I a maniac? But I will calm myself. Still how dreadful that it should be just he. My reason is at an end, my powers are at an end; but misfortune continues. Think that it should be just he. Forgive me all that I said before to thee, and save me; evil thoughts are coming to my head.

DOCTOR. Calm thyself, thou art mistaken.

YERZY. Show me that I am mistaken, and I will kneel before thee.

DOCTOR. Thou art mistaken. Dragomir is going away.

YERZY. He is going away! (*A moment of silence.*) Then I can live still like every man, not in torture, and have hope?

DOCTOR (*coldly and slowly*). He is not going away, it is true, for good. He said that he would return soon.

YERZY. Again thou art fastening me to the cross.

DOCTOR. Collect presence of mind, and do not let thyself be carried to madness. In every case thou wilt gain time. If he has shaken thy place in the heart of the Princess, thou canst win back what is lost.

YERZY. No! It is all over! I will go into the abyss.

DOCTOR. Everything may be settled by his departure.

YERZY (*with an outburst*). But thou hast said that he will return.

DOCTOR (*with power*). Listen, I will agree that thou hast paid Dragomir for thy life with suffering. Dragomir has betrayed and broken friendship by taking her heart from thee; but I reject the thought that he is going away to save his person from thy revenge.

YERZY. But to give her time to break with me! That is it! So I am cursed already to the hour of death; I will suspect him now of everything. He is fleeing from me.

DOCTOR. Yerzy!

YERZY. May God forgive me if something terrible happens here to Dragomir.

DOCTOR. Poor Yerzy!

YERZY. Enough, enough! I will go to ask him when he returns. He saved me one life and killed ten.

[*Wishes to go out.*

DOCTOR. Where art thou going?

YERZY. To ask him how long he will be gone.

DOCTOR. One moment. Of what dost thou wish to ask, madman? He may be innocent; but pride will close his lips and destroy both of you. Stay here, thou wilt pass only over my corpse. I am not afraid of thee — dost understand! In a moment they are to talk here. If thou need proofs, thou shalt have them. From the garden porch thou wilt not hear, but thou wilt see them; thou wilt convince thyself with thy own eyes, and perhaps regret violent words.

YERZY (*after a while*). Agreed! that is well. O God grant that there is no fault there! I thank thee, but do not leave me now.

DOCTOR One word more: Whatever happens, it would be contemptible if thou shouldst endanger her life with an outburst.

YERZY. Agreed, let us go.

DOCTOR. They will be here alone.

YERZY. I shall correct everything yet. Whither shall we go?

DOCTOR. To the garden porch.

YERZY. May God have mercy on me, and on them.

DOCTOR. You are feverish. You are trembling already as in a fever.

YERZY. I will stuff my mouth with a handkerchief. Then from the porch —

DOCTOR. Yes, among the cypresses.

YERZY. I lack breath. Some one is coming. Let us go out.

SCENE VIII.

DRAGOMIR, *then*, STELLA.

DRAGOMIR. The last evening, and the last time. (*After a while.*) Let the will of God be done; let all suffering fall on me.

STELLA (*enters*). The doctor told me that you wished to see me.

DRAGOMIR. Yes, important reasons call me home for a time. I have come to take farewell of you.

STELLA. To take farewell?

DRAGOMIR. To-day I go to Svetlenitse, and to-morrow farther. (*A moment of silence.*)

STELLA. So, it is necessary.

DRAGOMIR. Life has passed like a dream here; it is time to wake up.

STELLA. But you say that we shall see each other again?

DRAGOMIR. If God permits.

STELLA. Then I give you my hand in parting, and with it eternal friendship. Friendship, like an immortelle, is a pale flower, but it never withers. May God conduct and guard you. The heart of a sister will go with you everywhere, I beg you to remember —

DRAGOMIR. I take farewell of you.

STELLA. I take farewell of you as if forever. (*She goes

away and then returns with tears in her voice.) Count, why do you deceive me, you are going away forever.

DRAGOMIR. Have pity on me!

STELLA. You are going away forever?

DRAGOMIR. Yes, it is true.

STELLA. I divined that. But perhaps it is better for us both.

DRAGOMIR. Oh, yes, there are things which cannot be told, though the heart should be rent. A moment ago you said that you would remember me; recall that gift, forget.

STELLA. I shall not be able. (*She bursts into tears.*)

DRAGOMIR. Then I love thee, angel, as if mad, and that is why I flee from thee and from myself. (*He presses her to his breast.*)

STELLA (*wakening*). O God!   [*She runs away.*

SCENE IX.

DRAGOMIR, YOZVOVICH, YERZY. YERZY *stops with the* DOCTOR *near the door.*

DRAGOMIR. Ah! is that thou, Yerzy?

YERZY. Do not approach me. I saw all! Thou art contemptible and a coward!

DRAGOMIR. Yerzy!

YERZY. Broken friendship, trampled happiness, lost faith in God and man, perfect contempt for thee and myself, — these I cast in thy face, so as not to soil my hands by slapping it.

DRAGOMIR. Enough!

YERZY. Do not approach me, or I shall lose presence of mind and sprinkle these walls with thy brains. No! no! I do not want that; I have promised. I slap thee on the face, contemptible! Dost hear?

DRAGOMIR (*after a moment's struggle with himself*). Before God and men, I declare that blood will wash out such words.

YERZY. Blood! (*Pointing to the* DOCTOR.) Here is the witness of those words.

DOCTOR. I am at your service, gentlemen.

(*Curtain falls.*)

END OF FOURTH ACT.

ACT V.

The same drawing-room.

SCENE I.

DOCTOR (*enters reading a despatch*). "The result as far as known : Yozvovich, 613 votes ; Husarski, 604. Ten o'clock : Yozvovich, 700 ; Husarski, 700. Eleven : Yozvovich, 814 ; Husarski, 750. The battle an obstinate one. Final result will be known about three o'clock." (*He looks at his watch.*)

SCENE II.

YOZVOVICH, YERZY.

DOCTOR. Thou art here !

YERZY. Thou withdrawest before the ghost ?

DOCTOR. But is it to-day ?

YERZY. I go straight from here to the place of meeting. I have one hour yet. The duel will be in Dombrova on the land of the Milishevskis, so not far off.

DOCTOR. It is too near.

YERZY. Milishevski, as second, insisted. Besides, thou art in the affair, so that the news should be known in this house as late as possible.

16

DOCTOR. But Doctor Krytski will be on the spot according to agreement.

YERZY Yes.

DOCTOR. Beg him once more to send me the news immediately. I would go with you, but I must be here.

YERZY. Very properly. If I die —

DOCTOR. Do not admit that in advance.

YERZY. There are people condemned by fate at birth, for whom the only ransom is death. I am one of those. I have thought over everything long and calmly. God knows that I fear life more than death. There is no escape for me; even should I survive what will happen, tell me, what awaits me if I kill a man whom she loves? I shall live without her and be cursed by her. Dost know that when I think of my position, when I think of what has happened, it seems to me that some demon has come between us, and so involved all things, that death alone can straighten them.

DOCTOR. A duel ends frequently in maiming.

YERZY. I gave the lie to Dragomir cruelly, and such an insult is not washed out by a wound. Believe me that one of us must die. But I have come to speak of something else.

DOCTOR. I hear thee.

YERZY. To tell the truth, since I know not whether I shall be alive in an hour, I have come to look once more on her, for I loved her above everything in the world. I was perhaps too abrupt for her, too unhappy, too dull, but — I loved her. Then let God, who is looking now into my heart, condemn me forever if I did not desire her happiness. As thou seest me here this moment, I am grieved most because of her, and I suffer greatly when I think of her future. Listen! whether I perish or not, she is lost to me; Dragomir will not marry her, for he cannot marry a woman whose betrothed he has killed.   Of us three, thou alone wilt remain near her, guard her, watch over her.   She was the only treasure which I had ; I give her into thy honest hands.

DOCTOR.   I will carry out all thy wishes.

YERZY.   And now, since I may die, I wish to die as a Christian.   If thou hast any feeling against me, if I have been to blame regarding thee at any time, forgive me !

[*He presses the* DOCTOR'S *hand and goes out.*

DOCTOR (*alone*).   Yes !   Of us three, I alone remain near her.

SCENE III.

ANTONI, YOZVOVICH.

ANTONI (*rushing in quickly*).   Man, you are mad ! Every moment there is precious, and thou art sitting here.   The cause is trembling; new hand-bills are posted up.   Husarski's partisans are seizing people by their coats.   In God's name come with me !   A drosky is waiting below.   Why art thou sitting here ?

DOCTOR.   I must stay here.   I will not go for anything on earth ; I will not go, let happen what may.

ANTONI.   But I swear, if I expected this !   Show thyself even for a moment, and thou wilt win surely !   Lungs and voice are gone from me.   Art thou mad ?   There they are working for him, and shouting for him, and this man is clinging to a petticoat, and sitting here.   We are choosing a pretty deputy !

DOCTOR.   Antoni !   Even though the election were to be lost, I would not move a step.   I cannot, I will not go !

ANTONI.   Is this true ?

DOCTOR.   It is !

ANTONI.   Well, do what may please thee.   Well !   I wish — (*He walks through the room, after a while puts his hands in his pockets, and stands before the* DOCTOR.) Well, what does this mean?

DOCTOR. It means that I must be here. At this moment Dragomir and Pretvits are face to face with arms in their hands. If news should reach the Princess, she might pay for it with her life.

ANTONI. Are they shooting?

DOCTOR. For life and death. News will be here in a moment telling which of the two is dead.

ANTONI. Yozvovich, who did this?

DOCTOR. I! I crushed those who stood in my road, and I shall crush them always. Thou seest me as I am.

ANTONI. Well, if that is so, neither am I in a hurry. Dost thou know what I will say?

DOCTOR. Withdraw for a while; the Princess is coming. (*He opens the door of a side chamber.*) Go in there.

SCENE IV.

YOZVOVICH, STELLA.

STELLA. My doctor, what is happening in this house?

DOCTOR. Of what do you ask, Princess?

STELLA. Pan Yerzy came to me somehow excited; he took farewell of me, begged me to forgive him if he had ever offended me —

DOCTOR (*aside*). Sentimental fool!

STELLA. He told me that he might be forced to go away for a number of days. I have the feeling that you are hiding something from me. What does this mean, doctor? Do not torture me longer. I am so weak already that, in truth, it is proper to have a little pity on me.

DOCTOR. Be not concerned. What could happen? Pure imagination. The care of tender hearts surrounds you. Whence could such a strange supposition come? Go now to your own room, and receive nobody. I will come soon.

STELLA. Then there is really no trouble, doctor?

DOCTOR. And what is this again! I beg you to believe that I should be able to set aside everything which might threaten your happiness.

STELLA (*giving him her hand*). Oh, Pan Stanislav, happiness is too difficult a thing; but let peace not desert us.

[*She wishes to go out through the room where* ANTONI *is.*

DOCTOR. This way, Princess. In that room a man is waiting for me. I will come to you soon. Receive no one, I beg you. Antoni!   [PRINCESS *goes out.*

SCENE V.

ANTONI, DOCTOR YOZVOVICH, *afterwards*, SERVANT.

ANTONI. Poor, poor child!

DOCTOR. For her sake I cannot go away. I must be here and not let news of the misfortune reach her, that might kill her.

ANTONI. How? — knowing this, thou art exposing her? Thou lovest her, and art sacrificing her to thyself?

DOCTOR (*feverishly*). I love her and must have her, even if this house were to fall on our heads.

ANTONI. Man, thou art speaking like one who has lost his mind.

DOCTOR. Man, thou speakest like an incompetent, not like a man. Thou hast a mouthful of phrases and strength, but knowest not how to look facts in the eyes. Who dares say to me, "Thou hast not the right to defend thyself"?

ANTONI. Farewell!

DOCTOR. Where art thou going?

ANTONI. I return to the city.

DOCTOR. Art thou with me, or against me? I am an honest man.

SERVANT (*enters*). A messenger has brought a letter from Milishevski.

DOCTOR. Give it here! (SERVANT *goes out; he breaks the seal and reads.*) "The duel has taken place. Pretvits is no longer living." (*After a while.*) Ah!—

ANTONI. Before I go, I owe thee an answer, for thou hast inquired what my going means. I have served thee as faithfully as a dog, for I believed in thee. Thou hast known how to use, and perhaps to abuse me. I knew that I was a tool, but I care not for such things; still now—

DOCTOR. Now thou wilt leave the cause?

ANTONI. Thou dost not know me. What should I do in the world if I were to desert it? And finally dost thou think that thou alone art the cause? I will not leave the cause because I was deceived in thee. But for me, it is a question of something else. I was so foolish as to attach myself to thee, and now I am sorry; for as a private man, I must tell thee, thou hast exceeded the measure, thou hast used for evil the power which is in thee. Oh, I know, I know, perhaps for me it would be more profitable not to say this to thee. Perhaps to cling to thee would be a future for a ragged man like me, who has not very much at home to give wife and children to eat. But I cannot, I cannot! I am naked, and naked I shall remain; let me have at least a clear conscience. This is what I will say: Thou wert as near to me as my wife and children, nearer too! From this day forward thou art only a political figure; but as to friendship, seek some one else. Know that I am not particular; a man rubs against people, and rubs more than one thing into himself; but thou hast exceeded the measure. Hang me, if I do not prefer to love people rather than crush them. Men say that honesty and politics are different. Here and there it may be so. But with us those things must be connected. Why should they not go together? I shall not desert the cause; but there is an end to the friendship between me and thee, for the man who says that he loves people, and lurks and strikes them on the head by deceit, is a liar, dost understand?

DOCTOR. I shall not attract thy friendship by superior force; but listen to me for the last time. If a period of defeats begins for me, it will begin because men like thee cease to understand me. Behold, this man who has died went suddenly, blindly, and fatally against my success, my right to happiness, my future, and took all from me. He appeared with wealth, a name, relatives, and all that invincible armor which fortune and birth give. What had I against him? With what could I do battle? What could I put against his power? Nothing, but that which is the armor of new men, — that little intelligence acquired by bloody toil and effort. He declared a silent war against me. I defended myself. With what? With the armor which nature gave me. When thou tramplest a worm, do not take it ill that it defends itself with a sting, for it has nothing else with which to defend itself. When thou hast to remove a stone lying in the way, remove it as may please thee. That is a human right! Yes, I put everything on a single card, and I won; but it was not I, it was reason which overcame strength, the new time past ages. And thou takest that ill of me? What is thy wish? I am true to my principle; but ye draw back, I do not. That is one side, but what is the other? That woman was necessary to me, to my happiness; I love her, for

my plans, for her property, her relations. Give me such
weapons, and I will accomplish and carry out everything! Dost understand what a gigantic labor, what
great objects and plans are before me? Ye wish that I
should break the wall of darkness, hesitation, sloth, that
I should breathe life into that which is withered; I call
for means. Ye have none! Hence I will get them or
perish. But what? One little noble, one pallid knight,
one adventurer, whose only service is that he was born
with an escutcheon, stands in the way of these great
plans, of that bright future, not only for me, but for
society, and I have not the right to crush him. And ye
wish that I should fall at his great, mighty feet, that I
should sacrifice everything to him? No, ye do not know
me! Enough of sentiment. Strength is needed, and I
have it, and I will open a way for myself and others
even though I had to trample a hundred Pretvitses.

ANTONI. No, Yozvovich! Thou hast always done
with me whatever pleased thee, but now thou wilt not
overcome me. While it was a question of convictions, I
was with thee; but thou hast assaulted certain principles
which are greater than thou and I, and more enduring
and more unchangeable. Thou wilt not explain thy
position to me, and have a care for thyself. At any
slight cause, thou wilt fall with all thy energy. Principles change, my dear man, but simple honesty is always
the same. Do what may please thee, but guard thyself.
What the deuce! the blood of men is avenged; that is
also a right of nature. Thou hast asked if I desert
thee? Perhaps thou wouldst like to be free to shoot
people from behind a fence, whenever that might suit
thee! No, brother! Henceforth begins between us a
close account, for we cannot trust thee. Thou wilt
be a deputy; but if thou thinkest that we shall serve

thee, and thou not us, thou art mistaken. What hast thou supposed, that the rounds of this ladder on which thou art climbing is made up of rascals? Halt there! We, who make thee a deputy, we, in whose honesty thou dost not believe, perhaps, will watch now and judge thee. If thou do mischief, we will grind thee to dust. The cause is not for thee, but thou art for the cause. We elected thee, now serve.

DOCTOR (*violently*). Andrei!

ANTONI. Quietly! In the evening thou wilt stand before the electors in the city. Till we see each other, Doctor Yozvovich —   [*Goes out.*

DOCTOR (*alone*). He is the first.

SCENE VI.

DOCTOR YOZVOVICH, YAN MILISHEVSKI.

YAN (*appears in a half-open door*). Pst!

DOCTOR. Who is there?

YAN. I, Milishevski. Are you alone?

DOCTOR. Come in! Well, what is it?

YAN. It is finished. Ah, doctor, he did not live five minutes! I commanded to take the body to Milishevo, to the church.

DOCTOR. But your mother is not here?

YAN. I sent her to the city. This is election day, and mamma does not know that I have withdrawn; so she will wait for the evening papers, hoping that my name will be among the elected.

DOCTOR. No one has seen him on the road?

YAN. I am afraid that people will see blood. He bled terribly on the road.

DOCTOR. Strange thing! He was such a good shot.

YAN. He let himself be killed purposely. I was

there; I saw perfectly that he did not put his finger on the trigger. He did not wish to kill Dragomir. Six steps, such a close mark! Oh. it is ghastly to look at the death of another man! In truth, I would rather have died myself. They fired at command: one! two! three! — we heard a shot, but only one. We flew forward. Pretvits advanced two steps and knelt; he wanted to speak, but blood gushed out of his mouth; then he took his pistol and fired to one side. We were already standing around, and he said to Dragomir, "You have done me a favor, I thank you. This life belonged to you, for you saved it. Forgive me — brother," said he; "give me your hand," ánd he began to die — (YAN *wipes his brow with his handkerchief.*) Dragomir threw himself on Yerzy's breast. Oh, doctor, indeed it was terrible! Poor Princess Stella, what will become of her now?

DOCTOR. For God's sake, silence, not a word before her. She is sick.

YAN. I shall be silent.

DOCTOR. Master your emotion.

YAN. I cannot control my legs, for they are trembling under me.

SCENE VII.

The same, the PRINCE, *leaning on* STELLA'S *arm*, PANI CHESKI.

PRINCE. I thought that Pretvits was here with you. Doctor, where is Pretvits?

DOCTOR. I know not.

STELLA. Did he not tell you where he was going?

DOCTOR. I know not.

PANI CHESKI (*to* YAN). What is the matter, Count, you are so pale?

YAN. Not at all, that is from fever.

PRINCE. Doctor, Pretvits told me —

SCENE VIII.

The door opens suddenly; COUNTESS MILISHEVSKI *rushes in.*

COUNTESS. Jean! where is my Jean? O God, what is happening! What a ghastliness!

DOCTOR (*running up to her quickly*). Be silent, Countess.

STELLA. What has happened?

COUNTESS. Then it was not thou who killed Pretvits? It was not thou who fought the duel?

DOCTOR. Silence, Countess.

STELLA. Who is killed?

COUNTESS. Then was it Dragomir? Stella dear, Dragomir has killed Pretvits.

STELLA. Killed! O God! O God! What has happened?

DOCTOR. Princess, this is not true!

STELLA. Killed? (*She staggers and falls.*)

DOCTOR. She has fainted. Let us carry her to her chamber.

PRINCE. My child!

PANI CHESKI. Stella dear!

[*The* PRINCE *and* DOCTOR *carry* STELLA *out; the* COUNTESS *and* PANI CHESKI *follow them.*

YAN (*alone*). Oh, this is ghastly! I sent mother purposely to the city; who could have expected that she would return? (*The* COUNTESS *appears in the door.*) Mamma, how is the Princess?

COUNTESS. The doctor is examining her. She has not regained consciousness. Jean, let us go from here.

YAN (*in despair*). I will not go from here. Why did you come back from the city?

COUNTESS. For thee. This is election day, hast forgotten?

YAN. I have no wish to be a deputy! Why did mamma tell of Pretvits' death?

SCENE IX.

The same, YOZVOVICH.

THE COUNTESS *and* YAN (*together*). What has happened there? What?

DOCTOR. There is nothing more to be done, all is over! (*They are ringing the chapel bell.*)

YAN (*in terror*). What is this? Ringing the chapel bell!

(YOZVOVICH *comes to the front of the stage and sits down.*)

SCENE X.

The same, PODCHASKI.

PODCHASKI (*rushes in on a sudden*). Victory along the whole line! The deputation is here! (*Voices behind the stage.* " Long life to him ! " " Long life to him !") He has won! Long life to him!

DOCTOR. I have lost dreadfully.

END.

YANKO THE MUSICIAN

YANKO THE MUSICIAN.

IT came into the world frail, weak. The gossips, who
had gathered around the plank bed of the sick
woman, shook their heads over mother and child. The
wife of Simon the blacksmith, who was the wisest among
them, began to console the sick woman.

"Let me," said she, " light a blessed candle above you;
Nothing will come of you, my gossip; you must prepare
for the other world now, and send for the priest to
absolve you from your sins."

"Yes!" said another, " but the boy must be christened
this minute: he cannot wait for the priest. It is well
even to stop him from becoming a vampire."

So saying, she lighted the blessed candle, and taking
the child sprinkled him with water till his eyes blinked;
and then she said, —

"I baptize thee in the name of the Father, Son, and
Holy Ghost. I give thee Yan as name; and now, Christian soul, go to the place whence thou camest. Amen !"

But the Christian soul had no wish whatever to go to
the place whence it came and leave its lean little body.
It began to kick with the legs of that body as far as it
was able, and to cry, though so weakly and pitifully that,
as the gossips said, " One would think 't is a kitten; 't is
not a kitten, — what is it?"

They sent for the priest; he came, he did his duty, he
went his way, — the sick woman grew better. In a week
she went out to her work. The little boy barely " puled,"
— still, he puled on till in the fourth year the cuckoo

brought him sickness in spring; but, he recovered, and
with some kind of health reached the tenth year of his
life.

He was always lean and sunburnt, with bloated stomach
and sunken cheeks; he had a forelock of hemp color
almost white and falling over clear, staring eyes, which
looked at the world as if gazing into some immense distance. In winter he used to sit behind the stove and cry
silently from cold, and from hunger too, at times when his
mother had nothing to put into the stove or the pot. During summer he went around in a shirt, with a strip of cloth
for a belt, and a straw hat, from beneath the torn brim
of which he looked with head peering upward like a bird.
His mother, a poor lodger, living from day to day, like a
sparrow under a stranger's roof, loved him perhaps in her
own way; but she flogged him often enough and called
him "giddy-head" generally. In the eighth year of his life
he went to herd cattle, or, when there was nothing to eat
in the cottage, to the pine woods for mushrooms. It was
through the compassion of God that a wolf did not eat
him.

He was a very dull little fellow, and, like village children, when spoken to put his finger in his mouth. People
did not even promise that he would grow up, and still less
that his mother could expect any good from him, for he
was a poor hand at work. It is unknown whence such
a creature could have come; but he was eager for one
thing, music. He listened to it everywhere, and when
he had grown up a little he thought of nothing else.
He would go to the woods for the cattle, or with a two-
handled basket for berries, but would come home without
berries and say, stammering, —

"Mamma, something was playing in the woods. Oi!
oi!"

And the mother would say, " I 'll play for thee, never fear!"

And in fact she made music for him, sometimes with the poker. The boy screamed and promised that he would not do it again, and still he was thinking, " Something is playing out there in the woods." What was it, — did he know? Pines, beeches, golden orioles, all were playing, — the whole forest was playing, and that was the end of it!

The echo, too! In the field the artemisia played for him; in the garden near, the sparrows twittered till the cherry-trees were trembling. In the evening he heard all the voices that were in the village, and thought to himself that surely the whole village was playing. When they sent him to work to spread manure, even then the wind played on the fork-tines.

The overseer caught him once standing with dishevelled forelock and listening to the wind on the wooden tines; he looked at the little fellow, unbuckled his own leather belt, and gave him a good keepsake. But what use in that? People called the boy " Yanko the musician." In the springtime he ran away from the house to make whistles near the river. In the night, when the frogs were croaking, the land-rail calling in the meadows, the bittern screaming in the dew, the cocks crowing behind the wicker fences, he could not sleep, — he did nothing but listen; and God alone knows what he heard in that playing. His mother could not take him to church, for as soon as the organ began to roar or the choir sang in sweet voices, the child's eyes were covered with mist, and were as if not looking forth out of this world.

The village policeman who walked through the place at night and counted stars in the sky to keep from sleeping, or conversed in a low voice with the dogs, saw more than

17

once the white shirt of Yanko stealing along in the dark toward the public house. But the boy was not going to the public house, only to a spot near it. There he would cower at the wall and listen. The people were dancing the *obertas;* at times some young fellow would cry, " U-ha ! " The stamping of boots was heard; then the querying voices of girls, " What ? " The fiddles sang in low tones, " We will eat, we will drink, we shall be merry ; " and the bass viol accompanied in a deep voice, with importance, " As God gave ! As God gave ! " The windows were gleaming with life, and every beam in the house seemed to tremble, singing and playing also ; but Yanko was listening.

How much would he give to have such a fiddle playing thinly, " We will eat, we will drink and be merry " ! Such singing bits of wood ! But from what place could he get them, — where were they made ? If some one would just let him hold such a thing in his hand even once ! How could that be ? He was only free to listen, and then to listen only till the voice of the watchman was heard behind him in the darkness, —

" Wilt thou go home, little devil ? "

Then he fled away home in his bare feet, but in the darkness behind him ran the voice of the fiddle, "We will eat, we will drink, we shall be merry," and the deep voice of the bass, "As God gave ! As God gave ! As God gave ! "

Whenever he could hear a fiddle at a harvest-home or some wedding, it was a great holiday for him. After that he went behind the stove and said nothing for whole days, looking like a cat in the dark with gleaming eyes. Then he made himself a fiddle out of a shingle and some horsehair, but it would not play beautifully like that one in the public house, — it sounded low, very low, just like mice of some kind, or gnats. He played on it however from morning till evening; though for doing that he got so many cuffs that at last he looked like a pinched, unripe apple. But such was his nature. The poor child became thinner and thinner, only he had always a big stomach; his forelock grew thicker and thicker, and his eyes opened more and more widely, though filled oftener with tears; but his cheeks and his breast fell in more and more.

He was not like other children at all; he was rather like that shingle fiddle of his, which hardly made a noise. Besides, he was suffering from hunger before harvest, for he lived mainly on raw carrots, and the wish to have a fiddle. But that wish did not turn out well for Yanko.

At the mansion the lackey had a fiddle and he played on it sometimes at twilight to please the waiting-maid. Yanko crept up at times among the burdocks as far as the open door of the pantry to gaze at the fiddle. It hung on the wall opposite the door; the boy would send his whole soul out through his eyes to it, for it seemed to him that that was some unattainable object, which he was unworthy to touch, that that was some kind of dearest love of his. Still he wanted it. He would like to have it in his hand at least one time, to look at it near by. The poor little fellow's heart quivered with happiness at the thought.

A certain night there was no one in the pantry. Their lordships had been in foreign countries for some time, the house was empty, the lackey was at the other side with the waiting-maid. Yanko, lurking in the burdocks, had been looking for a long time through the broad door at the object of all his desires. The moon in the sky was full, and shone in with sloping rays through the pantry window, which it reflected in the form of a great quadrangle on the opposite wall. The quadrangle approached the fiddle gradually and at last illuminated every bit of the instrument. At that time it seemed in the dark depth as if a silver light shone from the fiddle, — especially the plump bends in it were lighted so strongly that Yanko could barely look at them. In that light everything was perfectly visible, — the sides with incisions, the strings, and the bent handle. The pegs in it gleamed like fireflies, and at its side hung the bow which seemed a rod of silver.

Ah, all was beautiful and almost enchanted; and Yanko looked more and more greedily. He was crouched in the burdocks, with his elbows pressed on his lean knees; with open eyes he looked and looked. Now terror held him to the spot, now a certain unconquerable desire pushed him forward. Was that some enchantment, or what? But the fiddle in the bright light seemed sometimes to approach, as it were to float toward the boy. At times it grew darker, to shine up again still more. Enchantment, clearly enchantment! Then the breeze blew; the trees rustled quietly, there was a noise in the burdocks, and Yanko heard, as it were, distinctly, —

"Go, Yanko, there is no one in the pantry; go, Yanko!"

The night was clear, bright. In the garden a nightingale began to sing and whistled with a low voice, then louder, "Go! go in! take it." An honest wood-owl turned in flight around the child's head, and cried, "Yanko, no! no!" The owl flew away, but the nightingale and the burdocks muttered more distinctly, "There is no one inside!" The fiddle shone again.

The poor little bent figure pushed forward slowly and carefully; meanwhile the nightingale was whistling in a a very low voice, "Go! go in! take it!"

The white shirt appeared nearer and nearer to the pantry. The dark burdocks covered it no longer. On the threshold of the pantry was to be heard quick breathing from the weak breast of the child. A moment more the white shirt has vanished; there is only one naked foot outside the threshold. In vain, O wood-owl, dost thou fly once again and cry, "No! no!" Yanko is in the pantry.

The great frogs began to croak in the garden pond, as if frightened, but afterward grew silent. The nightingale ceased to sing, the burdocks to rustle. Meanwhile Yanko crept along silently and carefully, but all at once fear seized him. In the burdocks he felt at home, like a wild beast in a thicket; but now he was like a wild beast in a trap. His movements became hurried, his breath short and whistling; at the same time, darkness seized hold of him. A quiet summer lightning flashed between east and west, and lighted up once more the interior of the pantry, and Yanko on all fours with his head turned upward. But the lightning was quenched, a small cloud hid the moon, and nothing was to be seen or heard.

After a while a sound came out from the darkness, very low and complaining, as if some one had touched strings unguardedly, and on a sudden some rough, drowsy voice, coming out of the corner of the pantry, asked angrily, —

"Who is there?"

Yanko held his breath in his breast, but the rude voice inquires again, —

"Who is there?"

A match became visible on the wall; there was a light, and then — Oh, my God! curses, blows, the wailing of a child, and crying "Oh, for God's sake!" — the barking of dogs, moving of lights behind the window, a noise through the whole building!

The next day Yanko stood before the tribunal of the village mayor.

Was he to be tried as a criminal? Of course! The mayor and councilmen looked at him as he stood before them with his finger in his mouth, with staring and terrified eyes, small, poor, starved, beaten, not knowing where he was or what they wanted of him. How judge such a poor little misery, who was ten years of age, and barely able to stand on his legs? Send him to prison, — how help it? Still it was necessary to have some small mercy on children. Let the policeman take him and give him a flogging, so that he won't steal a second time, and that's the whole business.

It was indeed!

They called Stah, who was the village police.

"Take him and give him something for a keepsake."

Stah nodded his dull beastlike head, thrust Yanko under his arm as he would a cat, and took him out to the barn. The child, whether he failed to understand what the question was, or whether he was frightened — 't is enough that he uttered not a syllable; he merely stared like a bird. Did he know what they were doing with him? Only when Stah took the handful to the stable, stretched it on the ground, and raising the shirt from it struck a full blow, only then did Yanko scream, "Mamma!" and as long as Stah flogged him he cried, "Mamma! mamma!" but always lower and weaker, until after a certain blow the child called mamma no longer.

The poor broken fiddle!

Ai, stupid, angry Stah, who beats children that way? Besides, this one is small and weak, hardly living.

The mother came, took the little boy, but she had to

carry him home. The next day Yanko did not rise from the bed, and the third day, in the evening, he died quietly on the plank cot under hemp matting.

The swallows were twittering in the cherry-tree which grew at the cottage; the rays of the sun entered in through the window pane and colored with the brightness of gold the dishevelled hair of the little boy and his face in which not one drop of blood remained. That ray was as it were a road upon which the soul of the boy was to go away. It was well that it went by a broad shining road in the moment of death, for during life it went on a thorny one, truly. Meanwhile the emaciated breast moved with another breath, and the face of the child was as if absorbed in listening to the sounds of the village which came in through the open window. It was evening, so the girls coming back from hay-making were singing, "Oi, on the green field!" and from the stream came the playing of pipes. Yanko listened for the last time to the sounds of the village. On the matting lay the shingle fiddle at his side.

All at once the face of the dying boy lighted up, and from his whitening lips came out the whisper "Mamma!"

"What, my son?" answered the mother, whom tears were choking.

"Mamma, will the Lord God give me a real fiddle in heaven?"

"He will, my son, He will give thee one," answered the mother; but she could speak no longer, for suddenly in her hard breast burst the gathering sorrow, and groaning only, "O Jesus! O Jesus!" she fell with her face on a box, and began to wail as if she had lost her reason, or as a man wails who sees that he cannot wrest the beloved one from death.

In fact, she did not wrest him; for when she raised herself again she looked at the child. The eyes of the little musician were open, it is true, but fixed; his face was very dignified, gloomy, and rigid. The ray of the sun had gone also.

Peace to thee, Yanko.

. . . .

On the second day the master and mistress of the mansion returned to their residence from Italy, with their daughter and the cavalier who was paying court to her The cavalier said, —

"Quel beau pays que l'Italie !"

"And what a people of artists! On est heureux de chercher la-bas des talents et de les protéger," added the young lady.

The birches were murmuring above Yanko.

BARTEK THE VICTOR

BARTEK THE VICTOR.

I.

MY hero was Bartek Slovik; [1] but since he had the habit of staring when any one spoke to him, his neighbors called him Bartek the Starer. In truth he had little in common with the nightingale; on the contrary, his mental qualities and his real Homeric simplicity gained for him the nickname of Bartek the Stupid. The last name was the most popular, and without doubt is the only one that will pass into history, though Bartek had a fourth, an official name. Since the Polish words "chlovyek" [2] and "slovik" present no difference to the German ear, and since the Germans love to translate, in the name of civilization, barbarous Slav names into a more cultured language, the following conversation took place in its time while they were registering the army list : —

"What is thy name?" asked the officer of Bartek.

"Slovik."

"Shloik? Ach, ja! Gut!"

And the officer wrote down, "Mensch" (man).

Bartek came from the village of Pognembin; there are

---

[1] Slovik means in Polish "nightingale."

[2] Chlovyek (czlowiek) means "man." Owing to German incapacity to distinguish Slav sounds, the officer confounds the word which means nightingale with that which means man, and translates Slovik, nightingale, Batek's name, into Mensch, the German word for man.

very many villages of that name in the Principality of Poznan, and in other lands of the former Commonwealth. Besides his land, cottage, and two cows he had a pied horse, and a wife Magda.   Thanks to such a concurrence of circumstances, he could live quietly and according to the wisdom contained in the following lines : —

> " A horse a pied one, and a wife Magda,
>   What God is to give He will give anyway."

In fact, his life arranged itself completely as God gave, and when God gave war Bartek was grieved not a little. Notice came that he must join the regiment; he had to go from his cottage and land, and leave everything to the care of the woman.   The people in Pognembin were on the whole poor enough.   Bartek used to go to the mill to work in winter, and in that way helped his housekeeping; but what now ?   Who knows when the war with the French will be over ?   When `Magda read the ticket of summons, she began to curse : " May they — may they be blinded !   Though thou art stupid, Bartek, I am sorry to lose thee ; the French, too, will not let thee pass ; they will cut thy head off, or something."

Bartek felt that his wife spoke truly.   He feared the French like fire, and besides he was sorry to go.   What had the French done to him ?   Why go to that terrible, strange land, where there was not one soul friendly to him ?   In Pognembin life had seemed neither this nor that, nothing in particular; but when they commanded him to go, he saw for the first time that, people might say what they liked, but it was better in Pognembin than anywhere else.   There was no help though — such was his fate, he had to go.

Bartek embraced his wife, his ten-year old Franek ; then he spat, made the sign of the cross, went out of the

cottage, and Magda after him. They did not part with an
overflow of feeling. She and the boy sobbed. Bartek
repeated, " Now be quiet, now," and they found themselves
on the road. There they saw that the same visitation
had met all Pognembin. The whole village had come
out; the road was crowded with men summoned to the war.
They were going to the railroad station, and women, children, old men, and dogs were accompanying them. The
hearts of the summoned men were heavy. Pipes were
hanging from the mouths of only a few of the younger
ones; some were already drunk, to begin with; some were
singing, with hoarse voices, —

> " Skrynetski's hands and gold rings
>   Will not wield a sabre at the war."

A few Germans, too, of the Pognembin colonists were
singing from fear " Die Wacht am Rhein." All that
crowd, motley and many-colored, with the glittering
bayonets of police in the midst of it, was pushing forward
along the fences with cries, uproar, and hustling. The
women were holding their "soldier-boys" by the neck,
and weeping; one old woman, showing a yellow tooth,
shook her fist at something in space; another was
cursing, "May the Lord God pay you for our tears!"
Cries were heard of " Franek! Kasek! Jozek! farewell!"
Dogs are barking. The bell on the church is ringing.
The parish priest is reading prayers for the dying, for
not all who are going to the station will return from
it. War takes them all, but war will not give them all
back. The ploughs are rusting in the furrows, for Pognembin has declared war against France. Pognembin
cannot recognize the preponderance of Napoleon III., and
takes the cause of the Spanish succession to heart. The
sound of the bell conducts the crowd. which has come

out already from between the fences.   Figures pass; caps
and helmets fly from heads.   A golden dust rises on the
road, for the day is dry and sunny.   On both sides of
the way the ripening grain rustles with heavy head, and
bends beneath the light breeze, which blows mildly at
intervals.   In the blue sky the larks are soaring and
singing as if they had gone mad.

The station!   The crowds are still greater.   At the
station are men summoned from Upper Kryvda, Lower
Kryvda, from Vyvlashchyntse, from Nyedolya, from
Mizerov.   Movement, noise, disorder !   The walls of the
station are covered with proclamations.   War is present,
"in the name of God and the Fatherland."   The *Land-
wehr* will go to protect their native homes, their wives,
their children, their cottages, and fields.   The French, it
is clear, hold Pognembin in special hatred, as well as Upper
Kryvda, Lower Kryvda, Vyvlashchyntse, Nyedolya, and
Mizerov.   It seems so at least to those who read the proclamations.   New crowds are coming to the front of the
station.   In the hall the smoke of pipes fills the air and
hides the proclamations.   In the uproar it is difficult for
people to understand one another; everything is moving,
shouting, screaming.   On the platform are heard German
commands, the strong words of which have a peremptory,
brief, firm sound.

A bell is heard, a whistle! from a distance comes the
violent breath of the engine, — every moment nearer,
clearer.   It seems the war itself is approaching in person.

A second bell.   A quiver runs through every breast.
Some woman screams, " Yadom, Yadom !"   Evidently she
is calling her Adam.   But other women catch up the
word, and cry, " Yadan, Yadan !" (they are coming).   Some
voice more shrill than others adds, " Frantsuzy yadan !"
(the French are coming!) and in the twinkle of an eye a

panic seizes not only the women but the future heroes of Sedan. The crowd is stirred up. Meanwhile the train has stopped at the station. In all the windows uniforms and caps with red bands are visible. The troops are apparently as numerous as ants. In coal-cars sullen, long-bodied cannon seem black; on platforms a forest of bayonets is bristling. Evidently command has been given the soldiers to sing, for the whole train is just quivering from their strong, manly voices. A certain power and might issues from that train which is so long that its end is out of sight.

On the platform they are beginning to marshal the recruits; whoever has the chance takes farewell once again. Bartek, waving his paws like the wings of a wind-mill thrusts out his eyes.

"Now, Magda, farewell!"

"Oi, my poor fellow!"

"Thou wilt see me no more!"

"I shall see thee no more!"

"There is no help of any kind!"

"May the Mother of God guard and save thee!"

"Farewell! keep the cottage."

The woman caught him by the neck, with weeping.

"May God go with thee."

The last moment has come. For a while the whining and weeping, and lamenting of women drown everything. "Farewell! Farewell!" But now the soldiers are separated from the crowd, they are already a dark, dense mass which forms into squares and rectangles, and moves with the regularity and precision of a machine. The command comes, "Seats!" The squares and rectangles break in the centre, move toward the cars in narrow lines, and vanish inside them. In the distance the engine whistles, and puffs forth rolls of blue smoke.

Now it pants like a dragon, and ejects streams of vapor. The lamentation of women reaches the highest pitch. Some cover their eyes with their aprons; others stretch their hands toward the cars. With sobbing voices they repeat the names of their husbands and sons.

"Farewell, Bartek!" cries Magda from below; "and go not where thou'rt not sent. May the Mother of God — Farewell! O God help us!"

"But take care of the cottage!" calls Bartek.

The line quivers suddenly; the cars strike one another, and move.

"But remember that thou hast a wife and a child!" screams Magda, running after the train. "Farewell, in the name of the Father, Son, and Holy Ghost. Farewell!"

The train moves with increasing rapidity, bearing warriors from Pognembin, from both Kryvdas, from Nyedolya, and Mizerov.

II.

On one side, Magda is returning to Pognembin with a crowd of women, and crying; on the other, the train is rushing forth into the blue distance, bristling with bayonets, and on it is Bartek. The end of the blue distance is not to be seen. Pognembin is barely visible. One poplar-tree stands there looking gray, and the church-tower shines in gold, for the sun is playing on it. Soon the poplar has vanished, and the golden cross seems a mere shining point. While that point was shining, Bartek gazed at it; but when it also vanished, there was no end to the man's sorrow. A great faintness seized him, and he felt that he was lost. He began then to look at the corporal, for besides God there was no one else above him. What will happen now to him? The corporal's head is there to answer that question. Bartek himself knows nothing, understands nothing. The corporal sits on a bench, holds his musket, and smokes a pipe. The smoke, as if a cloud, shades every little while his serious and anxious face. Not Bartek's eyes alone are looking on that face; all eyes are looking on it from every corner of the car. In Pognembin or Kryvda every Bartek or Voitek is his own master, each must think of himself for himself; but now the corporal is there for that purpose. If he commands them to look toward the right, they look toward the right; if he commands them to look toward the left, they look toward the left. Each one asks him with a glance, " Well, what will happen to us?" and he himself knows as much as they, and would be glad also if a superior were to give him command or explanation in this regard. Besides, the men are afraid to ask in words, for it is war time, with the complete apparatus of courts-martial. What is permitted and what not is unknown,—at least to them; and they are alarmed by the sound of expressions such as " Kriegsgericht" (court-martial), which they do not understand well, but fear all the more.

At the same time they feel that this corporal is more needful to them now than at the manœuvres near Poznan, for he is the only one who knows everything, — he thinks for them; and without him not a stir. Meanwhile the musket has grown burdensome to the corporal, for he throws it to Bartek to hold. Bartek seizes the gun hurriedly, holds his breath, stares and looks at the corporal as at a rainbow; but he gains little comfort from that.

Oi! there must be bad news, for the corporal looks as if taken from a cross. At the stations there are songs and shouting; the corporal commands, hurries about, scolds, so as to exhibit himself to his superiors; but when

18

the train moves, all are silent, and so is he. For him, too, the world has two sides at present, one clear and understandable, — that is his cottage, his wife, and the feather-bed; the other, dark, perfectly dark, — that is France and the war. His ardor, like the ardor of the whole army, would be glad to borrow its gait from the crab. Their courage stirred the warriors of Pognembin the more evidently that it was sitting not in them, but on their shoulders. And since every soldier carried a knapsack, a cloak, and other military baggage, they all were uneasy.

Meanwhile the train roared, snorted, and flew into the distance. At every station new cars and engines were attached. At every station they saw only helmets, cannon, horses, the bayonets of infantry, and the flags of Ulans. A clear evening came down gradually. The sun lost its rays in a purple twilight; high in the heavens droves of light small clouds were moving with edges darkened by the sunset. The train ceased at last to take people at the stations; it only rattled, and flew farther into that redness as into a sea of blood. From the open car in which Bartek was sitting with the men of Pognembin, they saw villages, settlements, and towns, the towers on the churches, storks bent like hooks, standing on one leg at their nests, single cottages, cherry-gardens, — all gleamed in passing, and all were red. The soldiers began to whisper to one another, the more boldly that the corporal, having put his knapsack under his head, had fallen asleep, with his porcelain pipe between his teeth. Voitek Gvizdala, a man from Pognembin, sitting next to Bartek, pushed him with his elbow, —

"Bartek, but listen!"

Bartek turned his face toward him, with anxious staring eyes.

"Why look like a calf going to the slaughter?" whispered Voitek; "and thou, poor fellow, art going surely to the slaughter."

"Oi, oi!" groaned Bartek.

"Art afraid?" asked Voitek.

"Why shouldn't I be afraid?"

The twilight had become ruddier. Voitek stretched his hand toward it, and whispered on, —

"Seest thou that brightness? Know'st, stupid fellow, what that is? That is blood. This is Poland, our country. Dost understand? But there, far away where it shines so, that is France."

"But shall we get there soon?"

"Art in a hurry? They say 'tis terribly far away. But never fear: the French will come to meet us."

Bartek began to work heavily with his Pognembin head; after a while he asked, —

"Voitek!"

"What?"

"Well, for example, what kind of people are the French?"

Here Voitek's learning saw on a sudden in front of it an abyss into which it might plunge head-foremost more easily than fly back again. He knew that the French are French. He had heard something about them from older men, who said that they always conquered everybody; finally, he knew that they are some kind of very foreign people; but how was he to explain this to Bartek so that he might know how foreign they are? First of all he repeated the question, —

"What kind of people are they?"

"That's it."

Three nations were known to Voitek: in the middle were the Poles; on one side the "Moskale" (Muscovites);

on the other, the Germans, — but various kinds of Germans. Preferring to be clear rather than accurate, he said, —

"What kind of people are the French? How can I tell thee? they are just such Germans, only worse."

And Bartek in answer to that: "Oh, the carrion!"

Hitherto he had had only one feeling touching the French, — a feeling of indescribable fear; now that Prussian *Landwehrmann* began to feel toward them a rather distinct patriotic dislike. Still he did not understand it all clearly yet; hence he inquired again, —

"But will Germans fight against Germans?"

Here Voitek, like a second Socrates, determined to proceed by the method of comparison, and answered, —

"But does not thy Lysek fight with my Burek?"

Bartek opened his mouth, and looked awhile at his master, —

"Oh, that is true."

"Besides, the Austrians are Germans," said Voitek; "and have not our people fought with them? Old Sversch said that when he was at the war, Steinmetz shouted to them, 'Forward, boys, against the Germans!' But it won't be so easy with the French!"

"Oh, for God's sake!"

"The French have never lost a war. The man that they catch cannot get away, never fear. Every man of them is equal to two or three on our side; and they have beards like Jews. Sometimes they are as black as the Devil. At sight of such people commit thyself to God."

"Well, but why do we go against them?" asked Bartek, in desperation.

That philosophic question was not so stupid as it seemed to Voitek, who, under the evident influence of official inspiration, hastened with an answer, —

"I should rather not go against them. But if we don't go to them they'll come here. There is no help for it. Hast thou read what was printed? They hate our men terribly. People say that they are so hungry for the land here because they want to smuggle *vodka* out of the kingdom, and the Government will not let them; and that's the cause of the war. Well, dost understand?"

"Why shouldn't I understand?" said Bartek, with resignation.

Voitek continued, "And they are as greedy for women as a dog for cheese."

"In that case they would n't let Magda pass?"

"They would n't let even old women pass."

"Oh!" cried Bartek, in such a tone as if he wished to say, "If that is true I'll fight!"

And, in fact, it seemed to him that that was too much. Let them smuggle *vodka* from the kingdom, if they like; but let them keep away from Magda. Now my Bartek began to look on the whole war from the point of view of his own interest, and to feel a certain consolation in the thought that so many troops and cannon were moving forward to defend Magda, who was threatened by the seductions of the French. His fists were clinched involuntarily, and fear of the French was mingled in his mind with hatred of them. He came to the conviction that there was no escape; it was necessary to go.

Meanwhile the brightness of the sky had vanished. It was dark. The car, moving on rails of unequal elevation, began to sway greatly, and, in keeping with its motion, the helmets and bayonets nodded to the left and the right.

One hour passed, and a second. From the engine were showered millions of sparks, which crossed one another in the darkness like long golden streaks and

small serpents.   Bartek was unable to sleep for a long
time.   As those sparks shot through the air, so did
thoughts in his mind touching the war, Magda, Pognembin, the French, and the Germans.   It seemed to him
that even had he wished he could not raise himself from
the bench on which he was sitting.   He fell asleep; but
with an unwholesome half-sleep.   Immediately visions
flew to him; first of all he saw his Lysek fighting his
neighbor's Burek, till the dogs' hearts were flying in
them.   He grasps after his stick to stop them, but sees
all at once something else: at Magda's side a Frenchman
is sitting, black as the holy earth; and the satisfied
Magda is laughing, and showing her teeth.   Other Frenchmen are sneering at Bartek, and pointing at him.   Of
course it is the engine puffing; but it seems to him
the Frenchmen are calling, "Magda! Magda! Magda!"
Bartek screams, "Shut your snouts, you scoundrels! let the
woman go!"   But they cry, "Magda! Magda! Magda!"
Lysek and Burek are barking; all Pognembin is shouting,
"Don't give up the woman!"   Is Bartek tied, or what?
He struggles, pulls, his fetters break.   Bartek seizes the
Frenchmen by the head, and all at once —

All at once he is shaken by a violent pain as from a
heavy blow.   Bartek wakes and springs to his feet.   The
whole car is roused.   All ask what has happened.   But
poor Bartek has caught the corporal by the beard.
Now he is standing erect as a post, two fingers at his
temple, and the officer is waving his hand, and shouting
as if mad, —

"Ach Sie!   Dummes Vieh aus der Polakei!   Hau' ich
den Lümmel in die Fresse, das ihm die Zähne sektionen-
weise aus dem Maule herausfliegen werden!   [Oh, stupid
beast from Poland!   I will whack the clown in the snout
so that the teeth will fly out of his mouth in sections!]"

The corporal is hoarse from rage; but Bartek stands unmoved, with his fingers at his temple. The soldiers are biting their lips so as not to laugh; but they are afraid, for out of the corporal's mouth are falling yet the last arrows: "Ein polnischer Ochse! Ochse aus Podolien! (Polish ox, ox from Podolia!)"

At last everything is quiet. Bartek sits down on his old place again. He feels that his cheeks begin to tingle somehow, and the engine as if in spite repeats continually:

"Magda! Magda! Magda!"

He felt also some kind of great sorrow.

III.

MORNING! A scattered pale light shines on faces which are sleepy and weary from lack of rest. The soldiers are sleeping on the bench, without order; some with their heads on their breasts, others with their heads dropped back. The morning comes, and fills the whole world with rosy light. It is fresh and wholesome. The soldiers wake up. The bright morning brings out of shadow and mist a certain country unknown to them. Hei! but where now is Pognembin, where Upper and Lower Kryvda, where Mizerov? Here it is strange, and everything is different. The high land round about is shaded with oaks; in the valleys the houses are covered with red roofs, with black milkwort on the walls,— houses beautiful as palaces, grown around with grape-vines. Here and there are churches with pointed towers, here and there mill chimneys with plumes of rosy smoke. But somehow, it is crowded; there is a lack of grain-fields. The people are numerous as ants. Villages and

towns shoot by. The train, without stopping, passes
a number of smaller stations. Something must have
happened, for everywhere crowds are to be seen. The
sun comes up slowly from behind the hills; therefore,
one and another Matsek begin their "Our Father"
aloud. Others follow their example. The first rays
put their glitter on the prayerful and serious faces of
the men.

Meanwhile the train stops at the main station. A
throng of people surrounds it at once. News from the
seat of war, a victory! a victory! The despatches had
come some hours before. All were expecting defeat, and
when news of success waked them, their joy knew no
bounds. People half dressed left their beds and hurried
to the station. From some roofs flags are waving already,
and in all hands are handkerchiefs. They bring beer to
the cars, tobacco, and cigars. Their enthusiasm is beyond
speech, faces are radiant. "Die Wacht am Rhein" is
roaring like a storm. Some are weeping, others fall
into one another's embraces. "*Unser Fritz* has crushed
them to pieces! cannon and flags are captured!" With
noble enthusiasm the crowd give the soldiers everything
they have. Joy enters the hearts of the soldiers, and
they begin to sing too. The cars are trembling from the
deep voices of the men, and the crowds listen with wonder to the words of songs which they do not understand.
The Pognembin men are singing, "Bartosh! Bartosh!
O lose not thy hope." "Die Polen! Die Polen!" repeat
the crowd by way of explanation, and gather around
the cars, wondering at the appearance of the soldiers,
and at the same time strengthening themselves by
relating anecdotes of the terrible bravery of those Polish
regiments.

Bartek has swollen cheeks, which with his yellow

mustaches, staring eyes, and enormous bony form make him terrible. They look on him as a special beast. What defenders the Germans have! He will fix the French! Bartek smiles with satisfaction, for he too is glad that they have beaten the French, who at least will not come to -Pognembin to lead Magda astray; they won't take his land. He smiles then; but since his face pains him greatly, he twists it withal, and in truth he is terrible. But he eats with the appetite of an Homeric hero; pea-sausage and goblets of beer vanish in his mouth as in a cavern. They give him cigars, *pfennigs;* he takes everything.

"They are a good sort of people, these German fellows," says he to Voitek; but after a while he adds, "But seest thou they have beaten the French?"

The sceptical Voitek casts a shadow on his joy. Voitek is a Cassandra-like prophet.

"The French always let themselves be beaten in the beginning so as to lead men astray, but afterward when they go at it the chips fly."

Voitek did not know that the greater part of Europe shared his opinion; and still less did he know that all Europe was mistaken as well as he.

They went farther. Every house within eyesight was covered with flags. At some stations they were detained longer, for every place was filled with trains. Troops were hastening from all parts of Germany to strengthen their victorious brethren. The trains were adorned with green crowns. The Ulans held on their lances bouquets of flowers, given them on the road. Among the Ulans the majority were Poles also. Cries were heard often from the cars, —

"How are ye, boys? and whither is God leading you?"

Sometimes from a train flying past on a neighboring track came the well-known song:

> "From the other side of Sandomir
> The maiden calls her soldier —"

And then Bartek and his comrades catch up:

> "Oh, soldier, come and love me.
> I have not eaten yet — May God reward thee!"

In the same degree in which all had left Pognembin in sorrow were they now full of spirit and enthusiasm. The first train with the first wounded coming from France destroyed that good feeling, however. The train with the wounded halts at Deutz, and halts long to let those pass who are hastening to the field of combat. But before all can pass the bridge at Cologne some hours are consumed. Bartek rushes with others to look at the sick and wounded. Some are lying in covered cars, others for want of room in open ones, and the latter could be seen easily. At the first glance the heroic courage of Bartek flew out again to his shoulder.

"Come here, Voitek," cries he, with terror; "but see how many men these French have spoiled!" And there is something to look at! — pale suffering faces, some black from powder or pain, bespattered with blood. In answer to the general rejoicing these give only groans. Some of them curse the war of French against Germans. Parched and dry lips cry every moment for water; eyes gaze as in madness. Here and there among the wounded is to be seen the stiffened face of one dying, — sometimes calm, with blue around the eyes, sometimes distorted from convulsions, with wild stare and grinning teeth. Bartek sees for the first time the bloody fruits of war. A new chaos rises in his head; he looks as if stunned, and stands in the throng with mouth open; they knock

against him on every side; a policeman pushes him with
the butt of his musket in the shoulder. He seeks Voitek
with his eyes, finds him, and says, —

"Voitek, God save us! oh!"

"It will be that way with thee, too."

"Jesus Mary! And so people kill each other like
that! Why, when a man in a village strikes another the
police take him to the court and punish him."

"That may be; but now the best man is he who kills
most people. Didst think, stupid fellow, that thou
wouldst fire off powder as at the manœuvres or at a
mark, — not at men?"

Here, there was an evident difference between theory
and practice. Our Bartek was a soldier however. He
had been at manœuvres and musters, had fired guns, and
knew that war was for men to kill one another; but now
when he saw the blood of the wounded, the misery of
war, he felt so sick and faint that he could hardly stand
on his feet. He gained new respect for the French, which
decreased only when he crossed from Deutz to Cologne.
At the central station he saw prisoners for the first
time. They were surrounded by a multitude of soldiers,
and by people who looked at them with feelings of
importance, but still without hatred. Bartek pressed
through the crowd, pushing people aside with his elbow;
he looked at the car and was astonished.

The crowd of French infantrymen in torn cloaks, small,
dirty, suffering, filled the car as closely as herrings fill a
cask. Many of them stretched out their hands for the
scant gifts which the crowd bestowed on them so far as
the guards did not prevent. Bartek, according to what
he had heard from Voitek, had an altogether different
picture in his mind of the French. Courage returned
from his shoulder to his breast again. He looked around
for Voitek. Voitek was at his side.

"What didst thou tell me?" asked Bartek. "They are poor little fellows. If I should knock the head off one of them the life would go out of three others."

"They must have wasted away somehow," said Voitek, equally disenchanted.

"In what language are they chattering?"

"Be sure 't is not Polish."

Satisfied in this regard Bartek went farther along the cars.

"Miserable fellows!" said he, finishing his review of soldiers of the line.

But in the next cars sat Zouaves. These gave Bartek more to think of. Since they sat in covered cars it was impossible to determine whether each was as big as two or three common men; but through the windows could be seen the long beards and warlike, serious faces of old soldiers with dark complexions, and eyes gleaming terribly. Bartek's courage went again to his shoulder.

"Those are more dangerous," whispered he, as if fearing that they might hear him.

"Thou hast not seen those yet who would not let themselves be taken," said Voitek.

"God guard us!"

"Thou wilt see them!"

When they had looked at the Zouaves, they went farther. At the next car Bartek sprang back as if burned.

"Oh, rescue! Voitek, save me!"

In the open window was visible the dark, almost black, face of a Turko, with the whites of his eyes turned out. He must have been wounded, for his face was distorted from suffering.

"What is that?" asked Voitek.

"That is the Evil One, not a soldier. God be merciful to me a sinner!"

" But look at him; what teeth he has ! "

"Oh, devil take him ! I will not look at-him."

Bartek was silent, but after a while he asked, —

" Voitek ! "

" What ? "

" If such a one were christened, would n't it help ? "

" Pagans have no understanding of the holy faith."

The order was given to take seats. After a while the
train moved. When it grew dark, Bartek saw before him
continually the black face of the Turko and the terrible
whites of his eyes. From the feelings which at that
moment possessed this warrior of Pognembin, it was
not possible to prophesy much concerning his future
exploits.

IV.

AN intimate part in the general engagement at Gravelotte convinces Bartek at first of this only, — that in a
battle there is something to stare at, but nothing to do.
To begin with, he and his regiment are commanded to
stand with grounded arms at the foot of a hill covered
with grape-vines. From a distance cannon are playing ;
near by cavalry regiments are flying past with a thunder
from which the ground trembles ; now pennons are glittering, now the swords of cuirassiers. On the hill through
the blue sky grenades fly hissing in the form of white
cloudlets ; smoke fills the air, and hides the horizon. It
seems that the battle, like a storm, will go past at the
sides ; but doubt does not last long.

After a time certain wonderful movements rise around
Bartek's regiment. Other regiments begin to take their
places near it ; and in the interval between them cannon are swept in with all horse-speed, unlimbered in a
flash, and their jaws turned toward the hill-top. The

whole valley is filled with troops. Every place is thundering with commands; adjutants are flying. But our men in the ranks are whispering one to another, " Oi, we shall catch it, we shall!" or they ask one another with alarm, "Is it beginning?" — "Surely it is." Now comes uncertainty, a riddle, — maybe death. In the smoke which covers the hill-top something is seething and rattling terribly. Nearer and nearer are heard the deep roar of cannon and the rattling of musketry. From a distance comes, as it were, some undefined crashing; those are the *mitrailleuses*. Suddenly. when the newly-placed cannon roar, the earth and the air tremble together. Before Bartek's regiment there is a terrible hissing. They look: something is flying bright as a rose, like a cloudlet, and in that cloudlet something is hissing, laughing, gnashing its teeth, neighing, and howling. The men cry, "Grenade! grenade!" Then that bird of war, moving like a whirlwind, approaches, falls, bursts! A dreadful roar tears the ears, — an outburst as if the world were falling, and a blow as if from a wind-stroke. Disorder in the ranks standing near the cannon, a cry, and a command, "Attention!" Bartek stands in the first rank, his gun at his shoulder, his head erect, his beard motionless; therefore his teeth are not chattering. It is not permitted to tremble, it is not permitted to fire. Stand! Wait! The second grenade comes, the third, the fourth, the tenth! The wind blows the smoke away from the hill. The French have driven from it the Prussian batteries, have placed there their own, which are vomiting fire now into the valley. Every moment long white darts of smoke are shooting out of the vineyard. The infantry, under cover of the cannon, are descending lower and lower, so as to open a musketry-fire. Now they are perfectly visible; for the wind has

borne away the smoke. Has the vineyard bloomed with
poppies? No, those are the red caps of infantry. At
once they disappear among the tall grape-vines; they
are not to be seen, — only here and there a tri-colored
flag appears. The musketry-fire begins, — quick, feverish,
irregular; it bursts forth suddenly every moment in new
places. Above that fire, howling continually, come the
grenades, crossing one another in the air. On the hill
shouts burst forth, which are answered in the valley by
German hurrahs. Cannon from the valley roar uninter-
ruptedly. The regiment stands there immovable.

The circle of fire begins, however, to enclose it from
the flanks. Bullets from afar buzz like horse-flies or
shoot past with a terrible whistle. Every moment there
are more of them, — now they are whistling around the
heads, noses, eyes, shoulders of the men; thousands of
them, millions of them are coming. It is a marvel that
a man is left standing. All at once behind Bartek some
one groans, "Jesus!" then the command is heard, "Close!"
again a groan, "Jesus!" after that "Close!" At last
there is one unbroken groan; the commands come more
quickly; the ranks close; the whistling is more frequent;
then unceasing and awful. The slain are dragged out by
the feet. The judgment of God is there present.

"Art afraid?" asks Voitek.

"Why should n't I be?" answers our hero, with chattering teeth.

And both stand there, Bartek and Voitek, and it does
not even occur to them that it is possible to run. They
were ordered to stand; and that is the end of it! Bartek
did not tell the truth. He was not so much afraid as
thousands of others would have been in his place. Discipline lorded it over his imagination, and his imagination
did not paint to him the situation in its dreadful reality.

Still Bartek thought that they would kill him, and he conveyed that thought to Voitek.

"There will be no hole in heaven if such a fool is killed," answered Voitek, with vexation.

These words pacify Bartek considerably. It seems to him that the main question for him is whether there will be a hole in heaven. Pacified in this regard, he stands patiently; only feels terribly hot, and the sweat streams over his face. Meanwhile the fire becomes so murderous that the ranks are melting before their eyes. There is no one to drag away the killed and the wounded; the groans of the dying are mingled with the whistling of missiles and the roar of musketry. By the movement of the tri-colored flag it is clear that the infantry concealed in the vineyard are coming nearer and nearer. The crowds of *mitrailleuses* are decimating the ranks, which despair is now seizing.

But in the sounds of that despair is felt the muttering of impatience and rage. If they are commanded to advance they will go like a storm. Only they cannot stand in one place. Some soldier tears his cap from his head on a sudden, hurls it with all force to the ground, and says, —

"One death to the goat!"

Bartek found again a known consolation in these words, so that he ceased almost to fear. For if death must come once, it is no great question. That peasant philosophy is better than any other, since it gives consolation. Bartek knew before, of course, that death must come once; but it was pleasant for him to hear this, and to have complete certainty, especially since the battle had begun to turn into utter defeat. Think of it, — that regiment, without firing a shot, is already half annihilated! Crowds of soldiers from other scattered regiments

are rushing past in disorder; but these men from Pognembin, from Upper and Lower Kryvda and Mizerov,
held by the iron discipline of Prussia, are standing still.
But in their ranks a certain hesitation is felt. In a
moment the bonds of discipline will burst. The ground
under their feet is growing soft and slippery from blood,
the raw smell of which is mixed with the smell of the
powder-smoke. In certain places the ranks cannot close,
for corpses block the way. At the feet of those men
who are still standing, the other half of the regiment is
lying in blood, in groans, in convulsions, dying or in the
grasp of death. Air fails the breath. A murmur is
rising in the ranks, —

"They have brought us here to be slaughtered!"

"No one will go from this place."

"Still, Polnisches Vieh!" sounds the voice of an officer.

"It is well for you behind my collar!"

"Steht der Kerl da!"

Suddenly some voice begins to speak, —

"Under Thy protection — "

Bartek accompanies at once, "We take refuge, Holy
Mother of God!"

And soon a chorus of Polish voices is calling out on
that field of destruction to the Patroness of Chenstohova,
"Reject not our prayers!" And from under their feet
groans accompany them, "O Mary, O Mary!" And she
heard them evidently, for that moment an adjutant
rushes up on a foaming horse. "To the attack! Hurrah!
Forward!"

The ridge of bayonets is lowered suddenly; the rank
stretches in a long line, and rushes toward the hill, seeking with the bayonet those enemies which it could not
find with the eye. But from the foot of the hill our men
are divided yet by two hundred yards, and this distance

19

must be crossed under a murderous fire. Will they not
be slaughtered to the last man, or will they not run?
They may be exterminated; but they will not draw back,
for the Prussian commander knows what note to play for
the attack. Amid the bellowing of cannon, amid musketry-fire, smoke, confusion, and groans, louder than all
the trumpets and drums is rising to heaven the hymn at
which every drop of blood dances in their bosoms.
"Poland is not lost!" Hurrah! Not lost! "While we
are living!" answer the Matseks. Enthusiasm seizes
them; a flame is beating in their faces. They go like a
storm over prostrate bodies of men and horses, over fragments of cannon. They perish, but sweep forward with
shouting and singing. They have reached already the
edge of the vineyard. They vanish among the vines;
but the hymn rises. At once their bayonets are gleaming.
On the hill the fire is seething still more terribly. In the
valley the trumpets are playing continually. The French
discharges become quicker and quicker, feverish, and on
a sudden are silent.

Down in the valley Steinmetz — that old wolf of war —
lights a porcelain pipe, and speaks in tones of satisfaction, —

"Only give them that music! They have got there,
bold fellows!" In fact, the next instant one of the tri-
colored standards waving proudly springs up, stoops, and
vanishes.

"They are not joking!" said Steinmetz.

The trumpets play the same hymn again. Another
Poznan regiment rushes on to help the first. In the
thicket a battle with bayonets rages up.

O Muse! sing now, of my Bartek, that posterity may
know what he did! In his heart fear, terror, impatience,
despair, were blended in the single feeling of rage; and
when he heard that music, every nerve in him was as

rigid as steel wire. His hair was on end ; sparks flew
from his eyes. He forgot the world, — forgot that death
must come once ; and seizing in his mighty paws the
musket, he ran on with the others. When he had run to
the hill, he fell to the ground at least ten times, bruised
his nose, covered himself with earth and with the blood
which was running from his nose, and hurried forward,
mad, panting, catching the air with open mouth. He
was staring his eyes out to see in the thicket at the
soonest some Frenchman ; and at last he saw three at
once at a standard. They were Turkos. But do you
think that Bartek drew back ? No! he would have
taken Lucifer himself by the horns at that moment. He
rushed at the three men, and they with a howl rushed at
him ; two bayonets, like two stings, are already touching
his breast ; but my Bartek takes his musket like a club
by the small end, whirls it, strikes. A terrible cry answers him, a groan, — and two black bodies are quivering
on the ground.

That moment about ten comrades ran with assistance
to the third, who was holding a flag. Bartek sprang like
a fury on all at once. They fired ; there was a flash and
a report, and at the same time in the rolls of smoke
thundered the hoarse bellow of Bartek, —

"Ye have missed ! "

And again the musket in his hand described a terrible
half-circle ; again groans answered his blows. The Turkos
drew back in terror at sight of this giant, wild with rage ;
and whether Bartek heard wrongly, or they cried out
something in Arabic, 't is enough that it seemed to him
distinctly that from their broad lips came the cry, —

" Magda ! Magda ! "

" Ye want Magda ! " howled Bartek, and with one
spring he was in the midst of the enemy.

Happily a number of Matseks and Voiteks and other Barteks hurried up in that moment to aid him. In the midst of the thicket of vines a battle sprang up, hand to hand, close, which was accompanied by the crash of muskets, the whistling of nostrils, and the feverish puffing of the combatants. Bartek raged like a storm. Scorched with smoke, covered with blood, more like a beast than a man, caring for nothing, — he overturned enemies with every blow, broke muskets, smashed heads His hands moved with the terrible swiftness of a machine scattering destruction. He rushed to the standard-bearer, seized him with iron fingers by the throat. The eyes of the standard-bearer were bursting from his head, his face was blue, he coughed, and his hands dropped the staff.

"Hurrah!" cried Bartek; and raising the flag, he waved it in the air.

General Steinmetz saw from the valley that rising and falling standard; but he could see it only during one twinkle of an eye, for in the next twinkle Bartek, with that same standard, crushed in some head covered with a cap in gold lace.

Meanwhile his comrades had rushed ahead; Bartek was left for one instant alone. He tore off the flag, hid it in his bosom, and, seizing the staff with both hands, hurried after his comrades. Crowds of Turkos, howling with unhuman voices, rushed to the cannon standing on the summit of the hill; after them rushed the Poles, shouting, chasing, crushing them with gun-stocks, and stabbing with bayonets.

The Zouaves, standing at the guns, greeted pursuers and pursued with musketry-fire.

"Hurrah!" cried Bartek.

The Poles rushed to the cannon. A new battle rose, hand to hand. At this moment the second Pognem-

bin regiment came to support the first. The flag-staff
in Bartek's powerful paws was turned this time into a
kind of infernal flail. Every blow of it opened a free
road in the dense ranks of the Frenchmen. Fear began
to seize the Zouaves and the Turkos. In the place
where Bartek was fighting they fled. Bartek was the
first to sit on a cannon, as he would on his Pognembin
mare.

But before the soldiers had time to see him there he
was sitting on a second one, where he overturned the
flag bearer with his flag.

"Hurrah, Bartek!" repeated the soldiers.

The victory was complete. All the *mitrailleuses* were
captured. The fleeing infantry came upon a new Prussian regiment on the other side of the hill, and laid down
their arms.

Bartek in the pursuit captured a third flag. It was
necessary to see him when, wearied, covered with sweat
and blood, puffing like a blacksmith's bellows, he came
down with the others from the hill, bearing on his
shoulders three flags. The Frenchmen! hei! what had
he done with them? At his side walked the torn and
slashed Voitek. Bartek said to him:

"What didst thou say to me? They are only worms,
there is no strength in their bones. They scratched me
and thee like cats, but that is all; and when I struck a
man he went to the ground."

"Who knew that thou wert so venomous?" answered
Voitek, who had seen Bartek's deeds, and began to look
at him now with different eyes altogether.

But who had not seen those deeds? History, the
whole regiment, most of the officers, — all looked now
with wonder on that gigantic fellow with his thin yellow
mustaches and staring eyes.

"Ach! Sie verfluchter Polake (eh! cursed Pole)!"
said the major himself, and took him by the ear. And
Bartek showed his back teeth with delight. When the
regiment stood in line again at the foot of the hill, the
major pointed him out to the colonel and the colonel to
Steinmetz himself.

Steinmetz looked at the flags and gave command to
take them; then he began to look at Bartek. My Bartek
stretches out like a string again and presents arms; but
the old general looks at him and shakes his head with
satisfaction. At last he begins to say something to the
colonel. . The word *Unter-officier* (Under-officer) was
heard distinctly.

"Zu dumm, Excellenz (too stupid, your Excellency),"
answered the major.

"Let us try," said his Excellency, and turning his horse
approached Bartek.

Bartek himself knew not what was coming to him, —
a thing unheard of in the Prussian army: a general
speaks to a soldier! His Excellency does it the more
easily since he knows Polish. Besides, that soldier has
captured three flags and two cannon.

"From what place art thou?" asked the general.

"From Pognembin," answered Bartek.

"Well. And thy name?"

"Bartek Slovik."

"Mensch (man)," explained the major, who stood behind his Excellency.

"*Mens!*" repeated Bartek.

"Knowst why thou art beating the French?"

"I know, Tselentsiyo (Excellency)."

"Tell me."

Bartek began to stutter: "For — for —"

On a sudden the words of Voitek came by good luck

to his memory; he blurted them out quickly so as not to misplace them, —

"Because they are Germans too, — only worse, the carrion!"

The face of the old Excellency began to quiver as if he were about to burst into laughter. After a moment however he turned to the major and said, —

"You were right."

My Bartek, self-satisfied, stood straight as a string.

"Who won the battle to-day?" asked the general again.

"I, Tselentsiyo," answered Bartek, without hesitation.

The face of the general began to quiver again.

"True, true; and here is thy reward."

The old warrior unfastened the iron cross from his own breast, then bent and fastened it to Bartek. The good-humor of the general in a perfectly natural way was reflected on the faces of the colonel, the majors, the captains, and down to the corporals. When the general was gone, the colonel on his part gave ten thalers to Bartek, the major five, and so on. All repeat to him, laughing, that he had won the battle. In consequence of this Bartek was in the seventh heaven.

A wonderful thing, Voitek was the only man not very much pleased with our hero!

In the evening when they had taken their places at the fire and the noble countenance of Bartek was stuffed with pea-sausage as tightly as the sausage itself was stuffed with peas, Voitek called out with a tone of resignation, —

"Oh, thou, Bartek, art stupid, oh, stupid!"

"But why?" asked Bartek, through his sausage.

"Why, man, didst thou tell the general that the French were Germans?"

"But thou didst say so thyself."

"But thou shouldst know that the general and officers are Germans themselves.

"But what of that?"

Voitek began somehow to stutter something,—"Though they are Germans that is not to be said to them, for it is awkward."

"But I said that about the French, not about them."

"Ei, even if thou didst, still—"

Voitek stopped suddenly. Clearly he wished himself too to say something else,—he wished to explain to Bartek that in presence of the German it was not right to speak ill of Germans; but somehow his tongue became twisted.

V.

SOMETIME after, the Royal Prussian mail brought to Pognembin the following letter,—

MOST BELOVED MAGDA,—May Jesus Christ be praised and His Holy Mother! What is to be heard at home? It is well for thee in the cottage under the feathers, and I here fighting terribly. We were around the great fortress of Metz, and I so pounded the French that all the cavalry and infantry were astonished; and the general himself was astonished and said that I won the battle, and he gave me a cross. Now the officers and under-officers respect me greatly, and do not beat me on the snout much. After that we marched on, and there was a second battle; but I have forgotten how the place is called; and I fought also and took a fourth flag, and I seized and took captive the greatest colonel of cuirassiers. The under-officer advises me to write a petition and ask to be left here when our regiments are sent home. In war there is no place to sleep, but all a man can hold to eat; and there is wine in this

country everywhere, for the people are rich. When we
burned a village we did n't spare the children or women,
and I did like the rest. A church was burned to the
ground, for the French are Catholics, and not a few people
were burned. We are going now against the Kaiser himself, and there will be an end of the war; but do thou take
care of the cottage and Franek. If not, when I come home
I 'll so fix thee that thou wilt not know who I am. I
commit thee to God.

BARTEK SLOVIK.

Bartek had got a taste for war, evidently, and began
to look at it as his own special craft. He had gained
great confidence in himself, and went now to battle as
if to some work in Pognembin. After every engagement
medals and crosses flew to his breast; and though he
was not made an under-officer, he was held by all to be
the first soldier in the regiment. He was always obedient as before, and possessed the blind bravery of a man
who cannot estimate danger. His valor did not come
now, as in the first moments, from rage. The source of
it now was military practice, and faith in himself. Besides, his gigantic strength endured all hardships, marching and watching. Men perished around him, — he
alone endured without exhaustion; only he grew fiercer,
and became more and more a stern Prussian man-at-arms.
He began not only to beat the French, but to hate them.
His other ideas also were changed. He became a soldier-
patriot, and gave blind worship to his leaders. In the
next letter he wrote to Magda, —

"Voitek was torn into two pieces; but such is war, thou
knowest. Besides, he was a fool, for he said that the
French were Germans, while they are French, and the
Germans are our people."

Magda in answer to both letters railed at him as follows, —

MOST BELOVED BARTEK, — We were married before the holy altar! May God punish thee! Thou art a fool thyself, Pagan, for in company with Chestnuts thou art murdering a Catholic people. Thou dost not understand that the Chestnuts are Lutherans, and thou, a Catholic, art helping them. Thou wish'st war, lazy-bones, for thou canst do nothing but fight and drink and kill people, and not observe fasts but burn churches. God knows that thou'lt be burned in hell if thou boast of thy deeds, and hast pity neither for old people nor children. Remember, sheep, what is written for the Polish people in the holy faith with golden letters from the beginning of the world to the last day of judgment when the Highest God will have no mercy for such fellows, and restrain thyself, Turk, lest thou smash thy head. I send thee five thalers, though I am here in misery and know not what to do, and the household is falling away. I embrace thee, dearest Bartek.

MAGDA.

The teachings contained in this letter made small impression on Bartek. "Women don't know service," thought he to himself, "but are meddlesome." And he fought on in old fashion. He distinguished himself in almost every battle, so that finally eyes of higher rank than those of Steinmetz fell on him. At last, when the Poznan regiments, wellnigh annihilated, were sent to the interior of Germany, he at the advice of the under-officer sent in a petition and remained. In consequence of this he was outside Paris.

His letters were full of contempt now for the French. "In every battle they race away from a man like hares," wrote he to Magda. And he wrote the truth! But the siege did not suit his taste greatly. He had to lie in

the trenches whole days before Paris, and listen to the
thunder of artillery, often to make breastworks and be
drenched. Besides, he was sorry for his former regiment.
In the one to which he was transferred now as a volun-
teer he was surrounded for the greater part by Germans.
Of German he knew a little, for he had learned some
at the mill, but he knew it poorly. Now he began to
talk freely. Still they called him in the regiment, *Ein
polnischer Ochs*, and only his strong back and terrible
fists saved him from their biting jests. Still, after a
number of battles he acquired the respect of these new
comrades, and began to grow used to them slowly. At
last he was looked on as one of them, he had covered
the regiment with glory to such a degree. Bartek would
have held it an insult at all times to be called a German
(Niemets), but in distinction to the French he called himself "ein Deutscher." That seemed to him something
altogether different; and, besides, he did not wish to
appear worse than others. There was an event, however,
which would have given him much to think over, had
thinking been easier for his heroic mind. On a time
some men of his regiment were sent against Volunteer-
riflemen, *Franc-tireurs*. They made an ambush, and the
riflemen fell into it. But this time Bartek did not see
the red caps flying at the first shots, for the detachment
was composed of old soldiers, the remnant of some regiments in a foreign legion. When surrounded, they
defended themselves desperately, and at last rushed forward to open with the bayonet a way through the encircling ring of Prussian soldiers. They fought with such
fury that some of them broke through. Above all, they
did not let themselves be taken alive, knowing the fate
which awaited volunteers after capture. Therefore the
company in which Bartek served took only two prisoners.

In the evening these two men were placed in a room in the forester's house. They were to be shot on the following morning. Bartek was stationed as guard over the bound prisoners in a room which had a broken window.

One of the prisoners was a man not young, with iron-gray hair and a face indifferent to everything. The other seemed twenty and a few years; his bright mustaches were barely visible; he was more like a woman in the face than a man.

"Yes, here is the end," said the young man, after a while; "a bullet in the forehead, and all is over."

Bartek quivered so that the musket rattled in his hand. The young man spoke Polish.

"It is all one to me," said the other, with unwilling voice, — "as God lives, all one. I have struggled so long that I have enough."

Bartek's heart beat under his uniform more quickly every moment.

"Listen," continued the older; "there is no help. If thou art afraid, think of something else, or lie down to sleep. Life is wretched! As God is dear to me, it is all one."

"I am sorry for my mother," answered the younger one, gloomily.

And wishing evidently to overcome his emotion or to deceive himself, he began to whistle. Suddenly he stopped, and cried out in deep despair, —

"May the thunderbolt strike me! I did not even take farewell."

"Thou didst run away from home?"

"I did. I thought: They will beat the Germans, it will be better for the people of Poznan."

"And I thought so too; but now —"

The old man waved his hand, and finished by saying

something in a low voice; but the sound of the wind drowned his words. The night was cold. Fine rain swept forward in waves from time to time; the neighboring forest was black as a mourning robe. In the room the wind whistled in the corners, and howled in the chimney like a dog. The lamp, placed high above the window so the wind might not quench it, cast abundant but flickering light on the room. Bartek, who stood under the lamp by the window, was buried in darkness.

And perhaps it was better that the prisoners did not see his face. Wonderful things were happening to the man. At first astonishment took possession of him; he stared at the prisoners, and tried to understand what they were saying. They had come to beat the Germans so that it might go better with the Poznan people; and he had beaten the French so that it might go better with the Poznan people! And those two men will be shot in the morning. What does this mean? What is he, poor fellow, to think of this? And if he were to speak to them, — if he were to tell them that he is of their people, that he is sorry for them? Something seized him all at once by the throat. And what will he tell them, — that he will save them? Then he will be shot! Hei to the rescue! What is happening to him? Pity is so throttling him that he cannot stand in one place.

A certain terrible sadness settles on him from afar, from some place, from Pognembin. Pity, a strange guest in a soldier's heart, is crying to him: " Bartek, rescue thy own people; these are thy own." And the heart is tearing itself away to his cottage, to Magda, to Pognembin, and tearing itself away in such wise as never before. He has had enough of that France, of that war, and of battles. Every moment he hears a voice more distinctly: "Bartek, save thy own people!" May the earth swallow this war! Through the broken window the forest is black, and it roars like the pines in Pognembin; and in that roar something is crying again: "Bartek, save thy own people!"

What is he to do, — flee with them to the forest, or what? All that Prussian discipline had ever been able to drive into him trembled straightway at that thought. "In the name of the Father and the Son," — this was to defend himself from temptation. He, a soldier, to desert? Never!

Meanwhile the forest roars ever louder, and the wind whistles more and more mournfully.

The older prisoner speaks suddenly, —

"But that wind is as if in autumn at home."

"Spare me!" said the younger, in a broken voice.

But after a while he repeated a number of times, —

"At home, at home, at home! O God! O God!"

A deep sigh was mingled with the whistling, and the prisoners were lying in silence again. Fever began to shake Bartek.

It is worst of all when a man cannot tell what is the matter with him. Bartek had stolen nothing, and it seemed to him as if he had stolen, and as if he feared that they would seize him. Nothing was threatening him, and still he was terribly afraid of something. See, his legs are trembling under him; his musket weighs him down fearfully, and something is choking him, something which is like a great suppressed wailing. Is it for Magda, or for Pognembin? He is sorry for both prisoners, but so sorry for the younger one that he knows not what to do.

At times it seems to Bartek that he is sleeping. Meanwhile the uproar outside is increasing still further. In the whistling of the wind wonderful cries and voices are growing louder.

All at once every hair on Bartek's head stands under his helmet.

See! out there somewhere in the dark, dripping depths of the forest it seems to him that some one is groaning and repeating: "At home, at home, at home!"

Bartek shudders, and strikes the butt of his musket on the floor to wake himself. In fact, he returns to consciousness. He looks around; the prisoners are lying in the corner, the lamp is glittering, the wind is howling, everything is in order.

The light is falling now thickly on the face of the younger prisoner. He has the face of a child or a maiden. But his eyes are closed. There is straw under his head, and he looks as if dead already.

Since Bartek is Bartek never has sadness so dived into him. Something is squeezing him tightly by the throat, a weeping is going out of his breast. Meanwhile the older prisoner turns on his side with difficulty, and says, —

"Good-night, Vladek."

Silence follows. An hour passes. Something really painful has happened to Bartek. The wind is playing like the organs in Pognembin. The prisoners are lying in quiet. Suddenly the younger raises himself with an effort, and calls, —

"Karol!"

"What?"

"Art sleeping?"

"No."

"Listen. I'm afraid; say what may please thee, but I will pray."

"Pray, then."

"Our Father, who art in Heaven, hallowed be Thy name. Thy kingdom come — "

Sobbing interrupted the voice of the young prisoner suddenly; still the broken voice was audible yet, —

"Thy — will — be done —"

"O Jesus!" howled something in the breast of Bartek, "O Jesus!"

No, he will endure no longer! Another moment, and he will cry, "I too am a Pole!" Then, through the window to the forest, let happen what may!

Suddenly from the direction of the entrance are heard measured steps. That is the patrol, and with him the under-officer. They are changing guards.

On the morrow Bartek was drunk from the morning hour; the following day also.

. . . .

But on subsequent days new expeditions came, skirmishes, marches, and it is pleasant for me to relate that our hero returned to his balance. After that night, however, there remained with him a little fondness for the bottle, in which may be found always some savor and ofttimes forgetfulness. For the rest he grew still more unsparing in battle; victory followed his footsteps.

VI.

AGAIN some months passed. The spring was well advanced. In Pognembin the cherry-trees had blossomed in the garden, and were covered with leaves; the fields were green with a thick fleece. On a certain time Magda was sitting outside the cottage and preparing for dinner shrunken sprouted potatoes, fitter food for cattle than for men. But they were before the new ones. Want had begun to look in a little at Pognembin. This might be known, too, from the face of Magda, which was darkened and full of anxiety. Perhaps, also, to drive away this anxiety the woman, closing her eyes, was singing in a thin, strained voice, —

"Oï, oï, my Yasenko is at the war! oi! he writes to me,
   Oï! I write to him, oï! for I am his wife."

The sparrows on the cherry-trees were twittering as if they wished to drown her voice; she while singing was looking in thoughtfulness now on the dog sleeping in the sun, now on the road around the cottage, now on the path stretching from the road through the garden and the fields. Perhaps Magda was looking on the path for the reason that it reached across to the station; and God granted that she did not look that day in vain. In the distance appeared a certain form, and the woman shaded her eyes with her hand, but she could not distinguish, for the rays dazzled her; but Lysek the dog woke up, raised his head, barked a little, began to smell, and to incline his head to one side and then to the other. At the same time the uncertain words of a song came to Magda's ears. Lysek sprang away at once, and ran with all speed to the man drawing near. Then Magda grew a little pale.

"Bartek, isn't it Bartek?"

She stood up quickly, so that the dish with the potatoes rolled on the ground. Now there was no doubt Lysek sprang to the breast of the newly-arrived. The woman rushed forward, crying with all her strength and with joy, —

"Bartek! Bartek!"

"Magda! it is I!" cried Bartek, putting his palm to his lips and hurrying his steps.

He opened the gate, missed the bolt, staggered, almost fell, and they dropped into each other's arms.

The woman began to talk quickly.

"But I thought thou wouldst never come back. I thought to myself: 'They have killed him!' How art thou? Come into the cottage. Franek is at school. The German beats the children. The boy is well, but he has staring eyes like thee. Oh, it was time for thee to come, for there is no help, — misery, I say, misery. The poor cottage is rotting down. How art thou? Oh, Bartek, Bartek! That I should look on thee again! What trouble I had here with the hay! The Chermenitskis helped me, but, O my God! — And art thou all well? But I am glad to see thee, glad! God guarded thee. Come in. Oh, for God's sake! is this Bartek, or not Bartek? But what is the matter with thee? Help!"

Magda now noticed for the first time a long scar stretching over Bartek's face, across the left temple and cheek to his beard.

"That's nothing. A cuirassier touched me there, but I paid him. I have been in the hospital."

"O Jesus!"

"Ei, nothing."

"Thou art as thin as death."

"Ruhig (be quiet)!" answered Bartek.

He was swarthy and wounded, a real victor. Withal he was tottering on his feet.

"Art thou drunk?"

"I am weak yet."

He was weak, it is true, but drunk also; exhausted as he was, one measure of *vodka* was enough. Bartek, however, had drunk at the station something like four. But he had the spirit and bearing of a real victor. Such a mien he had never had before.

"Ruhig!" repeated he. "We have finished the *krieg* (war). Now I am a lord, dost understand? Seest this?" Here he pointed to the crosses and medals. "Knowst

who I am ? He ? Links, rechts. Heu, S'troh ! Halt !
(left, right, hay, straw !) "

He thundered out the last halt ! with such a piercing
voice that the woman sprang back a number of steps.

"Hast gone mad ?"

"How art thou, Magda ? When I say to thee, ' How
art thou ?' that means ' How art thou ?' And knowst
French, foolish woman ? *musyu, musyu !* who *musyu ?* I
musyu ! knowst ?"

"Man, what is the matter with thee ?"

"What 's that to thee ? *Was* (what) ? *Done diner*
(donnez diner, — give dinner) Dost understand ?"

On Magda's forehead a storm began to collect.

"In what language art thou bellowing ? What, knowst
thou not Polish ? Ha, thou chestnut, I was right to say !
What have they made of thee ?"

"Give me something to eat !"

"March into the cottage."

Every command made an impression on Bartek which
he could in no way resist. When he heard then "march"
he straightened himself, stretched his arms down along
his hips, and making a half turn marched in the indicated
direction. On the threshold he recovered, and began to
look at Magda with astonishment.

"Well, what 's the matter, Magda, what 's the matter ?"

"Forward, march !"

He entered the cottage, but fell at the threshold. The
vodka began then indeed to go to his head ; he fell to
singing and looking around the cottage for Franek. He
even said, "Morgen, Kerl !" though Franek was not there.
Then he laughed, made one long step and two very short
ones, shouted hurrah, and stretched his whole length on
the floor.

In the evening he woke up sober, refreshed, greeted

Franek, and taking some tens of *pfennigs* from Magda he made a triumphant campaign to the drinking-shop. The fame of his deeds had already preceded him in Pognembin, where some soldiers of the other companies of that same regiment, having returned earlier, told of his prowess at Gravelotte and Sedan. At present, when the news went out that the victor was in the shop, all his old comrades hurried to see him.

Our Bartek sits there at the table. No one recognizes him. He who had been so submissive in old times beats the table with his fist now, swells up like a gobbler, and gobbles like a gobbler.

"Do ye remember, boys, how I warmed up the Frenchmen, and what Steinmetz said ? "

" Why should n't we remember ? "

" People spoke in favor of the French, frightened us with them; but that is a weak people. *Was* (what)! They are salad. They ride like hares and run like hares, and they don't drink beer, only wine."

" Is that true ? "

" When we burned a village they folded their hands and cried out *pitié, pitié !* which seems to mean that they will give drink, but in that tongue it means to spare them. But we paid no attention."

"Can any one understand what they chatter?" asked a young fellow.

"Thou couldst not, for thou art stupid, but I can. *Done dipen* (give bread), — dost understand ? "

" What is that ? "

" But have ye seen Paris ? There were battles there one after another; but we won them all. They have no good leaders. People say that too, and the officers are fools, and the generals are fools."

Matseı Kerz, an old, wise peasant in Pognembin, began

to shake his head. "Oi, the Germans have conquered in a terrible war; they have conquered, and we have helped them. But what will come of that to us God alone knows."

Bartek stared at him. "What do you say?"

"The Germans before this would pay no regard to us, and now they have stuck up their noses as if even God were not above them. And they will insult us more than ever, for they are doing so already."

"That is not true!" said Bartek.

In Pognembin, old Kerz had such weight that the whole village thought according to his head, and it was insolence to contradict him; but Bartek was now a victor, himself an authority. Still they looked on him with astonishment, and even with a certain indignation.

"What! wilt thou dispute with Matseï? What meanest thou?"

"What is Matseï to me! I have spoken with men who are not the like of him. Do ye understand? Have I not spoken with Steinmetz? *Was!* But whatever Matseï invents is bosh. Now it will be better for us."

Matseï looked awhile at the victor

"Oi, but thou art stupid!" said he.

Bartek struck the table with his fist till all the goblets and mugs rattled, —

"Still der Kerl da! Heu, Stroh! (shut up, fellow, there! hay, straw!)"

"Be quiet; don't make an uproar. Put the question, thou fool, to some his grace; some lord, and thou wilt find out."

"Was his grace at the war, or was his lordship there? But I was at the war. Don't believe him, boys; now they will begin to respect us Who won the battle? We won it; I won it. Now whatever I ask for they will give; if I wanted to be an heir in France I should be one. The Government knows well who beat the French best; but our regiments were the best; thus it was written in the orders. Now the Poles are on top, do ye understand?"

Kerz waved his hand, rose and went out. Bartek had won the victory on the field of politics also. The young fellows who remained gazed at him now as at a rainbow.

"But whatever I might ask for they would give. If it had not been for me then! Old Kerz is a fool, do ye understand? The Government commands to fight, then fight! Who will make light of me,— a German? But what is this?"

Here he pointed to his crosses and medals again.

"But for whom did I beat the French,— not for the Germans, was it? I am now better than a German, for no German has so many of these. Give us beer! I talked with Steinmetz, and I talked with Podbielski. Give beer!"

Gradually they prepared for a drinking bout. Bartek began to sing,—

> "Drinks, drinks, drinks!
> While in my purse
> A thaler clinks."

Suddenly he drew out of his pocket a handful of *pfennigs*.

"Take these,— I am a lord now,— do ye not want them? Oh, not this kind of money did we get in France, but it is gone. Little that we did n't burn up and kill. God knows not some — *Frantsirerov* (Franc-tireurs)."

The humor of men in drink changes very suddenly. Unexpectedly Bartek gathered the money from the table and began to cry piteously,—

"God be merciful to my sinful soul!"

Then he placed his elbows on the table, hid his face in his paws, and was silent.

"What's the matter with thee?" asked some of the tipsy ones.

"How am I to blame?" muttered Bartek, gloomily. "They came themselves. But I was sorry for them, because they were both of my people. O God, be merciful! One of them was as ruddy as the dawn then, but next morning he was pale as a kerchief, and while still alive they were covered with earth. — Vodka!"

A moment of gloomy silence followed. The men looked at one another in astonishment.

"What is he saying?" asked some one.

"He is saying something to his conscience."

"War makes a man drink," muttered Bartek.

He drank *vodka* once, and a second time. He sat awhile in silence, then spat; and good humor returned to him suddenly.

"But have ye talked with Steinmetz? I have talked with him. Hurrah! Drink! Who will pay? I!"

"Thou wilt pay, drunkard, thou!" called the voice of Magda; "but I'll pay thee, never fear."

Bartek looked at the newly-arrived woman with glassy eyes.

"But hast thou talked with Steinmetz? Who art thou?"

Magda instead of answering him turned to his sensitive audience and fell to lamenting.

"Oh, people, people, ye see my shame and misfortune. He came home. I was glad as if something good had come; but he came drunk, and forgot God, forgot Polish. He lay down to sleep, grew sober; and now he is drinking again, and pays with my sweat. Where didst thou get that money; was that not my toil, my blood-sweat? Oh, people, people, he is no longer a Catholic, no longer a man. He is a raging German, he chatters German, he lies in wait to do evil; he is a turn-coat, he is a —"

Here the woman was covered with tears; then she raised her voice an octave higher, —

"He was stupid but good. Now what have they made of him? I waited for thee evenings, I waited for thee mornings, and waited till thou didst come home. From no place consolation, from no place mercy. God of might! God of patience! Mayst thou turn German altogether!"

She finished the last words so sorrowfully that she was almost whining. But Bartek in answer said, —

"Be quiet, or I will rush at thee!"

"Strike, cut off my head, cut it off right away, kill, murder!" called the woman, stubbornly, and stretching out her neck, turned to the men, —

"And you men look at him doing it."

But the men began to go out. Soon the shop was empty; only Bartek remained, and the woman with her neck stretched out.

"Why stretch out thy neck like a goose? Go to the cottage," muttered Bartek.

"Cut it off!" repeated Magda.

"But I will not cut it off," answered Bartek, and he thrust his hands into his pockets.

Here the shopkeeper, wishing to put an end to the incident, quenched the only candle. There was darkness and silence. After a time in the darkness was heard the whining voice of Magda, —

"Cut off my head."

"I will not cut it off," answered the triumphant voice of Bartek.

By the light of the moon two forms were visible going from the shop toward the cottages; one of them in advance, was lamenting audibly. That was Magda. After her, with drooping head, went submissively enough the victor of Gravelotte and Sedan.

VII.

BARTEK came home, but so weak that he could not work for a number of days. That was a great misfortune for the whole housekeeping, which had urgent need of a man's hand. Magda did the best she could, — worked from morning till night. Her neighbors the Chemernitskis helped her according to their power; but all that was not enough, and the place was inclining somewhat toward ruin. She had gone in debt too to the colonist Just, a German, who in his time had bought from the lord some acres of poor land, and had now the best place in the village, and ready money, which he lent at rather high interest. He lent first of all to Pan Yarzynski, whose name Yarzynski was gleaming in the "Golden Book," but who on that account had to maintain the splendor of his house in befitting style; but Just lent also to peasants. Magda owed him, for about half a year, a few tens of thalers, some of which she expended on the land, and some she sent to Bartek. That however was nothing. God had given a good harvest, and from the coming fruits the debt might be paid if there were only hands to labor. Unfortunately Bartek could not work. Magda was not greatly willing to believe this, and went to the priest to take counsel as to how she might rouse the man; but he was really ailing. Breath failed him when he labored a little, and his back ached.

He sat whole days therefore before the cottage, and smoked a porcelain pipe on which was a portrait of Bismarck, in a white uniform and a cuirassier's helmet. Bartek looked on the world with the wearied sleepy eye of a man out of whose bones toil has not gone yet. At the same time he pondered a little over the war, a little over victories, a little over Magda, a little over everything, a little over nothing.

Once as he was sitting thus he heard from a distance the crying of Franek.

Franek was coming from school, and bellowing to be heard all over the place. Bartek took the pipe from his mouth.

"Well, Franek, what is the matter?"

"But what dost thou care?" said Franek, sobbing.

"Why bellow?"

"Why shouldn't I bellow when I got a slap on the face?"

"Who gave thee a slap on the face?"

"Who, unless Pan Boege!"

Pan Boege performed the duties of teacher in Pognembin.

"And what right has he to beat thee on the face?"

"He has, for he beat me."

Magda, who was digging in the garden, came in through the fence, and with a spade in her hand came up to the boy.

"What hast thou done?" asked she.

"Nothing. But Boege called me a Polish pig, slapped me on the face, and said that now as they had beaten the French they would stamp on us, for they are stronger. I did nothing to him, but he asked who was the greatest person in the world, and I said 'The Holy Father.' Pan Boege slapped me on the face. I began to cry, and he

called me a Polish pig, and said that now as they had
beaten the French — "

Franek began to repeat what he had said before : "and
he said and I said." At last Magda covered his face with
her hand, and turning to Bartek, cried out, —

"Dost hear, dost hear? Go thou and beat the French
and then let the German beat thy child as he would the
dog there! Go thou! fight! Let a Schwab beat thy
child! Now thou hast a reward, thou lout."

Here Magda, moved by her own eloquence, began to cry
too, as well as Franek. Bartek stared, opened his mouth,
and was amazed so much that he could not speak, and
above all could not understand what had happened.
How is that? But his victories? He sat awhile longer
in silence. On a sudden something gleamed in his eyes,
blood rushed to his face. Amazement, as well as terror,
frequently passes into rage with simple people. Bartek
sprang up quickly, and rushed forth with set teeth.

"I'll talk to him!" and he went on. It was not far.
The school was right there beyond the church. Pan
Boege was standing at that moment before his own door,
surrounded by a crowd of pigs, among which he was throwing bits of bread. He was a large man about fifty years
old, strong yet as an oak. He was not over thick; but
he had a very full face, and in his face were great fish
eyes with an expression of boldness and energy. Bartek
came up very near him.

"Why dost thou, German, beat my child? *Was!*"
inquired he.

Pan Boege stepped back a few yards, measured him
with his eyes without a shadow of fear, and said phlegmatically: "Be off!"

"Why didst thou beat my child?" repeated Bartek.

"I'll beat thee too. Polish trash! Now we'll show

thee who is lord here. Go to the devil! Go and complain to the court! Be off!"

Bartek, seizing the teacher by the shoulders, began to shake him powerfully, crying with hoarse voice, —

"Knowest who I am? Knowest who pounded the French? Knowest who talked with Steinmetz? Why beat my child, Schwab, lout?"

The fish eyes of Pan Boege were coming out of his head not less than Bartek's; but he was a strong man, and determined to free himself from the aggressor with one blow.

This blow was a powerful slap on the face of the victor of Gravelotte and Sedan. Thereupon Bartek lost self-control. Boege's head was shaken with two heavy movements reminding one of the movement of a pendulum, with this difference, — that the shaking was astonishingly quick. In Bartek the terrible crusher of the Turkos and Zouaves was aroused anew. In vain did the twelve-year old Oscar, son of Boege, a boy strong like his father, hasten to help him. A struggle began, short and terrible, in which the son fell to the ground and the father felt himself raised in the air. Bartek, with arms stretched aloft, bore him, whither he knew not himself. Unfortunately there stood near the house a barrel of swill industriously poured in for the pigs by Pani Boege; and behold there was a plash in the barrel, and in a moment were seen the legs of Boege sticking out of it and kicking violently. Boege's wife rushed out of the house, —

"Help, rescue!"

The woman with presence of mind turned the barrel over in a moment and spilled out her husband together with the swill. The German colonists hastened from the houses near by to help their neighbor.

A number of Germans hurled themselves on Bartek and began to belabor him, some with clubs, others with fists. A general chaos arose, in which it was difficult to distinguish Bartek from his enemies. A number of bodies were entangled in one mass moving convulsively. But suddenly from out the mass of strugglers rushed forth Bartek, wild, shooting off with all power toward the fence.

The Germans sprang after him; but at the same moment a crash in the fence was heard, and that instant a strong pole was brandished in the iron paws of Bartek. He turned, foaming at the mouth, raging; he raised his hands with the club in the air; all fled. Bartek followed them. Happily he overtook no man. Presently he came to himself, and began to retreat toward his cottage. Ah, had he the French before him history would have immortalized that retreat!

It was as follows: The attackers, to the number of twelve men, rallied and pressed again on Bartek. He retreated slowly, like a wild boar pressed by dogs. At times he turned and halted; then the pursuers restrained themselves. The club had won their perfect respect.

But they threw stones. One of these stones wounded Bartek in the forehead. Blood covered his eyes. He felt that he was growing weak. He staggered once and a second time, dropped the club, and fell.

"Hurrah!" cried the colonists.

But before they came up Bartek had risen; that restrained them. The wounded wolf might be dangerous yet. Moreover the first cottages were not far, and from a distance were to be seen a number of Polish peasants running with all speed to the scene of combat. The colonists withdrew to their houses.

"What has happened?" asked those who ran up.

"Dressing the Germans," said Bartek, and he fainted.

VIII.

THE affair assumed threatening proportions. The German papers contained rousing articles about the persecutions which peaceable Germans were suffering from the barbarous and ignorant mass excited by agitation against the State and by religious fanaticism. Boege became a hero. He, the teacher mild and gentle, spreading enlightenment along the distant borders of the State; he, the true missionary of culture among barbarians, was the first to fall a victim to their fury. It was fortunate that behind him were a hundred millions of Germans who will not permit, etc.

Bartek knew not what a storm was gathering above his head; but he was of good heart, he felt sure of winning before the court. Boege had beaten his child and had struck him first, and afterward so many had attacked him. He had to defend himself of course. Besides, they opened his head with a stone. Whose head ? The head of the man distinguished in the orders of the day, of the man who had " gained " the battle of Gravelotte, who had talked with Steinmetz himself, and who had so many crosses. He could not in truth understand how the Germans could know all this and still work such injustice on him ; nor how Boege could promise the men of Pognembin that the Germans would trample them now because they, the men of Pognembin, had beaten the French so valiantly whenever opportunity offered. But as to himself he was certain that the court and the Government would take his part. They at least will know who he is, what he has done in the war ; even if no one else does, Steinmetz will take his part. Besides, Bartek has grown poor through the war; his cottage is mort-gaged. They will not deny him justice.

Meanwhile the police come to Pognembin for Bartek. They expected to find terrible resistance, for they came with five loaded muskets. They were mistaken. Bartek did not think of resistance. They ordered him to sit in a wagon. He sat in it. Magda was in despair, only she repeated persistently, —

"Oh, there was need of thy fighting the French so! thou hast got it now, poor man, — thou hast got it!"

"Be quiet, foolish woman," said Bartek; and he smiled along the road gladly enough at passers-by.

"I will show them who did the injustice!" cried he from the wagon.

And with his crosses on his breast he went to the court like a conqueror. In fact, the court showed itself gracious toward him; extenuating circumstances were found. Bartek was condemned to only three months' imprisonment; besides this, he was condemned to pay one hundred and fifty marks as a recompense to the family of Boege and to other corporeally injured col-onists.

"The criminal however," said the "Posener Zeitung" in the report of the case, "when the sentence was read to him, did not exhibit the least repentance, but burst out with such rude words, and began to reproach the State so shamefully with his pretended services, that there is rea-son to wonder why the attorney present did not begin a new suit against him for his insults to the court and the German race."

Meanwhile Bartek in prison meditated calmly over his deeds of Gravelotte, Sedan, and Paris. We should be unjust, however, were we to say that Boege's act called forth no public comment. It did, it did. On a certain rainy morning some Polish member in the German Parliament showed very eloquently how the treatment of Poles in Poznan had changed; and that for the bravery of the Poznan regiments, and the losses incurred by them during the war, it would be proper to think more of the rights of people in the province of Poznan; finally, how Pan Boege of Pognembin had abused his position of teacher by beating Polish children, calling them Polish swine, and promising that after such a war an intrusive element would trample under foot the original inhabitants.

While the member was speaking, the rain was falling; and since on such a day drowsiness seizes men, the Conservatives were yawning; the Centre — for the *Kultur Kampf* had not begun yet — was yawning.

At last, in answer to the Polish complaint, the House returned to the order of the day.

Meanwhile Bartek was sitting in prison, or rather lying in the prison hospital, for from the blow of the stone the wound he had received in the war opened. When he had not the fever, he was thinking like that turkey gobbler which died from thought. Bartek did not die however; still he thought out nothing. But sometimes in moments which science calls *lucid intervals*, it came to his head that perhaps he had pounded the French without need.

On Magda came grievous times. The fine had to be paid; there was no place in which to get the money. The priest of Pognembin wanted to help her; but it turned out that in his treasury there were not forty whole marks. The parish of Pognembin was a poor one; besides, the old man never knew how his money was expended. Pan Yarzynski was not at home; people said that he had gone to court some wealthy young lady in the Kingdom. Magda knew not what to do. An extension of the term was not to be thought of. What then? To sell the horse or a cow? and it was just before harvest, — the most difficult period. Grain-cutting was at hand. The woman needed money, and had spent all her store of it. She wrung her hands in despair; she sent a number of petitions to the court, asking for extension, recounting Bartek's services. She did not get even an answer. The term was approaching, and with it an execution. She prayed and prayed, thinking bitterly of times before the war when they were rich, and when Bartek was earning money in winter at the mill. She went to her friends to borrow money; but they had none. The war had paid all with marks of distinction. To Just she did not dare to go, for she was already in debt to him, and had not paid even the interest. But Just himself came to her unexpectedly.

On a certain afternoon she was sitting on the threshold of her cottage doing nothing, for the strength had gone out of her from despair. She was looking out at the golden flies chasing through the air, and she thought how happy are those insects, playing for themselves, and not crying. At times she sighed heavily, or from her pale lips came the quiet exclamation, "O God! O God!" All at once before the gate appeared the hanging nose of Just, under which was a hanging pipe. Just called out, —

"Morgen!"

"How is your health, Pan Just?"

"But my money?"

"Oh, my dear, golden Pan Just, be patient! What shall I, poor woman, do? They have taken my man; I must pay the fine for him. I don't know what to do.

21

Better die than suffer from day to day as I suffer. Wait a little, my golden Pan Just."

She burst into tears, and, bending down, kissed submissively the thick red hand of Pan Just.

"Pan Yarzynski will come; I will get money from him, and pay you."

"But how will you pay the fine?"

"How do I know unless I sell a cow?"

"Well, I will lend you more money."

"May the Lord God reward you, my golden Pan. Although a Lutheran, you are a good man; I say indeed that if other Germans were like you, a man might bless them."

"But I will not give it without interest."

"I know, I know."

"Then you write me one note for all you owe."

"I will, golden Pan; God reward you even for that!"

"I will be in town, and we will draw up the paper."

He went to town, and had the paper drawn up; but Magda went first to take counsel with the priest. But what counsel was there to be taken? The priest said that the term was too short, that the interest was too high, and grieved greatly that Pan Yarzynski was not at home; for if he had been at home, he might help. But Magda could not wait till the court sold her effects, and was forced to accept Just's conditions.

She went in debt three hundred marks; that is, twice the amount of the "fine," for she needed some money in the house to carry on affairs. Bartek, who had to confirm the act with his own signature, to give it validity, signed it. Magda for that purpose went to him in prison. The victor was greatly weighed down, crushed, and sick. He wrote another complaint, and set forth his wrongs; but his complaint was not received. The articles in the

"Posener Zeitung" had roused opinions in Government circles with too great unfriendliness toward him. Were the authorities to refuse protection to that peaceable German population, "which in the last war had given so many proofs of its love for the country and for enlightenment"? Justly, therefore, was Bartek's complaint rejected. But be not surprised if that crushed him completely.

"We shall be lost altogether," said he, to his wife.

"Altogether," repeated she.

Bartek began to think over something powerfully.

"I am terribly wronged," said he.

"Boege is tormenting the boy," said Magda. "I went to entreat him; he abused me more. 'Oi!' said he, 'the Germans are on top now in Poznan. They are afraid of nobody now.'"

"It is sure that they are stronger," said Bartek, gloomily.

"I 'm a simple woman; but I say this, that God is stronger."

"In Him is our refuge," added Bartek.

Both were silent awhile; then they asked again, —

"Well, and what of Just?"

"May the highest God give us harvest! perhaps we may pay him some way. Perhaps, too, Pan Yarzynski will help us, though he himself is in debt to the Germans. Even before the war it was said that he must sell Pognembin. Perhaps he will marry a rich woman."

"But will he come soon?"

"Who knows? They say at the mansion that he 'll come soon with his wife. The Germans will crowd him when he comes. Those Germans are crawling in everywhere like worms. Wherever thy eyes look, wherever thou canst turn, in the village or the town, — Germans!

It must be in punishment for our sins. And rescue from no side !"

"Maybe thou canst do something; thou art a wise woman."

"What can I do, what? Did I borrow money from Just of my own will? In good right, the cottage in which we are, and the land too, is his now. Just is a better German than others; but he has his own good in mind, and not ours. He will not spare us, as he has not spared others. Am I such a fool as not to know why he offers me money? But what is to be done! what is to be done!" said Magda, wringing her hands; "tell, tell, if thou art wise. Thou wert able to beat the French; but what wilt thou do when there is no roof above thy head, nor a spoonful of food for thy mouth?"

The victor of Gravelotte seized his head, —

"O Jesus! O Jesus!"

Magda had a good heart; Bartek's pain moved her; she said at once, —

"Be quiet, poor fellow, be quiet; do not seize thy head, for it is not healed yet. If God gives a harvest! The rye is so beautiful that one would like to kiss the land; and the wheat is beautiful. The land is not a German, — it will not wrong thee. Even though without thy war the field was worked stupidly, still there is such a growth that — "

Honest Magda laughed through her tears, —

"The land is not a German," repeated she again.

"Magda," said Bartek, looking at her with his staring eyes, " Magda!"

"What?"

"But thou art — as — "

Bartek felt for her great thankfulness; but he knew not how to express it.

IX.

MAGDA was, indeed, worth as much as ten women worse than herself. She held her Bartek rather strictly; but she was really attached to him. In moments of excitement, as, for instance, that time in the shop, she told him to his eyes that he was a fool; but in general she wished people to think otherwise. "My Bartek seems dull, but he is cunning," said she, frequently. Meanwhile Bartek was as cunning as his own horse; and without Magda he would not have been able to get on either in housekeeping or aught else. Now everything was on her honest head; and she began to hurry about, to run, to entreat, so that she found rescue at last. A week after her first visit to the prison hospital, she rushed in again to Bartek, panting, happy, radiant.

"How art thou, Bartek, thou Chestnut?" cried she with joy. "Pan Yarzynski has come, — knowest thou? He got married in the Kingdom; the young lady is a berry. And he got all kinds of riches with her."

"Well, but what of that?" inquired Bartek.

"Be quiet, stupid fellow!" answered Magda. "I went to bow down to the Pani; I look — she comes out to me like some queen, so young, as beautiful as the dawn."

Magda raised her apron, and began to wipe her face. After a while she spoke again, with a broken voice, —

"She wore a robe blue as a star-thistle. I fell at her feet, and she gave me her hand; I kissed it; and her hands are sweet and small as the hands of a child. She is like a saint in a picture; and she is good, and understands the sufferings of people. I entreated her to save us, may God reward her! And she said, 'What is in my power I will do.' And she has a dear voice; so that when she speaks a sweetness takes hold of thee. When I told how unhappy people were in Pognembin, she said, 'Ai, not only in Pognembin!' and when I broke out crying, she cried as well, till her husband came in, and saw that she was crying. Then he took her, and kissed her on the mouth and on the eyes. Lords are not like peasants! Then she said to him, 'Do what thou canst for this woman!' And he answered, 'Everything in the world according to thy wish.' May the Mother of God bless her, the golden berry! bless her with children, with health! 'Ye are greatly to blame,' said Pan Yarzynski, 'for putting yourselves into German hands; but,' said he, 'I will save you, and give you the money for Just.'"

Bartek began to scratch his neck.

"But the Germans had him in hand, too."

"What of that? But the lady is rich. Now they can buy out all the Germans in Pognembin, so he can talk that way. 'The election is coming,' said he; 'let the people be careful not to vote for Germans. I will give the money for Just, and tame Boege.' And the lady put her arms around his neck, and he inquired about thee, and said: 'If he is weak I will ask the doctor to write a certificate that he cannot sit out his term at present. If they do not free him entirely, let him stay out his term in winter; but now he is needed for the harvest.' Dost hear? Yesterday, Pan Yarzynski was in the town, and to-day the doctor will come to Pognembin on a visit, for he was asked. He is not a German, and he will write a certificate. In the winter thou 'lt be in prison like a king in his castle; it will be warm for thee there, and they 'll give thee food free of cost; and now thou 'lt go home to work, and we 'll pay Just, and maybe Pan Yarzynski will not want any interest. And if we do not pay all in the autumn I'll speak to the lady. May the Mother of God reward her! Dost hear?"

"She is a good lady; there is nothing to be said against that," said Bartek, quickly.

"Thou wilt fall at her feet, thou'lt fall; if not I'll twist thy yellow head off. If God gives a good harvest — Dost see where rescue came from? From the Germans? Did they give thee even one copper for thy stupid work, did they? They gave thee a blow on the head, that's all. Thou'lt fall at the lady's feet, I tell thee."

"Why not fall?" answered Bartek, resolutely.

Fate seemed to smile again on the victor. A few days later it was announced to him that for reasons of health he was liberated till winter. But the Landrath commanded Bartek to appear before him. Bartek came with his soul on his shoulder. That man who with bayonet in hand took standards and cannon, began to fear every uniform more than death, — began to bear in his heart a certain dull, unconscious feeling that they were persecuting him, that they could do what they liked with him, that there was above him a certain enormous power, hostile and malevolent, which would grind him if he opposed it. He stood then before the Landrath, as once he had stood before Steinmetz, erect, with his stomach drawn in, his breast pushed forward, without breath in his bosom. There were a number of officers there also; war and military discipline stood as if living before Bartek. The officers looked at him through their gold-rimmed glasses with the pride and contempt which should be shown a common soldier and a Polish peasant by Prussian officers. Bartek held his breath, and the Landrath spoke in a commanding tone. He did not request, he did not persuade; he commanded, he threatened. The member had died in Berlin, a new election was ordered.

"Du polnisches Vieh (Thou Polish beast)! just try
to vote for Pan Yarzynski, try!"

The brows of the officers were contracted at that
moment in terrible lion wrinkles. One, biting a cigar,
repeated after the Landrath, "try," and the breath died
in Bartek the victor. When he heard the desired "Go
out!" he made a half turn to the left, went out, and
drew breath.

The command was issued to him to vote for Pan Schulberg from Upper Kryvda. He did not think over the
command; but he breathed, he went to Pognembin, for
he could be home for the harvest. Pan Yarzynski had
promised to pay Just. Bartek went outside the town.
He was surrounded by fields of ripening grain. One head
heavy with the wind strikes another head and rustles
with a sound dear to the ear of the peasant. Bartek was
weak yet, but the sun warmed him. "Hei, how beautiful
it is in the world!" thought the broken soldier. And
it is not far now to Pognembin.

X.

THE election! the election! Pani Marya Yarzynski has
her head full of it; she thinks not, she speaks not, she
dreams not of anything else.

"The lady benefactress is a great politician," says a
neighboring noble, kissing like a dragon her small hands;
and the "great politician" blushes like a cherry, and
answers with a pretty smile, —

"We agitate as far as we are able."

"Pan Yozef will be elected," said the noble, convincingly, and the "great politician" answers, —

"I should like it greatly, though the question is not
merely of Yozio, but [here the "great politician" was

cooking again the unpolitical lobster] of the common
cause."

"A real Bismarck, as I love God!" cries the noble,
and again he kisses the small hand. Again the two take
counsel about the agitation. The noble takes on himself
Lower Kryvda and Mizerov (Upper Kryvda is lost, for
its owner is Pan Schulberg) and Pani Marya is to occupy
herself beyond all with Pognembin. Her head was on
fire because she was playing such a rôle. Indeed, she lost
no time. Every day she was to be seen on the high road
among the cottages, her skirt raised with one hand, her
little parasol in the other, and from under the skirt
peeped forth her dainty feet, trotting around eagerly for
great political objects. She enters the cottages of laboring people, says on the way, "God give assistance!" She
visits the sick, occupies herself with the people, helps
where she can ; she would have done that without politics,
for she has a good heart; but all the more for politics.
What would she not do for politics? But she does not
dare to confess to her husband that she has an irresistible
desire to go to the village court; she even put together
in her head a speech proper to be made there. What a
speech! what a speech! In truth she would not really
speak it; but if she should speak it, then ? When the
news came to Pognembin that the authorities had dissolved
the village court, the "great politician" burst out from
anger in her room, tore her handkerchief, and had red
eyes all day. In vain did her husband entreat her not to
demean herself to that degree. Next morning the agitation was carried on in Pognembin with still greater intensity. Pani Marya did not retreat before anything.
In one day she was at a number of cottages, and jeered at
the Germans so loudly that her husband had to restrain
her. But there is no danger; the people receive her

with joy, kiss her hands, and smile at her, for she is so shapely, so rosy, that when she enters a house it grows bright. In turn she came to Bartek's cottage. Lysek the dog would not let her in, but Magda in her anger gave him a blow of a club on the head.

"Oh, serene lady, my golden lady, my beauty, my berry!" cried Magda, nestling up to her hands.

Bartek, in obedience to command, throws himself at her feet; little Franek first of all kisses her hand, then puts his finger in his mouth, and buries himself wholly in wonderment.

"I hope," said the young lady, after the greetings were over, "I hope, my Bartek, that you will vote for my husband, not for Pan Schulberg."

"Oh, my dawn!" cried Magda, "who would vote for Schulberg? May the paralysis strike him! [Here she kissed the lady's hand.] Let not the serene lady be angry; but when a German is mentioned, it is hard to hold the tongue."

"My husband has told me that he will pay Just."

"May God bless him!" Here Magda turned to Bartek. "Why stand like a post? He, my lady, is terribly silent."

"You will vote for my husband," asked the lady, "will you not? You are Poles, we are Poles; we will hold together."

"I would twist his head off if he did n't vote," said Magda. "Why stand like a post? He is terribly silent. Stir up!"

Bartek kisses the hand of the lady again; but is silent all the time and gloomy as night. He is thinking of the Landrath.

.   .   .   .

The day of the election is coming, has come. Pan Yarzynski is certain of victory. The nobles have returned

from the town; they have already voted, and will wait
now in Pognembin for the news which the priest is to
bring. There will be a dinner after that; in the evening
the Yarzynskis will go to Poznan, and then to Berlin.
Some villages in the electoral district had voted the day
before; the result will be known to-day. The company,
however, is in good spirits. The youthful lady is a little
disquieted, but full of hope and smiles. She is such a
welcoming lady that all say, "Pan Yarzynski has found
a real treasure in the Kingdom." That "treasure" cannot indeed sit quietly in one place just now, but is
running from guest to guest, and commands each a hundred times to give the assurance that "Yozio will be
elected." She is not really ambitious, and not from
vanity does she wish to become the wife of a member;
but she has imagined·in her young head that she and
her husband have a real mission to perform. Her heart
therefore is beating as quickly as at the moment of her
marriage, and joy lights up her pretty face. Making her
way deftly through the guests, she approaches her husband,
draws him by the sleeve, and whispers into his ear like a
child who is nicknaming some one, "Pan Posel [Lord
Deputy]." He smiles, and both are happy beyond
expression. Both have a great desire to kiss each other,
but that is not proper before guests. All are looking
every moment through the window, for the cause is really
important. The member who had died recently was a
Pole, and this was the first time that the Germans had
brought out a candidate in the district. Clearly a victorious war had given them boldness; but for that reason
it was important to the company assembled in the
mansion of Pognembin that their candidate be chosen.
There was no lack either before the dinner, of patriotic
utterances, which moved especially the youthful lady, so

unaccustomed to them.   At moments she had attacks of
fear : But if some fraud should be committed in counting
the votes ?   But Germans are not alone in the committee.
The older inhabitants explained then to the lady how
the counting of votes is carried on.   She had heard it
about a hundred times, but wishes to hear it again, for
the question is : Are the people of that place to have
a defender in Parliament or an enemy ?   That will be
decided soon indeed, for on the road a cloud of dust rises
suddenly.   " The priest is coming, the priest is coming ! "
repeat those present.   The lady grows pale.   On all faces
excitement is evident.   They are certain of victory ; but
still the last moment increases the beating of hearts.
But that is not the priest ; it is the land-steward returning
on horseback from the town.   Maybe he knows something ?   He ties the horse to the ring and hurries to the
house.   The guests, with the lady in front of them, rush
out to the porch.

" Have you news ? Is our host elected ? What ?
Come here ! You know surely ? Is the result announced ? "

Questions cross each other and fall like rockets.   The
man throws his cap in the air.

" Our lord is elected."

The lady drops suddenly on the bench and presses her
swelling bosom with her hand.

" Vivat ! vivat ! " cried the neighbors. " Vivat ! "

The servants rush out of the kitchen : " Vivat ! The
Germans are beaten ! Long life to the new member and
the lady ! "

" But the priest ? " inquires some one.

" He will be here soon," said the land-steward ; " they
are still counting the last names."

" Bring in the dinner ! " cries the new member.

"Vivat!" repeat others.

All return from the porch to the hall. Congratulations to the lord and the lady are now flowing more calmly; but the lady herself is not able to restrain her joy, and without thinking of spectators throws her arms around her husband's neck. But they do not take that ill of her; nay, emotion seizes all.

"We shall live yet," says a neighbor from Mizerov.

That moment a rattling is heard at the porch; the priest enters the hall, and with him old Kyerz from Pognembin.

"We greet, we greet!" cry the guests. "Well, what was the majority?"

The priest, silent for an instant, casts as it were in the face of the general rejoicing harshly and briefly two words, —

"Schulberg elected!"

A moment of astonishment, a hail-storm of questions hurried and disturbed, to which the priest answers again, —

"Schulberg elected!"

"How? What has happened? In what way? The land-steward said he was not. What has happened?"

At that moment Pan Yarzynski conducted out of the hall poor Pani Marya, who was gnawing her handkerchief to avoid bursting into tears or fainting.

"O misfortune! misfortune!" repeat the guests, seizing themselves by their heads.

At that moment from the direction of the village comes the sound of distant voices as if joyous shouts. That is the Germans of Pognembin going around joyfully with their victory.

The Yarzynskis return to the hall. It was to be heard how at the door the young man said to the lady, "Il faut faire bonne mine (We must put a good face on it)." In fact the lady was weeping no longer; she had dry eyes, and was greatly flushed.

"Tell us now how it happened," said the host, calmly.

"How could it be otherwise, serene lord," said old Kerz, "when the peasants here in Pognembin voted for Schulberg?"

"Who, — these here? But how was that?"

"They did. I myself saw, ánd all saw, Bartek Slovik vote for Schulberg."

"Bartek Slovik?" said the lady.

"Of course. Now the others are railing at him, the man is rolling on the ground; he is weeping, his wife is abusing him. But I myself saw him vote."

"Such a man should be driven from the village," said a neighbor from Mizerov.

"Well, serene lord," said Kerz, "others too who were at the war voted that way as well as he. They say that they were commanded."

"Abuse, pure abuse! the election is not valid. Constraint, fraud!" cried various voices.

Not joyful was the dinner of that day in the Pognembin mansion. In the evening the Yarzynkis went away, — but not to Berlin, only to Dresden.

Miserable, cursed, despised, and hated, Bartek sat in his cottage, a stranger even to his own wife, for the whole day she had not spoken a word to him.

.   .   .   .

God gave a bountiful harvest, and in the autumn Pan Just, who had now taken possession of Bartek's place, was glad that he had done a business that was not at all bad.

On a certain day three people were going from Pognembin to the town, a man, a woman, and a boy. The man, greatly bent, was more like some old grandfather than a healthy person. They were going to the town, for in Pognembin they could not find work. The rain was falling; the woman was sobbing terribly in grief for the lost cottage and the village, the man was silent. The whole road was empty, neither a wagon nor a man, — only the cross stretched over the wayside, its arms wet from rain. The rain fell more and more densely, and it was growing dark in the world.

Bartek, Magda, and Franek were on their way to the town; the victor of Gravelotte and Sedan had to serve out his time in prison for the Boege affair.

The Yarzynskis were living in Dresden.

ACROSS THE PLAINS

ACROSS THE PLAINS.

DURING my stay in California I went with my worthy and gallant friend, Captain R., to visit Y., a compatriot of ours who was living in the secluded mountains of Santa Lucia. Not finding him at home, we passed five days in a lonely ravine, in company with an old Indian servant, who during his master's absence took care of the Angora goats and the bees.

Conforming to the ways of the country, I spent the hot summer days mainly in sleep, but when night came I sat down near a fire of dry " chamisal," and listened to stories from the captain, concerning his wonderful adventures, and events which could happen only in the wilds of America.

Those hours passed for me very bewitchingly. The nights were real Californian: calm, warm, starry ; the fire burned cheerily, and in its gleam I saw the gigantic, but shapely and noble form of the old pioneer warrior. Raising his eyes to the stars, he sought to recall past events, cherished names, and dear faces, the very remembrance of which brought a mild sadness to his features. Of these narratives I give one just as I heard it, thinking that the reader will listen to it with as much interest as I did.

CHAPTER I.

I CAME to America in September, 1849, said the captain, and found myself in New Orleans, which was half French at that time. From New Orleans I went up the Missis-

sippi to a great sugar plantation, where I found work
and good wages. But since I was young in those days,
and full of enterprise, sitting in one spot and writing
annoyed me; so I left that place soon and began life
in the forest. My comrades and I passed some time
among the lakes of Louisiana, amidst crocodiles, snakes,
and mosquitoes. We supported ourselves with hunting
and fishing, and from time to time floated down many
logs to New Orleans, where purchasers paid for them not
badly in money.

Our expeditions reached distant places. We went as far
as "Bloody Arkansas," which, sparsely inhabited even at
this day, was well-nigh a pure wilderness at that time.
Such a life, full of labors and dangers, bloody encounters
with pirates on the Mississippi, and with Indians, who
were numerous then in Louisiana, Arkansas, and Tennessee, increased my health and strength, which by nature
were uncommon, and gave me also such knowledge of
the plains, that I could read in that great book not
worse than any red warrior.

After the discovery of gold in California, large parties
of emigrants left Boston, New York, Philadelphia, and
other eastern cities almost daily, and one of these, thanks
to my reputation, chose me leader, or as we say here,
captain.

I accepted the office willingly, since wonders were told
of California in those days, and I had cherished thoughts
of going to the Far West, though without concealing
from myself the perils of the journey.

At present the distance between New York and San
Francisco is passed by rail in a week, and the real desert
begins only west of Omaha; in those days it was something quite different. Cities and towns, which between
New York and Chicago are as numerous as poppy-seeds

now, did not exist then ; and Chicago itself, which later on grew up like a mushroom after rain, was merely a poor obscure fishing-village not found on maps. It was necessary to travel with wagons, men, and mules through a country quite wild, and inhabited by terrible tribes of Indians : Crows, Blackfeet, Pawnees, Sioux, and Aricka-rees, which it was well-nigh impossible to avoid in large numbers, since those tribes, movable as sand, had no fixed dwellings, but, being hunters, circled over great spaces of prairie, while following buffaloes and antelopes.

Not few were the toils, then, that threatened us ; but he who goes to the Far West must be ready to suffer hardship, and expose his life frequently. I feared most of all the responsibility which I had accepted. This matter had been settled, however, and there was nothing to do but make preparations for the journey. These lasted more than two months, since we had to bring wagons, even from Pittsburgh, to buy mules, horses, arms, and collect large supplies of provisions. Toward the end of winter, however, all things were ready.

I wished to start in such season as to pass the great prairies lying between the Mississippi and the Rocky Mountains in spring, for I knew that in summer because of heat in those open places, multitudes of men died of various diseases. I decided for this reason to lead the train, not over the southern route by St. Louis, but through Iowa, Nebraska, and Northern Colorado. That road was more dangerous with reference to Indians, but beyond doubt it was healthier. The plan roused op-position at first among people of the train. I declared that if they would not obey they might choose another captain. They yielded after a brief consultation, and we moved at the first breath of spring.

Days now set in which for me were toilsome enough,

especially till such time as men had grown accustomed to me and the conditions of the journey. It is true that my person roused confidence, for my daring trips to Arkansas had won a certain fame among the restless population of the border, and the name of " Big Ralph," by which I was known on the prairies, had struck the ears of most of my people more than once. In general, however, the captain, or leader, was, from the nature of things, in a very critical position frequently with regard to emigrants. It was my duty to choose the camping-ground every evening, watch over the advance in the daytime, have an eye on the whole caravan, which extended at times a mile over the prairie, appoint sentries at the halting-places, and give men permission to rest in the wagons when their turn came.

Americans have in them, it is true, the spirit of organization developed to a high degree; but in toils on a journey men's energies weaken, and unwillingness seizes the most enduring. At such times no one wishes to reconnoitre all day on horseback and stand sentry at night, but each would like to evade the turn which is coming to him, and lie entire days in a wagon. Besides, in intercourse with Americans, a captain must know how to reconcile discipline with a certain social familiarity, — a thing far from easy. In time of march, and in the hours of night-watching, I was perfect master of the will of each of my companions; but during rest in the day at farms and settlements, to which we came at first on the road, my rôle of commander ended. Each man was then his own master, and more than once I was forced to overcome the opposition of insolent adventurers; but when in presence of numerous spectators it turned out a number of times that my Mazovian fist was the stronger, my significance rose, and later on I never had personal encounters. Besides, I knew American character thoroughly. I knew how to help myself, and, in addition to all. my endurance and willingness were increased by a certain pair of blue eyes, which looked out at me with special interest from beneath the canvas roof of a wagon. Those eyes looked from under a forehead shaded by rich golden hair, and they belonged to a maiden named Lillian Morris. She was delicate, slender, with finely cut features, and a face thoughtful, though almost childlike. That seriousness in such a young girl struck me at once when beginning the journey, but duties connected with the office of captain soon turned elsewhere my mind and attention.

During the first weeks I exchanged with Miss Morris barely a couple of words beyond the usual daily "good morning." Taking compassion, however, on her loneliness and youth, — she had no relatives in that caravan, — I showed the poor girl some trifling services. I had not the least need of guarding her with my authority of leader nor with my fist from the forwardness of young men in the train, for among Americans even the youngest woman is sure, if not of the over-prompt politeness for which the French are distinguished, at least of perfect security. In view, however, of Lillian's delicate health, I put her in the most commodious wagon, in charge of a driver of great experience, named Smith. I spread for her a couch on which she could sleep with comfort; finally, I lent her a warm buffalo-skin, of which I had a number in reserve. Though these services were not important, Lillian seemed to feel a lively gratitude, and omitted no opportunity to show it. She was evidently very mild and retiring. Two women, Aunt Grosvenor and Aunt Atkins, soon loved her beyond expression for her sweetness of character. "Little Bird,"

a title which they gave her, became the name by which
she was known in the caravan. Still, there was not
the slightest approach between Little Bird and me, till I
noticed that the blue and almost angelic eyes of that
maiden were turned toward me, with a certain special
sympathy and determined interest.

That might have been interpreted in this way: Among
all the people of the train I alone had some social refine-
ment; Lillian, in whom also a careful training was evident, saw in me, therefore, a man nearer to her than the
rest of the company. But I understood the affair somewhat differently. The interest which she showed pleased
my vanity; my vanity made me pay her more attention,
and look oftener into her eyes. It was not long till I
was striving in vain to discover why, up to that time,
I had paid so little attention to a person so exquisite, —
a person who might inspire tender feelings in any man
who had a heart.

Thenceforth I was fond of coursing around her wagon
on my horse. During the heat of the day, which in
spite of the early spring annoyed us greatly at noon, the
mules dragged forward lazily, and the caravan stretched
along the prairie, so that a man standing at the first
wagon could barely see the last one. Often did I fly at
such times from end to end, wearying my horse without
need, just to see that bright head in passing, and those
eyes, which hardly ever left my mind. At first my imagination was more taken than my heart; I received pleasant solace from the thought that among those strange
people I was not entirely a stranger, since a sympathetic little soul was occupied with me somewhat. Perhaps this came not from vanity, but from the yearning
which a man feels on earth to discover his own self in
a heart near to him, to fix his affections and thoughts

on one living beloved existence, instead of wasting them on such indefinite, general objects as plains and forests, and losing himself in remotenesses and infinities.

I felt less lonely then, and the whole journey took on attractions unknown to me hitherto. Formerly, when the caravan stretched out on the prairie, as I have described, so that the last wagons vanished from the eye, I saw in that only a lack of attention, and disorder, from which I grew very angry. Now, when I halted on some eminence, the sight of those wagons, white and striped, shone on by the sun and plunging in the sea of grass, like ships on the ocean, the sight of men, on horseback and armed, scattered in picturesque disorder at the sides of the wagons, filled my soul with delight and with happiness. And I know not whence such comparisons came to me, but that seemed some kind of Old Testament procession, which I, like a patriarch, was leading to the Promised Land. The bells on the harness of the mules and the drawling, "Get up !" of the drivers accompanied like music thoughts which came from my heart and my nature.

But I did not pass from that dialogue of eyes with Lillian to another, for the presence of the women travelling with her prevented me. Still, from the time when I saw that there was something between us for which I could not find a name yet, though I felt that the something was there, a certain strange timidity seized me. I redoubled, however, my care for the women, and frequently I looked into the wagon, inquiring about the health of Aunt Atkins and Aunt Grosvenor, so as to justify in that way and equalize the attentions with which I surrounded Lillian ; but she understood my methods perfectly, and this understanding became as it were our own secret, concealed from the rest of the people.

Soon, glances and a passing exchange of words and tender endeavors were not enough for me. That young maiden with bright hair and sweet look drew me to her with an irresistible power. I began to think of her whole days; and at night, when wearied from visiting the sentries, and hoarse from crying "All is well!" I came at last to the wagon, and wrapping myself in a buffalo-skin, closed my eyes to rest, it seemed to me that the gnats and mosquitoes buzzing around were singing unceasingly in my ears, "Lillian! Lillian! Lillian!" Her form stood before me in my dreams; at waking, my first thought flew to her like a swallow; and still, wonderful thing! I had not noticed that the dear attraction which everything assumed for me, that painting in the soul of objects in golden colors, and those thoughts sailing after her wagon, were not a friendship nor an inclination for an orphan, but a mightier feeling by far, a feeling from which no man on earth can defend himself when the turn has come to him.

It may be that I should have noticed this sooner, had it not been that the sweetness of Lillian's nature won every one to her; I thought, therefore, that I was no more under the charm of that maiden than were others. All loved her as their own child, and I had proof of this before my eyes daily. Her companions were simple women, sufficiently inclined to wordy quarrels, and still, more than once had I seen Aunt Atkins, the greatest Herod on earth, combing Lillian's hair in the morning, kissing her with the affection of a mother; sometimes I saw Aunt Grosvenor warming in her own palms the maiden's hands, which had chilled in the night. The men surrounded her likewise with care and attentions. There was a certain Henry Simpson in the train, a young adventurer from Kansas, a fearless hunter and an honest fellow at heart, but so self-sufficient, so insolent and rough, that during the first month I had to beat the man twice, to convince him that there was some one in the train who had a stronger hand than his, and who was of superior significance. You should have seen that same Henry Simpson speaking to Lillian. He who would not have thought anything of the President of the United States himself, lost in her presence all his confidence and boldness, and repeated every moment, " I beg your pardon, Miss Morris ! " He had quite the bearing of a chained mastiff, but clearly the mastiff was ready to obey every motion of that small, half-childlike hand. At the halting-places he tried always to be with Lillian, so as to render her various little services. He lighted the fire, and selected for her a place free from smoke, covering it first with moss and then with his own horse-blankets; he chose for her the best pieces of game, doing all this with a certain timid attention which I had not thought to find in him, and which roused in me, nevertheless, a kind of ill-will very similar to jealousy.

But I could only be angry, nothing more. Henry, if the turn to stand guard did not come to him, might do what he liked with his time, hence he could be near Lillian, while my turn of service never ended. On the road the wagons dragged forward one after another, often very far apart; but when we entered an open country for the midday rest I placed the wagons, according to prairie custom, in a line side by side, so that a man could hardly push between them. It is difficult to understand how much trouble and toil I had before such an easily defended line was formed. Mules are by nature wild and untractable; either they balked, or they would not go out of the beaten track, biting each other meanwhile, neighing and kicking; wagons, twisted by sudden movement, were turned over frequently, and the raising up of such real houses of wood and canvas took no little time; the braying of mules, the cursing of drivers, the tinkling of bells, the barking of dogs which followed us, caused a hellish uproar. When I had brought all into order in some fashion, I had to oversee the unharnessing of the animals and urge on the men whose work it was to drive them to pasture and then to water. Meanwhile men who during the advance had gone out on the prairie to hunt, were returning from all sides with game; the fires were occupied by people, and I found barely time to eat and draw breath.

I had almost double labor when we started after each rest, for attaching the mules involved more noise and uproar than letting them out. Besides, the drivers tried always to get ahead of one another, so as to spare themselves trouble in turning out of line in bad places. From this came quarrels and disputes, together with curses and unpleasant delays on the road. I had to watch over all this, and in time of marching ride in advance, immediately after the guides, to examine the neighborhood and select in season defensible places, abounding in water, and, in general, commodious for night camps. Frequently I cursed my duties as captain, though on the other hand the thought filled me with pride, that in all that boundless desert I was the first before the desert itself, before people, before Lillian, and that the fate of all those beings, wandering behind the wagons over that prairie, was placed in my hands.

CHAPTER II.

On a certain time, after we had passed the Mississippi, we halted for the night at Cedar River, the banks of which, grown over with cottonwood, gave us assurance of fuel for the night. While returning from the men on duty, who had gone into the thicket with axes, I saw, from a distance, that our people, taking advantage of the beautiful weather and the calm, fair day, had wandered out on the prairie in every direction. It was very early; we halted for the night usually about five in the afternoon, so as to move in the morning at daybreak. Soon I met Miss Morris. I dismounted immediately, and, leading my horse by the bridle, approached the young lady, happy that I could be alone with her even for a while. I inquired then why she, though alone and so young, had undertaken a journey which might wear out the strongest man.

"Never should I have consented to receive you into our caravan," said I, "had I not thought during the first few days of our journey that you were the daughter of Aunt Atkins; now it is too late to turn back. But, my dear child, will you be strong enough? You must be ready to find the journey hereafter less easy than hitherto."

"I know all this," answered she, without raising her pensive blue eyes, "but I must go on, and I am happy indeed that I cannot go back. My father is in California, and from the letter which he sent me by way of Cape Horn, I learn that for some months he has been ill of a fever in Sacramento. Poor father! he was accustomed to comfort and my care, — and it was only through love of me that he went to California. I do not know whether

I shall find him alive; but I feel that in going to him, I am only fulfilling a duty that is dear to me."

There was no answer to such words; moreover, all that I might object to this undertaking would be too late. I inquired then of Lillian for nearer details touching her father. These she gave with great pleasure, and I learned that in Boston Mr. Morris had been judge of the Supreme Court, or highest tribunal of the State; that he had lost his property, and had gone to the newly discovered mines of California in the hope of acquiring a new fortune, and bringing back to his daughter, whom he loved more than life, her former social position. Meanwhile, he caught a fever in the unwholesome Sacramento valley, and thinking that death was near, he sent Lillian his last blessing. She sold all the property that he had left with her, and resolved to hasten to him. At first she intended to go by sea; but an acquaintance with Aunt Atkins made by chance two days before the caravan started, changed her mind. Aunt Atkins, who was from Tennessee, having had her ears filled with tales which friends of mine from the banks of the Mississippi had told her and others of my daring expeditions to the famed Arkansas, of my experience in journeys over the prairies, and the care which I gave to the weak (this I consider as a simple duty), described me in such colors before Lillian that the girl, without hesitating longer, joined the caravan going under my leadership. To those exaggerated narratives of Aunt Atkins, who did not delay to add that I was of noble birth, it is necessary to ascribe the fact that Miss Morris was occupied with my person.

"You may be sure," said I, when she had finished her story, "that no one will do you wrong here, and that care will not fail you; as to your father, California is the healthiest country on earth, and no one dies there of fever. In every case, while I live, you will not be left alone; meanwhile may God bless your sweet face!"

"Thank you, captain," answered she, with emotion, and we went on; but my heart beat with more violence. Gradually our conversation became livelier, and no one could foresee that that calmness above us would grow cloudy.

"But all here are kind to you, Miss Morris, are they not?" asked I again, not supposing that just that question would be the cause of misunderstanding.

"Oh, yes, all," said she, "Aunt Atkins and Aunt Grosvenor, and Henry Simpson too is very good."

This mention of Simpson pained me suddenly, like the bite of a snake.

"Henry is a mule-driver," answered I curtly, "and has to care for the wagons."

But Lillian, occupied with the course of her own thoughts, had not noticed the change in my voice, and spoke on as if to herself, —

"He has an honest heart, and I shall be grateful to him all my life."

"Miss Morris," interrupted I, cut to the quick, "you may even give him your hand. I wonder, however, that you choose me as a confidant of your feelings."

When I said that she looked at me with astonishment but made no reply, and we went on together in disagreeable silence. I knew not what to say, though my heart was full of bitterness and anger toward her and myself. I felt simply conquered by jealousy of Simpson, but still I could not fight against it. The position seemed to me so unendurable that I said all at once briefly and dryly:

"Good night, Miss Morris!"

"Good night," answered she calmly, turning her head to hide two tears that were flowing down her cheeks.

I mounted my horse and rode away again toward the point whence the sound of axes came, and where, among others, Henry Simpson was cutting a cottonwood. After a while I was seized by a certain measureless regret, for it seemed to me that those two tears were falling on my heart. I turned my horse, and next minute I was near Lillian a second time.

"Why are you crying, Miss Morris?" asked I.

"Oh, sir," said she, "I know that you are of a noble family, Aunt Atkins told me that, and you have been so kind to me."

She did everything not to cry; but she could not restrain herself, and could not finish her answer, for tears choked her voice. The poor thing! she had been touched to the bottom of her pensive soul by my answer regarding Simpson, for there was evident in it a certain aristocratic contempt; but I was not even dreaming of aristocracy, — I was simply jealous; and now, seeing her so unhappy, I wanted to seize my own collar and throttle myself. Grasping her hand, I said with animation, —

"Lillian, Lillian, you did not understand me. I take God to witness that no pride was speaking through me. Look at me: I have nothing in the world but these two hands, — what is my descent to me? Something else pained me, and I wanted to go away; but I could not support your tears. And I swear to you also, that what I have said to you pains me more than it does you. You are not an object of indifference to me, Lillian. Oh, not at all! for if you were, what you think of Henry would not concern me. He is an honest fellow, but that does not touch the question. You see how much your tears cost me; then forgive me as sincerely as I entreat your forgiveness."

Speaking in this way I raised her hand and pressed it

to my lips; that high proof of respect, and the truthfulness which sounded in my request, quieted the maiden somewhat. She did not cease at once to weep, but her tears were of another kind, for a smile was visible through them, as a sun-ray through mist. Something too was sticking in my throat, and I could not stifle my emotion. A tender feeling had mastered my heart. We walked on in silence, and round about us the world was pleasant and sweet.

The day was inclining toward evening; the weather was beautiful, and in the air, already dusky, there was so much light that the whole prairie, the distant groups of cottonwood-trees, the wagons in our train, and the flocks of wild geese flying northward through the sky, seemed golden and rosy. Not the least wind moved the grass; from a distance came to us the sound of rapids, which the Cedar River formed in that place, and the neighing of horses from the direction of the camp. That evening with such charms, that virgin land, and the presence of Lillian, brought me to such a state of mind that my soul was almost ready to fly out of me to the sky. I thought myself a shaken bell, as it were. At moments I wanted to take Lillian's hand again, raise it to my lips, and not put it down for a long time; but I feared lest this might offend her. Meanwhile she walked on near me, calm, mild, and thoughtful. Her tears had dried already; at moments she raised her bright eyes to me; then we began to speak again, — and so reached the camp.

That day, in which I had experienced so many emotions, was to end joyfully, for the people, pleased with the beautiful weather, had resolved to have a "picnic," or open air festival. After a supper more abundant than usual, one great fire was kindled, before which there was to be danc-

23

ing. Henry Simpson had cleared away the grass purposely from a space of many square yards, and sprinkled it
with sand brought from Cedar River. When the spectators
had assembled on the place thus prepared, Simpson began
to dance a jig, with the accompaniment of negro flutes, to
the admiration of all. With hands hanging at his sides he
kept his whole body motionless; but his feet were working so nimbly, striking the ground in turn with heel and
toe, that the eye could hardly follow their movements.

The flutes played madly; a second dancer came out, a
third, then a fourth, — and the fun was universal. The
audience joined the negroes who were playing on the
flutes, and thrummed on tin pans, intended for washing
the gold-bearing earth, or kept time with pieces of ox-ribs
held between the fingers of each hand, which gave out a
sound like the clatter of castanets.

Suddenly the cry of "minstrels! minstrels!" was heard
through the whole camp. The audience formed a circle
around the dancing-place; into this stepped our negroes,
Jim and Crow. Jim held a little drum covered with
snake-skin, Crow the pieces of ox-rib mentioned already.
For a time they stared at each other, rolling the whites
of their eyes; then they began to sing a negro song, interrupted by stamping and violent springs of the body;
at times the song was sad, at times wild. The prolonged
"Dinah! ah! ah!" with which each verse ended, changed
at length into a shout, and almost into a howling like that
of beasts. As the dancers warmed up and grew excited,
their movements became wilder, and at last they fell to
butting each other with blows from which European skulls
would have cracked like nutshells. Those black figures,
shone upon by the bright gleam of the fire and springing
in wild leaps, presented a spectacle truly fantastic. With
their shouts and the sounds of the drum, pipes, and tin

pans, and the click of the bones, were mingled shouts of
the spectators, "Hurrah for Jim! Hurrah for Crow!"
and then shots from revolvers.

When at last the black men were wearied and had
fallen on the ground, they began to labor with their
breasts and to pant. I commanded to give each a drink
of brandy; this put them on their feet again. But at
that moment the people began to call for a "speech." In
an instant the uproar and music ceased. I had to drop
Lillian's arm, climb to the seat of a wagon, and turn to
those present. When I looked from my height on those
forms illuminated by the fires, forms large, broad-
shouldered, bearded, with knives at their girdles, and
hats with torn crowns, it seemed to me that I was in
some theatre, or had become a chieftain of robbers. They
were honest, brave hearts, however, though the rough life
of more than one of these men was stormy perhaps and
half wild; but here we formed, as it were, a little world
torn away from the rest of society and confined to ourselves, destined to a common fate and threatened by common dangers. Here shoulder had to touch shoulder;
each felt that he was brother to the next man; the road-
less places and boundless deserts with which we were
surrounded commanded those hardy miners to love one
another. The sight of Lillian, the poor defenceless maiden,
fearless among them and safe as if under her father's roof,
brought those thoughts to my head; hence I told everything, just as I felt it, and as befitted a soldier leader who
was at the same time a brother of wanderers. Every
little while they interrupted me with cries, "Hurrah for
the Pole! Hurrah for the captain! Hurrah for Big
Ralph!" and with clapping of hands; but what made me
happiest of all was to see between the network of those
sunburnt strong hands one pair of small palms, rosy with

the gleam of the fire and flying like a pair of white doves. I felt then at once, What care I for the desert, the wild beasts, the Indians and the "outlaws"? and cried with mighty ardor, "I will conquer anything, I will kill anything that comes in my way, and lead the train even to the end of the earth, — and may God forget my right hand, if this is not true!" A still louder "Hurrah!" answered these words, and all began to sing with great enthusiasm the emigrants' song, "I crossed the Mississippi, I will cross the Missouri." Then Smith, the oldest among the emigrants, a miner from near Pittsburgh in Pennsylvania, spoke in answer. He thanked me in the name of the whole company, and lauded my skill in leading the caravan. After Smith, from nearly every wagon a man spoke. Some made very amusing remarks, for intance Henry Simpson, who cried out every little while, "Gentlemen! I'll be hanged if I don't tell the truth!" When the speakers had grown hoarse at last, the flutes sounded, the bones rattled, and the men began to dance a jig again.

Night had fallen completely; the moon came out in the sky and shone so brightly that the flame of the fires almost paled before its gleams; the people and the wagons were illuminated doubly by a red and a white light. That was a beautiful night. The uproar of our camp offered a strange but pleasing contrast to the calmness and deep slumber of the prairie.

Taking Lillian's arm, I went with her around the whole camp; our gaze passed from the fires to the distance, and was lost in the waves of the tall and dark grasses of the prairie, silvery from the rays of the moon and as mysterious as spirits. We strolled alone in that way. Meanwhile, at one of the fires, two Scottish Highlanders began to play on pipes their plaintive air of "Bonnie Dundee."

We both stopped at a distance and listened for some time
in silence ; all at once I looked at Lillian, she dropped
her eyes, — and without knowing myself why I did so,
I pressed to my heart long and powerfully that hand
which she had rested on my arm. In Lillian too the poor
heart began to beat with such force that I felt it as clearly
as if on my palm ; we trembled, for we saw that something was rising between us, that that something was
conquering, and that we would not be to each other as
we had been hitherto. As to me I was swimming already
whithersoever that current was bearing me. I forgot
that the night was bright, that the fires were not distant,
and that there were people around them ; and I wanted
to fall at her feet immediately, or at least to look into
her eyes. But she, though leaning on my arm, turned her
head, as if glad to hide her face in the shade. I wished to
speak but I could not ; for it seemed to me that I should
call out with some voice not my own, or if I should say
the words "I love" to Lillian I should drop to the earth.
I was not bold, being young then, and was led not by my
thoughts simply, but by my soul too ; and I felt this also
clearly, that if I should say " I love," a curtain would fall
on my past ; one door would close and another would
open, through which I should pass into a certain new
region. Hence, though I saw happiness beyond that
threshold I halted, for this very reason it may be, — that
the brightness beating from out that place dazzled me.
Besides, when loving comes not from the lips, but the
heart, there is perhaps nothing so difficult to speak about.

I had dared to press Lillian's hand to my breast ; we
were silent, for I had not the boldness to mention love,
and I had no wish to speak of aught else, — I could not
at such a time.

It ended with this, that we both raised our heads and

looked at the stars, like people who are praying. Then some one at the great fire called me; we returned; the festival had closed, but to end it worthily and well, the emigrants had determined to sing a psalm before going to rest. The men had uncovered their heads, and though among them were persons of various faiths, all knelt on the grass of the prairie and sang "Wandering in the Wilderness." The sight was impressive. At moments of rest the silence became so perfect that the crackling of sparks in the fire could be heard, and from the river the sound of the waterfalls came to us.

Kneeling near Lillian, I looked once or twice at her face; her eyes were uplifted and wonderfully shining, her hair was a little disarranged; and, singing with devotion, she was so like an angel, that it seemed almost possible to pray to her.

After the singing, the people went to their wagons. I, according to custom, repaired to the sentries, and then to my rest, like the others. But this time when the mosquitoes began to sing in my ears, as they did every evening, "Lillian! Lillian! Lillian!" I knew that in that wagon beyond there was sleeping the sight of my eye and the soul of my soul, and that in all the world there was nothing dearer to me than that maiden.

CHAPTER III.

AT dawn the following day we passed Cedar River successfully and came out on a level, broad prairie, stretching between that river and the Winnebago, which curved imperceptibly to the south, toward the belt of forests lying along the lower boundary of Iowa. From the morning Lillian had not dared to look in my eyes. I saw that she was thoughtful; it seemed as though she were ashamed of something, or troubled for some cause; but still what sin had we committed the evening before? She scarcely left the wagon. Aunt Atkins and Aunt Grosvenor, thinking that she was ill, surrounded her with care and tenderness. I alone knew what that meant, — I knew that it was neither pangs of conscience, nor weakness; it was the struggle of an innocent being with the feeling that a power new and unknown is bearing it on, like a leaf, to some place far away. It was a clear insight that there was no help, and that sooner or later she would have to weaken and yield to the will of that power, forget everything, — and only love.

A pure soul draws back and is afraid on the threshold of love, but feeling that it will cross, it weakens. Lillian therefore was as if wearied by a dream; but when I understood all that, the breath in my breast was nearly stopped from joy. I know not whether it was an honorable feeling, but when in the morning I flew past her wagon and saw her, broken like a flower, I felt something akin to what a bird of prey feels, when it knows that the dove will not escape. And still I would not do an injustice to that dove for any treasure on earth, for with love I had in my heart at the same time an immense compassion. A wonderful thing however: notwithstanding my feeling for Lillian, the whole day passed for us as if in mutual offence, or at least in perplexity. I was racking my head to discover how I could be alone with her even for a moment, but could not discover. Fortunately Aunt Atkins came to my aid; she declared that the little one needed more exercise, that confinement in that close wagon was injuring her health. I fell upon the thought that she ought to ride on horseback, and ordered Simpson to saddle a horse for her; and though there were no side-saddles in the train, one of those Mexican saddles with a high pommel which women use everywhere on frontier prairies, could serve her very well. I forbade Lillian to loiter behind far enough to drop out of view. To be lost in the open prairie was somewhat difficult, because people, whom I sent out for game, circled about a considerable distance in every direction. There was no danger from Indians, for that part of the prairie, as far as the Winnebago, was visited by Pawnees only during the great hunts, which had not begun yet. But the southern forest-tract abounded in wild beasts, not all of which were grass eating; wariness, therefore, was far from superfluous.

To tell the truth I thought that Lillian would keep near me for safety; this would permit us to be alone rather frequently. Usually I pushed forward some distance in time of march, having before me only the two half-breed scouts, and behind the whole caravan. So it happened in fact, and I was both truly and inexpressibly happy the first day, when I saw my sweet Amazon coming on at a light gallop from the direction of the train. The movement of the horse unwound her tresses somewhat, and care for her skirt, which was the least trifle short for the saddle, had painted her face with a charming anxiety. When she had ridden up she was like a rose; for she knew that she was going into a trap laid by me so that we might be alone with each other, and knowing this she came, though blushing, and as if unwilling, feigning that she knew nothing. My heart beat as if I had been a young student; and, when our horses were abreast, I was angry with myself because I knew not what to say. At the same time such sweet and powerful desires began to pass between us that I, urged by some unseen power, bent toward Lillian as if to straighten something in the mane of her horse, and meanwhile I pressed my lips to her hand, which was resting on the pommel of the saddle. A certain unknown and unspeakable happiness, greater and keener than any delight that I had known in my life till that moment, passed through my bones. I pressed that little hand to my heart, and told Lillian, that if God had bestowed all the kingdoms of the earth on me, and all the treasures in existence, I would not give for anything one tress of her hair, for she had taken me soul and body forever.

"Lillian, Lillian," said I further, "I will never leave you. I will follow you through mountains and deserts; I will kiss your feet and I will pray to you; only love me a little, only tell me that in your heart I mean something."

Thus speaking, I thought that my bosom would burst, when she said with the greatest confusion, —

" O Ralph! you know well! you know everything!"

I did not know just this, whether to laugh or to cry, whether to run away or remain; and, as I hope for salvation to-day, I felt saved, for nothing in the world then was lacking to me.

Thenceforth, so far as my occupations permitted, we were always together. And those occupations decreased every day till we reached the Missouri. Perhaps no caravan had more success than ours during the first month of the journey. Men and animals were growing accustomed to order and skilled in travelling; hence I had less need to look after them, while the confidence which the people gave me upheld perfect order in the caravan. Besides, abundance of provisions and the fine spring weather roused joyfulness and increased good health. I convinced myself daily, that my bold plan of passing, not by the usual route through St. Louis and Kansas, but through Iowa and Nebraska, was best. There, heat almost unendurable tortured people, and in the unhealthy region between the Mississippi and Missouri, fevers and other diseases thinned the ranks of emigrants; here, because of a cooler climate, cases of weakness were fewer, and our labor was less.

It is true that the road by St. Louis was in the earlier part of it freer from Indians; but my train, composed of two or three hundred men well furnished with weapons and ready for fighting, had no cause to fear roving tribes, especially those inhabiting Iowa, who through meeting white men more frequently, and having greater experience of what white hands could do, had not the courage to rush at large parties. It was only needful to guard against stampedes, or night attacks on mules and horses, — the loss of draught-animals puts a caravan on the prairies in a terrible position. But against that we put diligence and the experience of sentries who, for the greater part, were as well acquainted with the stratagems of Indians as I was.

When once I had introduced travelling discipline and made men accustomed to it, I had incomparably less to do during daylight, and could give more time to the feelings which had seized on my heart. In the evening I went to sleep with the thought, "To-morrow I shall see Lillian;" in the morning I said to myself, "To-day I shall see Lillian;" and every day I was happier, and every day more in love. In the caravan people began by degrees to notice this; but no one took it ill of me, for Lillian and I possessed the good-will of those people. Once old Smith said in passing, "God bless you, captain, and you, Lillian." That connecting of our names made us happy all day. Aunt Grosvenor and Aunt Atkins whispered something frequently in Lillian's ear, which made her blush like the dawn, but she would never tell me what it was. Henry Simpson looked on us rather gloomily, — perhaps he was forging some plan in his soul, but I paid no heed to him.

Every morning at four I was at the head of the caravan; before me the scouts, some fifteen hundred yards distant, sang songs, taught them by their Indian mothers; behind me at the same distance moved the caravan, like a white ribbon on the prairie, — and what a wonderful moment, when, about two hours later, I hear on a sudden behind me the tramp of a horse. I look, and behold the sight of my soul, my beloved is approaching. The morning breeze bears behind her her hair, which either had been loosened from the movement, or badly fastened on purpose, for the little rogue knew that she looked better that way, that I liked her that way, and that when the wind threw the tress on me I pressed it to my lips. I feign not to notice her tricks, and in this agreeable meeting the morning begins for us. I had taught her the Polish phrase, "Dzien dobry" (good morning). When I hear her pronouncing those words, she seems still dearer; the memory of my country, of my family, of years gone by, of that which had been, of that which had passed, flies before my vision on that prairie like mews of the ocean. More than once I would have broken out in weeping, but from shame I restrained with my eyelids the tears that were ready to flow. She, seeing that the heart was melting in me, would repeat like a trained starling, "Dzien dobry! dzien dobry! dzien dobry!" and how was I not to love my starling beyond everything? I taught her then other phrases; and when her lips struggled with our difficult sounds, and I laughed at a faulty pronunciation, she pouted like a little child, feigning resentment

and anger. But we had no quarrels, and once only a
cloud flew between us. One morning I pretended to
tighten a strap on her stirrup, but in truth the leopard
Ulan was roused in me, and I began to kiss her foot, or
rather the poor shoe worn out in the wilderness. Then
she drew her foot close to the horse, and repeating, " No,
Ralph! no! no!" sprang to one side; and though I implored and strove to pacify her she would not come near
me. She did not return to the caravan, however, fearing
to pain me too much. I feigned a sorrow a hundred
times greater than I felt in reality, and sinking into
silence, rode on as if all things had ended on earth for me.
I knew that compassion would stir in her, as indeed it
did; for soon, alarmed at my silence, she began to ride up
at one side and look at my eyes, like a child which wants
to know if its mother is angry yet, — and I, wishing to
preserve a gloomy visage, had to turn aside to avoid
laughing aloud.

But this was only one time. Usually we were as gladsome as prairie squirrels, and sometimes, God forgive me,
I, the leader of that caravan, became a child with her.
More than once when we were riding side by side I would
turn on a sudden, saying to her that I had something
important and new to tell, and when she held her inquisitive ear I whispered into it, "I love." Then she also
whispered into my ear in answer, with a smile and
blush, "I also!" And thus we confided our secrets to
each other on the prairie, where the wind alone could
overhear us.

In this manner day shot after day so quickly, that, as
I thought, the morning seemed to touch the evening like
links in a chain. At times some event of the journey
would vary such pleasant monotony. A certain Sunday
the half-breed Wichita lassoed an antelope of a large

kind, and with her a fawn which I gave to Lillian, who made for it a collar on which was put a bell, taken from a mule. This fawn we called Katty In a week it was tame, and ate from our hands. During the march I would ride on one side of Lillian, and Katty would run on the other, raising its great black eyes and begging with a bleat for caresses.

Beyond the Winnebago we came out on a plain as level as a table, broad, rich, primeval. The scouts vanished from our eyes in the grass at times; our horses waded, as if in a river. I showed Lillian that world altogether new to her, and when she was delighted with its beauties, I felt proud that that kingdom of mine was so pleasing to her. It was spring, — April was barely reaching its end, the time of richest growth for grasses of all sorts. What was to bloom on the plains was blooming already.

In the evening such intoxicating odors came from the prairie, as from a thousand censers; in the day, when the wind blew and shook the flowery expanses, the eye was just pained with the glitter of red, blue, yellow, and colors of all kinds. From the dense bed shot up the slender stalks of yellow flowers, like our mullein; around these wound the silver threads of a plant called "tears," whose clusters, composed of transparent little balls, are really like tears. My eyes, used to reading in the prairie, discovered repeatedly plants that I knew: now it was the large-leaved kalumna, which cures wounds; now the plant called "white and red stockings," which closes its cups at the approach of man or beast; finally, "Indian hatchets," the odor of which brings sleep and almost takes away consciousness. I taught Lillian at that time to read in this Divine book, saying, —

"You will live in forests and on plains; it is well then to know them in season."

In places on the level prairie rose, as if they were oases, groups of cottonwood or alder, so wreathed with wild grapes and lianas that they could not be recognized under the tendrils and leaves. On the lianas in turn climbed ivy and the prickly, thorny "wachtia," resembling wild roses. Flowers were just dropping at all points; inside, underneath that screen and beyond that wall, was a certain mysterious gloom; at the tree trunks were sleeping great pools of water of the spring-time, which the sun was unable to drink up; from the tree-tops and among the brocade of flowers came wonderful voices and the calling of birds. When for the first time I showed such trees to Lillian and such hanging cascades of flowers, she stood as if fixed to the earth, repeating with clasped hands, —

"Oh, Ralph! is that real?"

She said that she was a little afraid to enter such a depth; but one afternoon, when the heat was great, and over the prairie was flying, as it were, the hot breath of the Texan wind, we rode in, and Katty came after us.

We stopped at a little pool, which reflected our two horses and our two forms; we remained in silence for a time. It was cool there, obscure, solemn as in a Gothic cathedral, and somewhat awe-inspiring. The light of day came in bedimmed, greenish from the leaves. Some bird, hidden under the cupola of lianas, cried, "No! no! no!" as if warning us not to go farther; Katty began to tremble and nestle up to the horses; Lillian and I looked at each other suddenly, and for the first time our lips met, and having met could not separate. She drank my soul, I drank her soul. Breath began to fail each of us, still lips were on lips. At last her eyes were covered with mist, and the hands which she had placed on my shoulders were trembling as in a fever: she was seized with a kind of oblivion of her own existence, so that she grew faint and placed her head on my bosom. We were drunk with each other, with bliss, and with ecstasy. I dared not move; but because I had a soul overfilled, because I loved a hundred times more than may be thought or expressed, I raised my eyes to discover if through the thick leaves I could see the sky.

Recovering our senses, we came out at last from beneath the green density to the open prairie, where we were surrounded by the bright sunshine and warm breeze; before us was spread the broad and gladsome landscape. Prairie chickens were fluttering in the grass, and on slight elevations, which were perforated like a sieve by prairie dogs, stood, as it were, an army of those little creatures, which vanished under the earth at our coming; directly in front was the caravan, and horsemen careering around it.

It seemed to me that we had come out of a dark chamber to the white world, and the same thought must have come to Lillian. The brightness of the day rejoiced me; but that excess of golden light and the memory of rapturous kisses, traces of which were still evident on her face, penetrated Lillian as it were with alarm and with sadness.

"Ralph, will you not take that ill of me?" asked she, on a sudden.

"What comes to your head, O my own! God forget me if in my heart there is any feeling but respect and the highest love for you."

"I did that because I love greatly," said she; and therewith her lips began to quiver and she wept in silence, and though I was working the soul out of myself she remained sad all that day.

CHAPTER IV.

At last we came to the Missouri. Indians chose generally the time of crossing that river to fall upon caravans; defence is most difficult when some wagons are on one bank, and some in the river; when the draught-beasts are stubborn and balky, and disorder rises among people. Indeed, I noticed, before our arrival at the river, that Indian spies had for two days been following us; hence I took every precaution, and led the train in complete military order. I did not permit wagons to loiter on the prairie, as in the eastern districts of Iowa; the men had to stay together and be in perfect readiness for battle.

When we had come to the bank and found a ford, I ordered two divisions, of sixty men each, to intrench themselves on both banks, so as to secure the passage under cover of small forts and the muzzles of rifles. The remaining one hundred and twenty had to take the train over. I did not send in more than a few wagons at once, so as to avoid confusion. With such an arrangement everything took place in the greatest order, and attack became impossible, for the attackers would have had to carry one or the other intrenchment before they could fall upon those who were crossing the river.

How far these precautions were from being superfluous the future made evident, for two years later four hundred Germans were slaughtered by the Kiowas, at the place where Omaha stands at this moment. I had this advantage besides: my men, who previously had heard more than once narratives, which went to the East, of the terrible danger of crossing the yellow waters of the Missouri, seeing the firmness and ease with which I solved the problem, gained blind confidence, and looked on me as some ruling spirit of the plains.

Daily did those praises and that enthusiasm reach Lillian, in whose loving eyes I grew to be a legendary hero. Aunt Atkins said to her, "While your Pole is with you, you may sleep out in the rain, for he won't let the drops fall on you." And the heart rose in my maiden from those praises. During the whole time of crossing I could give her hardly a moment, and could only say hurriedly with my eyes what my lips could not utter. All day I was on horseback, now on one bank, now on the other, now in the water. I was in a hurry to advance as soon as possible from those thick yellow waters, which were bearing down with them rotten trees, bunches of leaves, grass, and malodorous mud from Dakota, infectious with fever.

Besides this, the people were wearied immensely, from continual watching; the horses grew sick from unwholesome water, which we could not use until we had kept it in charcoal a number of hours.

At last, after eight days' time, we found ourselves on the right bank of the river without having broken a wagon, and with the loss of only seven head of mules and horses. That day, however, the first arrows fell, for my men killed, and afterward, according to the repulsive habit of the plains, scalped three Indians, who had been trying to push in among the mules. In consequence of this deed an embassy of six leading warriors of the Bloody Tracks, belonging to the Pawnees, visited us on the following day. They sat down at our fire with tremendous importance, demanding horses and mules in return for the dead men, declaring that, in case of refusal, five hundred men would attack us immediately. I made no great account of those five hundred warriors, since I had the train in order and defended with intrenchments. I saw well that that embassy had been sent merely because those wild people had caught at the first opportunity to extort something without an attack, in the success of which they had lost faith. I should have driven them away in one moment, had I not wished to exhibit them to Lillian. In fact, while they were sitting at the council-fire motionless, with eyes fixed on the flame, she, concealed in the wagon, was looking with alarm and curiosity at their dress trimmed at the seams with human hair, their tomahawks adorned with feathers on the handles, and at their faces painted black and red, which meant war. In spite of these preparations, however, I refused their demand sharply, and, passing from a defensive to an offensive rôle, declared that if even one mule disappeared from the train, I would go to their tribe myself and scatter the bones of their five hundred warriors over the prairie.

They went away, hardly repressing their rage, but when going they brandished their tomahawks over their heads in sign of war. However, my words sank in their memory; for at the time of their departure two hundred of my men, prepared purposely, rose up with threatening aspect, rattling their weapons. and gave forth a shout of battle. That readiness made a deep impression on the wild warriors.

Some hours later Henry Simpson, who at his own instance had gone out to observe the embassy, returned, all panting, with news that a considerable division of Indians was approaching us.

I, knowing Indian ways perfectly, knew that those were mere threats, for the Indians, armed with bows made of hickory, were not in numbers sufficient to meet long range Kentucky rifles. I said that to Lillian, wishing to quiet her, for she was trembling like a leaf; but all the others were sure that a battle was coming; the younger ones, whose warlike spirit was roused, wished for it eagerly.

In fact, we heard the howling of the red-skins soon after; still, they kept at the distance of some gun-shots, as if seeking a favorable moment.

In our camp immense fires, replenished with cotton-wood and willows, were burning all night; the men stood guard around the wagons; the women were singing psalms from fear; the mules, not driven out to the usual night pasture, but confined behind the wagons, were braying and biting one another; the dogs, feeling the nearness of Indians, were howling, — in a word, it was noisy and threatening throughout the camp. In brief moments of silence we heard the mournful and ominous howling of Indian outposts, calling with the voices of coyotes.

About midnight the Indians tried to set fire to the prairie, but the damp grass of spring would not burn, though for some days not a raindrop had fallen on that region.

When riding around the camp-ground before daybreak I had a chance of seeing Lillian for a moment. I found her sleeping from weariness, with her head resting on the knees of Aunt Atkins, who, armed with a bowie-knife, had sworn to destroy the whole tribe, if one of them dared to come near her darling. As to me, I looked on that fair sleeping face with the love not only of a man, but almost of a mother, and I felt equally with Aunt Atkins that I would tear into pieces any one who would threaten my beloved. In her was my joy, in her my delight; beyond her I had nothing but endless wandering, tramping, and mishaps. Before my eyes I had the best proof of this : in the distance were the prairie, the rattle of weapons, the night on horseback, the struggle with predatory redskin murderers; nearer, right there before my face, was the quiet sleep of that dear one, so full of faith and trust in me, that my word alone had convinced her that there could be no attack, and she had fallen asleep as full of confidence as if under her father's roof.

When I looked at those two pictures, I felt for the first time how that adventurous life without a morrow had wearied me, and I saw at once that I should find rest and satisfaction with her alone. " If only to California ! " thought I, "if only to California ! But the toils of the journey — merely one-half of which, and that half the easier, is over — are evident already on that pallid face ; but a beautiful rich country is waiting for us there, with its warm sky and eternal spring." Thus meditating, I covered the feet of the sleeper with my buffalo-robe, so that the night cold might not harm her, and returned to the end of the camp.

It was time, for a thick mist had begun to rise from the river; the Indians might really take advantage of it and try their fortune. The fires were dimmed more and more, and grew pale. An hour later one man could not see another even ten paces distant I gave command then to cry on the square every minute, and soon nothing was heard in that camp but the prolonged "All 's well ! " which passed from mouth to mouth like the words of a litany.

But the Indian camp had grown perfectly still, as if held by dumb occupants. This alarmed me. At the first dawn an immense weariness mastered us ; God knows how many nights the majority of the men had passed without sleep, — besides, the fog, wonderfully penetrating, sent a chill and a shiver through all of us.

Would it not be better, thought I, instead of standing

on one place and waiting for what may please the Indians, to attack and scatter them to the four winds? This was not simply the whim of an Ulan, but an absolute need; for a daring and lucky attack might gain us great glory, which, spreading among the wild tribes, would give us safety for a long stretch of road.

Leaving behind me one hundred and thirty men, under the lead of the old prairie wolf, Smith, I commanded a hundred others to mount, and we moved forward somewhat cautiously, but gladly, for the cold had become more annoying, and in this way we could at least warm ourselves. At twice the distance of a gun-shot we raced forward at a gallop with shouting, and in the midst of a musket-fire rushed, like a storm, on the savages. A ball, sent from our side by some awkward marksman, whistled right at my ear, but only tore my cap.

Meanwhile, we were on the necks of the Indians, who expected anything rather than an attack, for this beyond doubt was the first time that emigrants had charged the besiegers. Great alarm so blinded them, therefore, that they fled in every direction, howling from fright like wild beasts, and perishing without resistance. A smaller division of these people, pushed to the river and, deprived of retreat, defended themselves so sternly and stubbornly that they chose to rush into the water rather than beg for life.

Their spears pointed with sharpened deer-horns and tomahawks made of hard flint were not very dangerous, but they used them with wonderful skill. We burst through these, however, in the twinkle of an eye. I took one prisoner, a sturdy rascal, whose hatchet and arm I broke in the moment of fighting with hatchets.

We seized a few tens of horses, but so wild and vicious that there was no use in them. We made a few prisoners, all wounded. I gave command to care for these most attentively, and set them free afterward at Lillian's request, having given them blankets, arms, and horses, necessary for men badly wounded. These poor fellows, believing that we would tie them to stakes for torture, had begun to chant their monotonous death-songs, and were simply terrified at first by what had happened. They thought that we would liberate only to hunt them in Indian fashion; but seeing that no danger threatened, they went away, exalting our bravery and the goodness of "Pale Flower," which name they had given Lillian.

That day ended, however, with a sad event, which cast a shade on our delight at such a considerable victory, and its foreseen results. Among my men there were none killed; a number, nevertheless, had received wounds more or less serious; the most grievously wounded was Henry Simpson, whose eagerness had borne him away during battle. In the evening his condition grew so much worse, that he was dying; he wished, poor fellow, to make a confession to me, but could not speak, for his jaw had been broken by a tomahawk. He merely muttered, "Pardon, my captain!" Convulsions seized him immediately. I divined what he wanted, remembering the bullet which had whistled at my ear in the morning, and I forgave him, as becomes a Christian. I knew that he carried with him to the grave a deep, though unacknowledged feeling for Lillian, and supposed that he might have sought death.

He died about midnight; we buried him under an immense cottonwood, on the bark of which I carved out a cross with my knife.

CHAPTER V.

On the following day we moved on. Before us was a prairie still more extensive, more level, wilder, a region which the foot of a white man had hardly touched at that period, — in a word, we were in Nebraska.

During the first days we moved quickly enough over treeless expanses, but not without difficulty, for there was an utter lack of wood for fuel. The banks of the Platte River, which cuts the whole length of those measureless plains, were, it is true, covered with a dense growth of osier and willow; but that river had overflowed its shallow bed, as is usual in spring, and we had to keep far away from it. Meanwhile we passed the nights at smouldering fires of buffalo dung, which, not dried yet sufficiently by the sun, rather smouldered with a blue flame than burnt. We hurried on then with every effort toward Big Blue River, where we could find abundance of fuel.

The country around us bore every mark of a primitive region. Time after time, before the train, which extended now in a very loose line, rushed herds of antelopes with ruddy hair and with white under the belly; at times there appeared in the waves of grass the immense shaggy heads of buffaloes, with bloodshot eyes and steaming nostrils; then again these beasts were seen in crowds, like black, moving patches on the distant prairie.

In places we passed near whole towns formed of mounds raised by prairie dogs. The Indians did not show themselves at first, and only a number of days later did we see three wild horsemen, ornamented with feathers; but they vanished before our eyes in an instant, like phantoms. I convinced myself afterward that the bloody lesson which I had given them on the Missouri, made the name of " Big Ara " (for thus they had modified Big Ralph) terrible among the many tribes of prairie robbers ; the kindness shown the prisoners had captivated those people, wild and revengeful, though not devoid of knightly feeling.

When we had come to Big Blue River, I resolved to halt ten days at its woody banks. The second half of the road, which lay before us, was more difficult than the first, for beyond the prairie were the Rocky Mountains, and farther on the " Bad Lands " of Utah and Nevada. Meanwhile, our mules and horses, in spite of abundant pasture, had become lean and road-weary ; hence it was needful to recruit their strength with a considerable rest. For this purpose we halted in the triangle formed by the Big Blue River and Beaver Creek.

It was a strong position, which, secured on two sides by the rivers and on the third by the wagons, had become almost impregnable, especially since wood and water were found on the spot. Of camp labor there was scarcely any, excessive watching was not needed, and the emigrants could use their leisure with perfect freedom. The days, too, were the most beautiful of our journey. The weather continued to be marvellous, and the nights grew so warm that one might sleep in the open air.

The people went out in the morning to hunt, and returned at midday, weighed down with antelopes and prairie birds, which lived in millions in the country about ; the rest of the day they spent eating, sleeping, singing, or shooting for amusement at wild geese, which flew above our camp in whole flocks.

In my life there has never been anything better or happier than those ten days between the rivers. From morning till evening I did not part from Lillian, and that beginning not of passing visits, but, as it were, of life, convinced me more and more that I had loved once and forever her, the mild and gentle. I became acquainted with Lillian in those days more nearly and more deeply. At night, instead of sleeping, I thought frequently of what she was, and that she had become to me as dear and as needful in life as the air is for breathing. God sees that I loved greatly her beautiful face, her long tresses, and her eyes, — as blue as that sky bending over Nebraska, — and her form, lithe and slender, which seemed to say, "Support and defend me forever; without thee I cannot help myself in the world!" God sees that I loved everything that was in her, every poor bit of clothing of hers, and she attracted me with such force that I could not resist; but there was another charm in her for me, and that was her sweetness and sensitiveness.

Many women have I met in my life, but never have I met and never shall I meet another such, and I feel endless grief when I think of her. The soul in Lillian Morris was as sensitive as that flower whose leaves nestle in when you draw near it. Sensitive to every word of mine, she comprehended everything and reflected every thought, just as deep, transparent water reflects all that passes by the brink of it. At the same time that pure heart yielded itself to feeling with such timidity that I felt how great her love must be when she weakened and gave herself in sacrifice. And then everything honorable in my soul was changed into one feeling of gratitude to her. She was simply my one, my dearest in the world; so modest, that I had to persuade her that to love is not a sin, and I was breaking my head continually over this: how can I persuade her? In such emotions time passed for us at the meeting of the rivers, till at last my supreme happiness was accomplished.

One morning at daybreak we started to walk up Beaver Creek; I wanted to show her the beavers; a whole kingdom of them was flourishing not farther than half a mile from our wagons. Walking along the bank carefully, near the bushes, we came soon to our object. There was a little bay as it were, or a lakelet, formed by the creek, at the brink of which stood two great hickory-trees; at the very bank grew weeping-willows, half their branches in the water. The beaver-dam, a little higher up in the creek, stopped its flow, and kept the water ever at one height in the lakelet, above whose clear surface rose the round cupola-shaped houses of these very clever animals.

Probably the foot of man had never stood before in that retreat, hidden by trees on all sides. Pushing apart the slender limbs of the willows cautiously, we looked at the water, which was as smooth as a mirror, and blue. The beavers were not at their work yet; the little water-town slumbered in visible quiet; and such silence reigned on the lake that I heard Lillian's breath when she thrust her golden head through the opening in the branches with mine, and our temples touched. I caught her waist with my arm to hold her on the slope of the bank and we waited patiently, delighted with what our eyes were taking in at that moment.

Accustomed to life in wild places, I loved Nature as my own mother, though simply; but I felt that something like God's delight in Creation was present.

It was early morning; the light had barely come, and was reddening among the branches of the hickories; the dew was dropping from the leaves of the willows, and the world was growing brighter each instant. Later on, there came to the other shore prairie chickens, gray, with black throats, pretty crests on their heads, and they drank water, raising their bills as they swallowed.

"Ah, Ralph! how good it is here," whispered Lillian.

There was nothing in my head then but a cottage in some lonely canyon, she with me, and such a rosary of peaceful days, flowing calmly into eternity and endless rest. It seemed to us that we had brought to that wedding of Nature our own wedding, to that calm our calm, and to that bright light the bright light of happiness within us.

Now the smooth surface described itself in a circle, and from the water came up slowly the bearded face of a beaver, wet and rosy from the gleam of the morning; then a second, and the two little beasts swam toward the lake, pushing apart with their noses blue lines, puffing and muttering. They climbed the dam, and, sitting on their haunches, began to call; at that signal heads, larger and smaller, rose up as if by enchantment; a plashing was heard in the lake. The herd appeared at first to be playing, — simply diving and screaming from delight in its own fashion; but the first pair, looking from the dam, gave a sudden, prolonged whistle from their nostrils, and in a twinkle half of the beavers were on the dam, and the other half had swum to the banks and vanished under the willows, where the water began to boil, and a sound as it were of sawing indicated that the little beasts were working there, cutting bark and branches.

Lillian and I looked long, very long, at these acts, and at those pleasures of animal life until we disturbed it. Wishing to change her position, she moved a branch accidentally, and in the twinkle of an eye every beaver had vanished; only the disturbed water indicated that something was beneath; but after a while the water became smooth, and silence surrounded us again, interrupted only by the woodpeckers striking the firm bark of the hickories.

The sun had risen above the trees and began to heat powerfully. Since Lillian did not feel tired yet, we resolved to go around the little lake. On the way we came to a small stream which intersected the wood and fell into the lake from the opposite side. Lillian could not cross it, so I had to carry her; and despite her resistance, I took her like a child in my arms and walked into the water. But that stream was a stream of temptations. Fear lest I should fall made her seize my neck with both arms, hold to me with all her strength, and hide her shamed face behind my shoulder; but I began straightway to press my lips to her temple, whispering, "Lillian! my Lillian!" And in that way I carried her over the water.

When I reached the other bank I wished to carry her farther, but she tore herself from me almost rudely. A certain disquiet seized both of us; she began to look around as if in fear, and now pallor and now ruddiness struck her face. We went on. I took her hand and pressed it to my heart. At moments fear of myself seized me. The day became sultry; heat flowed down from the sky to the earth; the wind was not blowing, the leaves on the hickories hung motionless; the only sound was from woodpeckers striking the bark as before; all seemed to be growing languid from heat and falling asleep. I thought that some enchantment was in the air, in that forest, and then I thought only that Lillian was with me and that we were alone.

Meanwhile weariness began to come on Lillian; her breathing grew shorter and more audible, and on her face, usually pale, fiery blushes beat forth. I asked if she was not tired, and if she would not rest.

"Oh, no, no!" answered she quickly, as if defending herself from even the thought; but after a few tens of steps she tottered suddenly and whispered, —

"I cannot, indeed, I cannot go farther."

Then I took her again in my arms and carried that dear burden to the edge of the shore, where willows, hanging to the ground, formed a shady corridor. In this green alcove I placed her on the moss. I knelt down; and when I looked at her the heart in me was straitened. Her face was as pale as linen, and her staring eyes looked with fear at me.

"Lillian, what is the matter?" cried I. "I am with you." I bent to her feet then and covered them with kisses. "Lillian!" continued I, "my only, my chosen, my wife!"

When I said these last words a shiver passed through her from head to foot; and suddenly she threw her arms around my neck with a certain unusual power, as in a fever, repeating, "My dear! my dear! my husband!" Everything vanished from my eyes then, and it seemed to me that the whole globe of the earth was flying away with us.

I know not to this day how it could be that when I recovered from that intoxication and came to my senses twilight was shining again among the dark branches of the hickories, but it was the twilight of evening. The woodpeckers had ceased to strike the trees; one twilight on the bottom of the lake was smiling at that other which was in the sky; the inhabitants of the water had gone to sleep; the evening was beautiful, calm, filled with a red light; it was time to return to the camp.

When we had come out from beneath the weeping-willows, I looked at Lillian; there was not on her face either sadness or disquiet; in her upturned eyes was the light of calm resignation and, as it were, a bright aureole of sacrifice and dignity encircled her blessed head. When I gave her my hand, she inclined her face quietly to my shoulder, and, without turning her eyes from the heavens, she said to me, —

"Ralph, repeat to me that I am your wife, and repeat it often."

Since there was neither in the deserts, nor in the place to which we were going, any marriage save that of hearts, I knelt down, and when she had knelt at my side, I said, "Before God, earth, and heaven, I declare to thee, Lillian Morris, that I take thee as wife. Amen."

To this she answered, "Now I am thine forever and till death, thy wife, Ralph!"

From that moment we were married; she was not my sweetheart, she was my lawful wife. That thought was pleasant to both of us, — and pleasant to me, for in my heart there rose a new feeling of a certain sacred respect for Lillian, and for myself, a certain honorableness and great dignity through which love became ennobled and blessed. Hand in hand, with heads erect and confident look, we returned to the camp, where the people were greatly alarmed about us. A number of tens of men had gone out in every direction to search for us; and with astonishment I learned afterward that some had passed around the lake, but could not discover us; we on our part had not heard their shouts.

I summoned the people, and when they had assembled in a circle, I took Lillian by the hand, went into the centre of the circle, and said, —

"Gentlemen, be witnesses, that in your presence I call this woman, who stands with me, my wife; and bear witness of this before justice, before law, and before every one whosoever may ask you, either in the East or the West."

"We will! and hurrah for you both!" answered the miners.

Old Smith asked Lillian then, according to custom, if she agreed to take me as husband, and when she said "Yes," we were legally married before the people.

In the distant prairies of the West, and on all the frontiers where there are no towns, magistrates, or churches, marriages are not performed otherwise; and to this hour, if a man calls a woman with whom he lives under the same roof his wife, this declaration takes the place of all legal documents. No one of my men therefore wondered, or looked at my marriage otherwise than with the respect shown to custom; on the contrary, all were rejoiced, for, though I had held them more sternly than other leaders, they knew that I did so honestly, and with each day they showed me more good-will, and my wife was always the eye in the head of the caravan. Hence there began a holiday and amusements. The fires were stirred up; the Scots took from their wagons the pipes, whose music we both liked, since it was for us a pleasant reminiscence; the Americans took out their favorite ox-bones, and amid songs, shouts, and shooting, the wedding evening passed for us.

Aunt Atkins embraced Lillian every little while, now laughing, now weeping, now lighting her pipe, which went out the next moment. But I was touched most by the following ceremony which is a custom in that movable portion of the American population which spends the greater part of its life in wagons. When the moon went down the men fastened on the ramrods of their guns branches of lighted osier, and a whole procession, under the lead of old Smith, conducted us from wagon to wagon, asking Lillian at each of them, "Is this your home?" My beautiful love answered, "No!" and we went on. At Aunt Atkins' wagon a real tenderness took possession of us all, for in that one Lillian had ridden hitherto. When she said there also in a low voice, "No," Aunt Atkins bellowed like a buffalo, and seizing Lillian in her embrace, began to repeat, "My little one! my sweet!" sobbing meanwhile, and carried away with weeping. Lillian sobbed too; and then all those hardened hearts grew tender for an instant, and there was no eye to which tears did not come.

When we approached it, I barely recognized my wagon; it was decked with branches and flowers. Here the men raised the burning torches aloft, and Smith inquired in a louder and more solemn voice, —

"Is this your home?"

"It is, it is!" answered Lillian.

Then all uncovered their heads, and there was such silence that I heard the hissing of the fire and the sound of the burnt twigs falling on the ground; the old white-haired miner, stretching out his sinewy hands over us, said, —

"May God bless you both, and your house, Amen!"

A triple hurrah answered that blessing. All separated then, leaving me and my loved one alone.

When the last man had gone, she rested her head on my breast, whispering, "Forever! forever!" and at that moment the stars in our souls outnumbered the stars of the sky.

CHAPTER VI.

NEXT morning early I left my wife sleeping and went to find flowers for her. While looking for them, I said to myself every moment, "You are married!" and the thought filled me with such delight, that I raised my eyes to the Lord of Hosts, thanking Him for having permitted me to live to the time in which a man becomes himself genuinely and rounds out his life with the life of another loved beyond everything. I had something now of my own in the world, and though that canvas-covered wagon was my only house and hearth, I felt richer at once, and looked at my previous wandering lot with pity, and with wonder that I could have lived in that manner hitherto. Formerly it had not even come to my head what happiness there is in that word "wife," — happiness which called to my heart's blood with that name, and to the best part of my own soul. For a long time I had so loved Lillian that I saw the whole world through her alone, connected everything with her, and understood everything only as it related to her. And now when I said "wife," that meant, mine, mine forever; and I thought that I should go wild with delight, for it could not find place in my head, that I, a poor man, should possess such a treasure. What then was lacking to me? Nothing. Had those prairies been warmer, had there been safety there for her, had it not been for the obligation to lead people to the place to which I had promised to lead them, I was ready not to go to California, but to settle even in Nebraska, if with Lillian. I had been going to California to dig gold, but now I was ready to laugh at the idea. "What other riches can I find there, when I have her?" I asked myself. "What do we care for gold? See, I will choose some canyon, where there is spring all the year; I will cut down trees for a house, and live with her, and a plough and a gun will give us life. We shall not die of hunger —" These were my thoughts while gathering flowers, and when I had enough of them I returned to the camp. On the road I met Aunt Atkins.

"Is the little one sleeping?" asked she, taking the inseparable pipe from her mouth for a moment.

"She is sleeping," answered I.

To this Aunt Atkins, blinking with one eye, added, —

"Ah, you rascal!"

Meanwhile the "little one" was not sleeping, for we both saw her coming down from the wagon, and shielding her eyes with her hand against the sunlight, she began to look on every side. Seeing me, she ran up all rosy and fresh, as the morning. When I opened my arms, she fell into them panting, and putting up her mouth, began to repeat, —

"Dzien dobry! dzien dobry! dzien dobry!"

Then she stood on her toes, and looking into my eyes, asked with a roguish smile, "Am I your wife?"

What was there to answer, except to kiss without end and fondle? And thus passed the whole time at that meeting of rivers, for old Smith had taken on himself all my duties till the resumption of our journey.

We visited our beavers once more, and the stream, through which I carried her now without resistance. Once we went up Blue River in a little redwood canoe. At a bend of the stream I showed Lillian buffaloes near by, driving their horns into the bank, from which their whole heads were covered as if with armor of dried clay. But two days before starting, these expeditions ceased, for first the Indians had appeared in the neighborhood, and second my dear lady had begun to be weak somewhat. She grew pale and lost strength, and when I inquired what the trouble was, she answered only with a smile and the assurance that it was nothing. I watched over her sleep, I nursed her as well as I was able, almost preventing the breezes from blowing on her, and grew thin from anxiety. Aunt Atkins blinked mysteriously with her left eye when talking of Lillian's illness, and sent forth such dense rolls of smoke that she grew invisible behind them. I was disturbed all the more, because sad thoughts came to Lillian at times. She had beaten it into her head that maybe it was not permitted to love so intensely as we were loving, and once, putting her finger on the Bible, which we read every day, she said sadly, —

" Read, Ralph."

I looked, and a certain wonderful feeling seized my heart too, when I read, "Who changed the truth of God into a lie, and worshipped and served the creature more than the Creator, who is blessed forever." She said when I had finished reading, "But if God is angry at this, I know that with His goodness He will punish only me."

I pacified her by saying that love was simply an angel, who flies from the souls of two people to God and takes Him praise from the earth. After that there was no talk between us touching such things, since preparations for the journey had begun. The fitting up of wagons and beasts, and a thousand occupations, stole my time from me. When at last the hour came for departure we took tearful farewell of that river fork, which had witnessed so much of our happiness; but when I saw the train stretching out again on the prairie, the wagons one after another and lines of mules before the wagons, I felt a certain consolation at the thought that the end of the journey would be nearer each day, that a few months more and we should see California, toward which we were striving with such toil.

But the first days of the journey did not pass over-successfully. Beyond the Missouri, as far as the foot of the Rocky Mountains, the prairie rises continually over enormous expanses; therefore the beasts were easily wearied, and were often tired out. Besides, we could not approach the Platte River, for, though the flood had decreased, it was the time of the great spring hunts, and a multitude of Indians circled around the river, looking for herds of buffaloes then moving northward. Night service became difficult and wearying; no night passed without alarms.

On the fourth day after we had moved from the river fork, I broke up a considerable party of Indian plunderers at the moment when they were trying to stampede our mules. But worst of all were the nights without fire. We were unable to approach the Platte River, and frequently had nothing to burn, and toward morning drizzling rain fell; buffalo dung, which in case of need took the place of wood, got wet, and would not burn.

The buffaloes filled me with alarm also. Sometimes we saw herds of some thousands on the horizon, rushing forward like a storm, crushing everything before them. Were such a herd to strike the train, we should perish every one without rescue. To complete the evil, the prairie was swarming at that time with beasts of prey of all species; after the buffaloes and Indians, came terrible gray bears, cougars, big wolves from Kansas and the Indian Territory. At the small streams, where we stopped for the night sometimes, we saw at sunset whole menageries coming to drink after the heat of the day. Once a bear rushed at Wichita, our half-breed; and if I had not run up, with Smith and the other scout, Tom, to help him, he would have been torn to pieces. I opened the head of the monster with an axe, which I brought down with such force that the handle of tough hickory was broken; still, the beast rushed at me once more, and fell only when Smith and Tom shot him in the ear from rifles. Those savage brutes were so bold that at night they came up to the very train; and in the course of a week we killed two not more than a hundred yards from the wagons. In consequence of this, the dogs raised such an uproar from twilight till dawn that to close an eye was impossible.

Once I loved such a life; and when, a year before, I was in Arkansas, during the greatest heat, it was for me as in paradise. But now, when I remembered that in the wagon my beloved wife, instead of sleeping, was trembling about me, and ruining her health with anxiety, I wished all the Indians and bears and cougars in the lowest pit, and desired from my soul to secure as soon as possible the peace of that being so fragile, so delicate, and so worshipped, that I wished to bear her forever in my arms.

A great weight fell from my heart when, after three weeks of such crossings, I saw at last the waters of a river white as if traced out with chalk; this stream is called now Republican River, but at that time it had no name in English. Broad belts of dark willows, stretching like a mourning trail along the white waters, could afford us fuel in plenty; and though that kind of willow crackles in the fire, and shoots sparks with great noise, still it burns better than wet buffalo dung. I appointed at this place another rest of two days, because the rocks, scattered here and there by the banks of the river, indicated the proximity of a hilly country, difficult to cross, lying on both sides of the back of the Rocky Mountains. We were already on a considerable elevation above the sea, as could be known by the cold nights.

That inequality between day and night temperature troubled us greatly. Some people, among others old Smith, fell ill of fever, and had to go to their wagons. The seeds of the disease had clung to them, probably, at the unwholesome banks of the Missouri, and hardship caused the outbreak. The nearness of the mountains, however, gave hope of a speedy recovery; meanwhile, my wife nursed them with a devotion innate to gentle hearts only.

But she grew thin herself. More than once, when I woke in the morning, my first look fell on her beautiful face, and my heart beat uneasily at its pallor and the blue half-circles under her eyes. It would happen that while I was looking at her in that way she would wake, smile at me, and fall asleep again. Then I felt that I would have given half my health of oak if we were in California; but California was still far, far away.

After two days we started again, and coming to the Republican River at noon, were soon moving along the fork of the White Man toward the southern fork of the Platte, lying for the most part in Colorado. The country became more mountainous at every step, and we were really in the canyon along the banks of which rose up in the distance higher and higher granite cliffs, now standing alone, now stretching out continuously like walls, now closing more narrowly, now opening out on both sides. Wood was not lacking, for all the cracks and crannies of the cliffs were covered with dwarf pine and dwarf oak as well. Here and there springs were heard; along the rocky walls scampered wolverines. The air was cool, pure, wholesome. After a week the fever ceased. But the mules and horses, forced to eat food in which heather predominated, instead of the juicy grass of Nebraska, grew thinner and thinner, and groaned more loudly as they pulled our well filled and weighty wagons up the mountains.

At last on a certain afternoon we saw before us beacons, as it were, or crested clouds half melting in the distance, hazy, blue, azure, with white and gold on their crests, and immense in size, extending from the earth to the sky.

At this sight a shout rose in the whole caravan; men climbed to the tops of the wagons to see better, from every side thundered shouts, "Rocky Mountains! Rocky Mountains!" Caps were waving in the air, and on all faces enthusiasm was evident.

Thus the Americans greeted their Rocky Mountains; but I went to my wagon, and, pressing my wife to my breast, vowed faith to her once more in spirit before those heaven-touching altars, which expressed such solemn mysteriousness, majesty, unapproachableness, and immensity. The sun was just setting, and soon twilight covered the whole country; but those giants in the last rays seemed like measureless masses of burning coal and lava. Later on, that fiery redness passed into violet, ever darker, and at last all disappeared, and was merged into one darkness, through which gazed at us from above the stars, the twinkling eyes of the night.

But we were at least a hundred and fifty miles yet from the main chain; in fact, the mountains disappeared from our eyes next day, intercepted by cliffs; again they appeared and again they vanished, as our road went by turns.

We advanced slowly, for new obstacles stood in our

way; and though we kept as much as possible to the bed of the river, frequently, where the banks were too steep, we had to go around and seek a passage by neighboring valleys. The ground in these valleys was covered with gray heather and wild peas, not good for mules even, and forming no little hindrance to the journey, for the long and powerful stems, twisting around the wagon wheels, made the turning of them difficult.

Sometimes we came upon openings and cracks in the earth, impassable and hundreds of yards long; these we had to go around also. Time after time the scouts, Wichita and Tom, returned with accounts of new obstacles. The land was bristling with rocks, or it broke away suddenly.

On a certain day it seemed to us that we were going through a valley, when all at once the valley was missing; in place of it was a precipice so deep that the gaze went down with terror along a perpendicular wall, and the head became dizzy. Giant oaks, growing at the bottom of the abyss, seemed little black clumps, and the buffaloes pasturing among them like beetles. We entered more and more into the region of precipices, of stones, fragments, debris, and rocks thrown one on the other with a kind of wild disorder. The echo sent back twice and thrice from granite arches the curses of drivers and squealing of mules. On the prairie our wagons, rising high above the surface of the country, seemed lordly and immense; here before those perpendicular cliffs, the wagons became wonderfully small to the eye, and vanished in those gorges as if devoured by gigantic jaws. Little waterfalls, or as they are called by the Indians, "laughing waters," stopped the road to us every few hundred yards; toil exhausted our strength and that of the animals. Meanwhile, when at times the real chain of mountains appeared on the horizon, it seemed as far away and hazy as ever. Happily curiosity overcame in us even weariness, and the continual change of views kept it in practice. None of my people, not excepting those born in the Alleghanies, had ever seen such wild regions; I myself gazed with wonder on those canyons, along the edges of which the unbridled fancy of Nature had reared as it were castles, fortresses, and stone cities. From time to time we met Indians, but these were different from those on the prairies, very straggling and very much wilder.

The sight of white men roused in them fear mingled with a thirst for blood. They seemed still more cruel than their brethren in Nebraska; their stature was loftier, their complexion much darker, their wide nostrils and quick glances gave them the expression of wild beasts caught in a trap. Their movements, too, had almost the quickness and timidity of beasts. While speaking, they put their thumbs to their cheeks, which were painted in white and blue stripes. Their weapons were tomahawks and bows, the latter made of a certain kind of firm mountain hawthorn, so rigid that my men could not bend them. These savages, who in considerable numbers might have been very dangerous, were distinguished by invincible thievishness; happily they were few, the largest party that we met not exceeding fifteen. They called themselves Tabeguachis, Winemucas, and Yampas. Our scout, Wichita, though expert in Indian dialects, could not understand their language; hence we could not make out in any way why all of them, pointing to the Rocky Mountains and then to us, closed and opened their palms, as if indicating some number.

The road became so difficult, that with the greatest exertion, we made barely fifteen miles a day. At the same time our horses began to die, being less enduring than mules and more choice of food; men failed in strength too, for during whole days they had to draw wagons with the mules, or to hold them in dangerous places. By degrees unwillingness seized the weakest; some got the rheumatism, and one, through whose mouth blood came because of exertion, died in three days, cursing the hour in which it came to his head to leave New York. We were then in the worst part of the road, near the little river called by the Indians Kiowa. There were no cliffs there as high as on the Eastern boundary of Colorado; but the whole country, as far as the eye could reach, was bristling with fragments thrown in disorder one upon another. These fragments, some standing upright, others overturned, presented the appearance of ruined graveyards with fallen headstones. Those were really the "Bad Lands" of Colorado, answering to those which extended northward over Nebraska. With the greatest effort we escaped from them in the course of a week.

CHAPTER VII.

At last we found ourselves at the foot of the Rocky Mountains.

Fear seized me when I looked from a proximate point at that world of granite mountains, whose sides were wrapped in mist, and whose summits were lost somewhere in eternal snow and clouds. Their size and silent majesty pressed me to the earth; hence I bent before the Lord, imploring Him to permit me to lead, past those measureless walls, my wagons, my people, and my wife. After such a prayer I entered the stone gorges and cor-

ridors with more confidence. When they closed behind
us we were cut off from the rest of the world. Above
was the sky; in it a few eagles were screaming, around
us was granite and then granite without end, — a genuine
labyrinth of passages, vaults, ravines, openings, precipices,
towers, silent edifices, and as it were chambers, gigantic
and dreamy. There is such a solemnity there, and the
soul is under such pressure, that a man knows not himself why he whispers instead of speaking aloud. It
seems to him that the road is closing before him continually, that some voice is saying to him, "Go no
farther, for there is no passage!" It seems to him that
he is attacking some secret on which God Himself has
set a seal. At night, when those upright legions were
standing as black as mourning, and the moon cast about
their summits a silvery mantle of sadness, when certain
wonderful shadows rose around the "laughing waters,"
a quiver passed through the most hardened adventurers.
We spent whole hours by the fires, looking with a
certain superstitious awe at the dark depths of the
ravines, lighted by ruddy gleams; we seemed to think
that something terrible might show itself any moment.

Once we found under a hollow in the cliff the skeleton
of a man; and though from the remnant of the hair which
had dried to the skull, we saw that he was an Indian,
still an ominous feeling pressed our hearts, for that
skeleton with grinning teeth seemed to forewarn us that
whoso wandered in there would never come out again.

That same day the half-breed, Tom, was killed suddenly, having fallen with his horse from the edge of a
precipice. A gloomy sadness seized the whole caravan;
formerly we had advanced noisily and joyfully, now the
drivers ceased to swear, and the caravan pushed forward
in a silence broken only by the squeaking of wheels.

The mules grew ill-tempered more frequently, and when one pair stood as still as if lashed to the earth, all the wagons behind had to halt. I was most tortured by this, — that in those moments which were so difficult and oppressive, and in which my wife needed my presence more than at other times, I could not be near her; for I had to double and treble myself almost, so as to give an example, uphold courage and confidence. The men, it is true, bore toil with the endurance innate with Americans, though they were simply using the last of their strength. But my health was proof against every hardship. There were nights in which I did not have two hours of sleep; I dragged the wagons with others, I posted the sentries, I went around the square, — in a word, I performed service twice more burdensome than any one of the company; but it is evident that happiness gave me strength. For when, wearied and beaten down, I came to my wagon, I found there everything that I held dearest: a faithful heart and a beloved hand, that wiped my wearied forehead. Lillian, though suffering a little, never went to sleep wittingly before my arrival; and when I reproached her she closed my mouth with a kiss and a prayer not to be angry. When I told her to sleep she did so, while holding my hand. Frequently in the night, when she woke, she covered me with beaver skins, so that I might rest better. Always mild, sweet, loving, she cared for me and brought me to worship her simply. I kissed the hem of her garment, as if it had been a thing the most sacred, and that wagon of ours became for me almost a church. That little one in presence of those heaven-touching walls of granite, upon which she cast her upraised eyes, covered them for me in such a way, that in presence of her they vanished from before me, and amid all those immensities I saw only her. What is there wonderful, if when strength failed others, I had strength still, and felt that so long as it was a question of her I should never fail?

After three weeks' journey we came at last to a more spacious canyon formed by White River. At the entrance to it the Winta Indians prepared an ambush which annoyed us somewhat; but when their reddish arrows began to reach the roof of my wife's wagon, I struck on them with my men so violently that they scattered at once. We killed three or four of them. The only prisoner whom we took, a youth of sixteen, when he had recovered a little from terror, pointed in turn at us and to the West, repeating gestures similar to those made by the Yampa. It seemed to us that he wanted to say that there were white men near by, but it was difficult to give credit to that supposition. In time it turned out correct, and it is easy to imagine the astonishment and delight of my men on the following day, when, descending from an elevated plateau, we saw on a broad valley which lay at our feet, not only wagons, but houses built of freshly-cut logs. These houses formed a circle, in the centre of which rose a large shed without windows; through the middle of the plain a stream flowed; near it were herds of mules, guarded by men on horseback.

The presence of men of my own race in that valley filled me with astonishment, which soon passed into fear, when I remembered that they might be "criminal outlaws" hiding in the desert from death. I knew from experience that such outcasts push frequently to very remote and entirely desert regions, where they form detachments, on a complete military footing. Sometimes they are founders of new societies as it were, which at first live by plundering people moving to more inhabited places; but later, by a continual increase of population, they change by degrees into ordered societies. I met more than once with "outlaws" on the upper course of the Mississippi, when, as a squatter, I floated down logs to New Orleans; more than once I had bloody adventures with them, hence their cruelty and bravery were equally well known to me.

I should not have feared them had not Lillian been with us; but at thought of the danger in which she would be if we were defeated and I fell, the hair rose on my head, and for the first time in life I was as full of fear as the greatest coward. But I was convinced that if those men were outlaws, we could not avoid battle in any way, and that the conflict would be more difficult with them than with Indians.

I warned my men at once of the probable danger, and arranged them in order of battle. I was ready either to perish myself, or destroy that nest of wasps, and resolved to strike the first blow.

Meanwhile they saw us from the valley, and two horsemen started toward us as fast as their horses could gallop. I drew breath at that sight, for "outlaws" would not send messengers to meet us. In fact, it turned out that they were riflemen of the American Fur Company, who had their "summer camp" in that valley. Instead of a battle, therefore, a most hospitable reception was waiting for us, and every assistance from those rough but honest riflemen of the desert. Indeed, they received us with open arms, and we thanked God for having looked on our misery and prepared so agreeable a resting-place.

A month and a half had passed since our departure from Big Blue River. Our strength was exhausted, our mules were half alive merely; but here we might rest a whole week in perfect safety, with abundance of food for ourselves, and grass for our animals. For us that was simply salvation.

Mr. Thorston, the chief of the camp, was an educated man and enlightened. Knowing that I was not a common rough fellow of the prairies, he became friendly at once, and gave his own cottage to me and Lillian, whose health had suffered greatly.

I kept her two days in bed. She was so wearied that she barely opened her eyes for the first twenty-four hours; during that time I took care that nothing disturbed her. I sat at her bedside and watched hour after hour. In two days she was strengthened enough to go out; but I did not let her touch any labor. My men, too, slept for the first few days like stones, wherever each one dropped down. Only after they had slept did we repair our wagons and clothing and wash our linen. The honest riflemen helped us in everything earnestly. They were Canadians, for the greater part, who had hired with the company. They spent the winter in trapping beavers, killing skunks and minks; in summer they betook themselves to so-called "summer camps," in which there were temporary storehouses of furs. The skins, dressed there in some fashion, were convoyed to the East. The service of those people, who hired for a number of years, was arduous beyond calculation; they had to go to very remote and wild places, where all kinds of animals existed in plenty, and where they themselves lived in continual danger and in endless warfare with redskins. It is true that they received high wages; most of them did not serve for mere money, but from love of life in the wilderness, and adventures, of which there was no lack at any time. Men, too, of great strength and health had been chosen, men capable of enduring all hardships. Their great stature, fur caps, and long rifles reminded Lillian of Cooper's novels; hence she looked with curiosity on the whole camp and on all the arrangements. Their discipline was as absolute as that of a knightly order. Thorston, the chief agent of the company, and at the same time their employer, maintained complete military authority. Withal they were very honest people, hence time passed for us among them with perfect comfort; our camp, too, pleased them greatly, and they said that they had never met such a disciplined and well-ordered caravan. Thorston, in presence of all, praised my plan of taking the northern route instead of that by St. Louis and Kansas. He told us that on that trail a caravan of three hundred people, under a certain Marchwood, after numerous sufferings caused by heat and locusts, had lost all their draught-beasts, and were cut to pieces at last by the Arapahoe Indians. The Canadian riflemen had learned this from the Arapahoes themselves, whom they had beaten in a great battle, and from whom they had captured more than a hundred scalps, among others that of Marchwood himself.

This information had great influence on my people, so that old Smith, a veteran pathfinder, who from the beginning was opposed to the route through Nebraska, declared in presence of all that I was smarter than he, and that it was his part to learn of me. During our stay in the hospitable summer camp we regained our strength thoroughly. Besides Thorston, with whom I formed a lasting friendship, I made the acquaintance of Mick, famous throughout all the States. This man was not of the camp, but had wandered through the deserts with two other famous explorers, Lincoln and Kit Carson. Those three remarkable men carried on real wars with whole tribes of Indians; their skill and superhuman courage always secured them the victory. The name of Mick, of whom more than one book is written, was so terrible to the Indians, that with them his word had more weight than a United States treaty. The Government had often employed him as an intermediary, and finally appointed him Governor of Oregon. When I made his acquaintance he was nearly fifty years old; but his hair was as black as the feather of a raven, and in his glance was mingled kindness of heart with strength and irrestrainable daring. He passed also for the strongest man in America, and when we wrestled I was the first, to the great astonishment of all, whom he failed to throw. This man with a great heart loved Lillian immensely, and blessed her, as often as he visited us. In parting he gave her a pair of beautiful little moccasins made by himself from the skin of a doe. That present was very timely, for my poor wife had not a pair of sound shoes.

At last we resumed our journey, with good omens, furnished with minute directions what canyons to take on the way, and with supplies of salt game. That was not all. The kind Thorston had taken the worst of our mules and in place of them given us his own, which were strong and well rested. Mick, who had been in California, told real wonders not only of its wealth, but of its mild climate, its beautiful oak forests, and mountain canyons, unequalled in the United States. A great consolation entered our hearts, for we did not know of the trials which awaited us before entering that land of promise.

In driving away, we waved our caps long in farewell to the honest Canadians. As to me, that day of parting is graven in my heart for the ages, since in the forenoon that beloved star of my life, putting both arms around my neck, began, all red with embarrassment and emotion, to whisper something in my ear. When I heard it I bent to her feet, and, weeping with great excitement, kissed her knees.

CHAPTER VIII.

Two weeks after leaving the summer camp, we came out on the boundary of Utah, and our journey, as before, though not without labors, advanced more briskly than at the beginning. We had yet to pass the western part of the Rocky Mountains, forming a whole network of branches called the Wasatch Range. Two considerable streams, Green and Grand Rivers, whose union forms the immense Colorado, and numerous tributaries of those two rivers, cut the mountains in every direction, opening in them passages which are easy enough. By these passages we reached after a certain time Utah Lake, where the salt lands begin. A wonderful country surrounded us, monotonous, gloomy; great level valleys encircled by cliffs with blunt outlines, — these, always alike, succeed one another, with oppressive monotony. There is in those deserts and cliffs a certain sternness, nakedness, and torpor, so that at sight of them the Biblical deserts recur to one's mind. The lakes here are brackish, their shores fruitless and barren. There are no trees; the ground over an enormous expanse exudes salt and potash, or is covered by a gray vegetation with large felt-like leaves, which, when broken, give forth a salt, clammy sap. That journey is wearisome and oppressive, for whole weeks pass, and the desert stretches on without end, and opens into plains of eternal sameness, though they are rocky. Our strength began to give way again. On the prairies we were surrounded by the monotony of life, here by the monotony of death.

A certain oppression and indifference to everything took gradual possession of the people. We passed Utah, — always the same lifeless lands! We entered Nevada, — no change! The sun burnt so fiercely that our heads were bursting from pain; the light, reflecting from a surface covered with salt, dazzled the eye; in the air was floating a kind of dust, coming it was unknown whence, which inflamed our eyelids. The draught-beasts, time after time, seized the earth with their teeth, and dropped from sunstroke, as if felled by lightning. The majority of the people kept themselves up only with the thought that in a week or two weeks the Sierra Nevada would appear on the horizon, and behind that the desired California.

Meanwhile, days passed and weeks in ever-increasing labors. In the course of a certain week we were forced to leave three wagons behind, for there were no animals to draw them.

Oh, that was a land of misfortune and misery! In Nevada the desert became deeper, and our condition still worse, for disease fell upon us.

One morning people came to inform me that Smith was sick. I went to see what his trouble was, and saw with amazement that typhus had overthrown the old miner. So many climates are not changed with impunity; severe labor, in spite of short rests, makes itself felt, and the germs of disease are developed from hardship and toil. Lillian, whom Smith loved as if she had been his own daughter, and whom he blessed on the day of our marriage, insisted on nursing him. I, weak man, trembled in my whole soul for her, but I could not forbid her to be a Christian. She sat over the sick man whole days and nights, together with Aunt Atkins and Aunt Grosvenor, who followed her example. On the second day, however, the old man lost consciousness, and on the eighth he died in Lillian's arms. I buried him, shedding ardent tears over the remains of him who had been not only my assistant and right hand in everything, but a real father to me and to Lillian. We hoped that after such a sacrifice God would take pity on us; but that was merely the beginning of our trials, for that very day another miner fell ill, and almost every day after that some one lay down in a wagon, and left it only when borne to a grave.

And thus we dragged along over the desert, and after us followed the pestilence, grasping new victims continually. In her turn Aunt Atkins fell ill, but, thanks to Lillian's efforts, her sickness was conquered. The soul was dying in me every instant, and more than once, when Lillian was with the sick, and I somewhere on guard in front of the camp, alone in the darkness, I pressed my temples with my hands and knelt down in prayer to God. Obedient as a dog, I was whining for mercy on her without daring to say, "Let Thy will and not mine be done." Sometimes in the night, when we were alone, I woke suddenly, for it seemed to me that the pestilence was pushing the canvas of my wagon aside and staring in, looking for Lillian. All the intervals when I was not with her, and they formed most of the time, were for me changed into one torture, under which I bent as a tree bends before a whirlwind. Lillian, however, had been equal to all toils and efforts so far. Though the strongest men fell, I saw her emaciated it is true, pale, and with marks of maternity increasingly definite on her forehead, but in health, and going from wagon to wagon. I dared not even ask if she were well; I only took her by the shoulders and

pressed her long and long to my breast, and even had I
wished to speak, something so oppressed me, that I could
not have uttered a word.

Gradually, however, hope began to enter me, and in my
head were sounding no longer those terrible words of the
Bible, "Who worshipped and served the creature more
than the Creator."

We were nearing the western part of Nevada, where,
beyond the belt of dead lakes, the salt lands and desert
rocks find an end, and a belt of prairie begins, more
level, greener, and very fertile. During two days' journey no one fell ill; I thought that our misery was over.
And it was high time!

Nine men had died, six were ailing yet; under the
fear of infection discipline had begun to relax; nearly all
the horses were dead, and the mules seemed rather skele-
tons than beasts. Of the fifty wagons with which we
had moved out of the summer camp, only thirty-two
were dragging now over the desert. Besides, since no
one wished to go hunting lest he might fall somewhere
away from the caravan and be left without aid, our
supplies, not being replenished, were coming to an end.
Wishing to spare them, we had lived for a week past on
black ground squirrels; but their malodorous meat had
so disgusted us that we put it to our mouths with loath-
ing, and even that wretched food was not found in
sufficiency. Beyond the lakes, however, game became
more frequent, and grass was abundant. Again we met
Indians, who, in opposition to their custom, attacked us
in daylight and on the open plain; having firearms, they
killed four of our people. In the conflict I received such
a severe wound in the head from a hatchet that in the
evening of that day I lost consciousness from loss of
blood; but I was happy since Lillian was nursing me,

and not patients from whom she might catch the typhus. Three days I lay in the wagon, pleasant days, since I was with her continually. I could kiss her hands when she was changing the bandages, and look at her. On the third day I was able to sit on horseback; but the soul was weak in me, and I feigned sickness before myself so as to be with her longer.

Only then did I discover how tired I had been, and what weariness had gone out of my bones while I was lying prostrate. Before my illness I had suffered not a little concerning my wife. I had grown as thin as a skeleton, and as formerly I had been looking with fear and alarm at her, so now she was looking with the same feelings at me. But when my head had ceased to fall from shoulder to shoulder there was no help for it; I had to mount the last living horse and lead the caravan forward, especially as certain alarming signs were surrounding us on all sides. There was a heat well-nigh preternatural, and in the air a dull haze as if of smoke from a distant burning; the horizon became dull and dark. It was impossible to see the sky, and the rays of the sun came to the earth red and sickly; the draught-beasts showed a wonderful disquiet, and, breathing hoarsely, bared their teeth. As to us, we inhaled fire with our breasts. The heat was caused, as I thought, by one of those stifling winds from the Gila desert, of which men had told me in the East; but there was stillness round about, and not a grass blade was stirring on the plain. In the evening the sun went down as red as blood, and stifling nights followed. The sick groaned for water; the dogs howled. Whole nights I wandered around a number of miles from the camp to make sure that the plains were not burning; but there was no fire in sight anywhere. I calmed myself finally with the thought that the smoke must be from a fire that had gone out already. In the daytime I noticed that hares, antelopes, buffaloes, even squirrels, were hastening eastward, as if fleeing from that California to which we were going with such effort. But since the air had become a little purer and the heat somewhat less, I settled finally in the thought that there had been a fire which had ceased, that the animals were merely looking for food in some new place. It was only needful for us to push up as soon as possible to the burnt strip, and learn whether the belt of fire could be crossed or whether we should have to go around it. According to my calculation it could not be more than three hundred miles to the Sierra Nevada, or about twenty days' journey. I resolved, therefore, to reach it, even with our last effort.

We travelled at night now, for midday heat weakened the animals greatly, and among the wagons there was always some shade in which they could rest.

One night, being unable to remain on horseback because of weariness and my wound, I sat in the wagon with Lillian. I heard all at once a sudden wheezing and biting of the wheels striking on ground which was peculiar; at the same time shouts of "Stop! stop!" were heard along the whole length of the train. I sprang from the wagon at once. By the light of the moon I saw the drivers bent to the earth and looking at it carefully. At the same moment a voice called, —

"Ho, captain, we are travelling on coals."

I bent down, felt the earth, — we were travelling on a burnt prairie. I stopped the caravan at once, and we remained the rest of the night on that spot. With the first light of morning a wonderful sight struck our eyes: As far as we could see, there lay a plain black as coal, — not only were all the bushes and the grass burnt, but the earth was so glossy that the feet of our mules and the

wheels of the wagons were reflected in it as they might
have been in a mirror. We could not see clearly the
width of the fire, for the horizon was still hazy from
smoke; but I gave command without hesitation to turn
to the south, so as to reach the edge of that tract instead
of venturing on the burnt country. I knew from experience what it is to travel on burnt prairie land where
there is not a blade of grass for draught-beasts. Since
evidently the fire had moved northward with the wind, I
hoped by going toward the south to reach the beginning
of it.

The people obeyed my order, it is true, but rather
unwillingly, for it involved God knows how long a delay
in the journey. During our halt at noon the smoke
became thinner; but if it did, the heat grew so terrible
that the air quivered from its fervency, and all at once
something took place which might seem a miracle.

On a sudden the haze and smoke parted, as if at a
signal, and before our eyes rose the Sierra Nevada, green,
smiling, wonderful, covered with gleaming snow on the
summits, and so near that with the naked eye we could
see the dents in the mountains, the green lakes, and the
forests. It seemed to us that a fresh breeze filled with
odors from the pitchy fir was coming above the burnt
fields to us, and that in a few hours we should reach the
flowery foothills. At this sight the people, worn out
with the terrible desert and with labors, went almost
out of their minds with delight; some fell on the ground
sobbing, others stretched forth their hands toward heaven
or burst into laughter, others grew pale without power
to speak. Lillian and I wept from delight too, which in
me was mingled with astonishment, for I had thought
that a hundred and fifty miles at least separated us yet
from California; but there were the mountains smiling

at us across the burnt plain, and they seemed to approach as if by magic, and bend toward us and invite us and lure us on.

The hours fixed for rest had not passed yet, but the people would not hear of a longer halt. Even the sick stretched out their yellow hands from beneath the canvas roofs and begged us to harness the mules and drive on. Briskly and willingly we moved forward, and to the biting of the wheels on the charred earth were joined the cracking of whips, shouts, and songs; of driving around the burnt tract there was not a word now. Why go around when a few tens of miles farther on was California and its marvellous snowy mountains? We went straight across toward them.

The smoke covered the bright view from us again with a wonderful suddenness. Hours passed; the horizon came nearer. At last the sun went down; night came. The stars twinkled dimly on the sky, but we went forward without rest; still the mountains were evidently farther than they had seemed. About midnight the mules began to squeal and balk; an hour later the caravan stopped, for the greater number of the beasts had lain down. The men tried to raise them, but there was no possibility of doing so. Not an eye closed all night. At the first rays of light our glances flew eagerly into the distance and — found nothing. A dark mourning desert extended at far as the eye could see, monotonous, dull, defining itself with a sharp line at the horizon; of yesterday's mountains there was not a trace.

The people were amazed. To me the ominous word " mirage " explained everything, but also it went with a quiver to the marrow of my bones. What was to be done, — go on? But if that burnt plain extended for

hundreds of miles? Return, and then seek some miles
distant the end of the burnt tract? — but had the mules
strength to return over the same road? I hardly dared
to look to the bottom of that abyss, on the brink of
which we were all standing. I wished, however, to
know what course to take. I mounted my horse, moved
forward, and from a neighboring elevation took in with
my eye a wider horizon through the aid of a field-glass.
I saw in the distance a green strip. When I reached it,
however, after an hour's journey, the place turned out to
be merely a lake, along the bank of which the fire had
not destroyed vegetation completely. The burnt plain extended farther than I could see through the glass. There
was no help; it was necessary to turn back the caravan
and go around the fire. For that purpose I turned my
horse. I expected to find the wagons where I had left
them, for I had given command to wait for me there.
Meanwhile, disobeying my command, they had raised the
mules, and the caravan was advancing. To my questions
they answered moodily, "There are the mountains, we
will go to them."

I did not try even to struggle, for I saw that there was
no human power present to stop those men. Perhaps I
should have gone back alone with Lillian, but my wagon
was not there, and Lillian had gone on with Aunt
Atkins.

We advanced. Night came again, and with it a forced
halt. Out of the burnt plain rose a great lurid moon
and lighted the distance, which was equally black. In
the morning only half of the wagons could be moved,
for the mules of the others had died. The heat of that
day was dreadful. The sun's rays, absorbed by the
charred land, filled the air with fire   On the road one of
the sick men expired in dreadful convulsions, and no one

undertook his burial; we laid him down on the plain and went farther.

The water in the lake at which I had been the day before refreshed men and animals for a time, but could not restore their strength. The mules had not nipped a grass blade for thirty-six hours, and had lived only on straw which we took out of the wagons; but even that failed them now. We marked the road as we went with their bodies, and on the third day there was left one only, which I took by force for Lillian. The wagons and the tools in them, which were to give us bread in California, remained in that desert, — be it cursed for all ages!

Every one now except Lillian went on foot. Soon a new enemy looked us in the eyes, — hunger. A part of our provisions had been left in the wagons; that which each one could carry was eaten. There was not a living thing in the country around us. I alone in the whole caravan had biscuits yet and a piece of salt meat; but I hid them for Lillian, and I was ready to rend any man to pieces who would mention that food. I ate nothing myself, and that terrible plain stretched on without end.

As if to add to our torments the mirage appeared in the midday hours on the plain again, showing us mountains and forests with lakes; but the nights were more terrible than ever. All the rays which that charred land stole from the sun in the daytime came out at night, scorching our feet and parching our throats. On such a night one man lost his mind, and sitting on the ground burst into spasmodical laughter, and that dreadful laughter followed us long in the darkness. The mule on which Lillian was riding fell; the famishing people tore it to bits in a twinkle; but what food was that for two hundred!

The fourth day passed and the fifth. From hunger, the faces of the people became like those of birds of some kind, and they began to look with hate at one another. They knew that I had provisions; but they knew, too, that to ask one crumb of me was death, hence the instinct of life overcame in them hunger. I gave food to Lillian only at night, so as not to enrage them with the sight of it. She implored me by all that was holy to take my share, but I threatened to put a bullet in my brain if she even mentioned it. She was able, however, to steal from my watchfulness crumbs which she gave to Aunt Atkins and Aunt Grosvenor. At that time hunger was tearing my entrails with iron hand, and my head was burning from the wound.

For five days there had been nothing in my mouth but water from that lake. The thought that I was carrying bread and meat, that I had them with me, that I could eat, became a torture; I was afraid besides, that being wounded, I might go mad and seize the food.

"O Lord!" cried I in spirit, "suffer me not to become so far brutalized as to touch that which is to keep her in life!" But there was no mercy above me. On the morning of the sixth day I saw on Lillian's face fiery spots; her hands were inflamed, she panted loudly. All at once she looked at me wanderingly, and said in haste, hurrying lest she might lose presence of mind, —

"Ralph, leave me here; save yourself, there is no hope for me."

I gritted my teeth, for I wanted to howl and blaspheme; but saying nothing I took her by the hands. Fiery zigzags began to leap before my eyes in the air, and to form the words, "Who worshipped and served the creature more than the Creator?" I had broken like a bow too much bent; so, staring at the merciless heavens, I exclaimed with my whole soul in rebellion :

"I!"

Meanwhile I was bearing to the mount of execution my dearest burden, this my only one, my saint, my beloved martyr.

I know not where I found strength; I was insensible to hunger, to heat, to suffering. I saw nothing before me, neither people nor the burning plain; I saw nothing but Lillian. That night she grew worse. She lost consciousness; at times she groaned in a low voice, —

"Ralph, water!" And oh, torments! I had only salt meat and dry biscuits. In supreme despair I cut my arm with a knife to moisten her lips with my blood; she grew conscious, cried out, and fell into a protracted faint, from which I thought she would not recover. When she came to herself she wished to say something, but the fever had blunted her mind, and she only murmured, —

"Ralph, be not angry! I am your wife."

I carried her farther in silence. I had grown stupid from pain.

The seventh day came. The Sierra Nevada appeared at last on the horizon, and as the sun was going down the life of my life began to quench also. When she was dying I placed her on the burnt ground and knelt beside her. Her widely opened eyes were gleaming and fixed on me; thought appeared in them for a moment, and she whispered, —

"My dear, my husband!" Then a quiver ran through her, fear was on her face, — and she died.

I tore the bandages from my head, and lost consciousness. I have no memory of what happened after that. As in a kind of dream I remember people who surrounded me and took my weapons; then they dug a grave, as it

were; and, still later, darkness and raving seized me, and
in them the fiery words, "Who worshipped and served
the creature more than the Creator!"

.   .   .   .

I woke a month later in California at the house of
Moshynski, a settler.   When I had come to health somewhat I set out for Nevada; the prairie had grown over
with grass, and was abundantly green, so that I could
not find even her grave, and to this day I know not
where her sacred remains are.   What have I done, O
God, that Thou didst turn Thy face from me and forget
me in the desert? — I know not.   Were it permitted me
to weep even one hour at her grave, life would be easier.
Every year I go to Nevada, and every year I seek in
vain.   Since those dreadful hours long years have passed.
My wretched lips have uttered more than once, Let Thy
will be done!   But without her it is hard for me in the
world.   A man lives and walks among people, and laughs
even at times; but the lonely old heart weeps and loves,
and yearns and remembers.

I am old, and it is not long till I shall make another
journey, the journey to eternity; and for one thing alone
I ask God, — that on those celestial plains I may find my
heavenly one, and not part from her ever again.

FROM THE DIARY OF A TUTOR IN POZNAN.

FROM THE DIARY OF A TUTOR
IN POZNAN.

THE lamp, though shaded, roused me, and more than once I saw Mihas still working at two or three o'clock in the morning. His small, fragile figure, dressed only in sleeping clothes, was bent over a book; and in the stillness of the night his drowsy and wearied voice repeated Latin and Greek conjugations mechanically, and in that humdrum voice with which people at church respond to a litany. When I called him to go to bed the boy would answer: "I don't know my lessons yet, Pan Vavrykevich." I worked out his lessons however from four till eight, and then from nine till twelve o'clock, and did not go to bed myself till I was convinced that he had learned everything; but in truth all this was too much for the boy. When he had finished the last lesson he had forgotten the first; the conjugations of Greek, Latin, German, and the names of various districts brought his poor head into such confusion that he could not sleep. He crept out from under the quilt then, lighted his lamp, and sat down at the table. When I reproved him, he begged me to let him stay, and he shed tears. I grew so accustomed to those night sittings, to the light of the lamp and to the mumbling of conjugations, that when they were absent I myself could not sleep. Perhaps it was not right for me to permit the child to torture himself beyond his strength; but what was I to do? He had to learn his lessons daily even in some fashion, or he would be expelled from school; and God alone knows what a blow that would have been for Pani Marya, who, left with two orphans after the death of her husband, placed all her hopes on Mihas. The position was well-nigh without escape, for I saw that excessive mental effort was undermining the health of the boy, and might endanger his life. It was needful at the least to strengthen him physically, train him in gymnastics, make him walk a good deal, or ride on horseback; but there was no time for this. The child had so much to do, so much to learn by rote, so much to write every day, that on my conscience I say that there was no time. Every moment required for the recreation, health, and life of the boy was taken by Latin, Greek, and German.

In the morning, when I put his books into the satchel and saw his lean shoulders bending under the weight of those great volumes, my heart simply ached. At times I asked kindness and forbearance for him; but the German professors merely answered that I was spoiling and petting the child, that evidently Mihas was not working enough, and that he would cry for any cause. I am weak-breasted myself, solitary, and sensitive; hence these reproaches poisoned more than one moment for me. I knew best whether Mihas was working enough. He was a child of medium gifts, but so persevering, and, with all his mildness, gifted with such strength of character as I have never chanced to meet in another boy. Poor Mihas was attached to his mother passionately, blindly; and since people told him that she was very unhappy, and sickly, that, if in addition to other things, he would learn badly it might kill her, the boy trembled at the thought of this, and sat whole nights over his books, only to escape mortifying his mother. He burst into tears when he received a bad mark; but it did not come to the head of any one to inquire why he cried, or to what terrible responsibility he felt himself bound at such moments. Indeed, what did any one care? I was not spoiling him, nor petting him; only I knew him better than others. That I tried to comfort instead of scolding him for failures was my affair. I have toiled myself in life no little; I have suffered hunger and sorrow enough; I have not been happy; I shall not be happy, and — devils take it! — I do not even grit my teeth when I think of this. I do not believe that life is worth living; but perhaps for that very reason I have true sympathy for every misfortune.

At Mihas's age, when I ran after pigeons on the streets, or played wagtails under the town-hall, I had my hours of health and joyousness at least. A cough did not torment me. When some one flogged me I cried during the flogging; but I was as free as a bird and cared for nothing. Mihas had not even that. If life had put him on the anvil and beaten him with its hammer, he would have gained this much, — that as a boy he would have laughed heartily at that which amuses children; he would have played tricks, and tired himself in the open air, in the sunlight. But I had not before me such a union of labor with childishness. On the contrary, I saw a little boy going to school and coming home, gloomy, bent, straining under the weight of books, with wrinkles in the corners of his eyes, ever holding back, as it were, an outburst of weeping; therefore, I sympathized with him, and wished to be a refuge for him.

I am a tutor, though a private one, and I know not what I should do in the world were I to lose faith in the value of knowledge and the benefit which flows from it. But I think that study should not be the tragedy of our early years; that Latin cannot take the place of air and health; and that a good or bad accent should not decide the fate and life of children.

I think, too, that the task of instruction is better accomplished when a boy feels a hand leading him kindly, and not a foot pressing his breast and trampling everything which they teach him at home to love and revere. I am such an obscurant that I shall be sure not to change my opinion in this respect, for I become confirmed in it more and more when I remember my Mihas, whom I loved so sincerely. I taught him six years, first as a governor, and, when he entered the second class, as a tutor. I had time therefore to grow attached to him. Besides, why should I hide from myself that he was dear to me because he was the son of a being dear to me above all others. She has never known this, and never will. I remember that I am — well, Pan Vavrykevich, a private tutor, and a sickly man in addition; she the daughter of a rich, noble house, a lady to whom I dared not raise my eyes. But since a lone heart, dashed about by life as a mussel is dashed by the waves, must attach itself at last to something, my heart grew to her. How can I help it? And besides, how does that harm her? I do not deprive her of light, any more than I do the sun which warms my weak breast

I was six years in her house; I was present at the death of her husband; I saw that she was unhappy, alone, but always as kind as an angel; loving her children, well-nigh a saint in her widowhood; hence I was forced to this feeling. But it is not love on my part, — it is rather religion.

Mihas reminded me greatly of his mother. More than once when he raised his eyes to me I imagined that I was looking at her. The same delicate features were present, the very same forehead with a shadow of rich hair falling over it, the soft outline of brow, and above all a voice almost identical. In the disposition of the mother and child there was a likeness too, appearing in a certain tendency to exaltation of feelings and views. They belonged both of them to that species of nervous impressionable people, noble and loving, who are capable of the greatest sacrifices, but who in life and in contact with its reality find little happiness, giving, to begin with, more than they can receive in return. That kind of people perish, and I think now that some naturalist might declare them foredoomed to extinction, for they come into the world with a defect of heart, — they love too much.

Mihas's family was very wealthy at one time, but they loved too much; therefore various storms shattered their fortune, and what remained was not indeed want, — it was not even poverty; still in comparison with former days it was moderate. Mihas was the last of the family, therefore Pani Marya loved him not only as her own child, but also as her whole hope for the future. Unfortunately, with the usual blindness of mothers, she saw in him uncommon faculties. The boy was not dull indeed; but he belonged to that class of children whose powers, medium at first, develop only later, together with physical strength and with health. In other conditions he might have finished his course in the school and the University, and become a useful worker in any career. In existing conditions he simply tortured himself, and knowing his mother's high opinion of his powers, he strained them in vain.

My eyes have seen much in this world, and I have determined to wonder at nothing; but I confess that it was hard for me to believe that there could be a chaos, in which a boy's perseverance, strength of character, and industry would be against him. There is something unhealthy in this; and if words could repay me for sorrow and bitterness, I should say with Hamlet, that there are things in the world which have not been dreamed of by philosophers.

I worked with Mihas as if my own future depended on the marks which he got for his lessons, since my dear pupil and I had one object: not to afflict her, to show good rank, to call out a smile of happiness on her lips. When he succeeded in receiving good marks, the boy came from school radiant and happy. It seemed to me that in such cases he had grown on a sudden, had become erect; his eyes, usually cloudy, laughed now with the unaffected joy of childhood, and gleamed like two coals. He threw from his narrow shoulders his satchel laden with books, and blinking at me said while yet on the threshold,—

"Pan Vavrykevich, mamma will be satisfied! I got to-day in geography — guess how many?"

And when I pretended that I could not guess, he ran to me with a proud mien, and throwing his arms around my neck, said as if in a whisper, but very loud, —

"Five! truly five!"

Those were happy moments for us. In the evenings of such days Mihas fell to dreaming, and imagined to himself what would come to pass were he to receive excellent marks all the time, and said half to me, half to himself, —

"On Christmas we will go to Zalesin; the snow will fall, as it does always in winter; we'll go in a sleigh. We'll arrive at night, but oh! mamma will be waiting for me; she'll hug me and kiss me, then ask about my marks. I'll put on a sad face purposely; then mamma will read religion excellent, German excellent, Latin excellent, — most excellent! Oh, Pan Vavrykevich!"

The poor little boy! tears were in his eyes; and I, instead of restraining him, hurried after him with unwearied imagination, and recalled to myself the house in Zalesin, its dignity, its calm, that lofty, noble being who was mistress there, and the happiness which the return of the boy with his excellent rank would bring to her.

I took advantage of such moments, and gave Mihas advice, explaining to him that mamma cared greatly for his studies, but cared also for his health; hence he must not cry when I took him to walk, he must sleep as much as I prescribed, and not persist in sitting up at night. The boy, affected by this, embraced me and said, —

"I will obey, my golden Pan. I shall be so well that it will be a wonder to look at me, and I'll be so fat that neither mamma nor little Lola will know me."

I too received letters frequently from Pani Marya, recommending me to watch over the health of the child; but I convinced myself daily with despair that that was well-nigh impossible. If the subjects taught were too difficult I could have mended the matter by removing Mihas from the second to the first class; but those subjects, though dry, he understood perfectly. It was not a question of learning, but of time and of that unfortunate German language, which the child could not speak satisfactorily. In this I was powerless, and calculated only that when the holidays came, rest would fill out those breaches in the boy's health made by excessive labor.

If Mihas had been a child of less feeling I should have been less anxious about him; but he felt every failure almost more keenly than he did success. The moments of joy and those *fives* which I have mentioned were rare, unfortunately.

I had so learned to read his face that the moment he

came, I knew at the first glance of the eye that he had not succeeded. "Did you get a bad mark?" I asked.

"I did."

"You did n't know the lesson?"

Sometimes he answered, "I did n't know;" but oftener, "I knew, but I was n't able to tell it."

In fact little Ovitski, the first in the second class, whom I purposely brought in that Mihas might learn with him, said that Mihas received bad marks chiefly because he could not "tongue out."

As the child felt more and more wearied mentally and physically, such failures came oftener. I noticed that after having cried all he wanted he sat down to his lesson quietly and as though he were calm; but in that redoubled energy with which he turned to his tasks there was something both desperate and feverish. Sometimes he went into a corner, pressed his head with both hands, and was silent; the imaginative boy fancied that he was digging a grave under the feet of his darling mother, knew not how to escape this, and felt himself in a vicious circle from which there was no escape.

His night work became more frequent. Fearing that when I woke I would order him to bed, he rose in the dark, silently carried the lamp to the antechamber, lighted it there, and sat down to work. Before I caught him he had passed a number of nights in this way between unheated walls. I had no other resource than to rise, call him to the chamber, and go over all the lessons once more with him, to convince him that he knew them and that he exposed himself to cold without reason. But at last he did n't know himself what he did know. The child lost strength, grew thin, pale, and became more and more despondent. Something happened after a time to convince me that not work alone was exhausting him.

Once, while I was explaining to him the history that
"An Uncle told his Nephews," [1] which at the request of
Pani Marya I did daily, Mihas sprang up with flashing
eyes. I was frightened almost when I saw the inquiring
and stern look on his face as he cried, —

"Pan! is that really not a fable? For — "

"Why did you ask, Mihas?" inquired I, with astonishment.

Instead of an answer he gritted his teeth, and burst
out at last into such passionate weeping that for a long
time I was unable to quiet him.

I inquired of Ovitski touching the cause of this outburst. He either knew not, or would not tell; but I discovered myself. There was no doubt that in the German
school the Polish child had to hear many things that
wounded his feelings. Such teachings slipped over other
boys, leaving no trace except ill-will against the teachers
and their whole race; Mihas, a boy of such uprightness,
felt these teachings acutely, but dared not contradict
them. Two powers, two voices, obedience to which is the
duty of a child, but which for that very reason should be
in harmony, were tearing Mihas in two opposite directions. What one power called white, worthy, beloved,
the other called a stain vile and ridiculous; what one
called virtue the other called vice. Therefore in that
separation the boy followed the power to which his heart
was attracted, but he had to pretend that he obeyed and
took to heart words of the opposite meaning. He had to
pretend from morning till night, and to live in that torturing constraint days, weeks, months. What a position
for a child!

Mihas's fate was remarkable. Dramas of life begin later
usually, when the first leaves are falling from the tree of

[1] One of Lelewell's histories of Poland.

youth; for him everything which creates unhappiness —
such as moral constraint, concealed regret, trouble of
mind, vain efforts, struggling with difficulties, gradual loss
of hope — began in the eleventh year of his life. Neither
his slight form nor his weak forces could carry those
burdens. Days, weeks passed; the poor boy redoubled his
efforts, and the result was always less, always more
lamentable. The letters of Pani Marya, though sweet,
added weight to the burden. "God has gifted you, Mihas,
with uncommon capacities," wrote she; "and I trust that
you will not disappoint the hopes that I place in you,
that you will be a pleasure to me and the country."

When the boy received such a letter the first time he
seized my hand spasmodically, and borne away by weeping began to repeat, —

"What shall I do, Pan Vavrykevich, what can I do?"

In truth what could he do? How could he help it
that he had n't come into the world with an inborn
power over languages, and that he could not pronounce
German?

Before the recess at All Saints, the quarterly return
was not very favorable; in three of the most important
subjects he had low marks. At his most urgent prayers
and entreaties I did not send it to Pani Marya.

"Dear Pan," cried he, putting his hands together,
"mamma does n't know that they give rank at All Saints,
and before Christmas the Lord God may take pity on
me."

The poor child deluded himself with the hope that he
would raise his low rank; and to tell the truth, I deceived myself also. I thought that he would grow
accustomed to school routine, that he would grow accustomed to everything, be trained in German, and acquire
the accent; above all, that he would need less and less

time for his lessons. Had it not been for this I should have written long before to Pani Marya and laid before her the condition of affairs. In fact hopes did not seem vain. Just after All Saints Mihas received three perfect marks, one of which was in Latin. Of all the pupils in the class he alone knew that the perfect of *gaudeo* is *gavisus sum*, and he knew it because he had received before that two perfect marks and had inquired of me what "I rejoice" is in Latin. I thought that the boy would go wild from delight. He wrote a letter to his mother beginning with these words: "Does my beloved mamma know what the perfect of *gaudeo* is? Surely neither mamma nor little Lola knows, for in the whole class I was the only one who knew."

Mihas simply adored his mother. From that time he was inquiring of me continually about various perfects and participles. High marks had become the object of his life. But the gleam of fortune was brief. Soon his fatal Polish accent ruined all that effort had built up, and the excessive number of subjects did not permit the child to give each as much time as his strained memory needed. A circumstance caused also an increase of his failures. Mihas and Ovitski forgot to inform me of a certain task in writing, and omitted it. That passed for Ovitski, since he stood first the professors did not even ask him about it; but Mihas received a public admonition in school, with a threat of expulsion.

They seemed to think that he had concealed the task from me intentionally, so as not to perform it, and the boy, who was incapable of the least falsehood, had no means of proving his innocence. He might, it is true, say in self-defence that Ovitski had forgotten as well as he; but school honor would not permit such a statement. The Germans answered my assurances with the remark that

I encouraged the youngster to laziness. That was no slight offence to me; but the appearance of Mihas increased my anxiety. In the evening of that day I saw that he pressed his head with both hands, and whispered, thinking that I did not hear him, "It pains, it pains, it pains!" The letter from his mother, which came next day, and in which Pani Marya overwhelmed him with tenderness for those good marks, was a fresh blow for him.

"Oh, I am preparing nice consolation for mamma!" cried he, covering his face with his hands.

Next day, when I put the satchel of books on his shoulders, he tottered and came near falling. I wished to keep him from school, but he said that nothing was the matter; he merely asked me to go with him, for he feared dizziness. He came back in the evening with a new middling mark. He received it for a lesson which he knew perfectly, but according to Ovitski he grew frightened and could n't say a word. The opinion was confirmed decidedly, — "that he was a boy filled with retrograde principles and instincts, that he was lazy and dull."

The last two reproaches came to his knowledge, and he struggled with them desperately but vainly — as a drowning man struggles with a wave.

At last he lost all faith in himself, all confidence in his own powers; he came to the conviction that efforts and labor were useless, that he could n't help learning badly; and at the same time he imagined what his mother would say, what pain it would be for her, and how it might undermine her weak health.

The priest in Zalesin who wrote to him sometimes was very friendly, but incautious. Every letter of his finished with these words: "Let Mihas remember then that not only the joy but the health of his mother

depends on his progress in learning and in morality."
He remembered too much, for even in sleep he repeated
with sad voice: "Mamma, mamma!" as if begging her
forgiveness.

But when awake, he received lower and lower marks.
Christmas was coming quickly, and as to rank it was
impossible to be deceived. I wrote to Pani Marya, wishing to forewarn her, told her plainly and positively that
the child was weak and overburdened; that in spite of
the greatest effort he could not do his work; and that
probably it would be necessary to take him from school
after the holidays, to keep him in the country, and,
above all, to strengthen his health. Though I felt in
her answer that her motherly affection was wounded
somewhat, still she wrote like a sensible woman and a
loving mother. I did not mention this letter to Mihas,
nor the design of taking him from school, for I feared the
effect on him of every powerful excitement; I mentioned
only that, whatever might happen, his mother knew that
he was working, and she would be able to understand his
failure. That gave him evident comfort, for he wept long
and heartily, — which had not happened to him for some
time. While weeping, he repeated: "How much pain I
cause mamma!" Still at the thought that soon he
would return to the country, would see his mother and
little Lola and Father Mashynski, he laughed through
his tears. I too was in a hurry to go to Zalesin, for I
could hardly bear to look at the condition of the child.
There the heart of a mother was waiting for him, and the
good will of people, with calm and peace; there knowledge had for him a native air, well wishing, not strange
and repellent; there the whole atmosphere was familiar
and pure, — the boy's breast might breathe it.

I was looking to the holidays, therefore, as to salvation

for the boy; and I counted on my fingers the hours which separated us from them, but which brought more and more new vexation to Mihas. It seemed as though everything had conspired against him. Mihas had received again a public admonition for *demoralizing* others. That was just before the holidays; therefore it had the more significance. How the ambitious and impressionable boy felt the blow, I will not undertake to describe; what chaos must have risen in his mind! Everything was eager in that childish breast, and before his eyes he saw darkness instead of light. He bent then as an ear of grain before the blast. Finally, the face of that boy of eleven took on an expression simply tragic; he looked as if weeping were stopping his throat continually, as if he restrained sobbing by effort; at times his eyes looked like the eyes of a suffering bird; then a wonderful thoughtfulness and drowsiness took possession of him; his motions became as it were unconscious, and his voice mechanically obedient.

When I told him that it was time to walk, he did not resist as formerly, but took his cap and followed me in silence. I should have been content had that been indifference; but I saw that under the appearance of it was hidden an exalted and suffering resignation. He sat at his lessons, performed his tasks as before, but rather from habit. It was evident that, while repeating the conjugations mechanically, he was thinking of something else, or rather he was not thinking of anything. Once, when I asked whether he had finished everything, he answered in a slow voice, and as if sleepily: "I think, Pan Vavrykevich, that this is no use." I feared even to mention his mother before him, so as not to fill to overflowing that cup of bitterness from which his childish lips were drinking.

I was more and more alarmed about his health, for he grew thinner and thinner, and at last became almost transparent. The network of delicate veins, which appeared on his temples before when he was greatly excited, had now become permanent. He had grown so beautiful that he was almost like an image. It was painful to look at that childish head, half angelic, which produced the impression of a withering flower. Apparently it was as if nothing was the matter; but he sank, and lost power. He was able no longer to carry all his books in the satchel; hence I gave only some to him, and carried the others, for now I accompanied Mihas to and from school.

At last the holidays were at hand. The horses from Zalesin were waiting two days for us, and Pani Marya's letter, which came with them, stated that all were expecting us there with impatience. "I have heard," concluded Pani Marya, "that it goes hard with you, Mihas; I do not look for high marks; I wish only that the teachers should think with me that you have done what you could, and that with good conduct you have tried to atone for deficient progress."

But the teachers thought differently in every respect; therefore, his rank deceived even that expectation. The last public admonition touched the boy's conduct directly, —that conduct concerning which Pani Marya had such a high opinion. In the judgment of the German professors only that boy conducted himself well who repaid with laughter their jests at the "backwardness of the Poles," at their language and traditions. As a result of these ethical ideas Mihas, as not giving hopes of hearing their explanations in future with profit, and as occupying the place of another for nothing, was expelled from the school.

He brought the sentence in the evening. It had grown dark in the house, for very heavy snow was falling outside; hence I could not see the child's face. I saw only that he went to the window, stood in it, and looked without thought, in silence, on the snowflakes whirling in the wind. I did not envy the poor little fellow the thoughts which must have been whirling in his head like the snowflakes outside; but I preferred not to speak to him touching his rank and the sentence. In that way a quarter of an hour passed in bitter silence; but meanwhile it grew dark almost completely. I betook myself to packing the trunk; but seeing that Mihas was standing yet at the window, I said at last, —

"What are you doing there, Mihas?"

"Is it true," answered he, in a voice which quivered and hesitated at every syllable, "that mamma is sitting now with Lola in the green room before the fire, and thinking of me?"

"Perhaps she is. Why does your voice tremble so, — are you sick?"

"Nothing is the matter with me, Pan Vavrykevich; only I am very cold."

I undressed him, and put him straightway to bed; while undressing him, I looked with compassion on his emaciated knees, and his arms as thin as reed-stalks. I ordered him to drink tea, and covered him with what was possible.

"Are you warmer now?"

"Oh, yes! but my head aches a little."

Poor head! It had reason to ache. The suffering child fell asleep soon, and breathed laboriously in his sleep with his narrow breast. I finished packing his and my own things; then, since I did not feel well, I lay down at once. I blew out the light, and fell asleep almost that moment.

About three o'clock in the morning the lamp and the monotonous well-known muttering waked me. I opened my eyes, and my heart beat unquietly. On the table was the lighted lamp, and at the table sat Mihas over a book. He was in his shirt only; his cheeks were burning, his eyes partly closed as if for better exertion of his memory; his head was thrown back a little, and his sleepy voice repeated, —

"Subjunctive: Amem, ames, amet, amemus, ametis — "

"Mihas!"

"Subjunctive: Amem, ames — "

I shook him by the shoulder.

He woke up, and began to blink from astonishment, looking at me as if he did not know me.

"What are you doing? What is the matter, child?"

"Pan Vavrykevich," said he, smiling, "I am repeating everything from the beginning; I must get a perfect mark to-morrow."

I took him in my arms, and carried him to bed; his body burned me like fire. Happily the doctor lived in the same house; I brought him at once. He had no need to think long. He held the boy's pulse a moment, then put his hand on his forehead. Mihas had inflammation of the brain.

Ah, there were many things evidently which could not find place in his head!

His sickness acquired alarming proportions immediately. I sent a despatch to Pani Marya, and on the next day a violent pull at the bell in the antechamber announced her arrival. In fact, when I opened the door, I saw through the black veil her face, pale as linen. Her fingers rested on my shoulder with uncommon force, and her whole soul rushed out through her eyes, which were fixed on me, when she asked briefly, —

28

"Is he alive?"

"He is. The doctor says that he is better."

She threw aside the veil, on which hoar frost had settled from her breath, and hurried to the boy's chamber. I had lied. Mihas was alive, it is true; but he was not better. He did not even know his mother when she sat near him, and took his hand. Only when I had placed fresh ice on his head did he begin to blink, and look with effort at the face bent above him. His mind made an evident effort, struggling with fever and delirium; his lips quivered, he smiled once and a second time, and whispered at last, —

"Mamma!"

She seized both his hands, and sat in that way at his side a number of hours, not casting aside even her travelling costume. Only when I turned her attention to this, did she say, —

"True. I forgot to remove my hat."

When she took it off, my heart was oppressed with a wonderful feeling: among the blond hair adorning that young and beautiful head, silver threads were gleaming thickly. Three days ago, perhaps, there were none there.

She changed compresses for the boy herself, and gave him the medicine. Mihas followed her with his eyes wherever she moved, but again he did not recognize her. In the evening the fever increased; he declaimed in his raving the ballad about "Jolkevski from Nyemtsevich;" at times he spoke in the language of teaching; again he conjugated various Latin verbs. I left the room repeatedly, for I could not listen to this. While in good health, he had been learning in secret to serve at Mass, wishing to give his mother a surprise when he came home; and now a shiver passed through me when in the stillness of the evening I heard that boy of eleven years

repeating before his death with a monotonous and expir-
ing voice : " Deus meus, quare me repulisti, et quare
tristis incedo dum affligit me inimicus [My God, why hast
Thou rejected me, and why am I walking in grief while
my enemy afflicts me] ? "

I cannot tell what a tragic impression these words
produced. It was Christmas eve. From the street came
the hum of people and the tinkling of sleigh-bells. The
town had taken on a holiday and joyful exterior. When
it had grown dark completely, through the windows on
the other side of the street was to be seen an evergreen-
tree gleaming with lights, and hung with glittering gold
and silver nuts, and around it the heads of children
bright and dark, with locks flowing in the air, jumping
as if on springs. The windows were gleaming, and the
whole interior resounded with cries of delight and wonder. Among the voices coming from the street there
were none except joyous ones, gladness had become universal; our boy alone repeated, as if with great sorrow:
"Deus meus, Deus meus, quare me repulisti ? " At the
gate, boys halted with a little booth, and soon the song
reached us : "He is lying in the manger, who will run
to greet the little stranger ? " Christmas night was
approaching, and we trembled lest it should be a night
of death.

After awhile it seemed to us, however, that the boy
had become conscious, for he began to call Lola and his
mother; but that was of short duration. His quick
breathing stopped at times altogether. There was no
cause for self-deception ; that little soul was already only
half with us. His mind had flown away, and now he
was going himself into some dark distance and endlessness; already he saw no one, and felt nothing, — not
even the head of his mother, which was lying as if dead

at his feet. He had grown indifferent, and looked no longer at us. Every breath of his bosom removed him, and as it were pushed him out into the darkness. Disease was quenching spark after spark of his life. The hands of the child lying on the coverlet were outlined on it with heavy helplessness, the mark of death; his nose became sharp, and his face took on a certain cold seriousness. His breath became quicker, and at last was like the ticking of a watch. A moment more, another sigh, and the last grain of sand was to fall from the hourglass; the end was inevitable.

About midnight it seemed to us decisively that he was dying, for he began to rattle and groan like a man into whose mouth water is flowing, and then he was silent suddenly. But the glass which the doctor placed at his lips was covered yet with the mist of respiration. An hour later the fever decreased all at once; we thought that he was saved. The doctor himself had some hope. Poor Pani Marya grew faint.

In the course of two hours he was better and better. Toward morning, since that was the fourth night which I had spent near the boy without sleeping, and since a cough was stifling me with growing violence, I went to the anteroom, lay on a straw bed, and fell asleep. The voice of Pani Marya roused me. I thought that she was calling me, but in the stillness of night I heard clearly, "Mihas! Mihas!" The hair stood on my head, for I understood the terrible accent with which she cried to the child; before I sprang up, however, she ran in herself, holding the light in her hand, and whispered with quivering lips, —

"Mihas — is dead!"

I ran in a breath to the boy's bed. So it was. The head fallen back on the pillow, the mouth open, the eyes fixed without motion on one point, and the rigidity of every feature, left not the least doubt: Mihas was dead.

I covered him with the quilt, which his mother, in springing away from the bed, had pulled from his emaciated body. I closed his eyes, and then I had to rub Pani Marya a long time.

The first day of the Christmas season passed in preparations for the funeral, preparations which for me were terrible, since Pani Marya would not leave the corpse, and fainted continually. She fainted when men came to take the dimensions of the coffin, again when they began to prepare the body, finally when the catafalque was put up. Her despair was in continual clash with the indifference of the undertaker's assistants, accustomed as they were to similar sights, and passed almost into raving. She herself put shavings in the coffin under the satin, repeating, as if in a fever, that the child's head would be too low. And Mihas was lying meanwhile on his bed, in his new uniform and white gloves, rigid, indifferent, and calm. We placed the body at last in the coffin, put that on the catafalque, and set two rows of candles around it. The room in which the poor child had conjugated so many Latin verbs and worked out so many lessons had changed as it were into a chapel, for the closed windows did not admit sunshine, and the yellow, flickering light of the candles gave the walls a certain church-like and solemn appearance. Never since Mihas had received his last high mark had I seen his face so full of contentment. His delicate profile turned to the ceiling was smiling, as if in that eternal reaction of death the boy had pleased himself and felt happy. The flickering of the candles gave to his face and to that smile an appearance of life and sleep.

By degrees those of his schoolmates who had not gone home for the holidays began to assemble. The eyes of the children grew wide with wonder at sight of the candles, the catafalque, and the coffin. Perhaps the dignity and importance of their comrade astonished the little scholars. Not long since he was among them, bending like them under the weight of a satchel overladen with German books; he received bad marks, was scolded and admonished publicly; each might pull his hair or his ears. But now he lay there above them, dignified, calm, surrounded with light; all approached him with respect and a certain awe, — and even Ovitski, though the first scholar, did not mean much before him. The boys, pushing each other with their elbows, whispered that now he cared for nothing; that even if the "Herr Inspector" had come, he would not spring up nor be frightened, but would continue to smile quietly as before. "He can do just as he likes," said they; "he can shout as he likes, and talk to little angels with wings on their shoulders."

Thus they approached the rows of candles, and asked eternal rest for Mihas.

The next day the coffin was covered with the lid, fastened with nails, and taken to the cemetery, where lumps of sand mixed with snow soon concealed it from my eyes forever. To-day, as I write, almost a year has passed from that time; but I remember thee, and I mourn for thee, my little Mihas, my flower withered untimely. I know not where thou art, or if thou dost hear me; I know only that thy old teacher's cough is increasing, that the world seems more oppressive to him, that he is more lonely, and may go soon to the place whither thou hast gone.

THE LIGHT-HOUSE KEEPER
OF ASPINWALL.

THE LIGHT–HOUSE KEEPER
OF ASPINWALL.

CHAPTER I.

O N a time it happened that the light-house keeper in
Aspinwall, not far from Panama, disappeared without a trace. Since he disappeared during a storm, it was
supposed that the ill-fated man went to the very edge of
the small, rocky island on which the light-house is situated, and was swept out by a wave. This supposition
seemed the more likely as his boat was not found in its
rocky niche the next day. The position of light-house
keeper had become vacant. It was necessary to fill this
position at the earliest, since the light-house had no small
significance for the local movement as well as for vessels
going from New York to Panama. Mosquito Bay
abounds in banks and sandbars. Among these naviga-
tion even in the daytime is difficult; but at night, especially with the fogs which are so frequent on those
waters warmed by the sun of the tropics, it is almost
impossible. The only guide at that time for the numerous vessels is the light-house.

The task of finding a new keeper fell to the United
States consul in Panama, and this task was no small
one: first, because it was absolutely necessary to find
the man within twelve hours; second, the man must
be unusually conscientious, — it was not possible, of

course, to take the first comer at random; finally, there
was an utter lack of candidates. Life on a tower is
uncommonly difficult, and by no means enticing to people
of the South, who love idleness and the freedom of a
vagrant life. That light-house keeper is almost a prisoner. He cannot leave his rocky island except on Sun-
days. A boat from Aspinwall brings him provisions and
water once a day, and returns immediately; on the whole
island, one acre in area, there is no inhabitant. The
keeper lives in the light-house; he keeps it in order.
During the day he gives signals by displaying flags of
various colors to indicate changes of the barometer; in
the evening he lights the lantern. This would be no
great labor were it not that to reach the lantern at the
top of the tower he must pass over more than four
hundred steep and very high steps; sometimes he must
make this journey repeatedly during the day. In general
it is the life of a monk, and indeed more than that, — the
life of a hermit. It was not wonderful, therefore, that
Mr. Isaac Falconbridge was in no small anxiety as to
where he should find a permanent successor to the recent
keeper; and it is easy to understand his joy when a successor announced himself most unexpectedly on that very
day. He was a man already old, seventy years or more,
but fresh, erect, with the movements and bearing of a
soldier. His hair was perfectly white, his face as dark
as that of a creole; but judging from his blue eyes, he
did not belong to a Southern people. His face was
somewhat downcast and sad, but honest. At the first
glance he pleased Falconbridge. It remained only to
examine him. Therefore the following conversation
began, —

"Where are you from?"

"I am a Pole."

" Where have you worked up to this time ? "

" In one place and another."

" A light-house keeper should like to stay in one place."

" I need rest."

" Have you served? Have you testimonials of honorable government service ? "

The old man drew from his bosom a piece of faded silk resembling a strip of an old flag, unwound it, and said, —

" Here are the testimonials. I received this cross in 1830. This second one is Spanish, from the Carlist War; the third is the French legion ; the fourth I received in Hungary. Afterward I fought in the States against the South ; there they do not give crosses."

Falconbridge took the paper and began to read.

" H'm ! Skavinski ? Is that your name ? H'm ! Two flags captured in a bayonet attack. You were a gallant soldier."

" I am able to be a conscientious light-house keeper."

" It is necessary to ascend the tower a number of times daily. Have you sound legs ? "

" I crossed the plains on foot."   (The immense prairies between the East and California are called " the plains.")

" Do you know sea service ? "

" I served three years on a whaler."

" You have tried various occupations."

" The only one I have not known is quiet."

" Why is that ? "

The old man shrugged his shoulders. " Such is my fate."

" Still you seem to me too old for a light-house keeper."

" Sir," exclaimed the candidate suddenly, in a voice of emotion, " I am greatly wearied, knocked about. I have passed through much, as you see. This place is one of those which I have wished for most ardently. I am old, I need rest. I need to say to myself, 'Here you will remain; this is your port.' Ah, sir, this depends now on you alone. Another time perhaps such a place will not offer itself. What luck that I was in Panama! I entreat you — as God is dear to me, I am like a ship which if it misses the harbor will be lost. If you wish to make an old man happy — I swear to you that I am honest, but — I have enough of this wandering."

The blue eyes of the old man expressed such earnest entreaty that Falconbridge, who had a good, simple heart, was touched.

"Well," said he, "I take you. You are light-house keeper."

The old man's face gleamed with inexpressible joy.

"I thank you."

"Can you go to the tower to-day?"

"I can."

"Then good-by. Another word, for any failure in service you will be dismissed."

"All right."

That same evening, when the sun had descended on the other side of the isthmus, and a day of sunshine was followed by a night without twilight, the new keeper was in his place evidently, for the light-house was casting its bright rays on the water as usual. The night was perfectly calm, silent, genuinely tropical, filled with a transparent haze, forming around the moon a great colored rainbow with soft, unbroken edges; the sea was moving only because the tide raised it. Skavinski on the balcony seemed from below like a small black point. He tried to collect his thoughts, and take in his new position; but his mind was too much under pressure to move with regularity. He felt somewhat as a hunted beast feels when at last it has found refuge from pursuit on some inaccessible rock or in a cave. An hour of quiet had come to him finally; the feeling of safety filled his soul with a certain unspeakable bliss. Now on that rock he can simply laugh at his previous wanderings, his misfortunes and failures. He was in truth like a ship whose masts, ropes, and sails had been broken and rent by a tempest, and cast from the clouds to the bottom of the sea, — a ship on which the tempest had hurled waves and spat foam, but which had still wound its way to the harbor. The pictures of that storm passed through his mind quickly as he compared it with the calm future now beginning. A part of his wonderful adventures he had related to Falconbridge; he had not mentioned, however, thousands of other incidents. It had been his misfortune that as often as he pitched his tent and fixed his fireplace to settle down permanently, some wind tore out his tent-stakes, whirled away the fire, and bore him on toward destruction. Looking now from the balcony of the tower at the illuminated waves, he remembered everything through which he had passed. He had campaigned in the four parts of the world, and in wandering had tried almost every occupation. Labor-loving and honest, he had earned money more than once, but had always lost it in spite of every prevision and the utmost caution. He had been a gold-miner in Australia, a diamond-digger in Africa, a rifleman in public service in the East Indies. He had established a ranch in California, — the drought ruined him; he had tried trading with wild tribes in the interior of Brazil, — his raft was wrecked on the Amazon; he himself alone, weaponless, and nearly naked, wandered in the forest for many weeks, living on wild fruits, exposed every moment to death from the jaws of wild beasts. He established a forge in Helena, Arkansas, and that was burned in a great fire which consumed the whole town. Next he fell into the hands of Indians in the Rocky Mountains, and only through a miracle was he saved by Canadian trappers. Then he served as a sailor on a vessel running between Bahia and Bordeaux, and as harpooner on a whaling-ship; both vessels were wrecked. He had a cigar factory in Havana, and was robbed by his partner while he himself was lying sick with the vomito. At last he came to Aspinwall, and there was to be the end of his failures, — for what could reach him now on that rocky island? Neither water nor fire nor men. But from men Skavinski had not suffered much; he had met good men oftener than bad ones.

But it seemed to him that all the four elements were persecuting him. Those who knew him said that he had no luck, and with that they explained everything. He himself became somewhat of a monomaniac. He believed that some mighty and vengeful hand was pursuing him everywhere, on all lands and waters. He did not like, however, to speak of this; only at times, when some one asked him whose hand that could be, he pointed mysteriously to the Polar Star, and said, "It comes from that place." In reality his failures were so continuous that they were wonderful, and might easily drive a nail into the head, especially of the man who had experienced them. But Skavinski had the patience of an Indian, and that great calm power of resistance which comes from truth of heart. He had received once in Hungary a number of bayonet thrusts because he would not grasp at a stirrup which was shown as means of salvation to him, and implore quarter. In like manner he did not bend to misfortune. He crept up against the mountain as industriously as an ant. Pushed down a hundred times, he began his journey calmly for the hundred and first time.

He was in his way a most peculiar original. This old soldier, tempered God knows in how many fires, hardened in suffering, hammered and forged, had the heart of a child. In time of the epidemic in Cuba, the vomito attacked him because he had given to the sick all his quinine, of which he had a considerable supply, and left not a grain to himself.

There had been in him also this wonderful quality, — that after so many disappointments he was ever full of confidence, and did not lose hope that all would be well yet. In winter he grew lively, and foretold great events. He waited for these events with impatience, and lived through whole summers with the thought of them. But the winters passed one after another, and Skavinski lived only to this, — that they whitened his head. At last he grew old, began to lose energy; his endurance was becoming more and more like resignation, his former calmness was tending toward supersensitiveness, and that tempered soldier was degenerating into a man ready to shed tears for any cause. Besides this, from time to time he was weighed down by a terrible homesickness which was roused by any circumstance, — the sight of swallows, gray birds like sparrows, snow on the mountains, or melancholy music like that heard on a time. Finally, there was one idea which mastered him, — the idea of rest. It mastered the old man thoroughly, and swallowed all other hopes and desires. This ceaseless wanderer could not imagine anything more to be longed for, anything more precious, than a quiet corner in which to rest, and wait for the end in silence. Perhaps specially because some whim of fate had so hurried him over all seas and lands that he could hardly catch breath, did he imagine that the highest human happiness was simply not to wander. It is true that such modest happiness was due to him; but he was

so accustomed to disappointments that he thought of rest
as people in general think of a thing which surpasses
attainment. He dared not hope for it. Meanwhile, unexpectedly in the course of twelve hours he had gained a
position which was as if chosen for him out of all in the
world. We are not to wonder, then, that when he lighted
his lantern in the evening he was as if dazed, — that
he asked himself if that was reality, and dared not
answer that it was. But at the same time reality convinced him with incontrovertible proofs; hence hours
one after another passed while he was on the balcony.
He gazed, and convinced himself. It might seem that he
was looking at the sea for the first time in his life. The
lens of the lantern cast into the darkness an enormous
triangle of light, beyond which the eye of the old man
was lost in the black distance completely, in a distance
mysterious and awful. But that distance seemed to run
toward the light. The long waves following one another
rolled out of the darkness, and went bellowing toward
the base of the island; and then their foaming backs
were visible, shining rose-colored in the light of the lantern. The incoming tide swelled more and more, and
covered the sandy bars. The mysterious speech of the
ocean came with a fulness more powerful and louder, at
one time like the thunder of cannon, at another like the
roar of great forests, at another like the distant dull
sound of the voices of people. At moments it was quiet;
then to the ears of the old man came some great sigh,
then a kind of sobbing, and again threatening outbursts.
At last the wind bore away the haze, but brought black,
broken clouds, which hid the moon. From the west it
began to blow more and more; the waves sprang with
rage against the rock of the light-house, licking with foam
the foundation walls. In the distance a storm was be-

ginning to bellow. On the dark, disturbed expanse certain green lanterns gleamed from the masts of ships. These green points rose high and then sank; now they swayed to the right, and now to the left. Skavinski descended to his room. The storm began to howl. Outside people on those ships were struggling with night, with darkness, with waves; but inside the tower it was still and calm. Even the sounds of the storm hardly came through the thick walls, and only the measured tick-tack of the clock lulled the wearied old man to his slumber.

II.

Hours, days, and weeks passed. Sailors assert that at times when the sea is greatly roused, something from out the midst of night and darkness calls them by name. If the infinity of the sea may call out thus, perhaps when a man is growing old, calls come to him, too, from another infinity still darker and more deeply mysterious; and the more he is wearied by life the dearer become those calls to him. But to hear them quiet is needed. Besides, old age loves to seclude itself as if with a fore-knowledge of the grave. The light-house had become for Skavinski such a half grave. Nothing is more monotonous than life on a beacon-tower. If young people consent to take up this service they leave it soon after. Light-house keepers are generally men not young, gloomy, and confined to themselves. If by chance one of them leaves his light-house and goes among men, he walks in the midst of them like a person roused from deep slumber. On the tower there is a lack of minute impressions which in ordinary life teach men to adapt themselves to everything. All that a light-house keeper comes in contact

29

with is gigantic, and devoid of forms sharply outlined.
The sky is one whole, the water another; and between
those two infinities the soul of man is in loneliness. That
is a life in which thought is continual meditation, and
out of that meditation nothing rouses the keeper, not even
his work. Day is like day as two beads in a rosary, unless changes of weather form the only variety. But
Skavinski felt more happiness than ever in life before.
He rose with the dawn, took his breakfast, polished the
lens, and then sitting on the balcony gazed into the distance of the water; and his eyes were never sated with
the pictures which he saw before him. On the enormous
turquoise ground of the ocean were to be seen generally
flocks of swollen sails gleaming in the rays of the sun
with such brightness that the eyes blinked before the excess of light. Sometimes ships, favored by the so-called
trade winds, went in an extended line one after another,
like a chain of sea-mews or albatrosses. The red casks indicating the channel swayed on the light wave with gentle
movement. Among the sails appeared every afternoon
gigantic grayish feather-like plumes of smoke. That was
a steamer from New York which brought passengers
and goods to Aspinwall, drawing behind it a frothy path
of foam. On the other side of the balcony Skavinski saw
as if on his palm Aspinwall and its busy harbor, and in
it a forest of masts, boats, and craft; a little farther white
houses and the steeples of the town. From the height of
his tower the small houses were like the nests of sea-
mews, the boats were like beetles, and the people moved
around like small points on the white stone boulevard.
From early morning a light eastern breeze brought a confused hum of human life, above which predominated the
whistle of steamers. In the afternoon six o'clock came;
the movement in the harbor began to cease; the mews

hid themselves in the rents of the cliffs; the waves grew feeble and became in some sort lazy; and then on the land, on the sea, and on the tower came a time of stillness unbroken by anything. The yellow sands from which the waves had fallen back glittered like golden spots on the expanse of waters; the body of the tower was outlined definitely in blue. Floods of sunbeams were poured from the sky on the water and the sands and the cliff. At that time a certain lassitude full of sweetness seized the old man. He felt that the rest which he was enjoying was excellent; and when he thought that it would be continuous nothing was lacking him.

Skavinski was intoxicated with his own happiness; and since a man adapts himself easily to improved conditions, he gained faith and confidence gradually; for he thought that if men built houses for invalids, why should not God gather up at last his own invalids? Time passed, and confirmed him in this conviction. The old man grew accustomed to his tower, to the lantern, to the rock, to the sandbars, to solitude. He grew accustomed also to the sea-mews which hatched in the crevices of the rock and in the evening held meetings on the roof of the light-house. Skavinski threw to them generally the remnants of his food; and soon they grew tame, and afterward when he fed them a real storm of white wings encircled him, and the old man went among the birds like a shepherd among sheep. When the tide ebbed he went to the low sand-banks, on which he collected savory periwinkles and beautiful pearl shells of the nautilus, which receding waves had left on the sand. In the night by the moonlight and the tower he went to catch fish, which frequented the windings of the cliff in myriads. At last he was in love with his rocks and his treeless little island, grown over only with small thick plants exuding sticky resin. The distant views repaid him for the poverty of the island, however. During afternoon hours, when the air became very clear he could see the whole isthmus covered with the richest vegetation It seemed to Skavinski at such times that he saw one gigantic garden, — bunches of cocoa, and enormous musa, combined as it were in luxurious tufted bouquets, right there behind the houses of Aspinwall. Farther on, between Aspinwall and Panama, was a great forest over which every morning and evening hung a reddish haze of exhalations, — a real tropical forest with its feet in stagnant water, interlaced with lianas and filled with the sound of one sea of gigantic orchids, palms, milk-trees, iron-trees, gum-trees.

Through his field-glass the old man could see not only trees and the broad leaves of bananas, but even legions of monkeys and great marabous and flocks of parrots, rising at times like a rainbow cloud over the forest. Skavinski knew such forests well, for after being wrecked on the Amazon he had wandered whole weeks among similar arches and thickets. He had seen how many dangers and deaths lie concealed under those marvellous and smiling exteriors. During the nights which he had spent in them he heard close at hand the sepulchral voices of howling monkeys and the roaring of the jaguars; he saw gigantic serpents coiled like lianas on trees; he knew those slumbering forest lakes full of torpedo-fish and swarming with crocodiles; he knew under what a yoke man lives in those unexplored wildernesses in which are single leaves tenfold greater in size than a man, — wildernesses swarming with blood-drinking mosquitoes, tree-leeches, and immense poisonous spiders. He had experienced that forest life himself, had witnessed it, had passed through it; therefore it gave him the greater enjoyment to look from his height and gaze on those *matos*, admire their beauty, and be guarded from their treachery. His tower preserved him from every evil. He left it only for a few hours on Sunday. He put on then his blue keeper's coat with silver buttons, and hung his crosses on his breast. His milk-white head was raised with a certain pride when he heard at the door, while entering the church, the Creoles say among themselves, " We have an honorable light-house keeper and not a heretic, though he is a Yankee." But he returned straightway after Mass to his island, and returned happy, for still he distrusted the mainland. On Sunday also he read the Spanish newspaper which he bought in the town, or the " New York Herald," which he borrowed from Falconbridge ; and he sought in it European news eagerly. The poor old heart on that light-house tower and in another hemisphere was beating yet for its birthplace. At times too, when the boat brought his daily supplies and water to the island, he went down from the tower to talk with Johnson, the guard. But after a while he seemed to grow shy. He ceased to go to the town to read the papers and to go down to talk politics with Johnson. Whole weeks passed in this way, so that no one saw him and he saw no one. The only signs that the old man was living were the disappearance of the provisions left on shore, and the light of the lantern kindled every evening with the same regularity with which the sun rose in the morning from the waters of those regions. Evidently the old man had become indifferent to the world. Homesickness was not the cause, but just this, — that even homesickness had passed into resignation. The whole world began now and ended for Skavinski on his island. He had grown accustomed to the thought that he would not leave the tower till death, and he simply forgot that there was anything else in the world aside from it. Moreover, he had become a mystic; his mild blue eyes began to stare like the eyes of a child, and were as if fixed on something at a distance. In presence of a surrounding uncommonly simple and great, the old man was losing the feeling of personality; he was ceasing to exist as an individual, was becoming merged more and more into that which inclosed him. He did not understand anything beyond his environment; he felt only unconsciously. At last it seems to him that the heavens, the water, his rock, the tower, the golden sand-banks, and the swollen sails, the sea-mews, the ebb and flow of the tide, — all form one mighty unity, one enormous mysterious soul; that he is sinking in that mystery, and feels that soul which lives and lulls itself. He sinks and is rocked, forgets himself; and in that narrowing of his own individual existence, in that half-waking, half-sleeping, he has discovered a rest so great that it almost resembles half-death.

III.

BUT the awakening came.

On a certain day, when the boat brought water and a supply of provisions, Skavinski came down an hour later from the tower, and saw that besides the usual cargo there was an additional package. On the outside of this package were postage stamps of the United States, and the address, "Skavinski, Esq.," written on coarse canvas.

The old man with aroused curiosity cut the canvas, and saw books; he took one in his hand, looked at it, and put it back; thereupon his hands began to tremble greatly. He covered his eyes as if he did not believe them; it seemed to him as if he were dreaming. The book was

Polish, — what did that mean? Who could have sent the book? Clearly, he did not remember at the first moment that in the beginning of his light-house career he had read in the " Herald," borrowed from the consul, of the formation of a Polish society in New York, and had sent at once to that society half his month's salary, for which he had, moreover, no use on the tower. The society had sent him the books with thanks. The books came in the natural way; but at the first moment the old man could not seize those thoughts. Polish books in Aspinwall, on his tower, amid his solitude, — that was for him something uncommon, a certain breath from past times, a species of miracle. Now it seemed to him, as to those sailors in the night, that something was calling him by name with a voice greatly beloved and nearly forgotten. He sat for a while with closed eyes, and was almost certain that, when he opened them, the dream would be gone.

The package, cut open, lay before him, shone upon clearly by the afternoon sun, and on it was an open book. When the old man stretched his hand toward it again, he heard in the stillness the beating of his own heart. He looked; it was poetry. On the outside stood printed in great letters the title, underneath the name of the author. The name was not strange to Skavinski; he saw that it belonged to the famous poet,[1] whose productions he had read in 1830 in Paris. Afterward when campaigning in Algiers and Spain, he had heard from his countrymen of the growing fame of the great seer; but he was so accustomed to the musket at that time that he took no book in hand. In 1849 he went to America, and in the adventurous life which he led, he hardly ever met a Pole, and never a Polish book. With the greater

[1] Mickiewicz (pronounced Mitskevich), the greatest poet of Poland.

eagerness, therefore, and with a livelier beating of the heart, did he turn to the title-page. It seemed to him then that on his lonely rock some solemnity was about to take place. Indeed, it was a moment of great calm and silence. The clocks of Aspinwall were striking five in the afternoon. Not a cloud darkened the clear sky; only a few sea-mews were sailing through the air. The ocean was as if cradled to sleep. The waves on the shore stammered quietly, spreading softly on the sand. In the distance the white houses of Aspinwall, and the wonderful groups of palm, were smiling. In truth, there was something there solemn, calm, and full of dignity. Suddenly in the midst of that calm of Nature was heard the trembling voice of the old man, who read aloud as if to understand himself better, —

" Thou art like health, O Litva, my birth-land ! [1]
How much we should prize thee he only can know who has lost
    thee.
Thy beauty in perfect adornment this day
I see and describe, because I yearn for thee."

His voice failed Skavinski. The letters began to dance before his eyes; something broke in his breast, and went like a wave from his heart higher and higher, choking his voice and pressing his throat. A moment more he controlled himself, and read further, —

" O Holy Lady, who guardest bright Chenstohova,
Who shinest in Ostrobrama and preservest
The castle town Novgrodek with its trusty people,
As Thou didst give me back to health in childhood,
When by my weeping mother placed beneath Thy care
I raised my lifeless eyelids upward,
And straightway walked unto Thy holy threshold,
To thank God for the life restored me, —
So by a wonder now restore us to the bosom of our birthplace."

[1] Lithuania.

The swollen wave broke through the restraint of his will. The old man sobbed, and threw himself on the ground; his milk-white hair was mingled with the sand of the sea. Forty years had passed since he had seen his country, and God knows how many since he heard his native speech; and now that speech had come to him itself, — it had sailed to him over the ocean, and found him in solitude on another hemisphere, — it so loved, so dear, so beautiful! In the sobbing which shook him there was no pain, — only a suddenly aroused immense love, in the presence of which other things are as nothing. With that great weeping he had simply implored forgiveness of the beloved one, set aside because he had grown so old, had become so accustomed to his solitary rock, and had so forgotten it that in him even longing had begun to disappear. But now it returned as if by a miracle; therefore the heart leaped in him.

Moments vanished one after another; he lay there continually. The mews flew over the light-house, crying as if alarmed for their old friend. The hour in which he fed them with the remnants of his food had come; therefore, some of them flew down from the light-house to him; then more and more came, and began to pick and to shake their wings over his head. The sound of the wings roused him. He had wept his fill, and had now a certain calm and brightness; but his eyes were as if inspired. He gave unwittingly all his provisions to the birds, which rushed at him with an uproar, and he himself took the book again. The sun had gone already behind the gardens and the forest of Panama, and was going slowly beyond the isthmus to the other ocean; but the Atlantic was full of light yet; in the open air there was still perfect vision; therefore, he read further:

"Now bear my longing soul to those forest slopes, to those green
    meadows."

At last the dusk obliterates the letters on the white paper, — the dusk short as a twinkle. The old man rested his head on the rock, and closed his eyes. Then "She who defends bright Chenstohova" took his soul, and transported it to "those fields colored by various grain." On the sky were burning yet those long stripes, red and golden, and on those brightnesses he was flying to beloved regions. The pine-woods were sounding in his ears; the streams of his native place were murmuring. He saw everything as it was; everything asked him, "Dost remember?" He remembers! he sees broad fields, between the fields, woods and villages. It is night now. At this hour his lantern usually illuminates the darkness of the sea; but now he is in his native village. His old head has dropped on his breast, and he is dreaming. Pictures are passing before his eyes quickly, and a little disorderly. He does not see the house in which he was born, for war had destroyed it; he does not see his father and mother, for they died when he was a child; but still the village is as if he had left it yesterday, — the line of cottages with lights in the windows, the mound, the mill, the two ponds opposite each other, and thundering the whole night with a chorus of frogs. Once he had been on guard in that village all night; now that past stood before him at once in a series of views. He is an Ulan again, and he stands there on guard; at a distance is the public house; he looks with swimming eyes. There is thundering and singing and shouting amid the silence of the night with voices of fiddles and bass-viols "U-ha! U-ha!" Then the Ulans knock out fire with their horseshoes, and it is wearisome for him there on his horse. The hours drag on slowly; at last the lights are quenched; now as far as the eye reaches there is mist, and mist impenetrable; now the fog rises,

evidently from the fields, and embraces the whole world
with a whitish cloud. You would say, a perfect ocean.
But that is fields; soon the land-rail will be heard in
the darkness, and bitterns will call from the reeds. The
night is calm and cool, a true Polish night. In the distance the pine wood is sounding without wind, like the
roll of the sea. Soon dawn will whiten the East. In
fact, the cocks are beginning to crow behind the hedges.
One answers another from cottage to cottage; the storks
are screaming somewhere on high. The Ulan feels well
and bright. Some one had spoken of a battle to-morrow.
Hei! that will go on, like all others, with shouting, with
fluttering of pennons. The young blood is playing like a
trumpet, though the night cools it. But day is dawning.
Already night is growing pale; out of the shadows come
forests, the thicket, a row of cottages, the mill, the pop-
lars. The well is squeaking like a metal banner on a
tower. What a beloved land, beautiful in the rosy
gleams of the morning! Oh, the one land, the one
land!

Quiet! the watchful picket hears that some one is
approaching. Of course, they are coming to relieve the
guard.

Suddenly some voice is heard above Skávinski, —

"Here, old man! Get up! What's the matter?"

The old man opens his eyes, and looks with wonder at
the person standing before him. The remnants of the
dream-visions struggle in his head with reality. At last
the visions pale and vanish. Before him stands Johnson,
the harbor guard.

"What's this?" asked Johnson; "are you sick?"

"No."

"You did n't light the lantern. You must leave your
place. A vessel from St. Geromo was wrecked on the

bar. It is lucky that no one was drowned, or you would go to trial. Get into the boat with me; you'll hear the rest at the Consulate."

The old man grew pale; in fact he had not lighted the lantern that night.

A few days later Skavinski was seen on the deck of a steamer, which was going from Aspinwall to New York. The poor man had lost his place. There opened before him new roads of wandering; the wind had torn that leaf away again to whirl it over lands and seas, to sport with it till satisfied. The old man had failed greatly during those few days, and his body was bent, but his eyes were gleaming. On his new road of life he held at his breast a book, which from time to time he pressed with his hand as if fearing that that too might go from him.

YAMYOL.

A VILLAGE SKETCH

YAMYOL.[1]

A VILLAGE SKETCH.

IN the little town of Lupiskory, after the funeral of
widow Kaliksta, there were vespers, and after vespers old women, between ten and twenty in number,
remained in the church to finish the hymn. It was
four o'clock in the afternoon; but, since twilight comes
in winter about that hour, it was dark in the church.
The great altar, especially, was sunk in deep shade.
Only two candles were burning at the ciborium; their
flickering flames barely lighted a little the gilding of the
doors, and the feet of Christ, hanging on a cross higher
up. Those feet were pierced with an enormous nail,
and the head of that nail seemed a great point gleaming
on the altar.

From other candles, just quenched, streaks of smoke
were waving, filling the places behind the stalls with a
purely church odor of wax.

An old man and a small boy were busied before the
steps of the altar. One was sweeping; the other was
stretching the carpet on the steps. At moments, when
the women ceased their singing, either the angry whisper
of the old man was heard scolding the boy, or the hammering on the snow-covered windows of sparrows that
were cold and hungry outside.

[1] The Polish word for angel is *aniol*, distorted by the old woman
into *jamiol*, which is pronounced *yamyol*.

The women were sitting on benches nearer the door. It would have been still darker had it not been for a few tallow candles, by the light of which those who had prayer-books were reading. One of those candles lighted well enough a banner fastened to the seat just beyond; the banner represented sinners surrounded by devils and flames. It was impossible to see what was painted on the other banners.

The women were not singing; they were, rather, muttering with sleepy and tired voices a hymn in which these words were repeated continually, —

> " And when the hour of death comes,
> Gain for us, gain from Thy Son."

That church buried in shadow, the banners standing at the seats, the old women with their yellow faces, the lights flickering as if oppressed by the gloom, — all that was dismal beyond expression; nay, it was simply terrible. The mournful words of the song about death found there a fitting background.

After a time the singing stopped. One of the women stood up at the seat, and began to say, with a trembling voice, "Hail, Mary, full of grace!" And others responded, "The Lord is with Thee," etc.; but since it was the day of Kaliksta's funeral, each "Hail, Mary," concluded with the words, "Lord, grant her eternal rest, and may endless light shine on her!"

Marysia, the dead woman's daughter, was sitting on a bench at the side of one of the old women. Just then the snow, soft and noiseless, was falling on the fresh grave of her mother; but the little girl was not ten years old yet, and seemed not to understand either her loss, or the pity which it might rouse in another. Her face, with large blue eyes, had in it the calmness of childhood, and even a certain careless repose. A little curiosity was evident, — nothing beyond that. Opening her mouth, she looked with great attention at the banner on which was painted hell with sinners; then she looked into the depth of the church, and afterward on the window at which the sparrows were hammering.

Her eyes remained without thought. Meanwhile, the women began to mutter, sleepily, for the tenth time, —

" And when the hour of death comes."

The little girl twisted the tresses of her light-colored hair, woven into two tiny braids not thicker than mice tails. She seemed tired; but now the old man occupied her attention. He went to the middle of the church, and began to pull a knotty rope hanging from the ceiling. He was ringing for the soul of Kaliksta, but he did this in a purely mechanical manner; he was thinking of something else, evidently.

That ringing was also a sign that vespers were ended. The women, after repeating for the last time the prayer for a happy death, went out on the square. One of them led Marysia by the hand.

" But, Kulik," asked another, "what will you do with the girl?"

" What will I do? She will go to Leschyntsi. Voytek Margula will take her. But why do you ask me?"

" What will she do in Leschyntsi?"

" My dears, the same as here. Let her go to where she came from. Even at the mansion they will take in the orphan, and let her sleep in the kitchen."

Thus conversing, they passed through the square to the inn. Darkness was increasing every moment. It was wintry, calm; the sky was covered with clouds, the air filled with moisture and wet snow. Water was dropping from the roofs; on the square lay slush formed of ·snow and straw. The village, with wretched and tattered houses, looked as gloomy as the church. A few windows were gleaming with light; movement had ceased, but in the inn an organ was playing.

It was playing to entice, for there was no one inside. The women entered, drank vodka; Kulik gave Marysia half a glass, saying, —

"Drink! Thou art an orphan; thou wilt not meet kindness."

The word "orphan" brought the death of Kaliksta to the minds of the women. One of them said, —

"To you, Kulik, drink! Oh, my dears, how that *paralus* [paralysis] took her so that she couldn't stir! She was cold before the priest came to hear her confession."

"I told her long ago," said Kulik, "that she was spinning fine [near her end]. Last week she came to me. 'Ah, better give Marysia to the mansion!' said I. But she said, 'I have one little daughter, and I'll not give her to any one' But she grew sorry, and began to sob, and then she went to the mayor to put her papers in order. She paid four zloty and six groshes. 'But I do not begrudge it for my child,' said she. My dears, but her eyes were staring, and after death they were staring still more. People wanted to close them, but could not. They say that after death, even, she was looking at her child."

"Let us drink half a quarter over this sorrow!"

The organ was playing continually. The women began to be somewhat tender. Kulik repeated, with a voice of compassion, " Poor little thing! poor little thing!" and the second old woman called to mind the death of her late husband.

"When he was dying," said she, "he sighed so, oh, he
sighed so, he sighed so!—" and drawling still more, her
voice passed into a chant, from a chant into the tone of
the organ, till at last she bent to one side, and in following the organ began to sing, —

> "He sighed, he sighed, he sighed,
>   On that day he sighed."

All at once she fell to shedding hot tears, gave the
organist six groshes, and drank some more vodka. Kulik,
too, was excited by tenderness, but she turned it on
Marysia,—

"Remember, little orphan," said she, "what the priest
said when they were covering thy mother with snow,
that there is a yamyol above thee —" Here she stopped,
looked around as if astonished, and then added, with
unusual energy, "When I say that there is a yamyol,
there *is* a yamyol!"

No one contradicted her. Marysia, blinking with her
poor, simple eyes, looked attentively at the woman.
Kulik spoke on, —

"Thou art a little orphan, that is bad for thee! Over
orphans there is a yamyol. He is good. Here are ten
groshes for thee. Even if thou wert to start on foot to
Leschyntsi, thou couldst go there, for he would guide
thee."

The second old woman began to sing, —

> "In the shade of his wings he will keep thee eternally,
>   Under his pinions thou wilt lie without danger."

"Be quiet!" said Kulik. And then she turned again
to the child, —

"Knowest thou, stupid, who is above thee?"

"A yamyol," said, with a thin voice, the little girl.

"Oh, thou little orphan, thou precious berry, thou little worm of the Lord! A yamyol with wings," said she, with perfect tenderness, and seizing the child she pressed her to her honest, though tipsy, bosom.

Marysia burst into weeping at once. Perhaps in her dark little head and in her heart, which knew not yet how to distinguish, there was roused some sort of perception at that moment.

The innkeeper was sleeping most soundly behind the counter; on the candle-wicks mushrooms had grown; the man at the organ ceased to play, for what he saw amused him.

Then there was silence, which was broken by the sudden plashing of horses' feet before the door, and a voice calling to the horses, —

"Prrr!"

Voytek Margula walked into the inn with a lighted lantern in his hand. He put down the lantern, began to slap his arms to warm them, and at last said to the innkeeper, —

"Give half a quarter."

"Margula, thou chestnut," cried Kulik, "thou wilt take the little girl to Leschyntsi."

"I'll take her, for they told me to take her," replied Margula.

Then looking closely to the two women he added, —

"But ye are as drunk as —"

"May the plague choke thee," retorted Kulik. "When I tell thee to be careful with the child, be careful. She is an orphan. Knowest thou, fool, who is above her?"

Voytek did not see fit to answer that question, but determined evidently to raise another subject, and began, —

"To all of you —"

But he did n't finish, for he drank the vodka, made a wry face, and putting down the glass with dissatisfaction, said, —

"That 's pure water. Give me a second from another bottle."

The innkeeper poured from another. Margula twisted his face still more, —

"Ai! have n't you arrack?"

Evidently the same danger threatened Margula that threatened the women; but at that very time, in the mansion at Lupiskory, the landowner was preparing for one of the journals a long and exhaustive article, "On the right of landowners to sell liquor, this right being considered as the basis of society." But Voytek co-operated only involuntarily to strengthen the basis of society, and that all the more because the sale here, though in a village, was really by the landowner.

When he had co-operated five times in succession he forgot, it is true, his lantern, in which the light had gone out, but he took the half-sleeping little girl by the hand, and said, —

"But come on, thou nightmare!"

The women had fallen asleep in a corner, no one bade farewell to Marysia. The whole story was this: Her mother was in the graveyard and she was going to Leschyntsi.

Voytek and the girl went out, sat in the sleigh. Voytek cried to the horses, and they moved on. At first the sleigh dragged heavily enough through the slush of the town, but they came out very soon to fields which were broad and white. Movement was easy then; the snow barely made a noise under the sleigh-runners. The horses snorted at times, at times came the barking of dogs from a distance.

They went on and on. Voytek urged the horses, and sang through his nose, "Dog ear, remember thy promise." But soon he grew silent, and began to "carry Jews" (nod). He nodded to the right, to the left. He dreamt that they were pounding him on the shoulders in Leschyntsi, because he had lost a basket of letters; so, from time to time, he was half awake, and repeated: "To all!" Marysia did not sleep, for she was cold. She looked with widely opened eyes on the white fields, hidden from moment to moment by the dark shoulders of Margula. She thought also that her "mother was dead;" and thinking thus, she pictured to herself perfectly the pale and thin face of that mother with its staring eyes, — and she felt half consciously that that face was greatly beloved, that it was no longer in the world, and that never again would it be in Leschyntsi. She had seen with her own eyes how they covered it up in Lupiskory. Remembering this, she would have cried from grief; but as her knees and feet were chilled, she began to cry from cold.

There was no frost, it is true, but the air was penetrating, as is usual during thaws. As to Voytek he had, at least in his stomach, a good supply of heat taken from the inn. The landowner at Lupiskory remarked justly: "That vodka warms in winter, and since it is the only consolation of our peasants, to deprive landowners of the sole power of consoling peasants is to deprive them of influence over the populace." Voytek was so consoled at that moment that nothing could trouble him.

Even this did not trouble him, that the horses when they came to the forest slackened their pace altogether, though the road there was better, and then walking to one side, the beasts turned over the sleigh into a ditch. He woke, it is true, but did not understand well what had happened

Marysia began to push him.

"Voytek!"

"Why art thou croaking?"

"The sleigh is turned over."

"A glass?" asked Voytek, and went to sleep for good.

The little girl sat by the sleigh, crouching down as best she could, and remained there. But her face was soon chilled, so she began to push the sleeping man again.

"Voytek!"

He gave no answer.

"Voytek, I want to go to the house."

And after a while again: "Voytek, I'll walk there."

At last she started. It seemed to her that Leschyntsi was very near. She knew the road, too, for she had walked to church over it every Sunday with her mother. But now she had to go alone. In spite of the thaw the snow in the forest was deep, but the night was very clear. To the gleam from the snow was added light from the clouds, so that the road could be seen as in the daytime. Marysia, turning her eyes to the dark forest, could see tree-trunks very far away outlined distinctly, black, motionless, on the white ground; and she saw clearly also snow-drifts blown to the whole height of them. In the forest there was a certain immense calm, which gave solace to the child. On the branches was thick, frozen snow, and from it drops of water were trickling, striking with faint sound against the branches and twigs. But that was the only noise. All else around was still, white, silent, dumb.

The wind was not blowing. The snowy branches were not stirring with the slightest movement. Everything was sleeping in the trance of winter. It might seem that the snowy covering on the earth, and the whole silent and shrouded forest, with the pale clouds in the heavens, were all a kind of white, lifeless unity. So it is in time of thaw. Marysia was the only living thing, moving like a little black speck amid these silent greatnesses. Kind, honest forest! Those drops, which the thawing ice let down, were tears, perhaps, over the orphan. The trees are so large, but also so compassionate, above the little creature. See, she is alone, so weak and poor, in the snow, in the night, in the forest, wading along trustfully, as if there is no danger.

The clear night seems to care for her. When something so weak and helpless yields itself, trusts so perfectly in enormous power, there is a certain sweetness in the act. In that way all may be left to the will of God. The girl walked rather long, and was wearied at last. The heavy boots, which were too large, hindered her; her small feet were going up and down in them continually. It was hard to drag such big boots out of the snow. Besides, she could not move her hands freely, for in one of them, closed rigidly, she held with all her strength those ten groshes which Kulik had given her. She feared to drop them in the snow. She began at times to cry aloud, and then she stopped suddenly, as if wishing to know if some one had heard her. Yes, the forest had heard her! The thawing ice sounded monotonously and somewhat sadly. Besides, maybe some one else had heard her. The child went more and more slowly. Could she go astray? How? The road, like a white, broad, winding ribbon, stretched into the distance, lay well marked between two walls of dark trees. An unconquerable drowsiness seized the little girl.

She stepped aside and sat down under a tree. The lids dropped over her eyes. After a time, she thought that her mother was coming to her along the white road from the graveyard. No one was coming. Still, the child felt certain that some one must come. Who? A yamyol. Had n't old Kulik told her that a yamyol was above her? Marysia knew what a yamyol is. In her mother's cottage there was one painted with a shield in his hand and with wings. He would come, surely. Somehow the ice began to sound more loudly. Maybe that is the noise of his wings, scattering drops more abundantly. Stop! Some one is coming really; the snow, though soft, sounds clearly; steps are coming, and coming quietly but quickly. The child raises her sleepy eyelids with confidence.

"What is that?"

Looking at the little girl intently is a gray three-cornered face with ears, standing upright, — ugly, terrible!

THE BULL-FIGHT.

A REMINISCENCE OF SPAIN

THE BULL–FIGHT.

A REMINISCENCE OF SPAIN.

IT is Sunday! Great posters, affixed for a number of days to the corners of Puerta del Sol, Calle Alcala, and all streets on which there was considerable movement, announce to the city that to-day, " Si el tiempo lo permite " (if the weather permits), will take place bull-fight XVI, in which Cara-Ancha Lagartijo and the renowned Frascuello are to appear as " espadas " (swords).

Well, the weather permits. There was rain in the morning; but about ten o'clock the wind broke the clouds, gathered them into heaps, and drove them away off somewhere in the direction of the Escurial. Now the wind itself has ceased; the sky as far as the eye can reach is blue, and over the Puerta del Sol a bright sun is shining, — such a Madrid sun, which not only warms, not only burns, but almost bites.

Movement in the city is increasing, and on people's faces satisfaction is evident.

Two o'clock.

The square of the Puerta del Sol is emptying gradually, but crowds of people are advancing through the Calle Alcala toward the Prado. In the middle is flowing a river of carriages and vehicles. All that line of equipages is moving very slowly, for on the sidewalks there is not room enough for pedestrians, many of whom are walking along the sides of the streets and close to the carriages. The police, on white horses and in showy uniforms and three-cornered hats, preserve order.

It is Sunday, that is evident, and an afternoon hour; the toilets are carefully made, the attire is holiday. It is evident also that the crowds are going to some curious spectacle. Unfortunately the throng is not at all many-colored; no national costumes are visible, — neither the short coats, yellow kerchiefs *á la contrabandista*, with one end dropping down to the shoulder, nor the round Biscay hats, nor girdles, nor the Catalan knives behind the girdles.

Those things may be seen yet in the neighborhood of Granada, Seville, and Cordova; but in Madrid, especially on holidays, the cosmopolitan frock is predominant. Only at times do you see a black mantilla pinned to a high comb, and under the mantilla eyes blacker still.

In general faces are dark, glances quick, speech loud. Gesticulation is not so passionate as in Italy, where when a man laughs he squirms like a snake, and when he is angry he gnaws off the top of his hat; still, it is ener-getic and lively. Faces have well-defined features and a resolute look. It is easy to understand that even in amusement these people retain their special and definite character.

However, they are a people who on week-days are full of sedateness, bordering on sloth, sparing of words, and collected. Sunday enlivens them, as does also the hope of seeing a bloody spectacle.

Let us cut across the Prado and enter an alley leading to the circus.

The crowd is becoming still denser. Here and there shouts are rising, the people applauding single members of the company, who are going each by himself to the circus.

Here is an omnibus filled with "capeadors," that is, partakers in the fight, whose whole defence is red capes with which they mislead and irritate the bull. Through the windows are visible black heads with pigtails, and wearing three-cornered hats. The coats of various colors worn by the capeadors are embroidered with gold and silver tinsel. These capeadors ride in an omnibus, for the modest pay which they get for their perilous service does not permit a more showy conveyance.

Somewhat farther, three mounted "picadors" push their way through the people. The sun plays on their broad-brimmed white hats. They are athletic in build, but bony and lean. Their shaven faces have a stern, and, as it were, concentrated look. They are sitting on very high wooden saddles, hence they are perfectly visible over the crowd. Each of them holds in his hand a lance, with a wooden ball at the end of it, from which is projecting an iron point not above half an inch long. The picador cannot kill a bull with a weapon like that, — he can only pierce him or stop him for a moment; but in the last case he must have in his arm the strength of a giant.

Looking at these men, I remember involuntarily Doré's illustrations to "Don Quixote." In fact, each of these horsemen might serve as a model for the knight "of the rueful visage." That lean silhouette, outlined firmly on the sky, high above the heads of the multitude, the lance standing upright, and that bare-boned horse under the rider, those purely Gothic outlines of living things, — all answer perfectly to the conception which we form of the knight of La Mancha, when we read the immortal work of Cervantes.

But, the picadors pass us, and urging apart the crowd slowly, push forward considerably. Now only three lances are visible, three hats, and three coats embroidered on the shoulders. New men ride up, as incalculably similar to the first as if some mill were making picadors for all Spain on one pattern. There is a difference only in the color of the horses, which, however, are equally lean.

Our eyes turn now to the long row of carriages. Some are drawn by mules, but mules so large, sleek, and beautiful that, in spite of the long ears of the animals, the turn-out does not seem ridiculous. Here and there may be seen also Andalusian horses with powerful backs, arched necks, and curved faces. Such may be seen in the pictures of battle-painters of the seventeenth century.

In the carriages are sitting the flower of Madrid society. The dresses are black, there is very black lace on the parasols, on the fans, and on the heads of ladies; black hair trimmed in forelocks, from under which are glancing eyes, as it were, of the lava of Vesuvius. Mourning colors, importance, and powder are the main traits of that society.

The faces of old and of young ladies too are covered with powder, all of them are equally frigid and pale. A great pity! Were it not for such a vile custom, their complexion would have that magnificent warm tone given by southern blood and a southern sun, and which may be admired in faces painted by Fortuni.

In the front seats of the carriages are men dressed with an elegance somewhat exaggerated; they have a constrained and too holiday air, — in other words, they cannot wear fine garments with that free inattention which characterizes the higher society of France.

But the walls of the circus are outlined before us with growing distinctness. There is nothing especial in the building: an enormous pile reared expressly to give seats to some tens of thousands of people, — that is the whole plan of it.

Most curious is the movement near the walls. Round about, it is black from carriages, equipages, and heads of people. Towering above this dark mass, here and there, is a horseman, a policeman, or a picador in colors as brilliant as a poppy full blown.

The throng sways, opens, closes, raises its voice; coachmen shout; still louder shout boys selling handbills. These boys squeeze themselves in at all points among footmen and horsemen; they are on the steps of carriages and between the wheels; some climb up on the buttresses of the circus; some are on the stone columns which mark the way for the carriages. Their curly hair, their gleaming eyes, their expressive features, dark faces, and torn shirts open in the bosom, remind me of our gypsies, and of boys in Murillo's pictures. Besides programmes some of them sell whistles. Farther on, among the crowds, are fruit-venders; water-sellers with bronze kegs on their shoulders; in one place are flower dealers; in another is heard the sound of a guitar played by an old blind woman led by a little girl.

Movement, uproar, laughter; fans are fluttering everywhere as if they were wings of thousands of birds; the sun pours down white light in torrents from a spotless sky of dense blue.

Suddenly and from all sides are heard cries of "mira, mira!" (look, look!) After a while these cries are turned into a roar of applause, which like real thunder flies from one extreme to another; now it is quiet, now it rises and extends around the whole circus.

What has happened? Surely the queen is approaching, and with her the court?

No! near by is heard "eviva Frascuello!" That is the

most famous espada, who is coming for laurels and applause.

All eyes turn to him, and the whole throng of women push toward his carriage. The air is gleaming with flowers thrown by their hands to the feet of that favorite, that hero of every dream and imagining, that "pearl of Spain." They greet him the more warmly because he has just returned from a trip to Barcelona, where during the exhibition he astonished all barbarous Europe with thrusts of his sword; now he appears again in his beloved Madrid, more glorious, greater, — a genuine new Cid el Campeador.

Let us push through the crowd to look at the hero. First, what a carriage, what horses! More beautiful there are not in the whole of Castile. On white satin cushions sits, or reclines, we should say, a man whose age it is difficult to determine, for his face is shaven most carefully. He is dressed in a coat of pale lily-colored satin, and knee-breeches of similar material trimmed with lace. His coat and the side seams of his breeches are glittering and sparkling from splendid embroidery, from spangles of gold and silver shining like diamonds in the sun. The most delicate laces adorn his breast. His legs, clothed in rose-colored silk stockings, he holds crossed carelessly on the front seat, — the very first athlete in the hippodrome at Paris might envy him those calves.

Madrid is vain of those calves, — and in truth she has reason.

The great man leans with one hand on the red hilt of his Catalan blade; with the other he greets his admirers of both sexes kindly. His black hair, combed to his poll, is tied behind in a small roll, from beneath which creeps forth a short tress. That style of hair-dressing and the shaven face make him somewhat like a woman, and he reminds one besides of some actor from one of the provinces; taken generally, his face is not distinguished by intelligence, a quality which in his career would not be a hindrance, though not needed in any way.

The crowds enter the circus, and we enter with them.

Now we are in the interior. It differs from other interiors of circuses only in size and in this, — that the seats are of stone. Highest in the circle are the boxes; of these one in gold fringe and in velvet is the royal box. If no one from the court is present at the spectacle this box is occupied by the prefect of the city. Around are seated the aristocracy and high officials; opposite the royal box, on the other side of the circus, is the orchestra. Half-way up in the circus is a row of arm-chairs; stone steps form the rest of the seats. Below, around the arena, stretches a wooden paling the height of a man's shoulder. Between this paling and the first row of seats, which is raised considerably higher for the safety of the spectators, is a narrow corridor, in which the combatants take refuge, in case the bull threatens them too greatly.

One-half of the circus is buried in shadow, the other is deluged with sunlight. On every ticket, near the number of the seat, is printed "sombra" (shadow) or "sol" (sun). Evidently the tickets "sombra" cost considerably more. It is difficult to imagine how those who have "sol" tickets can endure to sit in such an atmosphere a number of hours and on those heated stone steps, with such a sun above their heads.

The places are all filled, however. Clearly the love of a bloody spectacle surpasses the fear of being roasted alive.

In northern countries the contrast between light and shadow is not so great as in Spain; in the north we find always a kind of half shade, half light, certain transition tones ; here the boundary is cut off in black with a firm line without any transitions. In the illuminated half the sand seems to burn ; people's faces and dresses are blazing ; eyes are blinking under the excess of glare ; it is simply an abyss of light, full of heat, in which everything is sparkling and gleaming excessively, every color is intensified tenfold. On the other hand, the shaded half seems cut off by some transparent curtain, woven from the darkness of night. Every man who passes from the light to the shade, makes on us the impression of a candle put out on a sudden.

At the moment when we enter, the arena is crowded with people. Before the spectacle the inhabitants of Madrid, male and female, must tread that sand on which the bloody drama is soon to be enacted. It seems to them that thus they take direct part, as it were, in the struggle. Numerous groups of men are standing, lighting their cigarettes and discoursing vivaciously concerning the merits of bulls from this herd or that one. Small boys tease and pursue one another. I see how one puts under the eyes of another a bit of red cloth, treating him just as a " capeador " treats a bull. The boy endures this a while patiently ; at last he rolls his eyes fiercely and runs at his opponent. The opponent deceives him adroitly with motions of a cape, exactly again as the capeador does the bull. The little fellows find their spectators, who urge them on with applause.

Along the paling pass venders of oranges proclaiming the merits of their merchandise. This traffic is carried on through the air. The vender throws, at request, with unerring dexterity, an orange, even to the highest row ; in the same way he receives a copper piece, which he catches with one hand before it touches the earth.

Loud dialogues, laughter, calls, noise, rustling of fans, the movement of spectators as they arrive, — all taken together form a picture with a fulness of life of which no other spectacle can give an idea.

All at once from the orchestra come sounds of trumpets and drums. At that signal the people on the arena fly to their places with as much haste as if their lives were in danger. There is a crush. But after a while all are seated. Around, it is just black: people are shoulder to shoulder, head to head. In the centre remains the arena empty, deluged with sunlight.

Opposite the royal box a gate in the paling is thrown open, and in ride two "alguazils." Their horses white, with manes and tails plaited, are as splendid as if taken from pictures. The riders themselves, wearing black velvet caps with white feathers, and doublets of similar material, with lace collars, bring to mind the incomparable canvases of Velasquez, which may be admired in the Museo del Prado. It seems to us that we are transferred to the times of knighthood long past. Both horsemen are handsome, both of showy form. They ride stirrup to stirrup, ride slowly around the whole arena to convince themselves that no incautious spectator has remained on it. At last they halt before the royal box, and with a movement full of grace uncover their heads with respect.

Whoso is in a circus for the first time will be filled with admiration at the stately, almost middle-age, ceremonial, by the apparel and dignity of the horsemen. The alguazils seem like two noble heralds, giving homage to a monarch before the beginning of a tournament. It is, in fact, a prayer for permission to open the spectacle, and at the same time a request for the key of the stables in which the bulls are confined. After a while the key is let down from the box on a gold string; the alguazils incline once again and ride away. Evidently this is a mere ceremonial, for the spectacle was authorized previously, and the bulls are confined by simple iron bolts. But the ceremony is beautiful, and they never omit it.

In a few minutes after the alguazils have vanished, the widest gate is thrown open, and a whole company enters. At the head of it ride the same two alguazils whom we saw before the royal box; after them advance a rank of capeadors; after the capeadors come "banderilleros," and the procession is concluded by picadors. This entire party is shining with all the colors of the rainbow, gleaming from tinsel, gold, silver, and satins of various colors. They come out from the dark side to the sun-lighted arena, dive into the glittering light, and bloom like flowers. The eye cannot delight itself sufficiently with the many colors of those spots on the golden sand.

Having reached the centre, they scatter on a sudden, like a flock of butterflies. The picadors dispose themselves around at the paling, and each one, drawing his lance from its rest, grasps it firmly in his right hand; the men on foot form picturesque groups; they stand in postures full of indifference, waiting for the bull.

This is perhaps the most beautiful moment of the spectacle, full of originality, so thoroughly Spanish that regret at not being a painter comes on a man in spite of himself. How much color, what sunlight might be transferred from the palette to the canvas!

Soon blood will be flowing on that sand. In the circus it is as still as in time of sowing poppy seed, — it is barely possible to hear the sound of fans, which move only in as much as the hands holding them quiver from impatience. All eyes are turned to the door through which the bull will rush forth. Time now is counted by seconds.

Suddenly the shrill, and at the same time the mournful, sound of a trumpet is heard in the orchestra; the door of the stable opens with a crash, and the bull bursts into the arena, like a thunderbolt.

That is a lordly beast, with a powerful and splendid neck, a head comparatively short, horns enormous and turned forward. Our heavy breeder gives a poor idea of him; for though the Spanish bull is not the equal of ours in bulk of body, he surpasses him in strength, and, above all, in activity. At the first cast of the eye you recognize a beast reared wild in the midst of great spaces; consequently with all his strength he can move almost as swiftly as a deer. It is just this which makes him dangerous in an unheard-of degree. His forelegs are a little higher than his hind ones; this is usual with cattle of mountain origin. In fact, the bulls of the circus are recruited especially from the herds in the Sierra Morena. Their color is for the greater part black, rarely reddish or pied. The hair is short, and glossy as satin; only the neck is covered somewhat with longer and curly hair.

After he has burst into the arena, the bull slackens his pace toward the centre, looks with bloodshot eyes to the right, to the left, — but this lasts barely two seconds; he sees a group of capeadors; he lowers his head to the ground, and hurls himself on them at random.

The capeadors scatter, like a flock of sparrows at which some man has fired small-shot. Holding behind them red capes, they circle now in the arena, with a swiftness that makes the head dizzy; they are everywhere; they glitter to the right, to the left; they are in the middle of the arena, at the paling, before the eyes of the bull, in front, behind. The red capes flutter in the air, like banners torn by the wind.

The bull scatters the capeadors in every direction; with lightning-like movements he chases one, — another thrusts a red cape under his very eyes; the bull leaves the first victim to run after a second, but before he can turn, some third man steps up. The bull rushes at that one! Distance between them decreases, the horns of the bull seem to touch the shoulder of the capeador; another twinkle of an eye and he will be nailed to the paling, — but meanwhile the man touches the top of the paling with his hand, and vanishes as if he had dropped through the earth.

What has happened? The capeador has sprung into the passage extending between the paling and the first row of seats.

The bull chooses another man; but before he has moved from his tracks the first capeador thrusts out his head from behind the paling, like a red Indian stealing to the farm of a settler, and springs to the arena again. The bull pursues more and more stubbornly those unattainable enemies, who vanish before his very horns; at last he knows where they are hidden. He collects all his strength, anger gives him speed, and he springs like a hunting-horse over the paling, certain that he will crush his foes this time like worms.

But at that very moment they hurl themselves back to the arena with the agility of chimpanzees, and the bull runs along the empty passage, seeing no one before him.

The entire first row of spectators incline through the barrier, then strike from above at the bull with canes, fans, and parasols. The public are growing excited. A bull that springs over the paling recommends himself favorably. When people in the first row applaud him with all their might, those in the upper rows clap their hands, crying, "Bravo el toro! muy bien! Bravo el toro!" (Bravo the bull! Very well, bravo the bull!)

Meanwhile he comes to an open door and runs out again to the arena. On the opposite side of it two capeadors are sitting on a step extending around the foot of the paling, and are conversing without the slightest anxiety. The bull rushes on them at once; he is in the middle of the arena, — and they sit on without stopping their talk; he is ten steps away, — they continue sitting as if they had not seen him; he is five steps away, — they are still talking. Cries of alarm are heard here and there in the circus; before his very horns the two daring fellows spring, one to the right, the other to the left. The bull's horns strike the paling with a heavy blow. A storm of hand-clapping breaks out in the circus, and at that very moment these and other capeadors surround the bull again and provoke him with red capes.

His madness passes now into fury: he hurls himself forward, rushes, turns on his tracks; every moment his horns give a thrust, every moment it seems that no human power can wrest this or that man from death. Still the horns cut nothing but air, and the red capes are glittering on all sides; at times one of them falls to the ground, and that second the bull in his rage drives almost all of it into the sand. But that is not enough for him, — he must search out some victim, and reach him at all costs.

Hence, with a deep bellow and with bloodshot eyes he starts to run forward at random, but halts on a sudden; a new sight strikes his eye, — that is, a picador on horseback.

The picadors had stood hitherto on their lean horses, like statues, their lances pointing upward. The bull, occupied solely with the hated capes, had not seen them, or if he had seen them he passed them.

Almost never does it happen that the bull begins a fight with horsemen. The capes absorb his attention and rouse all his rage. It may be, moreover, that the picadors are like his half-wild herdsmen in the Sierra Morena, whom he saw at times from a distance, and before whom he was accustomed to flee with the whole herd.

But now he has had capes enough; his fury seeks eagerly some body to pierce and on which to sate his vengeance.

For spectators not accustomed to this kind of play, a terrible moment is coming. Every one understands that blood must be shed soon.

The bull lowers his head and withdraws a number of paces, as if to gather impetus; the picador turns the horse a little, with his right side to the attacker, so the horse, having his right eye bound with a cloth, shall not push back at the moment of attack. The lance with a short point is lowered in the direction of the bull; he withdraws still more. It seems to you that he will retreat altogether, and your oppressed bosom begins to breathe with more ease.

Suddenly the bull rushes forward like a rock rolling down from a mountain. In the twinkle of an eye you see the lance bent like a bow; the sharp end of it is stuck in the shoulder of the bull, — and then is enacted a thing simply dreadful: the powerful head and neck of the furious beast is lost under the belly of the horse, his horns sink their whole length in the horse's intestines; sometimes the bull lifts horse and rider, sometimes you see only the up-raised hind part of the horse, struggling convulsively in the air. The rider falls to the ground, the horse tumbles upon him, and you hear the creaking of the saddle; horse, rider, and saddle form one shapeless mass, which the raging bull tramples and bores with his horns.

Faces unaccustomed to the spectacle grow pale. In Barcelona and Madrid I have seen Englishwomen whose faces had become as pale as linen. Every one in the circus for the first time has the impression of a catastrophe. When the rider is seen rolled into a lump, pressed down by the weight of the saddle and the horse, and the raging beast is thrusting his horns with fury into that mass of flesh, it seems that for the man there is no salvation, and that the attendants will raise a mere bloody corpse from the sand.

But that is illusion. All that is done is in the programme of the spectacle.

Under the white leather and tinsel the rider has armor which saves him from being crushed, — he fell purposely under the horse, so that the beast should protect him with his body from the horns. In fact the bull, seeing before him the fleshy mass of the horse's belly, expends on it mainly his rage. Let me add that the duration of the catastrophe is counted by seconds. The capeadors have attacked the bull from every side, and he, wishing to free himself from them, must leave his victims. He does leave them, he chases again after the capeadors; his steaming horns, stained with blood, seem again to be just touching the capeadors' shoulders. They, in escaping, lead him to the opposite side of the arena; other men meanwhile draw from beneath the horse the picador, who is barely able to move under the weight of his armor, and throw him over the paling

The horse too tries to raise himself; frequently he rises for a moment, but then a ghastly sight strikes the eye. From his torn belly hangs a whole bundle of intestines with a rosy spleen, bluish liver, and greenish stomach. The hapless beast tries to walk a few steps; but his trembling feet tread on his own entrails, he falls, digs the ground with his hoofs, shudders. Meanwhile the attendants run up, remove the saddle and bridle, and finish the torments of the horse with one stab of a stiletto, at the point where head and neck come together.

On the arena remains the motionless body, which, lying now on its side, seems wonderfully flat. The intestines are carried out quickly in a basket which is somewhat like a wash-tub, and the public clap their hands with excitement. Enthusiasm begins to seize them : "Bravo el toro! Bravo picador!" Eyes are flashing, on faces a flush comes, a number of hats fly to the arena in honor of the picador. Meanwhile "el toro," having drawn blood once, kills a number of other horses. If his horns are buried not in the belly but under the shoulder of the horse, a stream of dark blood bursts onto the arena in an uncommon quantity; the horse rears and falls backward with his rider. A twofold danger threatens the man : the horns of the bull or, in spite of his armor, the breaking of his neck. But, as we have said, the body of the horse becomes a protection to the rider; hence, every picador tries to receive battle at the edge of the arena, so as to be, as it were, covered between the body of the horse and the paling. When the bull withdraws, the picador advances, but only a few steps, so that the battle never takes place in the centre.

All these precautions would not avail much, and the bull would pierce the horsemen at last, were it not for the capeadors. They press on the bull, draw away his attention, rush with unheard-of boldness against his rage, saving each moment the life of some participant in the struggle. Once I saw an espada, retreating before the raging beast, stumble against the head of a dead horse and fall on his back; death inevitable was hanging above him, the horns of the bull were just ready to pass through his breast, when suddenly between that breast and the horns the red capes were moving, and the bull flew after the capes. It may be said that were it not for that flock of chimpanzees waving red capes, the work of the picadors would be impossible, and at every representation as many of them as of horses would perish.

It rarely happens that a picador can stop a bull at the point of a lance. This takes place only when the bull advances feebly, or the picador is gifted with gigantic strength of arms, surpassing the measure of men. I saw two such examples in Madrid, after which came a hurricane of applause for the picador.

But usually the bull kills horses like flies; and he is terrible when, covered with sweat, glittering in the sun, with a neck bleeding from lances and his horns painted red, he runs around the arena, as if in the drunkenness of victory. A deep bellow comes from his mighty lungs; at one moment he scatters capeadors, at another he halts suddenly over the body of a horse, now motionless, and avenges himself on it terribly, — he raises it on his horns, carries it around the arena, scattering drops of stiff blood on spectators in the first row; then he casts it again on the stained sand and pierces it a second time. It seems to him, evidently, that the spectacle is over, and that it has ended in his triumph.

But the spectacle has barely passed through one-half of its course. Those picadors whose horses have survived the defeat, ride out, it is true, from the arena; but in place of them run in with jumps, and amid shouts, nimble banderilleros. Every one of them in his upraised hands has two arrows, each an ell long, ornamented, in accordance with the coat of the man, with a blue, a green, or a red ribbon, and ending with a barbed point, which once it is under the skin will not come out of it. These men begin to circle about the bull, shaking the arrows, stretching toward him the points, threatening and springing up toward him. The bull rolls his blood-shot eyes, turns his head to the right, to the left, looking to see what new kind of enemies these are. "Ah," says he, evidently, to himself, "you have n't had blood enough, you want more — you shall have it!" and selecting the man, he rushes at him.

But what happens? The first banderillero, instead of fleeing, runs toward the bull, — runs past his head, as if he wished to avoid him; but in that same second something seems hanging in the air like a rainbow: the man is running away empty-handed with all the strength of his legs, toward the paling, and in the neck of the bull are two colored arrows.

After a moment another pair are sticking in him, and then a third pair, — six altogether, with three colors. The neck of the beast seems now as if ornamented with a bunch of flowers, but those flowers have the most terrible thorns of any on earth. At every movement of the bull, at every turn of his head, the arrows stir, shake, fly from one side of his neck to the other, and with that every point is boring into the wound. From pain the animal is evidently falling into the madness of rage; but the more he rushes the greater his pain. Hitherto the bull was the wrong-doer, now they wrong him, wrong him terribly. He would like to get rid of those torturing arrows; but there is no help for him. He is growing mad from mere torment, and is harassed to the utmost. Foam covers his nostrils, his tongue is protruding; he bellows no longer, but in the short intervals between the

wild shouts, the clapping, and the uproar of the spectators, you may hear his groans, which have an accent
almost human. The capeadors harassed him, every
picador wounded him, now the arrows are working into
his wounds; thirst and heat complete his torments.

It is his luck that he did not get another kind of "banderille." If — which happens rarely, however, — the bull
refuses to attack the horses and has killed none, the
enraged public rise, and in the circus something in the
nature of a revolution sets in. Men with their canes and
women with their parasols and fans turn to the royal
box; wild, hoarse voices of cruel cavaliers, and the shrill
ones of señoritas, shout only one word: "Fuego! fuego!
fuego!" (Fire, fire, fire!)

The representatives of the government withhold their
consent for a long time. Hence "Fuego!" is heard ever
more threateningly, and drowns all other voices; the
threat rises to such an intensity as to make us think that
the public may pass at any instant from words to a mad
deed of some kind. Half an hour passes: "Fuego!
fuego!" There is no help for it. The signal is given,
and the unfortunate bull gets a banderille which when
thrust into his neck blazes up that same instant.

The points wound in their own way, and in their own
way rolls of smoke surround the head of the beast, the
rattle of fireworks stuns him; great sparks fall into his
wounds, small congreve rockets burst under his skin; the
smell of burnt flesh and singed hair fill the arena. In
truth, cruelty can go no further; but the delight of the
public rises now to its zenith. The eyes of women are
covered with mist from excitement, every breast is heaving with pleasure, their heads fall backward, and between
their open moist lips are gleaming white teeth. You
would say that the torment of the beast is reflected in

the nerves of those women with an answering degree of delight. Only in Spain can such things be seen. There is in that frenzy something hysterical, something which recalls certain Phœnician mysteries, performed on the altar of Melitta.

The daring and skill of the banderilleros surpass every measure. I saw one of them who had taken his place in the middle of the arena in an arm-chair; he had stretched his legs carelessly before him, — they were in rose-colored stockings, — he crossed them, and holding above his head a banderille, was waiting for the bull. The bull rushed at him straightway; the next instant, I saw only that the banderille was fastened in the neck, and the bull was smashing the chair with mad blows of his head. In what way the man had escaped between the chair and the horns, I know not, — that is the secret of his skill. Another banderillero, at the same representation, seizing the lance of a picador at the moment of attack, supported himself with it, and sprang over the back and whole length of the bull. The beast was dumfounded, could not understand where his victim had vanished.

A multitude of such wonders of daring and dexterity are seen at each representation.

One bull never gets more than three pairs of banderilles. When the deed is accomplished, a single trumpet is heard in the orchestra with a prolonged and sad note, — and the moment the most exciting and tragic in the spectacle approaches. All that was done hitherto was only preparation for this. Now a fourth act of the drama is played.

On the arena comes out the "matador" himself, — that is, the espada. He is dressed like the other participants in the play, only more elaborately and richly. His coat is all gold and tinsel: costly laces adorn his breast.

He may be distinguished by this too, — that he comes out bareheaded always. His black hair, combed back carefully, ends on his shoulders in a small tail. In his left hand he holds a red cloth flag, in his right a long Toledo sword. The capeadors surround him as soldiers their chief, ready at all times to save him in a moment of danger, and he approaches the bull, collected, cool, but terrible and triumphant.

In all the spectators the hearts are throbbing violently, and a moment of silence sets in.

In Barcelona and Madrid I saw the four most eminent espadas in Spain, and in truth I admit, that besides their cool blood, dexterity, and training, they have a certain hypnotic power, which acts on the animal and fills him with mysterious fear. The bull simply bears himself differently before the espada from what he did before the previous participants in the play. It is not that he withdraws before him; on the contrary, he attacks him with greater insistence perhaps. But in former attacks, in addition to rage, there was evident a certain desire. He hunted, he scattered, he killed; he was as if convinced that the whole spectacle was for him, and that the question was only in this, that he should kill. Now, at sight of that cold, awful man with a sword in his hand, he convinces himself that death is there before him, that he must perish, that on that bloody sand the ghastly deed will be accomplished in some moments.

This mental state of the beast is so evident that every man can divine it. Perhaps even this, by its tragic nature, becomes the charm of the spectacle. That mighty organism, simply seething with a superabundance of vitality, of desire, of strength, is unwilling to die, will not consent to die for anything in the world! and death, unavoidable, irresistible, is approaching; hence unspeakable

32

sorrow, unspeakable despair, throbs through every movement of the bull. He hardly notices the capeadors,
whom before he pursued with such venom; he attacks
the espada himself, but he attacks with despair completely evident.

The espada does not kill him at once, for that is not
permitted by the rules of the play. He deceives the bull
with movements of the flag, himself he pushes from the
horns by turns slight and insignificant; he waits for the
moment, withdraws, advances. Evidently he wishes to
sate the public; now, this very instant, he'll strike, now
he lowers his sword again.

The struggle extends over the whole arena; it glitters
in the sun, is dark in the shade. In the circus applause
is heard, now general, now single from the breast of some
señorita who is unable to restrain her enthusiasm. At
one moment bravos are thundering; at another, if the
espada has retreated awkwardly or given a false blow,
hissing rends the ear. The bull has now given some tens
of blows with his horns, — always to the flag; the public
are satisfied; here and there voices are crying: " Mata el
toro! mata el toro!" (Kill the bull! kill the bull!)

And now a flash comes so suddenly that the eye cannot follow it; then the group of fighters scatter, and in
the neck of the bull, above the colored banderilles, is
seen the red hilt of the sword. The blade has gone
through the neck, and, buried two thirds of its length,
is planted in the lungs of the beast.

The espada is defenceless; the bull attacks yet, but he
misleads him in the old fashion with the flag, he saves
himself from the blows with half turns.

Meanwhile it seems that people have gone wild in the
circus. No longer shouts, but one bellow and howl are
heard, around, from above to below. All are springing

from their seats. To the arena are flying bouquets, cigar-cases, hats, fans. The fight is approaching its end.

A film is coming over the eyes of the bull; from his mouth are hanging stalactites of bloody saliva; his groan becomes hoarse. Night is embracing his head. The glitter and heat of the sun concern him no longer. He attacks yet, but as it were in a dream. It is darker and darker before him. At last he collects the remnant of his consciousness, backs to the paling, totters for a moment, kneels on his fore feet, drops on his hind ones, and begins to die.

The espada looks at him no longer; he has his eyes turned to the spectators, from whom hats and cigar-cases are flying, thick as hail; he bows; capeadors throw back to the spectators their hats.

A mysterious man dressed in black now climbs over the paling in silence and puts a stiletto in the bull, where the neck-bone meets the skull; with a light movement he sinks it to the hilt and turns it.

That is the blow of mercy, after which the head of the bull drops on its side.

All the participants pass out. For a moment the arena is empty; on it are visible only the body of the bull and the eviscerated carcasses of four or five horses, now cold.

But after a while rush in with great speed men with mules, splendidly harnessed in yellow and red; the men attach these mules to the bodies and draw them around so that the public may enjoy the sight once again, then with speed equally great they go out through the doors of the arena.

But do not imagine that the spectacle is ended with one bull. After the first comes a second, after the second a third, and so on. In Madrid six bulls perish at a representation. In Barcelona, at the time of the fair, eight were killed.

Do not think either that the public are wearied by the monotony of the fight. To begin with, the fight itself is varied with personal episodes caused by temperament, the greater or less rage of the bull, the greater or less skill of the men in their work; secondly, that public is never annoyed at the sight of blood and death.

The "toreadores" (though in Spain no participant in the fight is called a toreador), thanks to their dexterity, rarely perish; but if that happens, the spectacle is considered as the more splendid, and the bull receives as much applause as the espada. Since, however, accidents happen to people sometimes, at every representation, besides the doctor, there is present a priest with the sacrament. That spiritual person is not among the audience, of course; but he waits in a special room, to which the wounded are borne in case of an accident.

Whether in time, under the influence of civilization, bull-fights will be abandoned in Spain, it is difficult to say. The love of those fights is very deep in the nature of the Spanish people. The higher and intelligent ranks of society take part in them gladly. The defenders of these spectacles say that in substance they are nothing more than hazardous hunting, which answers to the knightly character of the nation. But hunting is an amusement, not a career; in hunting there is no audience, — only actors; there are no throngs of women, half fainting from delight at the spectacle of torment and death; finally, in hunting no one exposes his life for hire.

Were I asked if the spectacle is beautiful, I should say yes; beautiful especially in its surroundings, — that sun, those shades, those thousands of fans at sight of which it seems as though a swarm of butterflies had settled on the seats of the circus, those eyes, those red moist lips. Beautiful is that incalculable quantity of warm and strong tones, that mass of colors, gold, tinsel, that inflamed sand, from which heat is exhaling, — finally those proofs of bold daring, and that terror hanging over the play. All that is more beautiful by far than the streams of blood and the torn bellies of the horses.

He, however, who knows these spectacles only from description, and sees them afterwards with his own eyes, cannot but think: what a wonderful people for whom the highest amusement and delight is the sight of a thing so awful, so absolute and inevitable as death. Whence comes that love? Is it simply a remnant of Middle-age cruelty; or is it that impulse which is roused in many persons, for instance at sight of a precipice, to go as near as possible to the brink, to touch that curtain, behind which begin the mystery and the pit? — that is a wonderful passion, which in certain souls becomes irresistible.

Of the Spaniards it may be said, that in the whole course of their history they have shown a tendency to extremes. Few people have been so merciless in warfare; none have turned a religion of love into such a gloomy and bloody worship; finally, no other nation amuses itself by playing with death.

SACHEM

SACHEM.

IN the town of Antelope, situated on a river of the same name in the State of Texas, every living person was hurrying to the circus. The inhabitants were interested all the more since from the foundation of the town that was the first time that a circus had come to it with dancing women, minstrels, and rope-walkers. The town was new. Fifteen years before not only was there not one house there, but in all the region round about there were no white people. Moreover, on the forks of the river, on the very spot on which Antelope was situated, stood an Indian village called Chiavatta. That had been the capital of the Black Snakes, who in their time were such an eyesore to the neighboring settlements of Berlin, Gründenau, and Harmonia, that these settlements could endure them no longer. True, the Indians were only defending their "land," which the State government of Texas had guaranteed to them forever by the most solemn treaties; but what was that to the colonists of Berlin, Gründenau, and Harmonia? It is true that they took from the Black Snakes earth, air, and water, but they brought civilization in return; the redskins on their part showed gratitude in their own way, — that is, by taking scalps from the heads of the Germans. Such a state of things could not be suffered. Therefore, the settlers from Berlin, Grundenau, and Harmonia assembled on a certain moonlight night to the number of four hundred, and, calling to their aid Mexicans from La Ora, fell upon sleeping Chiavatta.

The triumph of the good cause was perfect. Chiavatta was burned to ashes, and the inhabitants, without regard to sex or age, were cut to pieces. Only small parties of warriors escaped who at that time were absent on a hunt. In the town itself not one soul was left alive mainly because the place lay in the forks of a river, which, having overflowed, as is usual in spring-time, surrounded the settlement with an impassable gulf of waters. But the same forked position which ruined the Indians, seemed good to the Germans. From the forks it was difficult to escape, but the place was defensible. Thanks to this thought, emigration set in at once from Berlin, Gründenau, and Harmonia to the forks, in which in the twinkle of an eye, on the site of the wild Chiavatta, rose the civilized town of Antelope. In five years it numbered two thousand inhabitants.

In the sixth year they discovered on the opposite bank of the forks a quicksilver mine; the working of this doubled the number of inhabitants. In the seventh year, by virtue of Lynch law, they hanged on the square of the town the last twelve warriors of the Black Snakes, who were caught in the neighboring "Forest of the Dead,"—and henceforth nothing remained to hinder the development of Antelope. Two "Tagblätter" (daily papers) were published in the town, and one "Montagsrevue" (Monday Review). A line of railroad united the place with Rio del Norte and San Antonio; on Opuncia Gasse (Opuncia Street) stood three schools, one of which was a high school. On the square where they had hanged the last Black Snakes, the citizens had erected a philanthropic institution. Every Sunday the pastors taught in the churches love of one's neighbor, respect for the property of others, and similar virtues essential to a civilized society; a certain travelling lecturer read a dissertation "On the rights of nations."

The richest inhabitants had begun to talk of founding a university, to which the government of the State was to contribute. The citizens were prosperous. The trade in quicksilver, oranges, barley, and wine brought them famous profits. They were upright, thrifty, industrious, systematic, fat. Whoever might visit in later years Antelope with a population nearing twenty thousand would not recognize in the rich merchants of the place those pitiless warriors who fifteen years before had burned Chiavatta. The days passed for them in their stores, workshops, and offices; the evenings they spent in the beer-saloon "Golden Sun" on Rattlesnake Street. Listening to those sounds somewhat slow and guttural of "Mahlzeit, Mahlzeit!" (meal-time, meal-time), to those phlegmatic "Nun ja wissen Sie, Herr Müller, ist das aber möglich?" (Well, now, Herr Muller, but is that possible?), that clatter of goblets, that sound of beer dropping on the floor, that plash of overflowing foam; seeing that calm, that slowness, those Philistine faces covered with fat, those fishy eyes, — a man might suppose himself in a beer-garden in Berlin or Munich, and not on the ruins of Chiavatta. But in the town everything was "ganz gemüthlich" (altogether cosey), and no one had a thought of the ruins. That evening the whole population was hastening to the circus, first, because after hard labor recreation is as praiseworthy as it is agreeable; second, because the inhabitants were proud of its arrival. It is well-known that circuses do not come to every little place; hence the arrival of the Hon. M. Dean's troupe had confirmed the greatness and magnificence of Ante-

lope.   There was, however, a third and perhaps the
greatest cause of the general curiosity.

No. Two of the programme read as follows, —

"A walk on a wire extended fifteen feet above the
ground will be made to the accompaniment of music by the
renowned gymnast Black Vulture, sachem of the Black
Snakes, the last descendant of their chiefs, the last man of
the tribe.   1. The walk ; 2. Springs of the Antelope ;
3. The death-dance and death-song."

If that "sachem" could rouse the highest interest in any
place, it was surely in Antelope.   Hon. M. Dean told at
the "Golden Sun" how fifteen years before, on a journey
to Santa Fé, he had found, on the Planos de Tornado, an
old dying Indian with a boy ten years of age.   The old
man died from wounds and exhaustion ; but before death
he declared that the boy was the son of the slain sachem
of the Black Snakes, and the heir to that office.

The troupe sheltered the orphan, who in time became
the first acrobat in it.   It was only at the "Golden Sun,"
however, that Hon. M. Dean learned first that Antelope
was the former Chiavatta, and that the famous rope-walker
would exhibit himself on the grave of his fathers.   This
information brought the director into perfect humor ; he
might reckon now surely on a *great attraction*, if only he
knew how to bring out the effect skilfully.   Of course
the Philistines of Antelope hurried to the circus to show
their wives and children, imported from Germany, the
last of the Black Snakes, — those wives and children who
in their lives had never seen Indians, — and to say: "See,
we cut to pieces men just like that fellow, fifteen years
ago !"   "Ach, Herr Je !"   It was pleasant to hear such
an exclamation of wonder from the mouth of Amalchen,
or little Fritz.   Throughout the town, therefore, all were
repeating unceasingly, "Sachem ! Sachem !"

From early morning the children were looking through cracks in the boards with curious and astonished faces; the older boys, more excited by the warrior spirit, marched home from school in terrible array, without knowing themselves why they did so.

It is eight o'clock in the evening, — a wonderful night, clear, starry. A breeze from the suburbs brings the odor of orange groves, which in the town is mingled with the odor of malt In the circus there is a blaze of light. Immense pine-torches fixed before the principal gate are burning and smoking. The breeze waves the plumes of smoke and the bright flame which illuminates the dark outlines of the building. It is a freshly erected wooden pile, circular, with a pointed roof, and the starry flag of America on the summit of it. Before the gate are crowds who could not get tickets or had not the wherewithal to buy them; they look at the wagons of the troupe, and principally at the canvas curtain of the great Eastern door, on which is depicted a battle of the whites with the redskins. At moments when the curtain is drawn aside the bright refreshment-bar within is visible, with its hundreds of glasses on the table. Now they draw aside the curtain for good, and the throng enters. The empty passages between the seats begin to resound with the steps of people, and soon the dark moving mass fills all the place from the highest point to the floor. It is clear as day in the circus, for though they had not been able to bring in gas pipes, a gigantic chandelier formed of fifty kerosene lamps takes its place. In those gleams are visible the heads of the beer drinkers, fleshy, thrown back to give room to their chins, the youthful faces of women, and the pretty, wondering visages of children, whose eyes are almost coming out of their heads from curiosity. But all the spectators have the curious, self-satisfied look that

is usual in an audience at a circus. Amid the hum of
conversation interrupted by cries of " Frisch wasser! frisch
wasser!" (fresh water), all await the beginning with
impatience.

At last a bell sounds, six grooms appear in shining
boots, and stand in two ranks at the passage from the
stables to the arena. Between those ranks a furious
horse rushes forth, without bridle or saddle; and on him,
as it were a bundle of muslin ribbons and tulle, is the
dancer Lina. They begin manœuvring to the sound of
music. Lina is so pretty that young Matilda, daughter of
the brewer on Opuncia Gasse, alarmed at sight of her
beauty, inclines to the ear of Floss, a young grocer from
the same street, and asks in a whisper if he loves her yet.
Meanwhile the horse gallops, and puffs like an engine;
the clowns, a number of whom run after the dancer, crack
whips, shout, and strike one another on the faces. The
dancer vanishes like lightning; there is a storm of applause. What a splendid representation! But No. One
passes quickly. No. Two is approaching. The word
"Sachem! sachem!" flies from mouth to mouth among
the spectators. No one gives a thought now to the
clowns, who cease not to strike one another. In the
midst of the apish movements of the clowns, the grooms
bring lofty wooden trestles several yards in height, and
put them on both sides of the arena. The band stops
playing Yankee Doodle, and gives the gloomy aria of the
Commandore in Don Juan. They extend the wire from one
trestle to the other. All at once a shower of red Bengal
light falls at the passage, and covers the whole arena with
a bloody glare. In that glare appears the terrible sachem,
the last of the Black Snakes. But what is that? The
sachem is not there, but the manager of the troop himself, Hon. M. Dean. He bows to the public and raises his

voice. He has the honor to beg "the kind and respected gentlemen, as well as the beautiful and no less respected ladies, to be unusually calm, give no applause, and remain perfectly still, for the chief is excited and wilder than usual." These words produce no little impression, and — a wonderful thing! — those very citizens of Antelope who fifteen years before had destroyed Chiavatta, feel now some sort of very unpleasant sensation. A moment before, when the beautiful Lina was performing her springs on horseback, they were glad to be sitting so near, right there close to the parapet, whence they could see everything so well; and now they look with a certain longing for the upper seats of the circus, and in spite of all laws of physics, find that the lower they are the more stifling it is.

But could that sachem remember? He was reared from years of childhood in the troupe of Hon. M. Dean, composed mainly of Germans. Had he not forgotten everything? This seemed probable. His environment and fifteen years of a circus career, the exhibition of his art, the winning of applause, must have exerted their influence.

Chiavatta, Chiavatta! But they are Germans, they are on their own soil, and think no more of the fatherland than *business* permits. Above all, man must eat and drink. This truth every Philistine must keep in mind, as well as the last of the Black Snakes.

These meditations are interrupted suddenly by a certain wild whistle in the stables, and on the arena appears the sachem expected so anxiously. A brief murmur of the crowd is heard: "That is he, that is he!" — and then silence. But there is hissing from Bengal lights, which burn continually at the passage. All eyes are turned toward the chief, who in the circus will appear on the graves of his fathers. The Indian deserves really that men should look at him. He seems as haughty as a king. A mantle of white ermine — the mark of his chieftainship — covers his figure, which is lofty, and so wild that it brings to mind a badly tamed jaguar. He has a face as it were forged out of bronze, like the head of an eagle, and in his face there is a cold gleam; his eyes are genuinely Indian, calm, indifferent, and ominous. He glances around on the assembly, as if wishing to choose a victim. Moreover, he is armed from head to foot. On his head plumes are waving, at his girdle he has an axe and a knife for scalping; but in his hand, instead of a bow, he holds a long staff to preserve his balance when walking on the wire. Standing in the middle of the arena he gives forth on a sudden a war cry. *Herr Gott!* That is the cry of the Black Snakes. Those who massacred Chiavatta remember clearly that terrible howl, — and what is most wonderful, those who fifteen years before had no fear of one thousand such warriors are sweating now before one. But behold! the director approaches the chief and says something to him, as if to pacify and calm him. The wild beast feels the bit; the words have their influence, for after a time the sachem is swaying on the wire. With eyes fixed on the kerosene chandelier he advances. The wire bends much; at moments it is not visible, and then the Indian seems suspended in space. He is walking as it were upward; he advances, retreats, and again he advances, maintaining his balance. His extended arms covered with the mantle seem like great wings. He totters! he is falling! — No. A short interrupted bravo begins like a storm and stops. The face of the chief becomes more and more threatening. In his gaze fixed on the kerosene lamps is gleaming some terrible light. There is alarm in the circus, but no one breaks the silence. Meanwhile the sachem approaches the end of the wire, stops; all at once a war-song bursts forth from his lips.

A strange thing! The chief sings in German. But that is easy to understand. Surely he· has forgotten the tongue of the Black Snakes. Moreover, no one notices that. All listen to the song, which rises and grows in volume. It is a half chant, a kind of half call, immeasurably plaintive, wild, and hoarse, full of sounds of attack.

The following words were heard : " After the great yearly rains, five hundred warriors used to go from Chiavatta on the war-path or to spring hunts; when they came back from war they brought scalps, when they came back from a hunt they brought the flesh and the skins of buffaloes; their wives met them with gladness, and they danced in honor of the Great Spirit.

" Chiavatta was happy. The women worked in the wigwams, the children grew up to be beautiful maidens, to be brave, fearless warriors. The warriors died on the field of glory, and went to the silver mountains to hunt with the ghosts of their fathers. Their axes were never dipped in the blood of women and children, for the warriors of Chiavatta were high-minded. Chiavatta was powerful; but pale-faces came from beyond distant waters and set fire to Chiavatta. The white warriors did not destroy the Black Snakes in battle, but they stole in as do jackals at night, they buried their knives in the bosoms of sleeping men, women, and children.

" Now there is no Chiavatta. In place of it the white men have raised their stone wigwams. The murdered nation and ruined Chiavatta cry out for vengeance."

The voice of the chief became hoarse. Standing on

33

the wire, he seemed a red archangel of vengeance floating above the heads of that throng of people. Evidently
the director himself was afraid. A silence as of death
settled down in the circus. The chief howled on, —

"Of the whole nation there remained only one little
child. He was weak and small, but he swore to the
spirit of the earth that he would have vengeance, — that
he would see the corpses of white men, women, and
children, that he would see fire and blood."

The last words were changed into a bellow of fury.
In the circus murmurs were heard like the sudden puffs
of a whirlwind. Thousands of questions without answer
came to men's minds. What will he do, that mad tiger?
What is he announcing? How will he accomplish his
vengeance, — he alone? Will he stay here or flee?
Will he defend himself, and how? "Was ist das, was
ist das?" is heard in the terrified accents of women.

All at once an unearthly howl was rent from the
breast of the chief. The wire swayed violently, he
sprang to the wooden trestle, standing at the chandelier,
and raised his staff. A terrible thought flew like a flash
through all heads. He will hurl around the lamps and
fill the circus with torrents of flaming kerosene — From
the breasts of the spectators one shout was just rising;
but what do they see? From the arena the cry comes,
"Stop! stop!" The chief is gone! Has he jumped
down? He has gone through the entrance without
firing the circus! Where is he? See, he is coming,
coming a second time, panting, tired, terrible. In his
hand is a pewter plate, and extending it to the spectators, he calls in a voice of entreaty: "Was gefällig für
den letzten der Schwarzen Schlangen?" (What are you
pleased to give to the last of the Black Snakes?)

A stone falls from the breasts of the spectators. You

see that was all in the programme, it was a trick of the director for effect. The dollars and half dollars came down in a shower. How could they say "No" to the last of the Black Snakes, in Antelope reared on the ruins of Chiavatta ? People have hearts.

After the exhibition, the sachem drank beer and ate dumplings at the "Golden Sun." His environment had exerted its influence, evidently. He found great popularity in Antelope, especially with women, — there was even scandal about him.

A COMEDY OF ERRORS

A COMEDY OF ERRORS.

FIVE or six years since it happened that oil springs were discovered in a certain place in Mariposa County, California. The enormous profits which such springs yield in Nevada and other States, induced a number of men to form a company for the purpose of working the newly-discovered springs. They brought in various machines, — pumps, engines, ladders, barrels, kegs, drills, and kettles; they built houses for laborers, and called the place Struck Oil. After a certain time a desert and uninhabited neighborhood, which a year before was inhabited only by coyotes, became a settlement composed of a number of tens of houses occupied by several hundred laborers.

Two years later, Struck Oil was called Struck Oil City. In fact it was a "city" in the full meaning of that term. I beg the reader to note that there were living in the city a shoemaker, a tailor, a carpenter, a blacksmith, a butcher, and a doctor, — a Frenchman, who in his time had shaved beards in France, but for the rest a "learned man," and harmless, which in an American doctor means a great deal.

The doctor, as happens very often in small American towns, kept also a drug store and a post-office; therefore he had a triple practice. He was as harmless an apothecary as he was a doctor, for it was possible to buy only two kinds of medicine in his drug store, — sugar sirup and leroa.[1] This quiet and mild old man said usually to his patients, —

"You need not fear my prescriptions, for when I give medicine to a patient I always take the same dose myself; I understand that if it will not hurt me while in health it will not harm a sick man. Is n't that true?"

"True," answered the reassured citizen, to whom somehow it did not occur that it was not only the duty of a doctor to avoid injuring a sick man, but to help him.

Monsieur Dasonville, such was the doctor's name, believed especially in the miraculous effects of leroa. More than once at meetings he removed the hat from his head, and turning to the public said, —

"Ladies and gentlemen, convince yourselves concerning leroa. I am eighty-four years of age and use leroa every day. Look at me, I have not one gray hair on my head."

The ladies and gentlemen might discover that the doctor had not one gray hair; but then he had no hair at all, for his head was as bald as a lamp globe. But since discoveries of that kind contributed in no way to the growth of Struck Oil City, no one made them.

Meanwhile Struck Oil City grew and grew. At the expiration of two years a branch railroad was built to it. The city had its elective officers also. The doctor, whom everybody loved, was chosen judge, as a representative of the intelligence; the shoemaker, a Polish Jew, Mr. Davis (David was his real name) was chosen sheriff, that is, chief of the police, which was composed of the sheriff and no one else; they built a schoolhouse, for the management of which a "schoolma'am" was imported on purpose, — a maiden born before man reckoned time, and who

---

[1] Leroa is, no doubt, the French *Le roi*, the King.

had an eternal toothache; finally, the first hotel rose, and was named United States Hotel.

"Business" was lively beyond measure. The export of oil brought good profit. It was noticed that Mr. Davis had put out before his shop a glass showcase, like those which adorn the shoeshops in San Francisco. At the following meeting the inhabitants thanked Mr. Davis publicly for this "new ornament to the city." Mr. Davis answered with the modesty of a great citizen, "Thank you! thank you!"

Where there is a judge and a sheriff there are lawsuits. These require writing and paper. Therefore, on the corner of First and Coyote streets there arose a "stationery," that is a paper shop, in which were sold also political daily papers and caricatures, one of which represented President Grant in the form of a man milking a cow, which in her turn represented the United States. The duties of the sheriff did not enjoin on him at all to forbid the sale of such pictures, for that does not pertain to the police.

But this was not the end yet. An American city cannot exist without a newspaper. At the end of the second year, therefore, a paper appeared called the "Saturday Weekly Review," which had as many subscribers as there were inhabitants in Struck Oil City. The editor of that paper was its publisher, printer, business manager, and carrier. The last duty came to him the more easily, since in addition to his business he kept cows, and had to deliver milk every morning at the houses of citizens. But this did not prevent him in any way from beginning his leading political articles with the words: "If our miserable President of the United States had followed the advice which we gave him in the last number," etc.

As we see, nothing was wanting in blessed Struck Oil

City. Besides, since men who work at getting oil are not distinguished either by the violence or rude manners which mark gold-diggers, it was peaceful in the city. No man had a fight with another; there was not a word spoken of "lynching;" life flowed on calmly. One day was as much like another as one drop of water is like another. In the morning every man occupied himself with "business;" in the evening the inhabitants burned sweepings on the street; and, if there was no meeting, they went to bed, knowing that on the following evening they would burn sweepings again.

But the sheriff was annoyed by one thing, — he could not break the citizens from firing at wild geese which flew over the place in the evening. The laws of the city prohibited shooting on the streets. "If this were some mangy little village," said the sheriff, "I would n't say anything; but in such a great city to have pif! paf! pif! paf! is very unbecoming."

The citizens listened, nodded, and answered, "Oh, yes;" but in the evening when on the blushing sky the white and gray lines appeared, stretching from the mountains to the ocean, every man forgot his promise, seized his carabine, and shooting began in good earnest.

Mr. Davis might, it is true, have summoned each tres- passer before the judge, and the judge could punish him with a fine; but it must not be forgotten that the offenders were in case of sickness patients of the doctor, and in case of broken shoes customers of the sheriff; since then hand washes hand, hand did not offend hand. Hence, it was as peaceful in Struck Oil City as in heaven; still, those halcyon days had a sudden end.

A man who kept a grocery was inflamed with mortal hatred toward a woman who kept a grocery, and the woman with hatred toward him.

Here it may be needful to explain what that is which in America is called "a grocery." A grocery is a place in which they sell goods of all kinds. In a grocery you can find flour, caps, cigars, brooms, buttons, rice, sardines, stockings, ham, garden seeds, coats, pantaloons, lamp chimneys, axes, crackers, crockery, paper-collars, dried fish; in a word, everything which a man can use.

At first there was only one grocery in Struck Oil City. It was kept by a German named Hans Kasche. He was a phlegmatic German from Prussia, thirty-five years of age, and had staring eyes; he was not fat, but portly; he went about always in his shirt-sleeves, and never let the pipe out of his mouth. He knew as much English as was needed in business; beyond that not a toothful. But he managed his business well, so that in a year people said in Struck Oil City that he was worth several thousand dollars.

On a sudden, however, a second grocery was opened. And marvellous thing! a German man kept the first grocery, a German woman established the second. *Kunegunde und Eduard, Eduard und Kunegunde!* Straightway a war was begun between the two sides; it began from this, — that Miss Neumann, or, as she called herself, "Miss Newman," gave at her opening "lunch" pancakes baked from flour mixed with soda and alum. She would have injured herself in the highest degree by this in the opinion of the citizens, were it not that she stated, and then proved by witnesses, that, as her flour had not been opened, she had bought this from Hans Kasche. It came out then that Hans Kasche was an envious man and a villain, who wished from the very first to ruin his rival in public estimation. Of course, it was to be foreseen that the two groceries would be rivals; but no one could foresee that the rivalry would pass into such terrible personal hatred. Soon that hatred increased to such a degree that Hans burned sweepings only when the wind blew the smoke from his shop to that of his rival; and the rival had no other name for Hans than "Dutchman," which he considered as the greatest insult.

At the beginning, the citizens laughed at both, all the more since neither of them knew English; gradually, however, through daily relations with the groceries, two parties were formed in the city, — the Hansites and the Newmanites, who began to look at each other askance, which might have injured the happiness and peace of Struck Oil City, and brought dreadful complications for the future. Mr. Davis, the profound politician, was anxious to cure the evil at its source; hence he strove to reconcile the German woman with the German man. More than once he stood in the middle of the street, and said to them in their native tongue, —

"Well, why do you fight? Is it because you do not patronize the same shoemaker? I have such shoes now that in all San Francisco there are no better."

"It is useless to recommend shoes to him who will be barefoot before long," replied Miss Newman, sourly.

"I do not win credit with my feet," answered Hans, phlegmatically.

And it is necessary to know that Miss Newman, though a German, had really pretty feet; therefore such a taunt filled her heart with mortal anger.

In the city the two parties began to raise the question of Hans and Miss Newman; but since no man in America can obtain justice against a woman, the majority inclined to the side of Miss Newman.

Soon Hans saw that his grocery was barely paying expenses.

But Miss Newman too did not win such brilliant victories, for soon all the married women in the city took the side of Hans, for they noticed that their husbands made purchases too often from the fair German, and sat too long at each purchase.

When no one was in either shop, Hans and Miss Newman stood in their doors, one opposite the other, casting mutual glances filled with venom. Miss Newman sang at such times to herself to the air of " Mein lieber Augustin," —

" Dutchman, Dutchman, Du-u-u-u-tchman, Du-u-u-u-tchman ! "

Hans looked at her feet, at her figure, at her face with an expression such as he would have had in looking at a coyote killed outside the city; then, bursting into demonic laughter, he exclaimed, —

" *Mein Gott !* "

Hatred in that phlegmatic man rose to such a pitch that when he appeared at the door in the morning, and Miss Newman was not there, he was as fidgety as if he missed something.

There would have been active collisions between them long before, were it not that Hans was sure of defeat in every official decision, and that all the more since Miss Newman had on her side the editor of the " Saturday Weekly Review." Hans convinced himself of this when he spread the report that Miss Newman wore a false bust. That was even likely, for in America it is a common custom. But on the following week there appeared in the " Saturday Weekly Review " a thundering article, in which the editor, speaking generally of the slanders of "Dutchmen," ended with the solemn assurance " of one well informed " that the bust of a certain slandered lady is genuine.

From that day forward Hans drank black coffee every morning instead of white, for he would take milk no longer from that editor; but to make up for the loss, Miss Newman took milk for two. Moreover, she ordered at the dressmaker's a robe, which, by the cut of its bosom, proved convincingly to all that Hans was a slanderer.

Hans felt defenceless before woman's cunning; meanwhile his opponent, standing before her shop every morning, sang louder and louder, —

"Dutchman, Dutchman, Du-u-u-u-tchman, Du-u-u-u-tchman!"

"What am I to do?" thought Hans. "I have wheat poisoned for rats; let me poison her hens with it? No, the justice would sentence me to pay for them. But I know what to do."

And in the evening Miss Newman, to her great astonishment, saw Hans carrying bunches of wild sunflowers, and laying them out as if in a row under the barred window of his cellar. "I am curious to know what is coming," thought she to herself, — "surely something against me." Meanwhile night came. Hans had put the sunflowers in two rows, so that only between them was there an open path to the window of the cellar; then he brought some object covered with cloth, and turned his back to Miss Newman. He took the cloth from the mysterious object, covered it with sunflower leaves, then approached the wall, and began to make certain letters on it.

Miss Newman was dying with curiosity. "Of course he is writing something about me," thought she; "but only let all go to sleep, I'll walk over there and see, even if it kills me."

When Hans had finished his work, he went upstairs,

and soon after put his light out. Then Miss Newman threw on her wrapper quickly, put slippers on her bare feet, and went across the street. When she came to the sunflowers, she went straight to the window, wishing to read the writing on the wall. Suddenly the eyes went up into her head; she threw back the upper half of her body, and from her mouth came with pain, "Ei! ei!" then the despairing cry, "Help! help!"

The window above was raised. "*Was ist das?*" was heard in the quiet voice of Hans. "*Was ist das?*"

"Cursed Dutchman," screamed the lady, "you have murdered me, destroyed me! You'll hang to-morrow. Help! help!"

"I'll come down right away," said Hans.

In fact he appeared after a while with a light in his hand. He looked at Miss Newman, who was as if spiked to the earth; then he caught his sides, and began to laugh.

"What is this? Miss Newman? Ha! ha! ha! Good evening, Miss Newman! Ha! ha! ha! I put out a skunk-trap, and caught Miss Newman. Why did you come to look at my cellar? I wrote a notice on the wall to keep away. Scream now; let people crowd up here; let all see that you come at night to look into the Dutchman's cellar. *O mein Gott!* Cry away; but stay there till morning. Good-by, Miss Newman, good-by!"

The position of Miss Newman was dreadful. If she screamed, people would collect, — she would be compromised; if she didn't cry, she'd stay all night caught in a trap, and next day make a show of herself. And there her foot was paining her more and more. Her head whirled around; the stars were confused with one another, and the moon with the ominous face of Hans Kasche. She fainted.

"*Herr Je!*" cried Hans to himself, "if she dies, they will lynch me in the morning without trial;" and the hair rose on his head from terror.

There was no help for it. Hans looked for his key as quickly as possible to open the trap; but it was n't easy to open it, for Miss Newman's wrapper was in the way. He had to put it aside somewhat; and, in spite of all his hatred and fear, Hans could n't help casting an eye at the feet beautiful as if of marble, — those feet of his enemy lighted by the red gleam of the moon.

A man might say that in his hatred then there was compassion. He opened the trap quickly; and, since Miss Newman made no movement, he took her in his arms, and carried her to her dwelling. On the way he felt compassion again. Then he went home, and could n't close an eye all that night.

Next morning Miss Newman did not appear before her grocery to sing, —

"Dutchman, Dutchman, Du-u-u-u-tchman, Du-u-u-u-tchman!"

Maybe that she was ashamed, and maybe that in silence she was forging revenge.

It turned out that she was forging revenge. On the evening of that same day the editor of the "Saturday Weekly Review" challenged Hans to fight with fists, and at the very beginning of the battle he gave him a black eye. But Hans, brought to despair, gave so many terrible blows to the editor that, after a short and vain opposition, the editor fell his whole length, crying, "Enough! Enough!"

It is unknown by what means, — for it was n't through Hans, — the whole city heard about the night adventure of Miss Newman. After the fight with the editor, compassion for his enemy vanished again from Hans's heart, and there remained only hatred.

Hans Kasche had a foreboding that some unexpected blow would strike him from the hated hand. In fact he did not have to wait long. Grocery-keepers paste up on their shops advertisements of various articles entitled usually "Notice." Besides, it is necessary to know that usually they sell ice to saloon-keepers, — without ice no American drinks either whiskey or beer. All at once Hans noticed that people stopped taking ice of him. The immense blocks, which he had brought by railroad and put in the cellar, thawed; there was a loss of several dollars. Why was that? How was it? Hans saw that even his partisans bought ice every day from Miss Newman; he did n't know what this meant, especially since he had not quarrelled with a single saloon-keeper. He determined to clear up the matter.

"Why don't you take ice of me?" asked he, in broken English, of a saloon-keeper, Peters, who was just passing his grocery.

"Because you don't keep any."

"Why don't I keep any?"

"How do I know?"

"*Aber* I keep it."

"But what is that?" asked the saloon-keeper, pointing to the notice stuck up on the grocery.

Hans looked, and grew green from rage; from his "Notice" some one has scratched out the letter *t* from the middle of the word, in consequence of which "Notice" became "No ice."

"*Donnerwetter!*" screamed Hans, and all blue and trembling, he rushed to Miss Newman's grocery.

"That 's scoundrelism!" cried he, foaming at the mouth. "Why did you scratch out a letter in the middle from me?"

34

"What did I scratch out from you in the middle?" asked Miss Newman, with a look of innocence.

"The letter *t*, I say. You scratched out *t* from me! *Aber* Gottam! this cannot last longer. You must pay me for that ice, Miss Newman! Gottam! Gottam!"

And losing his ordinary cool blood, he began to roar like a madman, whereupon Miss Newman fell to screaming; people flew together in a crowd.

"Help!" cried Miss Newman. "The Dutchman is raving! He says that I scratched something out of his middle, and I haven't scratched anything from him. What was I to scratch? I haven't scratched anything. In God's name! I'd scratch his eyes out if I could, but nothing else. I am a poor lone woman! he'll kill me, he'll murder me!"

Screaming in this way, she covered herself with hot tears. The Americans didn't know, in fact, what the question was; but Americans will not endure woman's tears; therefore they took the German by the neck, and through the door with him. He wanted to resist; little use in that! he flew as out of a sling, flew through the street, flew through his own door, and dropped at full length.

A week later there hung an immense painted sign on his shop. The sign represented an ape in a striped dress, with a white apron and shoulder straps, — in one word, exactly like Miss Newman. Underneath stood an inscription in great golden letters, —

"GROCERY UNDER THE APE."

The people collected to look at it. Their laughter brought Miss Newman to the door. She came out, looked, grew pale, but without losing presence of mind called out at once. —

"Grocery under the ape ?   No wonder, for Hans Kasche lives over the grocery.   Ha !"

The blow however pierced her to the heart.   In the afternoon she heard how crowds of children passing the grocery on their way from school, and stopping before the sign, cried, —

"Oh, that's Miss Newman!   Good evening, Miss Newman!"

This was too much.   In the evening when the editor came to her, she said to him, —

"That ape means me, I know that; but I will not give up my own.   He must take down that ape and lick it off before me with his own tongue."

"What do you wish to do, Miss Newman ?"

"I'll go this minute to the judge."

"How this minute ?"

"To-morrow."

In the morning she went out, and walking up to Hans, said, —

"Listen to me, Mr.-Dutchman, I know that that ape means me.   Come with me to the judge.   We'll see what he'll say to this."

"He will say that I am free to paint on my shop what I like."

"We'll see about that very soon."   Miss Newman was hardly able to breathe.

"But how do you know that that ape means you ?"

"Conscience tells me.   Come, come to the judge; if not, the sheriff will take you in chains."

"Very well, I'll go," said Hans, certain of victory.

They shut up their groceries and went, meditating for themselves along the road.   Only wnen they were at Judge Dasonville's door did they remember that neither of them knew English enough to explain the affair.

What were they to do? The sheriff, being a Polish Jew, knew German and English. They went to the sheriff; but the sheriff was just getting into his wagon to drive off.

"Go to the devil!" said he, in a hurry. "The whole city is disturbed by you! You wear the same shoes whole years! I am going for lumber. Good-by!" And he drove away.

Hans put his hands on his hips. "You must wait till to-morrow," said he, phlegmatically.

"I wait? I'd die first, unless you take down the ape."

"I won't take it down."

"You'll hang, Dutchman. We'll do without the sheriff. The judge knows already what the matter is."

"We'll go without the sheriff," said the German.

Miss Newman was mistaken, however. The judge was the only man in the whole city who didn't know one word of their quarrels. The old man was busy in preparing his leroa, and thought he was saving the world. He received them as he received every one usually, with kindness and politely.

"Show your tongues, my children!" said he; "I will prescribe for you this minute."

Both waved their hands in sign that they didn't want medicine. Miss Newman repeated, "Not that, not that!"

"What then?"

They interrupted each other. When Hans said a word the lady said ten. At last she fell upon the idea of pointing to her heart as a sign that Hans had offended her mortally.

"I understand! I understand now!" cried the doctor.

Then he opened his book and began to write. He asked Hans how old he was, — thirty-six. He asked the lady; she did n't remember exactly, — something about twenty-five. All right! What were their names? Hans, — Lora. All right! What was their occupation? They kept grocery. All right! Then other questions. Neither of them understood, but they answered yes. The doctor nodded. All was over.

He stopped writing, rose on a sudden, to the great astonishment of Lora put his arm around her waist and kissed her. She took this as a good omen, and went home full of rosy hopes.

On the road she said to Hans, "I 'll show you!"

"You 'll show some one else," said the German, calmly.

Next morning the sheriff passed in front of the groceries. The German man and woman were before their own doors. Hans was smoking his pipe, and Miss Newman was singing, —

"Dutchman, Dutchman, Du-u-u-u-tchman, Du-u-u-u-tchman!"

"Do you want to go to the justice?" asked the sheriff.

"We have been there."

"Well, and what?"

"My dear sheriff! My dear Mr. Davis!" cried Miss Newman, "go and find out. I just need some shoes; and speak a word for me to the justice. You see I am a poor, lone woman."

The sheriff went, and came back in a quarter of an hour. But it is unknown why he was surrounded by a crowd of people.

"Well, what? how was it?" both began to inquire.

"All is right," said the sheriff.

"Well, what did the justice do?"

"Well, what harm had he to do? He married you."

"Married!"

"Well, don't people marry?"

If a thunderbolt had burst on a sudden, Hans and Miss Newman would n't have been astonished to that degree. Hans stared, opened his mouth, hung out his tongue, and looked like a fool at Miss Newman; Miss Newman stared, opened her mouth, hung out her tongue, and looked like a fool at Hans. They were petrified. Then both screamed, —

"Am I to be his wife?"

"Am I to be her husband?"

"Murder! murder! Never! A divorce right away! I won't have a marriage!"

"No, it 's I that won't have it!"

"I 'll die first! murder! A divorce, a divorce!"

"My dears," said the sheriff, quietly, "what good will screaming do you? The judge marries, but the judge cannot divorce. What 's the use in screaming? Are you millionnaires from San Francisco, to get a divorce; or don't you know what that costs? Ai! What 's the use in screaming? I have nice children's shoes for sale cheap. Good-by!"

When he had said that he went away. The people too went away laughing; the newly married remained alone.

"That Frenchman," cried the married lady, "did this purposely, because we are Germans."

"Richtig [correct]," answered Hans.

"But we 'll go for a divorce."

"I first! You took me that *t* from the middle."

"No! I 'll go first! You caught me in the trap."

"I don't want you."

"I can't bear you."

They separated and closed their shops. She sat at

home thinking all day ; he sat at home. Night came. Night brought no rest ; neither could think of sleep. They lay down, but their eyes would not close. He thought, " My wife is sleeping over there ; " she, " My husband is sleeping over there." And some strange feeling rose in their hearts. It was hatred, anger, together with a feeling of loneliness. Besides, Hans began to think of the ape on his grocery. How keep it there when it was now a caricature of his wife ? It seemed to him that he had played a very ugly trick when he gave an order to paint the ape. But again that Miss Newman ! But he hates her ; through her his ice thawed ; he caught her during moonlight in a trap. Here again those outlines came to his mind, which he saw in the moonlight. " But, really, she is a brave girl," thought he. " But she can't stand me and I can't stand her. That's a position ! *Ach ! Herr Gott !* I am married. To whom ? To Miss Newman ! And here a divorce costs so much that the whole grocery would n't pay for it."

" I am the wife of that Dutchman," said Miss Newman to herself. " I 'm no longer a maiden, — that is, I mean to say single, — but married ! To whom ? To Kasche, who caught me in a trap. It is true that he took me up and brought me home. And how strong he is ! Just took me up. — What 's that ? Is there some noise here ? "

There was no noise whatever ; but Miss Newman began to be afraid, though up to that time she had never been afraid.

" But if he should dare now — O God — " Then she added, with a voice in which was heard a certain strange note of disappointment, " But he won't dare. He — "

With all that her fear increased. " That's always the way with a lone woman," thought she. " If there was a man in the house it would be safer. I've heard of murders in the neighborhood [Miss Newman had not heard of murders]. I swear that if they kill me here — Ah, that Kasche! that Kasche! has stopped my road. But it's necessary to take measures for a divorce."

Thinking thus she turned sleeplessly on her wide American bed, and really felt very lonely. She sprang up again suddenly. This time her fear had a real foundation. In the silence of night was heard distinctly the pounding of a hammer.

"Heaven!" cried Miss Newman, "they are breaking into my grocery!"

She sprang out of bed and ran to the window; but when she looked out she was at rest in a moment. By the light of the moon a ladder was visible, and on it the portly white figure of Hans drawing with a hammer the nails fastening the sign of the ape.

Miss Newman opened the window quietly.

"He is taking down the ape, — that is honorable on his part," thought she. And she felt all at once as if something were melting around her heart.

Hans drew out the nails one after another. The plate fell to the ground with a rattle; then he came down, took off the frame, folded up the plate in his strong hands, and began to remove the ladder.

Miss Newman followed him with her eyes. The night was quiet and warm.

"Herr Hans," called she, in a low voice.

"You are not sleeping?" answered Hans, in an equally low tone.

"No; good evening, Herr."

"Good evening."

"What are you doing?"

"Taking down the ape."

"Thank you, Herr Hans."

A moment of silence.

"Herr Hans," said the maiden again.

"What is it, Fraulein Lora?"

"We must arrange for the divorce."

"Yes."

"To-morrow?"

"To-morrow."

A moment of silence; the moon was laughing, the dogs not barking.

"Herr Hans!"

"What, Fräulein Lora?"

"I should like to have that divorce right away." Her voice had a melancholy tone.

"I too, Fräulein Lora." His voice was sad.

"So there should be no delay, you see."

"Better not delay."

"The sooner we talk the question over the better."

"The better, Fräulein Lora."

"Then we may talk it over right away."

"If you permit."

"Then come over here."

"Only let me dress."

"No need of ceremony."

The door below opened. Herr Hans vanished in the darkness, and after a while found himself in the young woman's chamber, which was quiet, warm, tidy. She wore a white dressing-gown, and was enchanting.

"I am listening to you," said Hans, with a broken, soft voice.

"But, you see, I should like very much to get a divorce, but — I am afraid somebody on the street will see us."

"But it is dark in the window," said Hans.

"Ah, that is true!" answered she.

Thereupon began a conversation concerning divorce which does not belong to this narrative.

Peace returned to Struck Oil City.

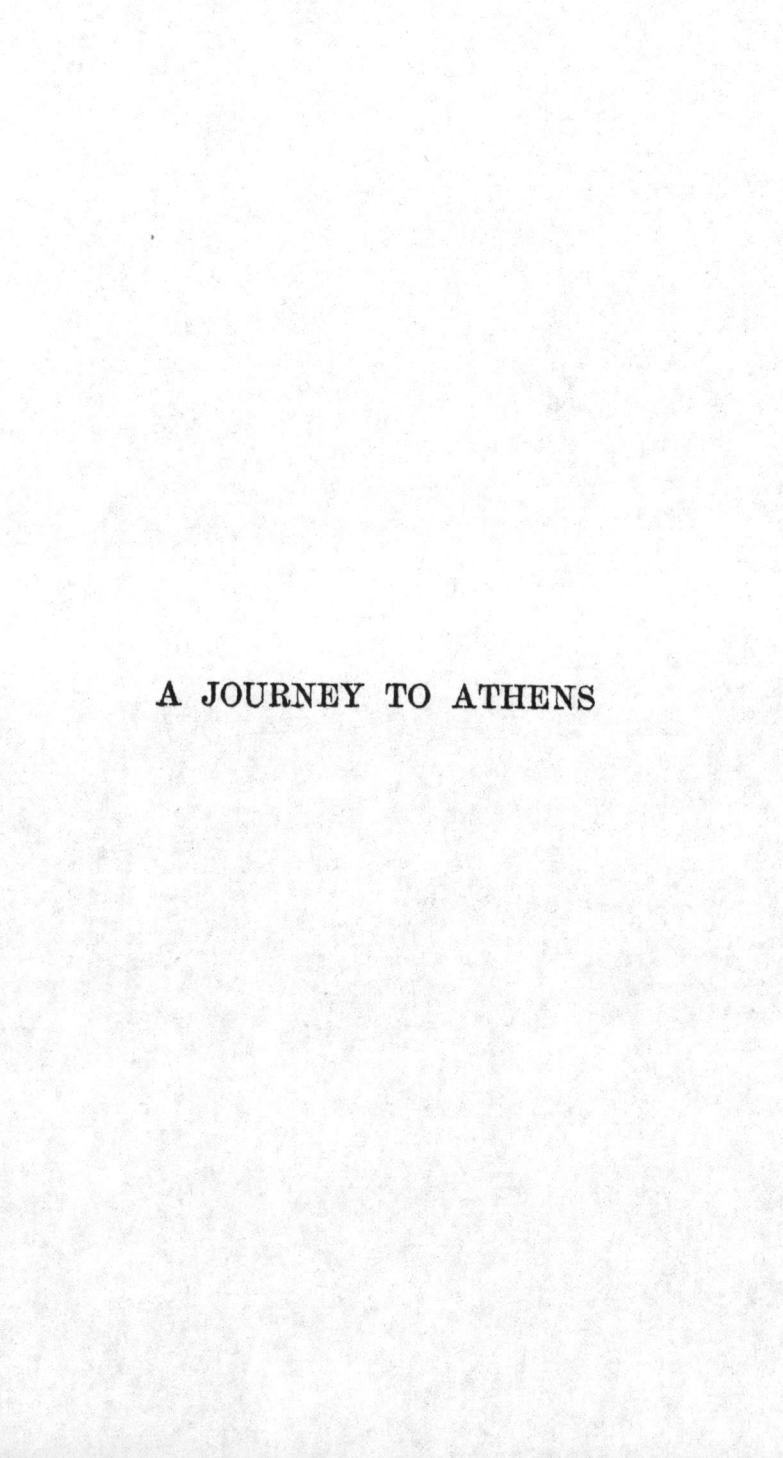

A JOURNEY TO ATHENS

A JOURNEY TO ATHENS.

IN leaving Stambul for Athens on the French steamer
Donnaı, I had before me the most beautiful view
which it is possible to have in the world. The sky,
rainy for a number of weeks, had at last become perfectly clear, and was reddened with a splendid evening.
The neighboring Asiatic shore was flooded with light;
the Bosphorus and Golden Horn looked like gigantic
ribbons of fire; Pera, Galata, Stambul, with their towers
and domes, and minarets of mosques, were sunk in purple
and gold.

The Donnaĭ turned her prow toward the Sea of Marmora and began to stir the water lightly, pushing with
care through the crowd of steamers, sailing vessels, small
boats, and kayuks. Constantinople is one of the best
anchoring places in Europe, and at the foot of this city,
which from its steep slopes rules over two seas, there is
another crowded city of ships. As over the first one
tower minarets, over the second tower masts, on these
masts is a rainbow of flags, and this lower city is not less
noisy than the other. Here, as well as there, is a mixture of tongues, races, complexions, garments. One sees
here all types of men who inhabit the adjoining three
parts of the earth, beginning with Englishmen, and ending with those half-savage dwellers of Asia Minor, who
have come to the capital to earn a morsel of bread, as
" kayukjis."

We passed the point on which stands the old Serai.

Pera, Galata, and Stambul began to merge into one terraced city, the borders of which the eye could not reach. Neither Naples nor any other place on earth can compare with that magnificent panorama. All descriptions, from those of Lamartine to those of De Amicis, are simply pale reflections of reality, for the words of men are but sound, hence unable to present to us either colors or those forms, now slender and aerial, now immense and tremendous. At times it seemed that a whole city of enchanted palaces was hanging in the air; then again I was under the impression of such majesty, greatness, and might, as if from that city terror were still going forth over Europe, and as if in the tower of the Seraskierat to-day, just as in past times, the fates of the world were in balance.

From the Sea of Marmora the naked eye could distinguish only the larger buildings, that is, the old Serai, a part of the walls of the Seven-towered Castle, Saint Sophia, Suleimanie, and the tower of the Seraskierat. The foundations of the city seemed to sink slowly; first the encircling walls hid themselves, then the lower rows of houses, then the higher, then the mosques and their domes. The city seemed to be drowning. It was growing dark in the sky, but on the arrow-like minarets the last ruddy and golden gleams were still falling. One might have said that they were a thousand gigantic torches burning above a city now invisible.

That is the hour in which the muezzins go out on the balconies of minarets and call the faithful to prayer, announcing to the four corners of the world that God is great and that God's night is coming down to us.

In fact night was coming, not only God's night, but a serene and a starry one. Night is a time for meditation; and because the fates of future peace or war are weighed really in the neighborhood of these straits, it is difficult to keep from political soothsaying. Still I will not occupy myself with it.

Let the daily papers do that work. Should future events give the lie to them, they will not be disgusted, I think, with their specialty. To me, as a novelist, comes a thought more literary in character, which, moreover, I throw out in parenthesis.

Well, it occurs to me that those gleams of the evening, those flaming waters, those palaces and minarets bathed in gold and purple, are something as real and actual as the dead dogs lying by tens on the streets of Stambul. But there are novelists of a certain school, especially those forming the gray end of it, who prefer the description of dead dogs, to the no less real sunsets, blue expanses of the sea, and other wonderful aspects of nature. Why is this? Of course there are various causes, but among them doubtless is this one, that to depict the beautiful in all its splendor a man needs more power and more colors on his palette than to depict the disgusting, and that in general it is easier to make a man's mouth water than to move his soul.

But I have no thought of raising a polemic, hence I touch these thing only in passing; now I shall follow the course of the steamer.

Mail steamers leaving Stambul in the evening are in the Dardanelles at dawn, with daylight they enter the Archipelago. We are in the Dardanelles then. Our steamer pushes forward between two shores lying close to each other; on those shores fortresses are visible and the black jaws of cannon which look forth from both sides at the straits. After a while we stop, for the steamer before issuing from that gorge must show papers and clear itself: whence has it come and whither is it

sailing ? The shores appear barren, covered with cliffs
which crumble, are ground fine and piled into stone
drifts. The whole landscape is melancholy and sterile,
though the sun is just rising and sculptures every outline beautifully. The straits themselves are narrower
than the Bosphorus, or even the Vistula. On the right
side the houses of Gallipoli stand out in whiteness ; their
squalor and misery is evident even from afar. And
again the question occurs to one, which in the East
occurs almost everywhere, — in Rustchuk, in Varna, in
Burgas, in Stambul itself : Are these the countries for
which human blood has been spilt in quantity sufficient
to fill the whole straits ? Is it for these half-ruined cities,
inhabited by semi-pauperous people, for those barren
plains and sterile cliffs, that millions are expended and
immense armies supported ; that the lives of generations
of people pass in uncertainty of the day and hour ? In
the Dardanelles more than in any place must a man
give himself this question. There are regions whose
main expression is wildness or melancholy ; but I have
never seen a landscape which said so clearly : I am age
and exhaustion ; I am abandonment and misery ! And
still in those straits lies the heart of the whole question.
It is not so much a question of the Bosphorus, or of
Tsargrad [1] itself, as it is of the Dardanelles. That narrow
shaft of water, that rocky corridor, is the one window and
also the door leading from regions behind to the world.

"Have you read of those cords," said to me a fellow-
traveller, an Englishman, "which the Sultans used to
send on a time to Grand Viziers, or unsuccessful com-
manders ? These straits are such cords ; it is possible to
choke the Black Sea with them, and even Constantinople
itself."

[1] Constantinople, the Tsar's city.

Meanwhile we sailed out into the Archipelago, to that famous sea which the ancient Greeks called a picture of the heavens, for it is dotted with islands as the heavens are dotted with stars. It is for this reason likely that they named it Arch-sea. Soon we saw the cliffs of Lemnos in front of us, the first island that is seen after issuing from the Dardanelles. Nothing in the north is delineated with definiteness equal to that of pearly Imbros; on the other side, nearer the Asiatic shore, stands Tenedos, on which the standard of the Prophet still waves, but above the whole Archipelago floats the soul of ancient Greece, with its songs and traditions. Under the influence of such memories, perhaps, these shores seem somehow different from all others which we see before coming here, and they answer to the outlines in which imagination paints the Grecian shores. Everything visible is naked, barren, just as it is near the Dardanelles, — neither tree nor human habitation; the region is gray olive in color, as if sunburnt and faded, but extended in long and bold direct lines like the prototypes of Doric architecture. One hill rears itself above another; here and there the peak of some height peers up, hardly visible in the blue curtain of distance; farther on, the background is entirely concealed. Above all is a simple and dignified melancholy. Once, according to tradition, the hammers of Hephaistos pounded in the volcano of Lemnos. Perhaps it was here that he forged the famous shield of Achilles ? To-day the crater of Mosychlos is silent, for the volcano is extinct; tradition has outlived the volcano and even the god.

On the right and the left appear islands continually; with the enumeration of these I shall not trouble the memory or attention of any man. The eye sees farther on the Archipelago than on other European waters.

Even the remotest islands are seen so clearly and definitely that one may distinguish almost every fissure in the rocks, and plants covering the brinks of precipices. So much light is poured down to the earth from the heavens here, that Italy itself can give no idea of it. The sea and the sky are not merely blue, they are luminous. In other lands, the sun seems to scorch and to shine; here, it penetrates the whole landscape, soaks in, permeates, coalesces with it, excluding absolutely every shadow. Therefore, nothing is defined here so sharply as on the shores of the Mediterranean for example. Every outline on which the eye rests is immensely expressive, and still mild, for it is embraced by a single tone which is very clear and also tender.

The Arch-sea is not always calm. Those same whirlwinds which bore the ship of Odysseus to the Cyclops rush on at times among the islands in the guise of wild horses; the waves thunder and hurl snow-white foam to the summits of cliffs on the shore. But at the moment of which I am speaking, the blue expanse was as smooth as a mirror, and only after the ship came a broad foaming pathway. There was not the least breeze during daylight. The steamer advanced as if on a lake, so the deck was swarming with passengers. There was no lack even of elegant toilets, for the women of Athens like, more than other daughters of Eve, to wear their best on every occasion.

That assembly on deck lasted till late in the evening. The Greeks form acquaintance easily, to gratify their love of talk, perhaps. Their politeness is even too effusive for sincerity. In general, they boast immeasurably, not only of their ancient but their present civilization. From moment to moment they enumerate to strangers Greek celebrities of the day, scientific and artistic, known loudly as it were in all Europe; and they are astonished if any one has not heard of them. This or that painter with his latest picture has destroyed Gérôme utterly; this or that scientist inoculated for hydrophobia years earlier than Pasteur, which, speaking in parenthesis, is the more wonderful as there is no hydrophobia in southern countries. One might think, while hearing them, that as God once acted solely through the Franks, so now He makes use of the Greeks with far greater effectiveness. If anything of prime importance happens in the world, search carefully, and thou wilt find a Greek there.

Night in the Archipelago is as beautiful as the day. Such nights Homer called "ambrosial." The bases of the islands are wrapped in mist the most delicate; the moon whitens the summits of the mountains; but not the least cloud is visible on the sky, and the whole sea is covered with silvery trails, — the widest made by the moon, others by stars. That phenomenon is unknown in the North; but more than once in Southern seas I have seen those silver trails, or rather stripes, playing from the stars on the water.

We are sailing amid such silence that every turn of the screw is heard. On the horizon we see a number of ships, or rather their lanterns, which seem from afar like many colored swaying points suspended in the atmosphere.

These ships for the greater part are making, as we are, for the Piræus, where they will be at daylight. At the first dawn in fact the screw ceases to roar and that sudden silence rouses all passengers We dress; we hurry to the deck, — the Piræus, Attica.

I suppose that the most callous of visitors must stand on this soil with a certain emotion, face to face with Athens. Envoys once carried to the Pope the great banner of all Islam taken at Vienna, and asked relics in return for it. "You have no need to seek relics," replied the Pope; "take a handful of your own earth, it is soaked in the blood of martyrs." So we may say in like manner of the soil of Attica: every handful of it is penetrated with Grecian thought and Grecian art. You will recall, surely, "the mothers" in the second part of Faust, those prototypes and first patterns of everything existing beyond the world and space, so majestic in their indefinite loneliness that they are terrible. Attica, while neither indefinite nor terrible, is the intellectual mother of all who are civilized. Without her, it is unknown where we might be at present, or what we might have become. Attica is the sun of the ancient world; and after its historical setting there remained so mighty an effulgence behind, that from it came the Renaissance or rebirth after the darkness of the Middle Ages. I say, Attica, and not Greece, for Attica was to Hellas what Hellas was to the world. In one word, when we enter that land we are at the source. Other civilizations on the neighboring shores of Africa and Asia, among other races of people, were developed into monsters; Grecian civilization alone remained human. Others were lost in phantasms; it was unique in this that it took the existent world as the basis for art and science, and was able from elements purely actual to develop the loftiest harmony; a harmony truly divine. Greece had the mind to be godlike without ceasing to be human, and this explains her significance.

At the moment when we touched Grecian soil "rosy fingered Aurora" was entering the sky. From the Piræus to Athens one may go by rail, but it is incomparably better to take a carriage and see accurately everything which may be seen in half an hour on the way. The road from the Piræus is occupied on both sides by sycamores; it passes through the so-called plain of Attica, which the Cephissus waters, or, rather, might water. Every name here rouses an echo in the memory and an historical reminiscence. Were it not for this, the Cephissus would rouse no very great regard; for as there are bridges in Poland which do not exist, so the Cephissus is a non-existent river; this means that in the parched and burnt bed of it not one drop of water is flowing. The plain is narrow. On the left hand, in the direction of the Bay of Eleusis, we see the mountains of Daphne and the Poikilon; on the right is honey-bearing Hymettus, and Pentelicus, which to-day, as in old times, furnishes Athenians with marble. The country seems sun-parched, empty, sterile. The fields, mountains, and cliffs have an ashen hue, immeasurably delicate, with a tinge somewhat bluish. This is a color into which all others merge in Greece; and it predominates everywhere, on the islands as well as the mainland.

Half-way on the road, the olive grove also seems covered with light ashes. Above everything is a cloudless, azure sky, not so deep a blue as in Italy, but, as I have stated, more radiant a hundred times. The earth is as if rent. The rocks crumble, turn to dust, and are scattered. This gives the whole region an aspect of ruin and desertion. But this aspect becomes it. Silence, decrepitude, sleepy olive-trees, and barren cliffs befit its complexion.

The main road passes the railway station which stands at the end of Hermes Street; but near the city our carriage turns to the right, and we enter the boulevard, which is lined on both sides with pepper-trees. Then on a steep cliff we see a row of columns of pale-gold color joined by battered architraves. All this is ruddy from the morning light, and is outlined against the sky with indescribable sweetness and purity, not too large in its proportions, great beyond every estimate in its repose, in its harmony, simply godlike.

The dragoman, sitting with the driver, turns and says, —

"The Acropolis."

Nearer the cliff, on the Ceramicus, is the temple of Theseus, relatively the best preserved monument of antiquity. Afterward, at every step, there are fragments: Pelasgic walls, the rock of the Pnyx, the prison of Socrates, and other grottos, looking out from amid their rocks through dark openings into daylight. At the foot of the cliff itself, the edge of the precipice hides the lines of the Parthenon; but one sees the whole disorder of the ruins of the Odeon of Herod, and the theatre of Bacchus. The eye runs from one fragment to another; the imagination labors, striving to reconstruct vanished life; the mind cannot embrace everything, and a man limits himself involuntarily to the simple acceptance of impressions. But you feel that it was worth while to come here, that this is not a hurried look at ruins, "Baedecker" in hand, and the desire in your soul of getting back to the hotel at the earliest. But the carriage passes those half divine rocks too quickly, and soon we are in the new city, modern Athens.

Let us speak of it before we go back to the Acropolis.

I had come prepared for Eastern filth, — the filth of Stambul, which conquers the nerves of an average person. I was most agreeably disappointed. First, it is not true that in Athens one sees only as much green as there is salad served at dinner. It may be that just because there is little of it in the country, the city has made an effort to shade streets and squares with trees. I entered the city near the Acropolis and the temple of Olympian Zeus, by the Panhellenic Boulevard, which is one strip of verdure. The pepper-trees, with bright-green, delicate leaves, call to mind weeping willows, and give this street the look of spring-time, of May. Everywhere one sees pleasure-grounds, in them palm-trees, black oaks, cactuses, and aloes. It is true that all these are covered with a gray dust coming from rocks and ruins, as if those dead remnants wished to say to every living being: "Dust thou art, and unto dust thou shalt return;" but, at present, shade and coolness may be found everywhere in Athens. The chief streets of the city are broad; the houses are large, of dazzling whiteness, the richer ones faced with marble obtained from the naked flanks of Pentelicus. Those buildings are not devoid of charm and elegance. The king's palace forms the exception. Its walls are of Pentelicus marble also, but the style heavy, like that of barracks, renders this residence not only no ornament to the grand square of the Constitution, but a deformity. As a recompense, behind the palace, and at one side of it, are the really splendid gardens of the king; but in front of the palace lies a genuine, gray, burning desert which extends to the chief public gardens of the city. So that nothing might spoil the impression of a desert, there are a few large palms in it, lofty, and delineated firmly in the middle of the barrenness. Add an Arab with a camel, and you might think yourself in Egypt. For the rest, the city is bright, clean, out and out European, but built (this we can understand easily) under the influence and on the model of the ancient architecture of Greece, which gives it a splendid aspect. Everywhere one sees Doric, Ionic, and Corinthian columns, friezes which man began to carve and which the sun has finished. The University, and especially the Academy of Fine Arts, has the splendid and harmonious forms of a Greek temple.

At the side of the portico stand two mighty columns

of the marble of Pentelicus with gilded abaci. On one of
them stands the gigantic Pallas Athene, with a helmet on
her head and a spear in her hand; on the other, an
immense Apollo with a phorminx. In the night, by
moonlight, these marbles seem bright green, and so charmingly light that they appear not to weigh on the earth.
Perhaps a specialist in architecture might object this and
that to those buildings; but in every case, they are a
decoration to the city, and one of the most beautiful
which it has happened me to see.

The richest part of Athens is nearest the square of the
Constitution and the palace of the king, then the Pan-
hellenic Boulevard, the University Boulevard, Stadin
Street, and many others adjoining, up to the Square of
Concord. These streets were laid out by rich Greeks,
living some in the Phanar of Stambul, some in Odessa,
Marseilles, and other seaport cities.

These people, with the inborn Greek genius for traffic,
accumulated millions; but, we should do them justice in
this, they have not bartered away the Greek spirit. A
money-changer of Marseilles or Odessa who might claim
descent from Miltiades, appeal to Marathon, Leonidas,
Thermopylæ, Themistocles, Salamis, Phidias, or Apelles,
and turn to the ruins of the Acropolis, had that which
no money in the world could purchase. And because of that claim, because of the glorious past, millions
from all lands flowed into Attica; amid its wild defiles
appeared macadamized roads and railways; in cities
inhabited by half-savage palicars, schools were founded;
and on the ruins of ancient Athens rose the Athens of
our day.

Merchants and traders at present are established mainly
on Hermes Street. Hermes, as we know, was the patron
of merchants when Zeus was in power. In general, the

whole lower part of the city, toward Gara and the Ceramicus, was under his patronage. Here is situated the bazaar, which calls to mind other Eastern bazaars; here a vivacious population swarm in great numbers, gesticulating and talking as loudly as if they intended to stun passers-by. Life and trade are on the street here, as everywhere in Southern cities; in the evening, when the heat of the day has passed, movement is greatest. The shops are open till late. Flaming jets of gas illuminate exhibitions of goods, splendid fruits, and flowers.

From four in the afternoon, not only Hermes Street and the business part of the city is swarming with people, but they fill also the wealthy divisions. Stadin Street, on which I lodged, is a fashionable promenade, in the forenoon it was difficult to pass on the sidewalks, and in the middle of the street carriages followed each other closely. There were fewer women present than men, especially among pedestrians. Perhaps this is a remnant of Oriental influence, or perhaps the custom of hiding women at home began and was fixed during Turkish rule, since it was not over safe for young women to show themselves before beys and bimbashis. There are few beautiful faces among the women. The type is less Greek than Armenian. The days of Phryne and Lais are far distant, and no Areopagus now would declare a Greek woman innocent because of her beauty. I have read that the inhabitants of Megara and ancient Laconia, as well as some of the islands, have preserved the ancient type still; but in Megara I have not found it, and I have not been on the banks of the Eurotas, or on the islands.

Among men there are many at once beautiful and wild looking. It is certain that the bright-haired Achilles must have looked otherwise; but Canaris might have resembled these. Many, too, wear yet the Albanian costume, composed of pustanelli, that is, a white skirt reaching almost to the knees, a fez, and a jacket embroidered with silk or gold. The loins are encircled by a belt, behind which was thrust formerly a whole arsenal of pistols and daggers, where to-day they carry handkerchiefs. In spite of the handkerchief, which, in comparison with past times, is undeniably a progress, they are inveterate conservatives and hostile to Western influence.

But one meets men in ancient costume, mainly among the aged. Still, whole divisions of the army are uniformed after the fashion of the palicars, and this gives Athens an appearance different from other cities.

Rural Greeks, despite robber instincts, which, as it seems, have not died out yet in all places, are perhaps honest, industrious, and faithful to their duties; yet city dwellers have the world over a fixed reputation which is far from favorable. As I passed not quite a month in the midst of them, I cannot judge from my own observation. But even in that brief stay one might observe that in no other city do merchants, hotel-keepers, guides, liverymen, and money-changers speak so much of their own honesty as in Athens. This seems a trifle suspicious.

More recent travellers, who have either spent a longer time in Greece, or who after a short stay have had the boldness to give a decisive opinion, make unfavorable mention of Greeks in general.

Edmond About, who died recently, wrote a book which is shallow, but curious, and full of witty remarks touching Greece. But the malicious "grandson of Voltaire," as he has been nicknamed, despite this, that he strives to be impartial, judges the descendants of the ancient Demos of Athens too sneeringly. According to him, the Greeks of to-day, in capacity for lying, might put their ancestor Ulysses to shame, as well as Pallas Athene, his patroness, and also the ancient Cretans, who, according to Epimenides, surpassed all men in this art. Besides, they are greedy beyond every expression; people of other nationalities they endure in so far as they can plunder them. As to bravery, Canaris, according to About, was exceptional, hence they made such an outcry concerning him; but the Greeks if considered in general are cowardly. About goes so far even as to state that they have been so at all times, even during the siege of Troy; that they lack knightly feeling, the appreciation of a good cause, and of justice; that they show a blind respect for power of all kinds, and a corresponding contempt for weakness, misfortune, and poverty.

Among thousands of anecdotes About cites one which I may be permitted to repeat, as it concerns us Poles more nearly.

After the storms in 1848, which shook the dynasty of the Hapsburgs, a handful of Poles settled in Athens. Some died of hunger and fever, for the climate of Athens, if they stay in it long, is injurious to foreigners. But even the slight means afforded the Poles was as salt in the eyes of the Greeks. At every step they insulted those refugees. They challenged them to duels; but the Poles acted prudently, and did not accept. Once a fire broke out in Athens, and threatened the whole city. The Greeks hurried together from all sides to look at the burning, gesticulate, and shout. The Poles (I beg to remember that I am quoting About) rushed into the flames and extinguished them with great peril to themselves. And now let any one guess what reward they received.

Well, command was given them to leave Greece!

The Greeks acted thus because after this deed the

Poles were celebrated at the expense of the Greeks, and because news of their exploit, hence of their presence in Athens, passed around Europe, and might attract later attention, and perhaps, too, a diplomatic note from the government of Austria, at that time exceedingly unfavorable to the refugees.

And that reason sufficed.

If About's account be a true one, and he was not our friend to such a degree as to invent tales to glorify us, it must be confessed that the descendants of the father of logic have not ceased, it is true, to be as logical as the Stagirite himself; but the traditions of Aristides have perished forever among them.

Still in that which is stated by the above-mentioned author, and by others more recent, concerning the Greeks, there must be undoubtedly many exaggerations, and perhaps misunderstandings in still greater number. Above all, such travellers bring with them a ready-made ethical standard which is very broad, being the result of Western civilization and its elaborate moral culture. With this scale, they measure a society which only in recent times freed itself from a bondage which was really debasing and shameful, and with a standard the more absolute because it is applied to foreigners, not to themselves. These men forget also this, that as, for instance, the conception of honor and knightliness was foreign to Antiquity, a whole sphere of moral conceptions may exist which is foreign to Orientals; those people, especially conquered ones, as were the Greeks, had, to speak strictly, no conception for a long time, and had to govern themselves solely by the animal instinct of self-preservation. That instinct was for them tone-giving, and decided equally questions of ethics and logic.

Savage people are the same everywhere. Once when

a missionary asked a negro converted by him to give a case of what to his thinking evil was, the savage meditated a while, and answered, —

"Evil is if some one steals my wife."

"Exactly!" said the delighted missionary. "And now give me a case of good."

The savage did not hesitate a moment, —

"Good is if I steal somebody else's wife."

Here is the logic of people who are savage, who have fallen into savagery, or who are becoming savage. It is also universal enough in the Orient.

But let us give peace to the Greeks. I have quoted Peschl's old anecdote because there is a logic contained in it, which we hear more and more, both in private and public. It thunders increasingly everywhere; it appears in the columns of daily papers; it swells like a wave; it drowns every day the difference between good and evil, between justice and injustice; it paralyzes the capacity of taking moral bearings in the mazes of public life, it destroys and brings to utter ruin the moral sense of public opinion, which at last knows not, and cares not to know, whom it should favor and whom it should execrate. The present world is not savage, but perhaps in a sense it is growing so.

About wrote his book thirty years ago. Greeks of the present generation would not act as did his contemporaries. They would not, because they are growing civilized in a good sense, for they are regenerated; youthful, enthusiastic, they work, they develop and perfect gradually all their spiritual capacities, hence among others the moral sense. Equilibrium among them is not destroyed yet. To be precise, they are ceasing to be savage, instead of becoming so; hence, they have shame in their eyes

Besides they have patriotism, one great quality which none will deny them.

This patriotism rests on love for ancient Hellas, as well as for Hellas of our day.

Though the thread of tradition was woven somewhat artificially; though scholars declare that the Greeks of to-day have in their veins hardly a small drop of the blood of the ancient Hellenes, and are pre-eminently a mixture of former slaves of various origins, Albanians and Slavs, — they, as heirs of the land, wish to be, and are, inheritors also of its traditions. For this reason, their patriotism is not like a plant which grasps only the surface, and which the first wind may tear out; but it has grown into the earth, and possesses immovable power. It possesses that power for this special cause, that it is historical, and wishes to go into the future with progress, but it knows that the ever-pulsating source and the reason of its existence is on the Acropolis. So we, too, will go to the Acropolis, for the source there is of this sort, that each of us can draw artistic impressions at least from it.

The whole plain of Attica is so small, and all things are so near one another, that travellers on steamers which stop at the Piræus only six hours have time to visit Athens, examine the sacred cliff, the Olympian, the temple of Theseus, the ruins surrounded by the new city, the ancient cemetery of the Hagia Trias, the museum, and return in time for sailing. All the more had I time therefore and opportunity not for scientific research, but for a minute examination, since I stayed about three weeks in Athens itself. But certainly it is easier to go from the square of the Constitution to the Acropolis, than to describe the Acropolis. Besides my labor moves by another road; I am not a Hellenist, so I prefer to give merely an account of impressions, and not describe minutely remains concerning which whole volumes have been written, — the fruit of difficult labor continued through long years.

We go up by a serpentine path overgrown by agaves and cactuses. Before and above us, we see merely a gigantic, gray, crumbling wall, which is only in part an Hellenic inheritance, some of it was reared by the Latins, and some by the Turks even. From behind this wall looks forth the three-cornered summits and the out-jutting architraves of the temples. It is empty when I go in, not a living soul present, for it is an afternoon hour, and the air burning, though in the first days of November. At a side gate an old veteran is slumbering; we pass him, go by a house where piles of marble fragments are heaped up. The road winds once more; we enter by steps ascending the hill, and are in the Propylæa, through which we embrace with the eye all the platform on the summit. The first impression is ruin! ruin! silence, death! Some external Doric and internal Ionic columns of the Propylæa are pushed apart, and are held in place only by the weight of rocks; the walls are split, dented, show the light through them, are broken round about; nowhere behind that glorious gate is there an ell of unoccupied earth. Scattered over the whole space on the flat summit, and piled on it, are the bases of columns, the remnants of architraves and friezes, the fragments of metopes, capitals, and facing stones. All this, except a few temples, thrown one on the other, hanging, bent, falling, piled up, lying in a wild disorder of which even the Roman Forum can give no idea. It occurs to the traveller that here must have happened some terrible battle of giants, or gigantic powers, from which the mountain split, the walls burst, and finally everything fell, and there remained only destruction.

So the first impression that we obtain on passing the Propylæa is the impression of a catastrophe.

The advance is silent; for everything around us is so perfectly dead that our own animation, our own movement, seems to us strange and inappropriate in those places.

Were we to meet an acquaintance, we should prefer not to speak to him, but merely to look him in the eyes inquiringly, pass on, sit down in the shade somewhere, and see how the sun bathes the ruins in light.

For, as I have said, light in this country does not fall, but at this hour, especially, it pours in a torrent. And it might seem that these burning, living springs of light weaken the impression of ruin, of destruction and deathly silence. But no! Ruin and destruction find only greater expression by means of them, — expression almost absolute.

So we sit and look at that stone mountain, on the bright marbles of the Parthenon and the Erechtheum, bathed in sunlight, until finally something rises out of the ruins and enters us. We begin to be in harmony with that world, and later to fraternize with it. Then we feel well; for an immense repose enters us, a repose great as stones and ruins can possibly have.

This repose and the repose of the traveller become one. I suppose that the more pained a man's soul is, the better he feels in those ruins. He would like to rest his head against the pilaster of a column, close and open his eyes in succession, and nestle there. One feels more and more at home; the wanderer looks with more and more friendliness on those extended lines of the Parthenon, on the white Erechtheum, and on the Propylæa lying lower. But one must see them to understand how those buildings, pale golden in color from age, are outlined in the sun and the blue; one must see them to understand the repose of those architraves, of those rows of columns and facades! Simplicity, repose, dignity, and true divine order, — there they are. It is difficult to see this immediately; the charm acts by degrees; but all the more mightily does it penetrate, and at last it intoxicates. And thou, O wanderer, wilt recognize that these masterpieces have given thee not only repose, but they have ravished thee with their beauty, and with that which goes with it, their sweetness.

These are the successive impressions through which a man passes on the Acropolis. When one is on the spot, these impressions are so powerful that it would come to no man's head to open a printed guide and look in it for details. Once at home, you will read that the temple Niké Apteros (Wingless Victory) was not long since raised up from its own ruins; that Lord Elgin took to the British Museum one of the marvellous caryatids supporting the right portico of the Erechtheum; and that thither also wandered the metopes of the Parthenon; that an explosion of Turkish powder caused the ruin of all the central part of that temple; that copies of the metopes may be seen in the museum on this cliff; and that pashas had their harems in the Erechtheum.

At the first moment it is all one to you that the Parthenon is built in a style purely Doric; that the Erechtheum and Niké Apteros are Ionic; and that in the Propylæa are columns of both styles. You knew that before you came to Athens. Here the universal spirit, or rather the genius of ancient Hellas, breathes on you first of all, and that breath you have no wish to ward off or analyze.

And soon the imagination begins to work, then it represents to itself that Acropolis in the days of Pericles, when everything stood in its own place, when there were temples of which there are no traces at present, and

36

when among them there was a forest of statues; when the Parthenon was not stripped of its ornaments; when from below it was possible to see on its front the birth of Athene, and on the other façade her dispute with Poseidon, and the spear of Athene Promachos was visible from the sea. Let us imagine to ourselves especially a Panathenic procession, — priests, archons, warriors, musicians, people, bulls with gilded horns led to the altars of the opisthodomos, garlands of flowers, and that classical drapery with statuesque folds. But I almost prefer to represent to myself in thought the night of that time, and the pale greenish light of the moon on the marbles, till it is difficult to believe that a people could create such a mountain of masterpieces; and still we may explain it. Grecian mythology was a worship of the powers of nature, or elemental Pantheism. But in the soul of the Greek, the artist preponderated always above the philosopher; so poets first of all arrayed phenomena in human bodies and feelings, later came plastic art, and thus rose those marvellous stone fables.

Athene knew how to choose a place for her capital; what a background was that for those temples and statues! On one side the sea, which in that transparent atmosphere seemed right before you; on the other, all Attica, like something on the palm of the hand, the hill of Hymettus, farther the Pentelicus; on the north, Parnassus; and southward, toward the straits of Salamis, Daphne. Overhead a sky ever serene, and eagles whose calls break to this day the silence on the Acropolis.

Our impressions at sight of other ruins are merely a fainter reflex of thoughts and feelings born in the soul at sight of those remnants on the Acropolis The works of Mnesicles, Ictinus and Callicrates were not equalled by any one either before Pericles or after him. They created

not only the Parthenon, the Erechtheum, and the Propylæa, but they established the architectural dogma which
thenceforth was to be accepted by all architects of antiquity. The Romans will permit themselves to add their
own arch ; they will rear Colosseums, Baths, Circuses,
and circular temples like the Pantheon of Agrippa, but
that is all. In other respects they will follow in the
footsteps of those immortal predecessors and not fall
away from the dogma. They can only exaggerate the
masterpieces of the Acropolis through size, and they do
that even in Athens itself.

Below the Acropolis, east of the cliff, the Romans
erected near the river Ilissus a temple to Olympian Zeus,
completed only during the time of the Emperor Hadrian.
To-day, of the hundred and twenty columns which composed it, there remain only sixteen, thirteen at one end,
and three at the other. These columns, purely Corinthian, are six feet in diameter and sixty feet high. That
was the largest temple on the plain watered by the
Cephissus and the Ilissus. Titus Livius, mentioning it,
declares that in dimensions it was the only temple worthy
of the majesty of the god to whom it was dedicated :
Unum in terris inchoatum pro magnitudine dei. And
perhaps Zeus, as the father of Athene and the mightiest
of the gods, deserved the largest temple ; but Athene, the
patroness of Athens, was also the goddess of wisdom, so
Zeus could only have, in gigantic form, the reflection from
prototypes and originals born directly of thoughts inspired
by the " owl-eyed " divinity.

It does not follow in the least from this that I consider
the creators of the temples of the Acropolis as the in-
ventors of the Grecian orders of architecture. I say only,
that they settled the rules ; for they knew how to give its
final and loftiest expression to Grecian architecture, as

Phidias in his time gave the highest expression to its sculpture. But the temple of Theseus, resembling the Parthenon on a smaller scale, was built before the Parthenon, as were surely many others of which only single columns remain here and there to us. That temple of Theseus is the best preserved remnant of the past. There was a fortress on the Acropolis, so the edifices which stood there were exposed to every blow of war, and in modern times to bombardment. The temple of Theseus was in the middle of the city. It was exposed mainly to internal changes, for from being a pagan temple it was modified into a Christian church. The internal columns of the pronaos were thrown down, and in place of them was erected a half-circular niche, in which an altar was placed; a large gate was opened in the wall, separating the cella from the opisthodomos, and evidently all the statues were thrown out of the interior of the temple, where to-day are seen only four naked walls. Light reaches with difficulty the interior, which is turned into a kind of museum; for there are set up in it either plaster of Paris copies or fragments of sculpture which adorned the temple in old times. As I have said, it recalls the Parthenon, but since it stands on level ground it does not produce that imposing impression, especially since its dimensions are much smaller. The Parthenon had seventeen columns at its sides; the temple of Theseus only thirteen, and they were much smaller. The Parthenon had eight columns at its ends; the temple of Theseus six. Finally, it was much less ornamented; for Phidias filled both façades of the temple on the Acropolis with statues, and all the metopes with sculptures in relief. The temple of Theseus had only frieze on the external wall of the cella, and metopes only on the eastern façade, covered with sculpture in relief, representing the exploits of Theseus accomplished through the aid of Heracles. The eastern façade had also sculpture, of which nothing is left.

But these are details which would have value only if I were to add to them at least drawings of these edifices. The temple of Theseus is interesting for this, that it is well preserved and gives us the most accurate idea of Doric architecture, which is at once so dignified and so full of repose. It stands on a broad square on which there is neither a tree nor a grass-blade; hence its columns, pale gold color from age, stand with a certain melancholy charm on that gray background.

From this square the rocks of the Pnyx are visible. The Pnyx was a meeting place once for multitudes. Stone steps hewn out in the rocks indicate the way where men passed to the upper terrace, from which Athens was seen below the spectator's feet. On the right hand was the Museum, directly in front the Acropolis. There are no buildings whatever at the Pnyx now, there are only traces of a gigantic tribune, called in antiquity the Bema, where people sat during deliberations. The rocks are stripped entirely of vegetation; they stand there eternally naked; I met no living soul on them. The noise of the city does not reach that far; the scream of eagles alone breaks the silence. A verse of Slovatski now occurred to me.

> "Here on the stones the breeze struggles
> With the work of Arachne and rends her web.
> Here is the odor of sad slopes, of parched mountains.
> Here the wind, when it has run around the gray pile of ruins,
> Blows over it the down of flowers,
> That down, advancing, flies among the tombs like spirits."

Not so silent, but equally desolate, is the Areopagus, situated near the cliff of the Acropolis. Besides the locality which tradition makes sacred, and the deep fissures in the rocks which are filled with refuse, there is nothing to be seen there.

In the city itself, and in its environs, are some remains which deserve attention, such as the Stoa of Hadrian, the Stoa of Attalus, the Tower of Winds, the little chapel of Lysicrates, the arch of Hadrian, and the monument of Philopappos; finally, the cemetery of the Hagia Trias, opened not long since, in which may be seen a number of beautiful, even very beautiful, monuments. But I shall not try to describe ruins. I have given an account merely of impressions which I received mainly on the Acropolis, which appeals most forcibly to the soul, for it contains all that Hellenic civilization has given of the most beautiful in plastic art, and she gave this with the whole power of Grecian genius. Surely Thucydides had the Acropolis in mind when he said that had Athens succumbed to a catastrophe, mankind would think from the ruins left behind by her that she was a city twofold more powerful than she was in reality. But Athens was four times more powerful than Thucydides imagined. Now the ancient city has succumbed to disaster, and is lying in ruins; but the genius of Athens created too much to let humanity forget what it owes to her. The debt was forgotten too long; but duties like that bind the memory as well as the conscience. Thanks to these feelings, this glorious land was snatched from the Turk. Not political interest alone commanded the resurrection of Greece; that was a debt which Europe had to pay, it was a question of shame simply. There are questions which the most dissolute conscience is unable to tolerate; and because of that a moment came when cannon roared at Navarino. But we may be sure that had it not been for the immense balance with which civilization had credited

Greece, had it not been for her glory and her deeds, had it not been for the poetry of Homer, for the memories of Marathon and Salamis, for those remains of the Acropolis masterpieces, pashas might have their harems yet in the Erechtheum, and the banner of the Prophet might be waving to-day from the summit of the Acropolis. So if we say that modern Greece was raised up by Homer, Miltiades, Leonidas, Themistocles, Phidias, Pericles, and other heroes or geniuses of similar stature, it will not be a figure of rhetoric, but a truth in history. While toiling for the glory of their people, they toiled, without knowing it, for their resurrection; and those immortal agents have made Greece a living fact at this moment.

ZOLA.

("DOCTOR PASCAL.")

ZOLA.

("DOCTOR PASCAL.")

YOU wish me to declare what I think of Zola's "Doctor Pascal," and in general of the whole "Rougon-Macquart" cycle. Perhaps because I come of a society in which so much power is wasted, every planned and completed work fills me with real respect, and has for me also some wonderful and exceptional charm. Whenever I write "The End" at the close of any work of mine, I feel something like a sensation of delight, not only because the labor is done, not only because of the possible success of the book, but also because of the sensation which comes of finished work. Every book is a deed, good or evil, but a deed that is done. A whole series of books, especially when written in the name of one leading idea, is a life task accomplished; it is a harvest-home festival at which the leader of the workmen has earned the right to a garland and the song, "I bring fruit, I bring fruit!"

But evidently the character of the service depends on the fruit. The career of a writer has difficulties of which readers do not even dream. The land-tiller who draws grain sheaves to his barn has this perfect certainty, that he is bringing in wheat, barley, buckwheat, or rye which will go to support people's health. An author, writing even in the very best faith, may have moments of doubt: Has he been giving poison instead of bread? Is not his work one great mistake, one great fault? Has it done good? Would it not have been better for men and for him if he had done nothing, if he had written nothing, if he had remained idle ?

Doubts are the enemy of human peace, but they are also a filter which lets no foul sediment pass. It is bad to have too many doubts, bad to have too few; in the first case, power of action is lost; in the second, conscience. Hence the need of an external regulator, — a need as old as humanity.

But French writers have ever distinguished themselves by a boldness incomparably greater than that of other authors; hence that regulator which in some countries has been religion has ceased long since to exist for them. Exceptions have appeared, it is true. Balzac asserted that his task was to serve religion and the monarchy. But even the works of those who proclaimed such principles were not always in accord with the principles. It might have been said that it suited authors to understand their activity in that way; but the reading public could understand it, and often did understand it, to be a negation of social, religious, and ethical principles. In the most recent epoch, however, such misunderstandings have become impossible, for authors began to appear openly, either in the name of their own personal convictions, which reckoned with nothing and were directly opposed to the bases and bonds of society, or with objective analysis, which in the examination of life notes good and evil as phenomena equally inevitable and equally justifiable. France, and through France the rest of Europe, was flooded with a deluge of books written so frivolously, freely, and offensively, books with no trace in them of a feeling of responsibility to mankind, that even those who took them up, also without scruple, were soon astounded. It seemed that every author had set out with the intent to go even farther than had been expected of him. In this way men acquired the reputation of daring thinkers and original artists. Boldness in the choice of subjects, and in the method of treating them, seemed the most precious quality of a writer. To this was added bad faith, or an unconscious deception of self and others — Analysis! They analyzed in the name of truth, — which, as it were, must and ought to be declared, — everything, but especially evil, dirt, human corruption, and foulness. They did not notice that this false analysis ceased to be an objective examination, and became a morbid fondness for decay, flowing from two causes: first, corruption of taste; second, from the greater ease of producing striking effects. They took advantage of this physiological peculiarity of the senses through which repulsive impressions seem more vigorous and real than agreeable ones, and they abused this peculiarity beyond measure. They created a certain kind of commercial travelling in the interests of rottenness, with a prompt use of subjects; it was a question to find something new, something which might draw yet. Truth itself, in whose name this was done, retired before these efforts. Take Zola's " La Terre." This novel was to contain the picture of a French village. Call to mind any village of France, or another country. What is it as a whole? A collection of cottages, trees, ploughed fields, stretches of grain, wild flowers, people, cattle, sunlight, blue skies, songs, petty village interests, and work. In all this doubtless manure plays no small part, but there is something beyond and aside from it. Meanwhile Zola's village looks as if composed only of ordure and crime. And this picture is false, it is truth perverted, for in nature the real relation of things is different. If any man were to give himself the trouble of making a list of the women in a French novel, he would be convinced that at least ninety-five per cent of them had fallen. Meanwhile in society it is not so, and cannot be so. Likely there has never been such a proportion even in countries where, on a time, Astarte was worshipped. And still authors wish to persuade us that they give a true picture of society, and that their analysis of morals is taken from life. Lying, exaggeration, admiration of rottenness, — that is an accurate picture of the literary harvest in most recent times. I know not what literature has gained from it; but I do know that the devil has lost nothing, for along that way a whole river of poison and mud has flowed, and the moral sense has become so blunted that at last it endures with ease books which a few tens of years ago would have brought an author to court. It is incredible at present that " Madame Bovary" once exposed the author to two law-suits. If it had been written twenty-five years later, it would have been considered too modest.

But the human mind, which never sleeps, and the organism which strives to live, cannot endure excess of poison. At last the moment comes to cough out disgust. Voices are rising at present which call for mental bread of another sort; an instinctive feeling is abroad that it is impossible to go farther in this way, that men must rise up, shake themselves free of mud, purify themselves, and change. People are crying for fresh air. In general, they cannot tell what they want; but they know what they do not want; they know that they have been breathing miasmas, and have a feeling of suffocation. Alarm possesses minds. In that very France, men are seeking for something, and calling for something. A sort of dull protest is rising against the prevailing order of things. Many writers feel this disquiet. Moments of doubt are coming on them, such as those which we have mentioned, and besides fear and bitterness, strengthened by uncertainty

as to new roads. Look at the last books of Bourget,
Rode, Barrès, Desjardins, at the poetry of Rimbaud, Ver-
laine, Heredes, Mallarme, and even Maeterlinck and his
school. What do they contain ? A search for new substance and new forms ; a feverish search for an issue of
some sort ; an uncertainty whither to turn and where to
look for salvation, whether in mysticism, or in faith, or in
the duties behind faith, or in patriotism, or in humanity ?
But, first of all, an immense disquiet is evident in them.
They find no issue, since to do that there is need of two
things : a great idea, and great talent, and they have
neither the idea nor the talent. Hence disquiet increases,
and these very same persons who step forth against the
rude pessimism of the naturalistic school fall into pessimism themselves, and thus is weakened the main significance and meaning which reform might have. For
what remains to them ? Grotesqueness of form. And
into this grotesqueness, whether it be called symbolism
or impressionism, they wade deeper and deeper ; they are
more and more perplexed, and lose artistic balance, sound
sense, repose of soul. Frequently they fall into the former
rottenness with respect to substance, and are almost always
in discord with themselves, for they have both the proper
and fundamental feeling that they must give the world
something new, but know not what it is.

Such is the present moment!

Any purloiner of public or private funds, any murderer,
may appeal to a neurotic grandmother ; but courts put
such people behind prison bars in spite of the "Rougon-
Macquart" cycle of volumes. The evil lies not in particular circumstances ; but in this, that an unparalleled
pessimism and depression is flowing into men's souls
from such literature, that life's charm, hope, energy,
the desire to live, and therefore the desire of all efforts

in the direction of good, disappears in them. What is the use? This is the question which thrusts itself forward. But a book is one agent in the education of the human soul. If at least the reader could find in Zola's books the good and bad sides of life in balancing relation, or at the worst in such relation as they are found in reality! Vain hope. One must reach high to get colors from the aurora or the rainbow; but every man has spittle in his mouth, and it is easier to paint with it. This painter from nature prefers cheap effects; he prefers foul odors to perfumes, rottenness to living blood, decayed wood to healthy sap, manure to flowers, *la bête humaine* to *l'âme humaine.*

If we could bring in some inhabitant of Mars or Venus, and command him to make a conclusion from Zola's novels touching life upon earth, he would answer undoubtedly: "Life is a little clean sometimes as *le rêve,* but in general it is something with a very bad odor; often it is slippery, oftenest of all it is terrible." And even if those theories on which Zola builds were recognized truths, as they are not, what a lack of mercy to represent life as he does to people who in every case must live! Did he do this to cast them down, disgust them, befoul them, poison every activity, paralyze every energy, and take away the desire for all thought? In view of this, his talent is evil indeed. Better for him, better for France, that he had it not. And at moments one is astonished that fear does not seize him, when even those are alarmed who had nothing to do with the analysis, he the only man with a calm forehead finishes his "Rougon-Macquart" as if he were strengthening instead of breaking the vital force of the French. Why does it not occur to him, that people, nourished on that foul bread and polluted water, will not only fail to resist the storm, but will not even have the wish to resist it? Musset, in his time, wrote the famous verse, " We have had your German Rhine." Zola so instructs his society that if all which he inculcates were really accepted a second verse of Musset's might sound as follows, " But to-day we give you even the Seine." But it is not so bad as that yet.

" La Débâcle," in spite of its blunders, is a famous book; but the soldiers who read it are inferior to those who at night sing, " Christ has arisen!"

If I were a Frenchman, I should consider Zola's talent a national misfortune, and rejoice that his epoch is passing, that even his most intimate disciples are abandoning their master, that he is left more and more to himself.

Will he remain in the memory of men, in literature; will his fame survive? It is difficult to foresee; it is permitted to doubt. In the cycle " Rougon-Macquart" are volumes really powerful, such as " Germinal" or " La Débâcle." But in general all that Zola's native talent has done to make him immortal has been ruined by his admiration for foul realism, and by his tongue, which is simply vile. Literature must not employ expressions which even boors are ashamed to use among themselves. Realistic truth, in so far as concerns criminals, the fallen, or wretches, is reached by another method, through truthful rendering of their conditions of mind, through acts, finally by the course of their speech, but not through a literal quotation of their curses and most repulsive phrases. So in the choice of images, as in the choice of words, there is a certain measure which is dictated by judgment and good taste. Zola has passed this measure to such a degree (in " La Terre") as no man had dared up to that time. Monstrosities are condemned to death, because they are monstrous. A book which rouses disgust must be cast aside. That lies also in the nature of things. Among produc-

37

tions of universal literature, rude things intended to rouse laughter have survived (Aristophanes and Rabelais), or wanton things written exquisitely (Boccaccio); but not one production has survived which was intended to rouse disgust. Zola, for the noise made by his books, for the scandal which every single volume called forth, killed his future. Therefore this wonderful thing happened, that he, a man writing on a settled plan, writing with deliberation, cool, and commanding his subject as few command, has produced the best things only when he had the least chance of carrying out his plans, doctrines, and methods; in a word, when he commanded his subject least, and when the subject commanded him most.

So it happened in "Germinal" and "La Débâcle." The immensity of socialism, and the immensity of the war, simply crushed Zola, with his entire mental apparatus. His doctrines were belittled before such proportions, and could hardly be heard in the roar of the deluge which filled up the mine, and in the thunder of the Prussian cannons. His talent alone remained. So in these two novels there are genuine pictures worthy of Dante. With "Doctor Pascal," the contrary happened. As the last volume of the cycle, it had to be the concluding induction from the whole work, — a synthesis of his doctrine, the tower finishing the structure. For this reason there is more mention made in it of doctrine than in any preceding volume; but since the doctrine is bad, pitiful, false, and empty, "Doctor Pascal" is the poorest and dreariest volume of the whole cycle. A series of empty, barren pictures, in which dreariness goes hand in hand with lack of moral sense, pallor of images with falseness, — that is Doctor Pascal. Zola wants to present him as a decent man. He is a degeneration of the Rougon-Macquarts. In heredity such happy degenerations are met, — the Doctor knows this; he looks on himself as a blessed degeneration, and this is for him a source of unceasing, heartfelt delight. Meanwhile he loves people, serves them, and injects into them a liquid discovered by himself, which is a cure for all ailments. He is a mild sage who investigates life, hence collects "human documents," fits together with toil a genealogical tree of the family Rougon-Macquart, of which he is a descendant; and, in virtue of his observations, he reaches the same conclusions as Zola. What are they? It is difficult to answer; they are, more or less, the following: Whoever is not well is generally ill; heredity exists, but mothers or fathers coming from other families bring in new elements to the blood of children, so that heredity may be modified to such a degree that, taking matters strictly, there is no heredity.

Doctor Pascal is, moreover, a positivist He does not wish to prejudge, but he asserts that the present condition of science will not let him make inferences which transcend known facts; therefore he must adhere to known facts and neglect others. In this regard his judgments tell us nothing newer than the articles of the newspapers written by young positivists. For people who are rushing forward because of spiritual needs which are as insistent as hunger and thirst, — needs in virtue of which a man is conscious of such conceptions as God, faith, immortality, — the Doctor has merely a smile of commiseration. And one might wonder at him somewhat. He would be understood better if he did not recognize the possibility of solving various abstract questions; but he asserts that the necessity of solving them does not exist, — by which he sins against evidence; for such a necessity exists, not farther away than under his own roof, in the person of his niece. That young lady, reared in his principles, loses the ground from under her feet all at once. More problems are born in her soul than the Doctor can answer. And from that moment the drama begins for them both.

" I cannot stop here," cries the niece, " I am suffocating; I must know something, be certain of something; and if thy science cannot pacify my pressing need, I will go to persons who will not only pacify it and explain everything, but make me happy, — I will go to the church!"

And she goes. The roads of the master and pupil diverge more. The pupil reaches the conviction that that science which is only a halter around the neck of people is simply an evil, and that it would be a service before God to burn those old papers on which the Doctor is writing his observations. And the drama intensifies; for, in spite of the sixty years of the Doctor and the twenty years and something of Clotilda, these two people now love each other, not merely as relatives, but as a man and woman love. That love adds bitterness to the battle, and hastens the catastrophe.

Amid those who grope in the dark, wandering and disquieted, one above all remains calm, sure of himself and his doctrine, unmoved and almost serene in his pessimism, — Emile Zola. A great talent, a power slow but immense and patient, an amazing power of observing feelings, for it almost equals indifference, a gift of seeing the collective soul of people and things, a power so exceptional that it brings this naturalistic writer near the mystics, and makes him an uncommon and very original figure.

The physical face of a man does not always reflect his spiritual personality. In Zola this connection appears very emphatically. A square face, a forehead low and covered with wrinkles, large features, high shoulders, and a short neck give his figure something rude. From his face, and the wrinkles around his eyes, you would divine that he is a man who can endure much, that he can bear much, — stubborn and enduring to fanaticism, not only in his plans and their realization, but, which is the main thing, in thought. There is no quickness in him. It is evident at the first glance that he is a *doctrinaire* shut up in himself, who, as a *doctrinaire*, does not take in broad horizons, — sees everything at a certain angle and narrowly, but definitely. His mind, like a dark lantern, casts a narrow light in one direction only, and goes in that direction with unswerving certainty. And this explains at once the history of that whole series of books bearing the general title, " Les Rougon-Macquart." Zola resolved to write the history of a given family during the Empire, on the basis of conditions which the Empire created, and to illustrate the law of heredity. It was even a greater question than to illustrate, for heredity was to become the physiological basis of the work.

There is a certain contradiction in the plan. The Rougon-Macquarts, taking them historically, were to be a picture of French society during recent times, and the normal phenomena of its life ; so they should themselves be a family more or less normal. But in such case, what would become of heredity? It is certain that normal families are such also by virtue of heredity. But to show it in those conditions is impossible ; so it must be done in deviations from the regular type. The Rougons are in fact a sickly family. They are children of neurosis. The ancestress of the family fell into it, and thenceforth her descendants were born with her brand on the forehead. Such is the wish of the author, and we must accept. But how the history of a family exceptionally affected with mental aberrations could be at the same time a picture of French society, the author does not explain to us. If he answered that during the Empire all

society was sick, that would be a subterfuge. Society
may go by a ruinous road, politically or socially, as Polish
society did in the eighteenth century, and be sick as a
whole, but be made up of individuals and families who
are healthy. These are two different things. One of two
issues, then : either the Rougons are sick, and the cycle
of novels concerning them is a psychological study, not a
picture of France during the Empire ; or, the whole psychological basis, all that heredity on which the cycle is
built, — in a word, Zola's entire doctrine, — is nonsense.
I do not know whether any one has ever turned Zola's
attention to this *aut aut* (either or). It is certain that
he himself has never turned his attention to it. Probably that would have had no influence on him, just as the
critics of his theory of heredity had not. Both literary
men and physiologists have appeared against him repeatedly with a whole supply of irresistible proofs. Nothing helped in any way. They contended in vain that in
exact science the theory of heredity had not been inves-
tigated or studied to the end, and, what was most important, it was impossible thus far to grasp it and to prove
it through facts ; in vain did they show that physiology
could not be fantastic, that its proofs could not be sub-
jected to the arbitrary ideas of an author. Zola listened,
wrote on, and in the final volume of his work added the
genealogical tree of the family of Rougon-Macquart with
as much calmness as if no one had ever brought his theory
into doubt.

That tree has one good side. It is so pretentious that
it is brought to ridicule, and deprives the theory of the
remnant of dignity which it might have had for minds
less independent. We learn from the tree that a stock
springs from a great-grandmother who is nervously ill,
also of light conduct. But the man who should think

that her neurosis would appear in her descendants, just as
might happen in the physical sphere, in a certain unmixed
manner, in some special inclination to something, or in
some passion, would be mistaken. On the contrary, the
wonderful tree produces the most varied fruit: red ap-
ples, peaches, plums, dates, and whatever any one wants.
And all this because of the great-grandmother's neurosis !
Does this happen in nature ? We do not know. Zola
himself has no data for it except pretended cuttings from
newspapers describing various crimes, which he preserves
carefully as " human documents," which he manipulates
according to his own fancy. And he is free to do this ;
only, let him not sell us these fancies as the eternal and
unchangeable laws of nature. The grandmother had
neurosis ; her nearest friends had the habit of seeking,
not in an apothecary shop, medicine for affliction ; hence
the descendants, male and female, are that which they
had to be, — namely, criminals, scoundrels, streetwalkers,
decent people, saints, statesmen, good-for-nothings, pro-
curesses, bankers, agriculturists, murderers, priests, soldiers, ministers: in a word, everything which in the
spheres of thought, soundness, property, position, and
career both men and women can be and are, the whole
world over. And we are amazed in spite of us. Well,
what is the position then ? All happens because the
great-grandmother was neurotic ? Yes ! answers the
author. But if Adelaide Fouqué had not been neurotic,
her descendants would have had to be good or bad,
and be occupied with that with which men or women
are occupied in the world usually ? Of course ! answers
Zola, but Adelaide Fouqué had the neurosis. And further discussion becomes simply impossible ; for we have
to do with a man who takes his own arbitrary fancy for
a law of nature. and whose mind does not answer to the

ordinary key furnished by logic. Well, he built a genealogical tree; the tree might have been different, but if
it had been, he would have contended that it could only
be as it is, and it would be easier to kill than convince
him that his theory was valueless.

For that matter, the theory is of this sort, — that there
is really nothing to dispute about. People have said
long ago that Zola had one good thing, his talent; and
one bad thing, his doctrine. If, as a result of neurosis
inherited from one and the same ancestor, one might be
as well a thief as an honest man, Nana as well as a sister
of charity, a brute as well as a sage, a laborer as well as
Achilles, then there is a bridge which does not exist, and
there is a heredity which is not. A man may be what he
wishes himself. The field for free-will and responsibility
is completely open, and all those moral bases on which
the life of man rests come uninjured from the fire. One
might say to the author, That is too "much ado about
nothing," finish with him as with a *doctrinaire*, and count
with him only as with a talent. But he wants something
else. Though his doctrine has no connection, and is simply
nothing, he draws other conclusions from it. His whole
cycle of books say expressly, and without double meaning:
"Whatever thou art, saint or criminal, thou art through
heredity: thou art that which thou must be, and in no
case is it thy fault or merit." Ah, this is the question
of responsibility! This is neither the time nor the
place to touch it. Philosophy has not found a proof
that man exists, unless the Cartesian "*cogito ergo sum*" is
proof sufficient. The question is still open. The same
thing with responsibility. Whole ages of philosophy
may assert what they like, man has the internal conviction that he exists, and the no less mighty conviction that he is responsible; and his whole life, without

reference to theory, is founded on such a conviction. Moreover, exact science has not decided the question of will and responsibility. Against considerations may be cited considerations; against opinions, opinions; against inferences, inferences. But for Zola the question is decided. There is no responsibility; there is only some grandmother Adelaide, or some grandfather Jacques, from whom all come. And here, to my thinking, begins the ruinous influence of this writer; for he not only prejudges undecided questions, but he popularizes his prejudices, ingrafts and facilitates dissolution.

A certain night the Doctor caught his niece in crime. She had made her way to his bureau, had drawn out his papers, and was preparing to burn them. He and she fell to fighting. A pretty picture! He in his linen, she in her nightdress; they wrestle, they pull, they scratch. He is stronger, and she, though he bruised her and drew blood, experienced a certain agreeableness in feeling on her own maiden skin the strength of a man. And in this is all Zola. But let us listen, for the decisive moment is approaching. The Doctor himself, after he has panted somewhat, talks to her solemnly. The reader is impatient. Is the Doctor, by the power of his genius, to rend the night sky and show her a wilderness beyond the stars, or, by the might of eloquence, to hurl into the dust her church, her beliefs, her impulses, her hopes? At once this verse occurs to one, —

> "Darkness on all sides, silence on all sides,
> What will come now, what will come now?"

In the silence was heard the low voice of the Doctor:
"I did not wish to show thee this, but it is not possible to live thus any longer; the hour has come. Give me the genealogical tree of the family Rougon-Macquart."

" What is that ?   What is that ? "

" Yes !   The genealogical tree of the family Rougon-Macquart !   The reading begins in silence : There was one Adelaide Fouqué who had as husband Rougon and a friend Macquart.   From Rougon was born Eugene Rougon, also Pascal Rougon, also Aristides, also Sidonia, also Martha.   From Aristides was born Maxim, also Clotilda, also Victor.   From Maxim was born Charles, and that is the end ; but Sidonia had a daughter Angela, and Martha, who married Mouret, who came from the Macquarts, she had three children, etc."

The night passes without incident, but the reading continues.   After the Rougons come the Macquarts ; later, the descendants of both families united.   Name follows name, surname surname.   They appear evil, they appear good, they appear indifferent ; all positions appear, ministers, bankers, great merchants, simple soldiers, or scoundrels without occupation ; finally the Doctor stops reading, and, looking with the eyes of a sage on his niece, asks, —

Well, and what now ?

But the beautiful Clotilda throws herself into his embraces.

" Thou hast conquered !   Thou hast conquered ! "

And her God, her faith, her church, her impulses toward ideals, her needs of soul scatter into dust.

Why ?   In virtue of what inferences ?   For what good reason ?   In that tree what could convince her or exercise any kind of influence save tedium ?   But why did not this question come from her lips which occurs to the reader invincibly, " But what of that ? "   It is unknown. I have never noted that any author obtained such great and immediate results from such an empty and remote cause.   This is something as astonishing as if Zola had commanded the faith and the principles of Clotilda to all into dust because the Doctor had read to her an almanac, a railroad guide, a bill of fare, or a catalogue of any museum. The arbitrariness passes all bounds, and is simply beyond understanding. The reader inquires if the author is deceiving himself, or casting dust in the eyes of the public. And this culminating point of the novel is its fall, and the fall of the whole doctrine. Clotilda ought to have answered as follows, —

"Thy theory does not stand in any relation to my faith in God and the church. Thy theory is so disconnected that by virtue of it one may be everything, and the theory itself becomes nothing; therefore all thy further inferences from it rest also on nothing. According to thee Nana is a streetwalker, and Angela a saint; Father Mouret an ascetic; Jacque Lotier a murderer, — and all because of grandmother Adelaide? But I will tell thee with a greater likelihood that the good are good because they have my faith, because they believe in responsibility and the immortality of the soul, and the sinners are sinners because they believe in nothing. How wilt thou prove to me that the reason of good and evil is Adelaide Fouqué? Wilt thou assure me with thy word simply, or repeat that it is so because it is so; but I can say to thee that faith and a feeling of responsibility have for ages been a barrier against evil, and if as a positivist thou wish to reckon even a little with reality, thou wilt not be able to contradict. In one word, I have objective proof, while thou hast only thy personal 'it seems to me;' that being the case, leave me my faith, and throw thy fantastic tree into the fire."

But Clotilda answers nothing of the kind. On the contrary, she eats immediately an apple from that vain tree, and goes over soul and body to the camp of the Doctor, and she acts thus only and exclusively because it pleases Zola. There is no other reason, and there cannot be.

If she had gone over out of love for the Doctor, if this reason, which in a woman can play such a great rôle, had really played it, I should have understood the matter. But no! For in such case what would have happened with Zola's whole doctrine? For it is the doctrine alone which influences Clotilda; it is her reasoning side which the Doctor wants to have so irresistible. And he does what he wants, but simply at the cost of logic and sound sense. From that moment, everything is possible; it is possible to persuade the reader that a man who is not loved makes a woman love him through showing her a price list of butter or of stearine candles. To such a plight is real and great talent brought by doctrinairism.

It leads also to a complete destruction of moral sense. That heredity is a wall through which as many windows may be pierced as one likes. The Doctor is such a window. He considers himself a degeneration from the family neurosis; that is, he considers himself a normal man, so he would like somehow to show his health to posterity. Clotilda is also of the opinion that it would not be out of the way, and, because love unites them, therefore they take each other. They take each other evidently as people took each other in the time of the cave-dwellers. Zola considers that perfectly natural, Doctor Pascal also, and, because Clotilda has gone over completely to his camp, neither does she protest. This seems a little more wonderful. Clotilda was religious so recently! Youth and inexperience do not explain it either.

Even girls at the age of eight have some instinctive feeling of modesty. A young lady of twenty years and something knows always what she is doing, and cannot become a victim: if she is at variance with the feeling of modesty, it is either through temperament or through love, which ennobles the transport, for it makes it an act of attachment and a duty, but also love itself wishes to be duty legalized. Though a woman be without religion, and renounce the consecration of love by religion, she may still wish her feeling to be legalized before people. The priest or the mayor. Clotilda, who loves Doctor Pascal, desires nothing. Marriage by a mayor seems of secondary value to her. And again, it is simply impossible to understand her, for genuine love should strive to strengthen the bond and make it permanent. Otherwise that happens which happened in this novel, that the first separation was the end of the connection. Had they been married even before a mayor, they would have remained man and wife, in separation they would not have ceased to belong to each other; since they had not been married, he was from the moment of her departure the unmarried Doctor Pascal, as before, she — the seduced Clotilda. Even during the time of their common life a thousand bitternesses rose from this, and moments really harrowing for both. A certain time Clotilda rushes in in tears, and flaming, and when the terrified Doctor asks what the matter is, she answers, —

"Oh, those women! While walking in the shade I closed my parasol and had the misfortune to hit some little child. Then all fell on me, and began to scream out such things! Oh, such things! That I never shall have children; that it is not for such a dishcloth as I am to have them — and other words, which I cannot repeat, and will not, which I did not even understand."

Her breast rose in sobbing; he grew pale, and, seizing her in his arms, covered her face with kisses; then he said. —

"This is my fault; thou art suffering through me! Listen, let us go to some place far off, where nobody will know thee, where every one will greet thee, and where thou wilt be happy."

But one thing does not come to the head of either: to marry. When Pascal's mother speaks to them of it, they have stone ears. Womanly modesty does not commend this method to Clotilda; care for her, and a desire to shield her from disrespect, does not commend it to him. Why? For a reason unjustified by anything. For the reason that it so pleases Zola.

But perhaps his object is to show what tragic results come of illegal connections? Not in the least. He is entirely on the side of the Doctor and Clotilda. If the mayor should marry them, there would be no drama, and the author wants one. That is the reason.

Later comes the Doctor's bankruptcy. They have to separate. This separation becomes the misfortune of their lives; the Doctor must die of the blow. Both feel that that must be the end; both do not wish it; still they do not imagine any method which would fix forever their mutual relations and change the separation only into a journey, not into a final parting: still they do not marry.

They were people without religion, so they did not want a priest; that we can understand. But why did they not want a mayor? This question is left without an answer.

Here, besides the want of moral feeling, is the lack of common sense. The book is not only immoral; it is a wretched hut built of planks which do not hold together, not suffering the least touch of logic and sound judgment. In this quagmire of nonsense even talent is submerged.

One thing remains: poison flows as formerly into the souls of readers, minds become accustomed to evil and cease to be indignant at it. The poison soaks in, destroys simplicity of soul, moral sensitiveness, and that delicacy of conscience which distinguishes good from evil.

The Doctor, in grief for Clotilda, gets the sclerosis and dies. She returns under the former roof and occupies herself with the rearing of the child. Nothing of what the Doctor had ingrafted into her soul went to nothing or withered. On the contrary, it grew stronger. He loved life; she also loves it now. She accepts it completely; not through resignation, but because she knows it; and the more she ponders over it, fondling the nameless child on her knee, the more she knows it. With this ends the cycle "Rougon-Macquart."

.   .   .   .

But this end is a new surprise. Now nineteen volumes lie before us, and in them, as Zola himself says: *Tant de boue, tant de larmes. C'était à se demander si d'un coup de foudre, il n'aurait pas mieux valu balayer cette four-milière gâtée et misérable.* It is true! The man who reads these volumes can arrive at no other conclusion than that life is a desperate and blind mechanical process in which one must share, to the greater misfortune of people, since it is impossible to do otherwise. In it mud predominates over green turf, rottenness over freshness; the odor of corpses over the perfume of flowers; sickness, madness, and crime over health and virtue. This Gehenna is not merely terrible, it is disgusting. The hair rises on the head, and at the same time saliva comes to the lips (to spit at it), and in fact the question springs up whether it would not be better if a lightning flash should sweep away *cette fourmilière gâtée et misérable?*

Another conclusion there cannot be; another would be a mad mental deviation, a simple breaking of the laws of reason and logic. And now do you know how this cycle of novels ends really? With a hymn in praise of life.

Here one's hands simply drop. It is useless labor to show again that the author arrives at something which is directly opposed to that which should flow from his work. We wish him no evil! But let him not be astonished if even his disciples desert him. People must think according to the laws of logic. And because they must also live, they want some consolation on the road of life. Masters, after the manner of Zola, give them only dissolution, chaos, a disgust for life, and despair. The rationalism of these masters can show the world nothing else; and these things it has always shown so eagerly that it has exceeded the measure. To-day those who are stifled with bad air need fresh air; the doubting need hope; those who are torn with unrest need a little repose, therefore they act properly when they turn thither whence hope and repose come, thither where they are blessed with the cross, and where it is said to them, as it was to the palsied : *Tolle grabatum tuum et ambula !* (Take up thy bed and walk !)

And thus is explained the newest evolution, the waves of which are beginning to pass through the world in every direction.

To my thinking, poetry and novels must also pass through this evolution ; nay more, they must strengthen and freshen it. To go on as hitherto is simply impossible! On an exhausted field only weeds grow. The novel should strengthen life, not undermine it; ennoble, not defile it; bring good "tidings," not evil. I care not whether the word that I say pleases or not, since I believe that I reflect the great and urgent need of the soul of humanity, which is crying for a change.

www.ingramcontent.com/pod-product-compliance
Lightning Source LLC
Chambersburg PA
CBHW011359010726
47495CB00009B/2696